For Jane Dashow, FQOTFU.
Love you, me gel.

continued . . .

"Ms. Martin always delivers heat and romance, with a very strong conflict to keep the reader engaged. *The Penalty Box* should be added to your 'must-read list.' "

—*Contemporary Romance Writers*

"An engrossing read . . . Left me cheering at the end!"

—*Joyfully Reviewed*

Total Rush

"*Total Rush* is just that—a total rush, an absolute delight. Deirdre Martin is the reason I read romance novels. This contemporary romance is so well written [and] has a hero to die for and a romance that turns you into a puddle. It fills your heart to overflowing with love, acceptance, and the beauty of uniqueness. I laughed, I cried, I celebrated. It's more than a read, it is a reread. Brava, Ms. Martin, you're the greatest!"

—*The Best Reviews*

"Well written . . . makes you want to keep turning the pages to see what happens next."

—*The Columbia (SC) State*

"Martin's inventive take on opposites attracting is funny and poignant."

—*Booklist*

"A heartwarming story of passion, acceptance, and most importantly, love, this book is definitely a *Total Rush*."

—*Romance Reviews Today*

"Fast paced, sexy, fun yet tender, the pages of *Total Rush* practically turn themselves. This is Deirdre Martin's third novel and [it] is as sensational as the first two . . . A definite winner."

—*Romance Junkies*

Fair Play

"Martin depicts the worlds of both professional hockey and ethnic Brooklyn with deftness and smart detail. She has an unerring eye for humorous family dynamics [and] sweet buoyancy."

—*Publishers Weekly*

Body Check

Titles by Deirdre Martin

BODY CHECK
FAIR PLAY
TOTAL RUSH
THE PENALTY BOX
CHASING STANLEY
JUST A TASTE

Deirdre Martin

BERKLEY SENSATION, NEW YORK

THE BERKLEY PUBLISHING GROUP
Published by the Penguin Group
Penguin Group (USA) Inc.
375 Hudson Street, New York, New York 10014, USA

Penguin Group (Canada), 90 Eglinton Avenue East, Suite 700, Toronto, Ontario M4P 2Y3, Canada
(a division of Pearson Penguin Canada Inc.)
Penguin Books Ltd., 80 Strand, London WC2R 0RL, England
Penguin Group Ireland, 25 St. Stephen's Green, Dublin 2, Ireland (a division of Penguin Books Ltd.)
Penguin Group (Australia), 250 Camberwell Road, Camberwell, Victoria 3124, Australia
(a division of Pearson Australia Group Pty. Ltd.)
Penguin Books India Pvt. Ltd., 11 Community Centre, Panchsheel Park, New Delhi—110 017, India
Penguin Group (NZ), 67 Apollo Drive, Rosedale, North Shore 0632, New Zealand
(a division of Pearson New Zealand Ltd.)
Penguin Books (South Africa) (Pty.) Ltd., 24 Sturdee Avenue, Rosebank, Johannesburg 2196,
South Africa

Penguin Books Ltd., Registered Offices: 80 Strand, London WC2R 0RL, England

This is a work of fiction. Names, characters, places, and incidents either are the product of the author's imagination or are used fictitiously, and any resemblance to actual persons, living or dead, business establishments, events, or locales is entirely coincidental. The publisher does not have any control over and does not assume any responsibility for author or third-party websites or their content.

PUBLISHER'S NOTE: The recipes contained in this book are to be followed exactly as written. The publisher is not responsible for your specific health or allergy needs that may require medical supervision. The publisher is not responsible for any adverse reactions to the recipes contained in this book.

JUST A TASTE

A Berkley Sensation Book / published by arrangement with the author

PRINTING HISTORY
Berkley Sensation mass-market edition / January 2008

Copyright © 2008 by Deirdre Martin.
Cover illustration by Sandy Haight.
Cover design by Lesley Worrell.
Interior text design by Laura K. Corless.

ISBN: 978-0-425-21897-6

BERKLEY® SENSATION
Berkley Sensation Books are published by The Berkley Publishing Group,
a division of Penguin Group (USA) Inc.,
375 Hudson Street, New York, New York 10014.
BERKLEY SENSATION and the "B" design are trademarks belonging to Penguin Group (USA) Inc.

PRINTED IN THE UNITED STATES OF AMERICA

10 9 8 7 6 5 4 3 2 1

Acknowledgments

Thanks to:

My husband, Mark, as always. The man has the patience of Job.

Miriam Kriss and Kate Seaver.

Binnie Braunstein.

Jeff Schwartzenberg, who did such a great job designing www.nyblades.com.

Mom, Dad, Bill, Allison, Beth, Jane, Dave, and Tom.

A number of publications were helpful in the creation of this book. They are:

The Perfectionist: Life and Death in Haute Cuisine by Rudolph Chelminski

French Women Don't Get Fat by Mireille Guiliano

Sixty Million Frenchmen Can't Be Wrong by Jean-Benoît Nadeau and Julie Barlow

Gourmet magazine

Essentials of Classic Italian Cooking by Marcella Hazan

Mastering the Art of French Cooking by Julia Child

HarperCollins French Dictionary

Chapter 1

"*Sorry I'm late,* Ang. They're doing construction on Metropolitan Avenue, and there's only one lane open. Traffic was backed up to the friggin' moon."

Anthony Dante set up a small canvas folding chair beside his wife Angie's grave and sat down, just as he'd done every Sunday morning for the past year. In one hand he clutched a foam cup of coffee; in the other, a ham and egg sandwich. He took a bite, disappointed to note it lacked the extra salt he always requested. He'd let it go this time, but if it happened again, he might have to say something to Al at the deli. It was important to get customers' orders right. If his staff was getting sloppy or lazy, Al needed to be told.

"So, let me tell you about my week . . ."

The vast cemetery was like a silent, sleeping city, the early morning mist draped like gossamer over the trees. Anthony took a moment to pass the steaming cup of coffee beneath his nose, reveling in its robust scent. Nothing like a perfectly brewed cup of coffee to start the day. At least Al had gotten that right. The coffee aroma mingled nicely with that of newly mown grass. The morning sun was a blazing ruby ball, bringing with it the first real hint of the day's heat. What was that old adage? "Red sky at night, sailor's delight. Red sky at morn, sailors be warned"? No doubt about it: today was going to be a scorcher. Not that Anthony minded. After years in a restaurant kitchen, heat and humidity didn't bother him the way it did some people.

"First, the veal chops." He threw a shot of coffee down his throat, sputtering as the scalding liquid burned the inside of his mouth. "Jesus," he gasped, running his burnt tongue over the roof of his mouth a few times for relief. "I think Al is trying to kill me."

He took the lid off the coffee, blowing onto the liquid to cool it. "Remember I told you I was going to switch up the recipe a little, maybe use a little more rosemary and a little less garlic to see if the customers would like it? Well, not only did they like it, they *loved* it." He smiled with satisfaction, imagining Angie's wide-eyed interest as she pulled one of their kitchen chairs closer to him, the better to listen. "Even Aldo gave it the thumbs-up, and you know what a crotchety old SOB he can be. By the way, he quit again yesterday. Second time this week."

Angie had always been amused at the way Anthony and the ancient waiter sparred, a tradition reaching all the way back to the restaurant's earliest days, when the old man had been young and used to mix it up with Anthony's father. "One of these days, I'm going to call his bluff," Anthony continued. "*Then* we'll see how quick he is to throw his apron at me and call me *un cazzone cafone*."

He paused for another sip of coffee, hearing voices behind him. He turned; two old women were slowly walking arm in arm toward a large, rectangular mausoleum whose double doors were flanked by enormous marble angels. It was rare to see anyone else at the cemetery at this hour, which was why Anthony liked coming so early. He could talk to Angie without having to worry about someone thinking he was a major nutcase, though if the past year of widowerhood had taught him anything, it was that grieving people were all a little unhinged. That, and everyone talked to their dead spouses all the time, whether they admitted it or not. He just chose to do it publicly once a week.

He glanced at his wife's headstone, at the carved words that read, "Angela Maria Dante, Beloved Wife, Daughter, Sister." He spoke to Angie all the time in his head. Maybe he was *ubatz*, but sometimes he swore she talked back. Not as a disembodied voice echoing through their dark bedroom or anything as crazy as that—it was more a coincidence thing.

Just the other week he'd lamented to Ang how he wasn't sure what christening gift to get for his cousin Gemma's new baby girl, Maeve. The next day, a Baby Gap catalog arrived in the mail. Some people might think it was nuts to believe the dead could influence the postal service, but since Ang died, Anthony found stuff like that happening all the time.

"Did I tell you about Mikey?" Anthony shook his head ruefully as he geared up to talk about his little brother, Michael, who had just retired from his career as a professional hockey player for the New York Blades. "Get this: he's going to stay home and be a full-time dad while Theresa goes back to work." Anthony snorted.

His gaze was pulled back to the mausoleum. The old ladies had slipped inside; he could picture them sitting on a glossy teak bench, staring at the smooth marble wall behind which their loved ones were interred. Sometimes he wished he'd chosen a mausoleum for Ang, if only because sitting out here when it rained or snowed was a big pain in the neck. Even so, he hadn't missed a Sunday yet. It was the least he could do for the woman snatched from his arms too soon, the angel who'd shown him there could be more to his life than his restaurant.

He continued chatting in between bites of his sandwich,

catching Angie up on both family and restaurant gossip. He liked concluding by sharing with her his ideas for shaking up the menu in the week to come. "I'm thinking of doing some kind of pork special this week, but I have to talk to Dom over at Santoro Brothers first."

Santoro Brothers! How could he have waited until now to share the most interesting piece of neighborhood gossip he'd heard in months? "I almost forgot! You know the old candy store next to Cuccio's, across the street from the restaurant? The one that's been for sale since Old Man Garlasco died? Well, according to Dom, someone bought it and is planning to turn it into a restaurant. Insane, right? Just what we need: another trattoria in Bensonhurst." He drained his coffee cup with a chuckle. "Good luck to them is what I say. They're about to enter the big leagues, eh, *cara*?"

"Can't you picture it? Couples staring dreamily into each other's eyes over a bottle of Bordeaux? The scent of apple *tartin* as it bakes? Oh, Natalie, it's going to be wonderful!"

Vivi Robitaille hugged herself tight, giving a small twirl in the center of the empty candy store she and her half sister planned on turning into a small bistro. All her life she'd dreamed of cooking in her own restaurant. Now it was going to happen—and in America!

Vivi dropped her arms and danced over to Natalie, who had yet to respond to her giddiness. "What? You can't imagine biting into a piece of my baguettes with creamed butter? Or ordering a bowl of my *bouillabaisse de poulet*?"

"Not as strongly as you can, obviously." Eyeing her surrounds critically, Natalie strolled the perimeter of the empty store, her high heels punching measured beats on the scuffed wooden floor. Unlike the high-spirited Vivi, Natalie was pragmatic, some might even say detached. Vivi was not surprised when Natalie concluded her stroll by asking, "Remind me again why we chose to open a restaurant in Brooklyn rather than Manhattan?"

"You know why," Vivi reminded her. "We—"

"*You*—"

"—wanted a small, intimate local place that would serve peasant food to regular people, not some fancy *haute* restaurant catering to Manhattan's rich."

"You have something against the rich?" Natalie asked wryly.

Vivi blushed. "You know what I meant." She regarded Natalie with unabashed appreciation. "I could never do this without you. You know that."

Natalie cracked a small smile. It saddened Vivi to think it, but sometimes she wasn't sure whether she liked her half sister at all. Now they'd embarked on a foreign adventure together, Natalie putting up the lion's share of the money for Vivi's restaurant. Amazing. Some would say that was only fair, since Natalie had received the lion's share of their papa's inheritance. But Vivi never felt entitled. Instead, she felt lucky to have Natalie there with her, both as a business partner and a friend, even though there were times a certain wariness could spring up between them. Vivi's mother claimed the beautiful, aloof Natalie was just running from her failed love affair, but Vivi knew better. Natalie wasn't running from, but toward. Both sisters wanted to reinvent themselves. What better place to do that than New York?

Still pensive, Natalie moved to look out the large front window, the one Vivi could picture with her own name stenciled across it in white script. Natalie's gaze remained critical as she peered up and down the street. "Not the most—how shall we say?—upscale area."

Vivi bristled. "That's the point."

"It's very bourgeois," Natalie continued as if she hadn't

heard. "Very *American* bourgeois," she concluded with a small sniff.

"What's wrong with that?" Vivi said. The disdain many of her fellow French had for America puzzled her. She loved the place! Her aunt Solange had moved to New York when Vivi was a child, and every other summer, Vivi and her mother came to visit. America always left her dizzied—not only by the sheer scale of the place, but the energy, the inventiveness. Some of her countrymen saw Americans as crude, but not Vivi. She found them spirited and comfortable in their own skins; a people willing to take risks and dream big. This was *exactly* the place she—and Natalie—needed to be.

Natalie sighed. "I suppose if we fail, it's better to fail here than in Manhattan."

"We're not going to fail."

Natalie eyed her with measured affection. "I'm amazed by your—what's the American expression?—pluck."

"You know what a great cook I am, Natalie. And you know how thoroughly I did my research."

"Just because this place is filled with 'average' people doesn't mean they'll want your food." She pointed out the window to the large, red brick restaurant across the street called Dante's Ristorante. "*That's* what they want: spaghetti, big fat meatballs . . . bah." She turned away in disgust.

"They'll want what I make, too," Vivi insisted stubbornly. "And if they don't, then the food will be good enough to draw people from Manhattan. I'm not worried. People want good, home-cooked food at reasonable prices. They want to sit down and relax over a simple, hearty meal at the end of the day."

"I hope you're right."

"I am."

Natalie studied her nails. "I still don't see why you insisted on renting an apartment here rather than in Manhattan with me."

"I want to live where I work, Natalie," said Vivi, tired of having to explain again. "I want to know the names and faces of my neighbors and future customers, and I want them to know me. Besides, getting into the city won't be a problem. I'll just hop on the Metro."

"Subway," Natalie corrected. "And it's filthy, by the way." She shuddered. *"Degoutante."*

"What are you saying?" Vivi teased. "That you're only going to travel by cab? Or hire a limo, perhaps?"

"Now there's an idea . . ."

Vivi furrowed her brows, worried that Natalie might be serious. Natalie caught her expression and chuckled.

"Don't worry. You concentrate on getting this place up and running, and making Vivi's the best it can be. I'll worry about the dollars and cents."

"If you say so."

Vivi took another tour of the space. The sweet smell of candy still lingered, bringing back pleasant memories of childhood. She'd been a happy little girl, never more so than when *maman* let her help out in the kitchen. Even as a small child, standing on a step stool beside the old gas stove, stirring potato soup under her mother's watchful eye, she knew she was destined to be a chef. Some people likened the clang of pots and pans to a headache, but not Vivi. To her, it was like church bells pealing in her ears, reminding her of her calling.

"Quick!" Natalie called from the window. "Come look!"

Vivi hustled to join her. Together they watched as a broadly built, dark haired, handsome man unlocked the door of the restaurant across the street, slipping inside.

"The owner," Natalie deduced.

"No doubt." Vivi tugged Natalie's sleeve and began pulling her toward the door. "Let's go introduce ourselves."

Natalie looked appalled. "What, *now*?"

"Yes, why not?"

"Let's wait half an hour or so. Otherwise, it will look like we were standing here spying on him."

"We were!"

The sisters laughed.

"Half an hour, then," Vivi agreed. Then she'd get to meet the first of her neighbors. She couldn't wait.

Chapter 2

"Hello. Can I help you?"

Vivi smiled at the handsome, rugged man standing in the doorway of Dante's Ristorante. He seemed slightly shorter than the man they'd seen enter just half an hour before. His expression was typically American: open and friendly. She felt reassured that her decision to open a bistro here rather than Paris, or even back home in Avignon, was the right one.

Vivi shot a quick sideways glance at Natalie to see if she wanted to field the man's question, but it was obvious from Natalie's ramrod posture that Vivi would be the one doing the talking. She was glad. Natalie could come across as imperious at first. Better she handle the initial introductions.

"My name is Vivi Robitaille, and this is my ha—my sister, Natalie." She pointed across the street. "We purchased the old candy store, and we just wanted to introduce ourselves."

The man looked delighted. "You're French, right?"

"Oui," said Vivi.

"I love your accent." The man extended his hand. "My name's Michael Dante. I'm half owner of this place with my brother, Anthony."

Vivi hesitated slightly. "Is he the tall man who arrived earlier?"

Michael laughed. "Yeah, that's Ant, all right. He's the head chef."

"I'm a chef, too!" Vivi said excitedly. "I would very much love to speak with him!"

"Come on in," said Michael, holding the door open wide. The inside of the restaurant surprised Vivi; it was much larger than it appeared from the outside. There were various-sized tables and a long, sleek wooden bar. Beyond the sea of tables was yet another dining room, probably used for private parties. Vivi took it as a good sign that a restaurant this large was thriving in the neighborhood. Natalie would say it was because it served Italian food in an Italian enclave, but Vivi had been working in restaurants long enough to know there was more to it than that. For a place this large to do well year in, year out, the food had to be outstanding.

Michael pointed to an empty table for four. "Have a seat. I'll go get my brother."

"Actually, could I see the kitchen?" Vivi could feel Natalie's eyes chastising her for being so pushy, but she didn't care.

"Sure, no problem. Just don't be surprised if Anthony's got his head stuck in a pot of sauce and he's less than cordial. He can be a little intense sometimes."

"All chefs are," Vivi said.

Michael looked thoughtful. "I guess you're right. You couldn't even *talk* to our father when he was in the middle of 'mangia making,' as he used to call it. He'd either bite your head off, or give you a chore and tell you to get busy."

Vivi laughed. "Sounds familiar."

Michael smiled, motioning for Vivi and her sister to follow him. Vivi ventured another quick glance at Natalie, who was clearly displeased that they weren't remaining in the dining room.

"Ten minutes," Natalie whispered in a warning voice. "That's it. I know how rapturous you get at the sight of industrial-sized gas ranges and Sub-Zero freezers! I don't want to be here all day!"

"We won't be," Vivi promised, though nothing would make her happier. She could feel the anticipation building inside her as Michael nudged open the swinging stainless steel doors of the kitchen with his hip. Vivi held her breath, her mouth falling open at the sight of the huge, well-lit, well-ventilated kitchen. It was as though Saint Peter had just permitted her to pass through the gates into heaven.

"Company, Ant," Michael announced.

The large man Vivi and Natalie had seen enter the restaurant earlier looked up from where he stood at the stove, peering into a large, stainless steel pot of sauce as if scrying. Vivi closed her eyes a moment and inhaled deeply, trying to pinpoint the individual ingredients making the sauce smell so inviting. Fresh garlic . . . basil . . . carrot . . . perhaps the slightest hint of nutmeg? Interesting.

"This is Vivi and Natalie," Michael continued as Anthony wiped his hands on the front of his apron. "They're the ones who bought Old Man Garlasco's candy store."

At the mention of the candy store, Vivi thought she saw a small smirk play across Anthony's lips. Arrogant, she thought, though on a certain level, she understood completely; all chefs were wary of new competition. Out of habit, her gaze was drawn to Anthony's hands. They were beautiful in the way a chef's hands should be: strong and scarred. Her eyes traveled back to his face. He was handsome, and judging from the slight upward tilt to his head, proud. She stole a quick glance at the prep cooks assembled in the kitchen, all of whom had greeted her and Natalie with pleasant smiles when they walked in. They seemed happily focused on their tasks. Of course, it was still early in the day. She knew that by the time the restaurant opened, nerves would be a bit frayed and a mild frenzy would prevail. She also knew that the minute she and Natalie left, they'd be back to chatting and gossiping, using the foulest words they could find where appropriate. Restaurant kitchens were not for the faint of heart, especially when it came to pressure and indelicate language.

Anthony joined the semicircle where Vivi, Natalie, and Michael stood by the kitchen door. "I hear you're opening a restaurant." His voice had a deep, rich timbre. He sounded self assured, and a little too cocky for Vivi's taste.

"Yes," Vivi answered, giving her head the same proud tilt as his. "A bistro."

"A bistro," Anthony repeated stonily. "Now there's an original concept."

"Anthony," Michael murmured under his breath, sounding embarrassed.

"You are afraid of some competition, maybe?" Vivi purred, teasing out the words slowly for maximum effect.

Anthony tilted his head a fraction higher. "I've got no competition. I'm peerless."

"Egocentrique," Natalie sniffed.

"And damn proud of it."

The enticing smell of the sauce on the stove was driving Vivi crazy. She had to know what, exactly, was giving it that wonderful tang. "Excuse me, is there nutmeg in that sauce?"

Anthony looked surprised—and impressed. "A little."

"Chianti, too, yes?"

Anthony frowned. "Of course there's Chianti. Who ever heard of making gravy without Chianti?"

Vivi and Natalie exchanged glances. "Gravy?"

"It's Italian slang for pasta sauce," Michael explained.

Anthony, meanwhile, seemed to be appraising Vivi suspiciously. "So, you're the chef, huh?"

"Yes," Vivi said. She glanced at the kitchen again in wonder. "This is a beautiful kitchen! So much room!"

"It started out strictly as a pizza joint," Anthony began to explain proudly, "and my folks built it up from there—"

"To the friggin' headache it is today," Michael joked.

Vivi blinked. *Friggin'*? A curse word?

"Speak for yourself," Anthony told Michael.

"Where did you train?" Natalie asked Anthony.

Anthony looked confused. "Train?"

"What cooking school did you go to?" Vivi clarified. She was glad Natalie asked, since she, too, was curious.

"You want to know where I trained?" Anthony pointed to the bank of stoves behind him. "Right there."

Vivi covered her surprise. "You didn't go to cooking school?"

"I didn't need to go to cooking school. Good cooking comes from here"—he tapped his chest over his heart—"not here." He tapped his forehead twice.

Against her better judgment, Vivi found herself impressed. "I guess . . . if one is nurtured young . . . cooking school isn't strictly necessary."

"Then why did you let Papa send you to Le Cordon Bleu?" Natalie snapped.

Vivi was dumbstruck. What business was it of Natalie's whether their father paid for her culinary education? Perhaps sensing the tension, Michael Dante smiled brightly and asked, "When are you ladies hoping to open?"

"About nine months from now," said Vivi.

"Why Bensonhurst?" Anthony asked.

"Why not?" Natalie retorted.

Vivi stared at her sister, wide eyed. Why was she being so *rude*? First the *egocentrique* comment, now this. Was she trying to show these brothers they weren't two fluffy little *mademoiselles*? Vivi was interested in making friends, not enemies. Anthony's wariness toward them seemed to grow with each of Natalie's waspish comments.

Vivi smiled at Anthony. "Maybe you could recommend some contractors to us? What suppliers you use?"

"Maybe."

"Of course we will," Michael said graciously, shooting his brother an annoyed look, which Anthony pointedly ignored.

Vivi gestured toward the stove. "Your sauce is done, I think. It smells done."

This time Anthony didn't hide his smirk. "It does, huh?"

"Yes," Vivi maintained primly.

"I'm pretty sure it's got five minutes or so to go before all the flavors have peaked."

Vivi shrugged. "It's your kitchen."

"That's right."

"But I still think it's done," she insisted. She could hear her mother's scolding voice in her head: "Don't be such a know-it-all when it comes to food, Vivi!" But she couldn't help it. Food was her passion, preparing it perfectly her obsession. Judging by the look of begrudging respect mingled with annoyance that flashed across Anthony Dante's face, he understood exactly where she was coming from, even if he didn't like it.

"Tell you what," Anthony challenged. "When it's your kitchen and you're making the gravy, you can decide how long it cooks. *Capisce?*"

Vivi regarded Anthony politely. "I'm sorry if you feel I insulted you. It's just important to me that things turn out right."

"I've been making the gravy since I was ten," Anthony replied. "I think I know when it's done."

"And I think—"

"Oh, my." Natalie looked at her Cartier watch and began nudging Vivi toward the door. "Look at the time. We've got to get going."

It was the last thing Vivi wanted. She wanted to wait and see whether she'd been right about the sauce. She wanted to chop, peel, flambé, roast, sear, blanch, fry, boil, bake, mix, blend, simmer. But most of all, she wanted to make it clear to Anthony Dante that she knew her way around a kitchen just as well as he did, if not better. Men! They always thought they knew better, they always thought—

Natalie began dragging her toward the doorway. "*Au revoir*, neighbors, *au revoir.*"

Vivi shook Natalie off. "Perhaps we can talk sometime," she said to Anthony.

He looked dubious. "About what?"

"Food." Bold though she knew it was, she plucked the pen held in place at his waist by the drawstring at the front of his apron. "Here's my address and cell phone number," she said, rummaging through her purse for a piece of scrap paper, upon which she scribbled furiously.

"Look, you can stop in here anytime you want," Michael offered graciously. This time it was Anthony who looked irked, not the other way around.

"I don't want to be a pest," said Vivi, holding out the paper with her address and phone number on it to Anthony. Their eyes locked. For a split second, it looked as if he might refuse, prompting a surge of anger within her. But then he reached out and took it, folding the paper into a careful square before tucking it into the back pocket of his pants.

"*Au revoir*," Natalie trilled desperately one final time, practically dragging Vivi by the hair.

"Nice meeting you," said Michael. "Right, Ant?"

"I've gotta go check the gravy, Mikey," is all Vivi heard as Natalie propelled her through the kitchen doors. Vivi smiled to herself. He was second-guessing himself, worried that perhaps she was right. Which she was, of course.

"She likes you."

Anthony ignored his brother's comment as he lifted a large wooden spoon to his lips to sample the gravy. Ha!

That obnoxious French woman was wrong; it still had a minute or two to go before the wine had completely evaporated. Still, she was in the ballpark, which was impressive, especially for someone who clearly didn't know her ass from her elbow when it came to Italian food.

He moved to check the progress of his new sous chef, Sam, who was busy dicing a small mountain of vegetables. Things seemed to be on schedule. Maybe tonight's typical Sunday rush wouldn't be too insane after all. Not that he really minded.

"Did you hear me?"

Anthony turned to Michael, who had taken a small spoon and was dipping it into a bowl of cannoli filling with alarming regularity, much to the annoyance of Anthony's pastry chef, Rocco. "If you want to keep all your fingers, Mikey, I suggest you stop what you're doing right now," Anthony warned.

Michael looked up guiltily into Rocco's scowling face and put down the spoon. "Sorry," he mumbled. Rocco grunted something unintelligible and picked up the next cannoli shell to fill.

"Did you hear me?" Michael repeated, annoying as a mosquito that wouldn't stop buzzing around your ears.

"I heard you," Anthony replied. "She's not my type."

"Why? Because she's alive?"

Anthony ignored the wisecrack and returned to the stove to reduce the heat under the gravy. The minute the first anniversary of Angie's death passed, Michael started riding his ass about dating, as if there were a statute of limitations on grief. You've mourned her a year! Time to go out and find a new wife. What Mikey didn't get was that Anthony was fine with his life as it was. He had his family, his restaurant, his friends; he didn't want to take another shot at love. Everyone knew lightning didn't strike twice, so why bother?

"You have to admit," Michael continued undeterred as

he sidled up beside his brother at the stove, "she was kind of cute."

Anthony thought a moment. He hadn't really paid close attention to how Vivi looked; he was too busy thinking of suitable retorts if she kept running off her mouth about the gravy. From what he could recall, she was willowy and blonde, her hair done in a long braid down her back. Pale-skinned. Delicate-looking. Anthony liked his women brunette and earthy, with flesh you could grab on to. Ang had hips. Hips and nice soft boobs and a ringing laugh that always made him want to join in.

"She was okay," Anthony allowed.

"The accent was kind of sexy, too," Michael continued in an insinuating voice. "Ooh la la."

"Ooh la listen to me, you pain in the ass," Anthony retorted. "Not. Interested."

Michael ignored him. "I think you should at least be neighborly."

" 'Neighborly'?" Anthony repeated with irritation. "What do you mean?"

"Pop in to say hello if you see her across the street. Whatever."

"Mike, the woman never met me before in her life, and has the *coglioni* to challenge me on my sauce, not to mention the fact that she and her sister are opening a competing restaurant right across from ours. Why the hell would I want to be neighborly?"

"You took her home address when she offered it," Michael pointed out.

"I was being polite."

"Let me see it."

Anthony pulled the slip of paper from his left back pocket and handed it to his brother, who eagerly unfolded it. "She's living here in Bensonhurst," Michael noted, nodding with approval. "Three blocks away on Twenty-third Avenue, as a matter of fact."

"That's nice."

"I'd bet my right nut the stuck-up sister isn't living with her," said Michael. "You see that watch? And those clothes? She looks like she stepped out of the pages of *Vogue*."

"You got that right. At least Fifi—"

"It's Vivi, Ant."

"At least Vivi was dressed like a normal woman." He took back the piece of paper with her address on it. He contemplated tossing it in the trash, but that seemed cold, so he just shoved it back in his pocket. "Pushy, though."

"Reminds me of someone."

"Excuse me?"

"How many times have you marched into my kitchen and told Theresa what you think she should be doing?"

"That's different! For one thing, Theresa is my sister-in-law. For another, I'm a friggin' chef!"

"So's Vivi."

"So she says," Anthony scoffed.

"Well, they're not going to go away, so we may as well try to get along with them."

"As long as she doesn't come barging into my kitchen, things will be fine." Anthony's fingers were itching to *do* something. Picking up his favorite knife, he helped himself to some onions in the prep area and began dicing. "I didn't get a chance to ask you, Mike: what the hell are you doing here?"

"Just stopping by to say hi."

Anthony nodded uneasily. The day he had always dreaded had finally arrived—his brother had retired from pro hockey. Michael had promised to keep out of Anthony's hair, but the fact was, Michael was half owner in the restaurant, and he'd always enjoyed popping in and schmoozing. Anthony worried the occasional schmooze was going to turn into a full-time presence. They'd nearly come to blows years before when expanding the place, with Michael throwing his weight around even though he didn't know a damn thing about the business. In the end, Michael conceded that Dante's was Anthony's domain, but Anthony had never forgotten Michael's comment that he'd been so invested in Dante's success because this was where he was "going to end up" when his hockey days were done. If Michael thought that he could come in here and start making executive decisions just because he'd hung up his skates, he was sorely mistaken.

"Shouldn't you be home with Theresa and the kids?" Anthony prodded.

"In a minute." Michael looked stricken. "I can do this stay-at-home dad thing, right?"

"Sure. How hard could it be?"

"Right. I mean, I get Dominica and Little Ant off to school, and then it's just me and the baby hanging out for the rest of the day. Pick up the kids, take Little Ant to hockey practice, Dominica to tap class, start dinner . . . piece of cake, right?"

"Definitely. Theresa excited about going back to work tomorrow?"

"She can't wait, though she's worried about being rusty."

"Ah, she'll be fine. She's a trouper."

Though their relationship had been rocky at the beginning, Anthony was now a big fan of his sister-in-law, both personally and professionally. Personally, she'd kept his *ubatz* brother sane and had created a nice life for him, with a great family. Professionally, she'd been one helluva publicist. He had no doubt that once she was back in the groove, she'd be unstoppable. It was thanks in part to Theresa that the restaurant's renovation a few years back was such a smashing success.

Anthony finished with the onions, adding them to the growing mound in the prep area. "You taking off soon?"

"Real subtle," Michael quipped. He locked Anthony in a big bear hug. "Maybe we'll stop by for dessert tonight, after dinner at my mother-in-law's."

"Sounds good. Hey, give Theresa's mom my love, will you? Hang on a minute." Knowing Theresa's mother loved his olive oil cake, he cut a big slab for her and wrapped it up for his brother.

"Tell her compliments of the chef."

"Too bad she's not thirty years younger," Michael teased. "You two would be a good match: Italian, widowed, both can cook . . ."

"Get of out here, Mikey. Before I toss you out."

"Later," Michael called as he left the kitchen, leaving Anthony shaking his head in amusement. Jesus, his brother was one pushy SOB. He returned to the stove to take another taste of the gravy. Perfect. Leaning against one of the kitchen's long, stainless steel tables, he pulled the pen from his apron to jot down his ideas for tomorrow's specials. Looking for scrap paper, he reached into his pocket and took out the sheet with Vivi's address and cell number. He was about to make notes on the blank side, but changed his mind, reaching instead for the small notepad lying on a nearby counter. He folded up the paper and put it back in his pocket. His father always said you should keep your friends close and your enemies closer. That's exactly what Anthony intended to do.

Chapter 3

Anthony preferred thinking he was on a reconnaissance mission rather than a social call. A week and a half had passed since Vivi and her sister had come barging into Dante's. Since then, he'd planned to follow his brother's advice and be "neighborly," but every time he casually strolled by to see what was up, Natalie was there, dressed to the teeth like she was still in gay Paree. Anthony decided to wait until he could catch Vivi alone. Today was his lucky day; crossing the street from Dante's to the old candy store, he could see Coco Chanel was nowhere in sight.

Anthony gently rapped on the window, startling Vivi where she sat in a folding chair frowning over some papers. She seemed surprised to see him, even hesitating a moment before getting up to let him in.

"Bonjour," she said politely as she ushered him inside. "How nice of you to come and say hello."

Anthony smiled sadly. He couldn't believe the candy store was gone. It had been a fixture of his childhood. How many Saturday afternoons had Nonna Maria given him,

Mikey, and their cousin Gemma money to go buy sweets? *Lazzaroni* dark chocolate, *torrone* . . . thinking about it still made his mouth water. It didn't help that there was still the faintest hint of chocolate in the air.

"I used to come here to buy candy when I was small," he told Vivi.

Vivi nodded sympathetically. "It's sad when a neighborhood business closes its doors." She unfolded a chair for him opposite hers. "We were told the old man died and the son didn't want the store?"

"Something like that," said Anthony, sitting down. He'd love to know how much Vivi and her sister paid for the space. His gaze traveled the room, though now it wasn't with nostalgia, but with a competitor's shrewd eye. Even with the shelves, counters, and bins removed, the space still wasn't big enough to fit more than seven or eight small tables, if that. Did Vivi realize that?

"Coffee?" Vivi offered, picking up the thermos at her feet. Her voice echoed slightly off the empty walls. Anthony nodded, looking up. The ceilings were high. She was definitely going to need fans if she wanted to keep the place at a decent temperature in both the summer and winter.

"Coffee sounds great. Where's your sister?" he asked casually.

"Running some errands in Manhattan. She'll be here this afternoon."

Anthony accepted the coffee-filled thermos lid from Vivi and took a sip. *Madonn'*. This was not coffee. This was brown water. Should he tell her? That would be rude. But she needed to know, didn't she? He decided to wait and see how their chat went.

"So, your 'gravy,' " Vivi began with a mischievous look. "Was I right? Was it done?"

"Not quite."

"But I was close," she insisted.

"I'll give you that," Anthony conceded reluctantly. He pointed to the papers in her hand. "Secret recipes?"

"Estimates from contractors." She frowned. "Dollar sign after dollar sign." She hesitated. "Is there someone you would recommend?"

Anthony could see it was hard for her to ask. She seemed proud, someone who would do everything herself if she could. He was torn. What if he gave her the name of the contractor who'd done the expansion on Dante's, and she was displeased with the results? He didn't want to be accused of sabotage. On the other hand, it was always good to do unto your neighbors as you would have them do unto you. But in this case, couldn't it be viewed as aiding and abetting the enemy?

Anthony held out his hand. "Here, let me see those," he said authoritatively. Vivi handed over the estimates. "Tony and Bob Mineo," he said, scanning the first estimate. "Totally overpriced, shoddy work." He slid the piece of paper to the bottom of the pile. "Jackson Morgan—it'll take you two years to get this place done if you're lucky. Forget him." Jackson went to the bottom of the pile with the Mineos. "Tippy Mottola. He does decent work." He picked up the next sheet of paper. "Ricky and Joey DiDinato. They're good, too." He handed the sheaf of papers back to her. "I'd go with either Tippy or the DiDinatos. You already had an architect in here, right?"

Vivi looked mildly insulted. "Of course. The whole time Natalie and I were getting ready to move, the plans were being prepared."

"Smart." Wanting to be polite, Anthony forced himself to take another sip of awful coffee and studied the delicate woman sitting across from him. He had a hard time imagining her commanding a restaurant kitchen, but you never knew. Sometimes the mildest mannered individuals turned into dictators once they put an apron on. God knows she had no problem giving her opinions. "You and your sister never really explained why you chose Bensonhurst."

Vivi considered the question carefully. "I wanted to be part of a close-knit community, with people who would appreciate good food."

"Have you ever even been out here before?"

"Yes. My aunt lived in New York, and a few times when I came to visit, we came out here to go to the Santa Rosalia Festival."

"Then you know the kind of people who live here."

Vivi's gaze hardened. "So?"

"They might not go for fancy French food."

"It's not going to *be* fancy," Vivi replied with mild irritation. "It's going to be simple. And affordable."

Anthony looked her straight in the eye. "You mean like Dante's."

"Simpler," Vivi insisted without blinking an eye. "Your restaurant is very large, Mr. Dante—"

"Please, call me Anthony—"

"And mine will be very small. You can accommodate large families and cater affairs. I won't be able to. My clients will be couples, small parties, who just want to relax over a bottle of wine and some good food."

"They can do that at Dante's, too, you know."

"Well, now they'll have two places to choose from," Vivi replied airily, though there was no mistaking the touch of challenge in her voice. "Variety is the spice of life. Don't you agree?"

No, he didn't. There was one restaurant around here that covered simple, affordable, family, single, parties, whatever, and it was his. Though if she served her coffee to customers, he might not have a problem.

Anthony forced a smile, wondering if he should choke down another sip. Vivi's gaze seemed locked on his hands.

"What?" Anthony asked, feeling self-conscious. "What are you looking at?"

"Your hands. Real chef hands."

"That's because I'm a real chef."

Vivi gave a small laugh. "Oh, and I'm not?" She held her own hands out for his inspection. She was right; though her fingers were long and delicate, there was some scarring. He nodded and said nothing.

"That's new," Vivi continued, pointing to his wedding ring.

"I take it off when I cook."

"Ah."

"You married?" Anthony asked, trying to imagine what kind of man could be attracted to someone so stuck up. *Variety is the spice of life, wouldn't you agree?* Gimme a break.

"Why do you ask?" Vivi replied coolly.

Anthony yawned. "Just making conversation."

"As it so happens, I'm not married, unless one can be married to their work." She gazed reverently at the bare walls surrounding them. "It's going to be beautiful in here when I'm done! Just wait and see."

Anthony smiled, squelching a feeling of envy. He tried to recall if he'd ever felt that kind of enthusiasm about Dante's. His situation was different, of course—Dante's had been family-owned and -run from the beginning—but he did remember how good it felt when his mother turned the kitchen over to him completely. He'd worked hard for it, and deserved it. "So, how are you adjusting to life here?" he asked curiously.

"I love it here," Vivi gushed. He must have given her an odd look, because she added, "Really! I do!"

"Most Americans think the French are snobs."

"Most French think Americans are rude. But I don't."

"Always a plus when you're opening a restaurant in the States."

They shared a laugh, and for a minute, Anthony felt like they could be friends.

"It's amazing to me you didn't formally train to be a chef," she said with a cool, appraising eye. "In France—"

"You're not in France," Anthony said tersely, abandoning the notion of friendship as quickly as it had appeared.

Vivi chuckled softly. *"Touche."*

"Here's what I don't get." Anthony was earnest as he leaned forward in his chair. "As a chef, why would you choose to leave the country that's supposedly the gastronomical capital of the world? Isn't France the place where the culinary *crème de la crème* strut their stuff?"

Vivi traced the top of her coffee mug with her finger. "Women don't get the same respect in France for cooking as men do. It's seen as a man's province. There are very, *very* few female chefs in France who have their own restaurants. I wanted to open a restaurant and be judged by the quality of the food, not my sex. So I chose America."

"Interesting," Anthony murmured. She had to be tough as nails. Not everyone could just pull up stakes and move to a foreign country. That took real guts. "And your sister?" he ventured. "She here for the same reasons?"

Vivi shifted uncomfortably in her chair. "She's also here to reinvent herself."

"What was she before?"

Vivi's gaze darted away.

"I'm sorry. Is that a rude question?"

"Yes."

"Does that mean you're not going to tell me?"

Vivi looked at him. "I shouldn't."

"But you want to."

Vivi smiled enigmatically. "There are lots of things I want to do. That doesn't mean I pursue them all."

"Tell you what," Anthony cajoled slyly. "You tell me what the deal is with your sister, and I'll tell you who renovated Dante's."

Vivi's jaw dropped. "That's blackmail!"

"No, that's what we call a quid pro quo. Come on."

Vivi clucked her tongue. "Honestly, you Americans are such gossips."

"Just spill it."

" 'Just spill it,' " Vivi repeated, sounding delighted. "I like that phrase."

"Here's another: quit stalling."

Vivi took a deep breath. "Natalie is—was—an official in the foreign ministry back home. She"—Vivi hesitated—"had an affair with a cabinet minister in the government. He told her he was in the process of divorcing his wife, but it wasn't true." She paused for a sip of coffee, and Anthony fought a wince. How could she drink that stuff? "Anyway, the affair became public knowledge, and it wrecked her career. She knew she'd never be judged on her own merits again. If she advanced, people would always suspect it was because she was sleeping with someone in a position above her."

"No pun intended."

Vivi looked confused. "What?"

"Never mind. Go on."

"Like me, she knew America is a place where there are no obstacles to one's ability to advance." She gave a shrug. "So, here we are."

Anthony couldn't hide his admiration. "You've both got guts, I'll give you that. But if you don't mind my saying, the similarity seems to end there."

Pink sprang to Vivi's cheeks. "We're very different, it's true." Vivi reached down to unscrew the thermos and refill her coffee cup. "Mmm, perfect," she said after taking a sip.

"Actually it's not," Anthony said politely. "No offense."

Vivi was taken aback. "What are you talking about? It's fine. You've been drinking it, haven't you?"

"To be polite."

Vivi's jaw clenched. "I made it myself this morning. It's delicious."

"If you're French, maybe. But we Italians like our joe a little more robust."

Vivi huffed indignantly. "Excuse me, but it's the French who are known for their coffee making expertise, and this coffee is perfect."

"I'm just telling you for your own good. If this is what you plan to serve in your bistro, you're going to hear some complaints. This is an Italian neighborhood, and Italians like their coffee strong."

"French coffee is strong. It's just not bitter."

"Italian coffee isn't bitter!"

"It's bitter, burnt-tasting sludge!"

"Speak for yourself!"

"I am." Vivi thrust out her hand. "If you're too much of a philistine to enjoy fine coffee, give it back to me. I don't want it wasted."

"Drink up," said Anthony, handing the thermos top back to her.

"I have work to do," Vivi snapped, gathering up her papers on the floor.

Anthony rose. "Sorry for interrupting you. Enjoy the rest of your day." He started toward the door, stopping to turn when Vivi sharply called out his name. "Yes?"

"I certainly hope you're nicer to your wife about her coffee than you were to me!"

Anthony swallowed, trying to beat back the feeling of being punched in the chest. "My wife is dead."

"*He insulted your* coffee? What a clod! I don't see why you served him any in the first place."

Vivi said nothing as she followed Natalie into the kitchen. It was her first time visiting her half sister's apartment in

Manhattan, and she was stunned. Not only was the place huge, but Natalie seemed to have spared no expense in furnishing it. Had their father really left *that* much money to Natalie? Enough for her to finance the restaurant and live this luxuriously? Vivi tried not to think about it, because if so, it meant their father had truly left her a pittance in comparison, and that hurt. Still . . .

"This place is so big," Vivi marveled, running her fingertips across the marble counters enviously. "Did it come furnished?"

"Of course not," Natalie scoffed, pouring a cup of coffee for each of them. "You think someone else would have such good taste?"

Vivi smiled uneasily as she accepted the coffee from her sister. "It must have cost a lot."

"It did, but so what? Honestly, Vivi," said Natalie as she flipped her long dark hair back over her shoulder, "your attitude toward money is so provincial sometimes."

That's because I've had to count every penny, Vivi thought angrily, *whereas you—*

She stopped herself, taking a deep breath. She should be grateful toward Natalie, not resentful. Still, it was hard. Natalie seemed to take her wealth and privilege for granted, whereas Vivi took nothing for granted. Perhaps she was being too touchy.

"I told you before," Natalie continued, motioning for Vivi to follow her into the plush living room, where a brand new white leather sofa dominated, "I don't understand why you insist on living out in Brooklyn and not here with me. Think of the fun we'd have as roommates." Natalie smiled fondly.

Generous and playful one moment, critical the next—it was so hard to read Natalie sometimes. So hard not to envy her, as well. She was so beautiful and composed, where Vivi was excitable and, if she was being generous, average looking. At least, that's how Vivi saw herself. It probably would be fun to live together. But truthfully, Vivi couldn't see herself here at all.

The size of the place struck her as ridiculous. Why would two people need so much space? Besides, her decorating taste was the opposite of Natalie's. Natalie favored a look that was elemental yet high tech—chrome, glass, leather, marble. Vivi liked fat, plump sofas with soft pillows, and windows filled with hanging plants. And a homey kitchen where something delicious was always baking in the oven. If this made her provincial, so be it. That's who she was.

She sat down on the couch beside her sister, carefully balancing the coffee mug on her lap. It was probably unwise to have told Natalie about Anthony's visit. But she couldn't help it; she wanted confirmation that her reaction to Anthony's criticism wasn't out of proportion. She still couldn't believe he'd had the gall to insult her to her face. Who did he think he was? It made her teeth grit.

"He's widowed, you know. The Italian."

Natalie clucked her tongue in exasperation. "We're back to him again, are we? Vivi, why do you care?"

"I don't! It's just . . . I embarrassed myself."

"How?"

"I saw he had a wedding ring on, and as he was leaving, I yelled, 'I hope you're nicer to your wife about her coffee than you were to me!' He turned around and told me his wife was dead."

Natalie gave a small wince. "Well, you didn't know."

"I know, but still."

Thinking about it made Vivi feel mortified all over again. But how was she supposed to know his wife had passed on? Still, the look on his face—the deep pain that swam to his eyes—revealed a sensitive man, at least when it came to matters of the heart. It was a pity he was such a fool when it came to food.

"Maybe I should apologize to him," Vivi thought aloud.

"What?" Natalie said indignantly. "If anything, he should apologize to you, flinging your hospitality back in your face!"

"I know, I just hate getting off on the wrong foot with our neighbors. It's not good."

"You should have thought of that before you challenged him in his own kitchen. Maybe that's why he made those comments about your coffee; he was swiping back at you."

Could someone be so petty? The answer, of course, was yes. Chefs could be a petty and vindictive lot. She'd seen grown men throw punches at each other over the correct way to prepare béchamel sauce. Being a chef was all about creativity and perfection. If he genuinely believed her coffee was subpar, then he wasn't out of line telling her so, but rather merely following the edicts of his calling—just as she'd been doing that day in his kitchen.

Vivi shielded her eyes from the bright morning sun flooding the apartment. One wall of the living room was pure glass, revealing a soaring landscape of skyscrapers. It was an impressive view. Even so, Vivi preferred the small apartment she'd rented in a five-story walk-up in Bensonhurst. She liked old places, places with a history. This steel and glass hothouse of Natalie's was a bit too *moderne* for her taste.

"I wonder how long the wife has been dead," Natalie mused. "A month? Five years? Either way, it's odd that he still wears his ring."

"I don't think so," Vivi disagreed, shifting so the sun wasn't in her eyes. It didn't seem to be bothering Natalie at all. In fact, with the morning sun shining on her face, Vivi could see how flawless Natalie's complexion was. "If I were married and my husband died, I'd keep wearing my ring."

"How romantic," Natalie said dryly.

"I do have a romantic streak."

"Well, you certainly didn't get it from Papa."

Vivi didn't respond. In fact, she thought the opposite. Her father was always buying little gifts for her mother, leaving little love notes for her around the house. Was it possible Natalie had never seen this side of his personality?

Natalie was regarding her sternly. "Promise me you won't let yourself get too close to that Dante. We can't have you distracted, Vivi. All our focus needs to be on getting the restaurant up and running."

All *our* focus?

"Stop worrying, Natalie. I'm here to cook, not find myself a new romance."

"Good. Who needs romance, anyway?" Natalie sneered.

The bitterness in Natalie's voice brought Vivi up short. She'd been so selfish, worrying about money and prattling on about the Italian, that she hadn't even stopped to think how Natalie was faring.

Vivi reached out to take her hand. "It still hurts, doesn't it, *cherie*?"

Natalie's eyes quickly filled with tears. "I was so stupid . . ."

"You were human and you made a mistake."

"A mistake that cost me my career."

"You'll begin a new career. Here," Vivi replied with absolute conviction. "You just need time to heal."

"And you need to learn not to listen to ignorant widowers who criticize your coffee!"

"You're right," Vivi agreed with a sigh. But she still felt badly about causing him pain.

Chapter 4

"You got company."

Anthony looked up from chopping basil with his mezzaluna to see Aldo—headwaiter, and the bane of his existence—scowling at him from the kitchen doorway. It was three thirty in the afternoon, which to Anthony's mind could only mean one thing: Vivi and her sister were launching another ambush.

Anthony frowned at the old man impatiently. "You can't handle it?"

"Asked for you," Aldo replied with a yawn.

"Jesus, Mary, and Joseph," Anthony muttered, putting down the curved steel blade in his hand. "How we doin' with that eggplant?" he asked Sam on his way out.

"Sliced, diced, and ready to go," Sam replied cheerfully.

"Sounds like you're describing your fingers rather than the eggplant," said Anthony. Sam grinned, which Anthony took as a good sign. Some people thought they wanted to be chefs, but the minute you gave them the grunt work, they gave up, not realizing the pecking order in a restaurant was a ladder to be scaled. Others were glad to do the work, but never quite got the hang of using the knives or coping with the nerve-shattering pace. Those were the ones that broke Anthony's heart—the ones who were willing to do what it took, but lacked the coordination or temperament.

He squared his shoulders, preparing for a face-off with Vivi. She'd been on his mind ever since their coffee brewing battle. He knew he'd taken a cheap shot at her. The polite thing would have been for him to pause and explain that his wife was dead, rather than storm out, leaving her sitting there with her face turning the color of a beet. But he was still steaming over her insults about Italian coffee. The woman wouldn't know a decent cup of joe if it came up and bit her on the *derriere*.

He pushed through the doors of the kitchen. It wasn't Vivi waiting there for him, but his seven-year-old nephew, Anthony, known in the family as "Little Ant." Though he and his nephew were close, Little Ant had never shown up at the restaurant on his own before, even though his elementary school was within walking distance. Something was wrong.

"Hey, big guy." Anthony tousled his nephew's dark curly hair while throwing Aldo a dirty look. "You couldn't tell me it was my nephew?" he called to him. "You had to act like it was a friggin' mystery?"

"I quit!" Aldo shouted as headed toward the banquet room, muttering a stream of Italian curses in his wake.

"Pain in my ass," Anthony growled as he watched the old man disappear. "You want a Coke or something?" he asked Little Ant.

Little Ant nodded. "Did Aldo really just quit?" he asked nervously.

"He quits every day," said Anthony as he went behind the bar to fetch the boy his soda. "Don't worry about it." The kid was the spitting image of Anthony's brother,

Michael, though father and son differed greatly in temperament. At seven, Michael had been a rambunctious little bastard, whereas Little Ant was a bit more studious and quiet.

Anthony handed his nephew the Coke and took a seat opposite him. "Where's the old man?"

"Home with the baby."

"Does he know you're here?"

"No." Little Ant slumped miserably in his chair. "He thinks I'm at hockey practice."

From the time Little Ant was born, Michael had started counting down the years until his son would be able to play youth hockey and carry on the "Dante legacy." Now the time had arrived, and Little Ant didn't look too thrilled.

"And you're not at practice because . . . ?" Anthony prodded.

"I hate it! I don't want to play hockey." Little Ant dipped his head shyly. "I want to learn to cook like you."

Anthony swallowed, surprised to find himself getting choked up. He and Angie had been trying to have a kid of their own when she died. Anthony had always loved hanging out with his nieces and nephew, now more than ever since it seemed likely they'd be the only children in his life. He and Little Ant were especially close. Not only did the kid love to eat, but he also loved knowing *how* the food he ate was made. From the time Little Ant could talk, it was "What's in this?" and "How do you make that?"

"Have you told your mom and dad you don't want to play?"

Little Ant looked tearful as he cracked an ice cube between his teeth. "I told Mom. She said I should at least give it a try."

"That sounds like good advice."

"But I hate it, Uncle Anthony. It's stupid." The agonized way he drew the word out—"stooooopid"—didn't bode well.

"Maybe you just hate watching it," Anthony offered,

knowing the boy had been watching his father play at Met Gar from the time he was small. "Maybe you'll feel different once you start playing yourself."

"I won't," Little Ant insisted miserably. "I'll never be as good as Dad, so why even try? I hate when he talks about me growing up and being on the Blades! Everyone on the team is like, 'Oooh, your dad is Michael Dante,' like they think I should play great or something. What if I mess up?"

"What if you do?"

"Dad'll get upset. He'll think I'm a loser."

"No, he won't," Anthony assured him, though he wasn't sure his words were helping. He couldn't even begin to imagine the pressure Little Ant had to be under with Michael as his father. He doubted Michael was in any way pressuring Little Ant on purpose. Michael worshipped the ground Little Ant walked on. But he also knew Michael had high hopes that his son might follow in his footsteps. How was the kid supposed to tell him he'd rather make meatballs?

"You want me to talk to your dad?" Anthony offered. "See if I can explain to him that hockey isn't your thing?"

Little Ant nodded vigorously. "Would you?"

"It's why you're here, right?"

"Well . . . yeah."

"Tell you what: You go back to hockey practice, and the next time I see your dad, I'll see what I can do."

Little Ant jumped up from the table. "Yippee! I can quit!"

"Hey!" Anthony said sharply. "No one said anything about quitting. Your mom's right; you need to at least give it a try. Have you even played a game yet?"

Little Ant's face fell. "No."

"Wait until you've played a few, and then we'll see what happens. In the meantime, I'll float the idea by your dad to let you hang out with me and learn to cook a few things."

"You think he'll let me?" Little Ant asked hopefully.

" 'Course he will," said Anthony. He saw some of himself

in Little Ant's eagerness, recalling how he'd hounded his father until he showed him how to properly assemble lasagna. And the first time his mother let him help with the gravy . . . *Madonn'*, it felt like Christmas. Cooking was in the Dante genes.

"What's the first thing you want to learn to make?"

"The gravy," Little Ant said reverently. "The family gravy."

" 'Atta boy," said Anthony, patting him proudly on the back. "Now scooch and get back to practice before your father finds out you went AWOL."

"Thanks, Uncle Anthony!" Little Ant threw his arms around Anthony's waist, hugging tight.

"Anytime," Anthony assured him. "Don't worry; we'll have you stirring the sauce in no time."

Vivi found herself having second thoughts as she walked into Dante's bearing her trademark *tarte aux pommes*. Perhaps she was crazy, seeking Anthony out after he'd had the audacity to criticize her coffee. But it bothered her that they'd parted on such strained terms. Plus, he'd promised to give her the name of his contractor if she told him about Natalie. The apple tart was an enticement to remind him to keep his word. It would also put to rest any doubts he might have about her culinary expertise.

The restaurant was in the early stages of springing to life before opening for dinner. God, how she missed that! The hustle, the bustle, the anticipation. *Patience,* she told herself. *You'll be back in the soup soon enough.*

"Can I help you?" A very old man with regal bearing slowly approached her.

"I'm here to see Anthony."

The old man's eyes flicked critically to the foil-covered pie tin in her hand. "Are you looking for a job of some sort? In the kitchen?"

"I'm a friend," Vivi fibbed, knowing she was using the term very loosely.

"Who should I tell him is here?" the old man asked irritably.

"Vivi. You're the headwaiter, yes?" It was a rhetorical question. She'd worked in enough restaurants to know the type immediately: peevish, territorial, and loyal to the chef unto death.

"I'm Aldo," the old man said, extending his hand for a shake. "And yes, this is my restaurant."

His restaurant. Oh, he was the top dog, all right. He asked Vivi to wait a moment as he went to fetch Anthony. His absence gave Vivi a chance to peruse her surroundings, and she found herself befuddled by the way Dante's was decorated. There seemed to be lots of autographed photos of priests, as well as photos of Frank Sinatra, Dean Martin, and some other men Vivi didn't recognize, but whom she assumed were Italians of note. The paintings weren't very enticing, either: watery reproductions of starry-eyed gondoliers punting Venice's canals, even a bad etching of the Leaning Tower of Pisa. The decor was—how should she put it?—*collant.* Tacky. Lacking in class. Perhaps this was supposed to be part of its charm?

"Well, this is a surprise." Anthony's tone was dry as he approached her. Vivi immediately began grinding her teeth. He couldn't open with a simple hello? He had to be sarcastic right from the start?

"Is this a bad time?" she asked, thinking, *Of course it is.* What a stupid idea this was.

"It's a restaurant. It's always a bad time."

They shared a chuckle as Vivi held the tart out to him. "A peace offering. I'm sorry we parted badly the other day."

"That was my fault."

"Yes, it was. What you said about my coffee wasn't very nice."

"I wasn't referring to the coffee," Anthony replied testily.

"I was referring to the thoughtless way I told you my wife was dead."

"No, the thoughtlessness on that count was mine. I—"

"You didn't know," Anthony interrupted, clearly uncomfortable with the subject.

Vivi longed to know more, but sensed she had to tread carefully. "Has she been gone long?" Such polite euphemisms people used when speaking of death, she thought. Gone. Departed. Crossed over. But what was the alternative? To say, "Has she been *dead* long?" That sounded awful. Heartless.

"She died a little over a year ago," said Anthony.

"I'm sorry to hear that," Vivi murmured.

Anthony glanced away. "Yeah, it was a shock."

Vivi held her breath, hoping he would elaborate further, but he didn't. A shock . . . well, that ruled out battling a long illness. Vivi was itching to ask him how she died, but if ever there was a rude question, that was it.

For a second, he seemed lost in thought . . . lost to *her*, his wife. But then he seemed to remember where he was, giving the pie plate in his hand a little shake. "What have we got here?"

"Apple tart. My own recipe."

"Oh yeah?" Anthony seemed intrigued. "Can I try it now?"

"After you tell me what contractor you used when you renovated Dante's," Vivi reminded him sweetly.

Anthony frowned. "Oh, that."

"Yes, that. You owe me in exchange for my telling you about Natalie, remember?"

"It's the DiDinato brothers."

It was Vivi's turn to frown. "Their estimate was the highest."

"Do you want the best or not?"

"Of course I do," she bristled.

"Then the double Ds are the go-to guys." He pointed to the pie plate. "May I?"

"Of course." Vivi couldn't wait to see the expression on his face when he took the first bite and his eyes glazed over with sheer pleasure. And sheer envy.

"Let me just grab a plate."

Vivi nodded, sitting down at a nearby table as Anthony fetched a plate and some cutlery. By the time he joined her, her heart was restless in her chest, obeying its own beat.

"Looks great," said Anthony, peeling back the foil and cutting into the pie. The sweet aroma of apples and sugar rose up. "Smells great, too."

Vivi watched as he cut a piece of pie for each of them. "No, none for me," she said quickly. She was actually nervous, so much so that she wasn't sure she could manage even the smallest bite. But Anthony wasn't having it.

"My mother always told me, 'Never trust a cook who won't sample their own creation in front of you.'"

Seeing no way out, she accepted the plate he slid across the table to her. "You first," she insisted.

"If you say so," said Anthony, taking a forkful of pie. Vivi's breath froze as she watched him chew slowly and deliberately, savoring the taste before swallowing. "Nice."

Vivi snorted. "'Nice'?"

"Nice," Anthony repeated mildly. He broke off a piece of the pastry, studying it. "This is really good. Sweet. How do you make it?"

"How do you think I make it?" Vivi shot back. Nice indeed.

Anthony popped the pastry into his mouth, chewing thoughtfully. "There's sugar in it."

"What kind?" Vivi pushed, folding her arms across her chest. He thought he was Mr. Hot Chef? Let's see how good he was at pinpointing ingredients in French pastry.

"Confectioner's sugar."

Bastard.

"Very good." She tensed as he took another bite of pie.

"How's that piece you're chewing on now?" she asked tartly. "Nice?"

"Very nice. But I think it would be better if you used a little more brown sugar, you know?"

Vivi contemplated picking up the pie plate and marrying it to his face. Instead, she picked up her fork and speared a bite of pie from his plate. "What you're saying is, you can do better." She popped the morsel into her mouth, raising an eyebrow. "Right?"

"Well . . ."

"Go on, then. I dare you. I dare you to do better."

Anthony reared back in his chair. "You're challenging me?" He seemed affronted. He *was* a raving egomaniac!

"Yes, I am," Vivi replied fiercely. "Bake me something better. Bake me a pie that will leave me drooling and begging you to share the recipe. I'll bet you can't."

Anthony's eyes seemed to ignite at the thought of competition. "That's a pretty big gauntlet you're throwing down there, *Ms.* Robitaille. You sure you're up for what we in the States call a major butt kicking?"

"Absolutely. There's no way you can best me. You know it, and I know it." She leaned across the table, staring hard into his big, brown eyes. "As you Americans say, 'Bring it over.'"

"I think you mean 'Bring it *on*.'" Anthony sprang to his feet. "When?"

Vivi rose, nimbly wrapping her own untouched slice of pie in tinfoil. "Surprise me."

Anthony had never been a fan of unexpected guests, which was why, showing up at work the day after Vivi's apple pie ambush, he almost turned around and walked right out when he saw his brother sitting in the dining room with baby Angelica. Three visits in one week! First Little Ant, then Vivi, now Mikey. Mother of God. Did he have an invisible sign over his head that read, "Please feel free to interrupt me at work"?

"What the hell are you doing here, Mike?" he asked his brother, bending down to kiss his youngest niece where she slept in her baby carrier atop a small table in the dining room. Michael was wolfing down the remainders of a tart. Vivi's tart.

"I was driving around trying to get Angelica to sleep, and thought I'd stop in," Michael mumbled, his mouth full of food.

"Lucky me." Anthony knew that sometimes the only way his brother and sister-in-law could get the little one to sleep was to drive around. But Anthony couldn't understand why, once the objective had been achieved, Mikey couldn't just drive back home and deposit Angelica back in her crib. Mikey knew what it was like at the restaurant. Did he really think Anthony had time to just shoot the breeze?

Oblivious to Anthony's annoyance, Michael tapped his plate with his fork enthusiastically. "Mmm. You make this? This is the most amazing apple pie I've ever tasted."

"Gimme that." Anthony grabbed the fork from his brother's hand and gouged a piece of tart for himself. "It's good, not great."

"You're wrong," Michael disagreed with a chortle, taking back his fork. "This pie is fucking great."

"Shut up, Mike."

"What?" Michael's eyes were wide and his mouth full. "I thought you'd be happy."

"I would if I'd made it. But I didn't."

"Who made it, then?"

Anthony just scowled until Michael figured it out.

"Ah, Vivi."

"Ah, Vivi," Anthony mimicked, stealing another bite of tart. Okay, it was great. But he still thought a little more brown sugar could make it even *greater*. He couldn't sleep last night, trying to figure out what he could make to prove his baking skills rivaled, if not exceeded, hers. So far he'd drawn a blank.

"I guess she really believes the way to a man's heart is through his stomach," Michael ribbed.

Anthony frowned. "She's not interested in my stomach, or any other part of me unless it's my head on a plate, and I feel the same way."

"Sure you do."

Anthony rolled his eyes. "Stop trying to create something where there's nothing, will you, please? The woman is a major pain in my ass, showing up here whenever she pleases, kinda like someone else I know."

"Might I remind you I'm half owner of this place?"

"Might I remind *you* our agreement was you'd keep out of my hair?"

Angelica stirred restlessly in her baby seat, and for a moment, Anthony and his brother held their breath, nervous she might awaken and start to bawl. Both sighed with relief once it became clear she was just getting comfortable.

"Why don't you take her home so she can sleep in her own crib?" Anthony asked.

"She's sleeping fine." Michael glanced around the dining room. "Look, I'm actually here to ask a small favor."

"What's that?"

"Could you put together some dinner for me that I can heat up later? You know, some spaghetti and meatballs? Something Dominica and Little Ant will eat?"

"The househusband thing is really working out for you, huh, Mike?"

Michael looked defensive. "It's working out fine," he insisted. "It's just been a crazy day, and I haven't had a chance to figure out dinner."

"So you had to come here?"

"That a problem?"

"Not yet. But it could be."

Anthony ignored the dark look his brother threw him as Michael wolfed down the remainder of the pie. Maybe doing all that homemaker stuff wasn't as easy as he and Michael thought. No wonder Little Ant was feeling the heat; the kid was Michael's lifeline to a world he knew inside and out, one in which Michael had excelled.

"How's Little Ant doing in hockey?" Anthony asked.

Michael puffed up with pride. "They don't play their first game until next week, but from what I've seen at the practices I've been able to catch, he's looking pretty good."

"The coach must *love* having you there," Anthony drawled sarcastically.

Michael frowned. "I keep telling the guy to look at me as a resource, but I get the sense he sees me as more of a liability than an asset. *Cafone.*"

"Maybe he's worried you're making Little Ant nervous."

"Nah. I've been playing hockey with Little Ant since he was three. He's not nervous."

"So, he's enjoying himself?"

"Yeah, of course." Michael's gaze turned suspicious. "What's with the fifty questions all of a sudden?"

"What, I can't show interest in my only nephew?"

"You're right." He patted Anthony's shoulder affectionately. "Didn't mean to bite your head off. I'm just a little tired."

"The kids are running your ass off, huh?"

"Pretty much. But that's the way it goes, right?"

"I guess." Anthony absently scratched behind his ear. "You know, last time I was at your place, Little Ant was asking me all sorts of questions about cooking."

"Yeah, I noticed that," said Michael, frowning a little.

"I was thinking—maybe I could show him how to prepare a few things."

Michael shrugged. "As long as it doesn't interfere with hockey, why not?"

Shit, thought Anthony, heart sinking on his nephew's behalf. This was going to be one uphill battle. Anthony didn't have any kids, so he sure as hell wasn't going to tell his brother how to raise his.

"Do you know what time his first game is next week?" Anthony asked.

"I can check. Why? You want to go?" The prospect seemed to make Michael happy.

"Yeah, I'd love to." The kid needed all the emotional support he could get. "It depends on whether I can get away."

"It'd be right after school, and the game usually doesn't last for more than an hour," Michael said eagerly. "You'd be back here in time for the beginning of the dinner rush."

"I'll try."

"Good. Little Ant would love it. You know how much he loves you."

"Yeah, I do," Anthony agreed proudly. He was a damn good uncle if he said so himself.

Michael slid out of his seat gingerly and picked up the baby carrier, regarding his slumbering daughter with affection. "I should probably get her home and settled. If she wakes up here, she'll freak out."

"I'll go put together some dinner for you. But first, let me ask you a question."

"Shoot."

"What do you think is the best dessert I make?" Anthony hated sounding like he was fishing for compliments, but he needed an objective opinion in choosing what to make that would blow Vivi's socks off, gastronomically speaking.

"No question, the ricotta fritters."

Anthony was pleasantly surprised. "Yeah? Not the olive oil cake?"

"Your olive oil cake is outstanding, but the fritters—oh man. Theresa says they're better than sex."

I remember sex, Anthony thought nostalgically. He hadn't been with anyone since Ang died. Friends urged him to find a friend with benefits, or even visit a hooker if he needed relief, but Anthony was not a sex for sex's sake kind of guy. Never had been.

"Right," Anthony said, tightening the ties of his apron. "You wait here, I'll get the chow."

"Mucho thanks, my man. I'll shoot you a call later about Little Ant's game."

"Sounds good."

"Oh, and Ant?"

"Yeah?"

Michael grinned. "Next time you see Vivi, tell her from me that her apple pie is outstanding."

Chapter 5

"*This estimate is* outrageous."

Vivi tried to cover her embarrassment over Natalie's pronouncement, smiling nervously at Ricky and Joey DiDinato. Vivi had agonized over whether to take Anthony's suggestion, precisely *because* the brothers DiDinato were the priciest contractors of the lot. But then she'd remembered Natalie telling her price was no object. When she'd mentioned the estimate to Natalie before contacting the brothers, Natalie's impatient response had been, "Yes, yes, whatever you want," her aversion to managing the myriad details clear. Yet now that it was actually time to sign the contract, Natalie was balking.

Joey DiDinato, a squat man with a pair of tattooed biceps that rivaled Popeye's and a face that looked like it had been flattened by a shovel, raised an unruly eyebrow. "We got a problem here, ladies?"

"No," said Vivi.

"Yes," Natalie countered, glaring at her. "This estimate seems very high to me."

"Compared to what?" asked Ricky DiDinato, whose physique matched his brother's but whose leathery face boasted more contour.

"Others we've received," said Natalie.

Joey snorted through his bulldog nose. "Hire the others, then." He started to rise from his folding chair, but Vivi waved him back down.

"Please," she said frantically. "Can you just wait one minute while I talk to my sister in private?"

"Sure." He stood again. "Me and Ricky'll go get a samwich. We'll be back in ten."

"Thank you," Vivi said as the men sauntered out of the empty candy store, their irritation obvious.

" 'Samwich'?" Natalie repeated disdainfully as they closed the door. "Can you believe—"

"Have you lost your mind?"

Natalie's mouth tightened. "I beg your pardon?"

"I told you what hiring the brothers would cost. You said it was fine. Now, all of a sudden, it's not fine?"

Natalie smoothed the front of her trousers. "Vivi, doesn't this estimate seem high to you? I mean, really."

"We agreed we wanted the best, Natalie. These brothers are supposed to be the best."

"According to whom?"

Vivi gestured across the street. "According to Anthony Dante."

"The Gravy Man?" Natalie hooted. "Oh, yes, I'm sure he steered you in the right direction!"

"What do you mean?" Vivi asked crossly.

Natalie looked at her like she was a simpleton. "Did it never cross your mind that he recommended the DiDinato brothers because they're the worst?"

Vivi shook her head in disbelief. No, it hadn't crossed her mind. Anthony Dante was an arrogant jackass—a jackass who'd yet to track her down bearing one of his own culinary creations, she noted with some satisfaction—but devious? He didn't seem the type.

"I don't think he would do that, Natalie."

"Did you even double check and ask them if they worked on Dante's?" Natalie questioned.

"There was no reason to. When they gave me a list of references, Anthony's name was on it."

"Maybe they're in league together."

"Natalie, listen to yourself. What you're saying is crazy."

"Maybe to you, but—" She broke off.

Vivi approached her with concern. "What is it, sweet girl? Why are you so upset?"

"I don't know." Natalie seemed anxious. "Sometimes I wonder if we haven't made a huge mistake, moving here without thinking things through."

"We did think things through," Vivi pointed out tersely. She was not about to let Natalie rewrite history just because she was experiencing a moment of doubt.

"Are you sure?" Natalie asked, sounding desperate for reassurance.

"More sure than I've ever been in my life," Vivi declared. She wasn't just saying it; with each passing day, she felt more confident in her surroundings. The people in Bensonhurst were so nice! They were hardworking, down to earth, and utterly without pretension—so different from so many of the people Vivi encountered when she moved from Avignon to Paris. She was starting to feel at home here, happy she'd chosen to live where she'd be working, rather than live with Natalie in Manhattan. She did get lonely sometimes, but that would change soon enough when the restaurant was up and running. She'd be living, eating, and breathing Vivi's; time alone would become something she yearned for. A memory.

She watched as Natalie's eyes slowly made a circuit

around the room, hopeful that Natalie's imagination was as strong as her own, and that she was seeing the room as Vivi saw it: alive with talk, laughter, and the smell of mouthwatering food prepared by Vivi. Instead, Natalie's mouth was pinched as she pointed to the back wall. "I'm not so sure having the kitchen there is a good idea. Maybe there would be better." She pointed to the left.

Vivi's hands curled at her sides. "Natalie, we discussed this. The architect drew up plans according to our specifications. You can't go changing things around now."

"Can't I? It's my money."

Vivi ignored the barb. "One minute you're saying the DiDinato brothers' estimate is too high; the next you're implying that we have enough money to tear up the original plans and start over because you're having second thoughts about the kitchen. Do we have enough money or not? Which is it?"

Natalie blinked with surprise. "Why are you upset, Vivi?"

"Why?" Vivi replied, trying not to sound shrill. "Because at every turn, you remind me that you hold the purse strings. I'm fully aware that I couldn't do this without you. But you said you wanted to be a silent partner, and leave all the details to me. Money is no object, you told me. But clearly it is."

"Look at the balance in the account. We have nothing to worry about."

"Then why nitpick over the brothers' price?"

Natalie hesitated. "I don't want us to be taken advantage of. I don't want people thinking they can push us around just because we're foreigners."

"Believe me, Natalie, no one would ever think that of us. That's one thing we both inherited from Papa: a 'don't fuck with me' attitude."

"Vivi!" Natalie looked horrified. "Watch your language. You're starting to sound a bit, well—"

"*Amerique?*" Vivi offered.

"*Oui.*"

"Good, I'm glad."

Natalie's eyes once again swept the empty store. "Don't you ever get homesick?"

"Of course I do," Vivi admitted quietly. She missed her mother and grandmother desperately. "Don't you?"

"Yes and no. I miss my mother"—her eyes glanced away from Vivi's—"and a few friends."

Vivi looked down at the floor. Things felt out of joint. Natalie must have felt it, too; she came over to Vivi and kissed her cheek.

"Let's make up."

Vivi lifted her head, bemused. "Are we fighting?"

"I don't know. Are we?"

"I'm not sure." Vivi knitted her brows. "Natalie, please. If you would like to be more involved in the day-to-day decisions regarding the restaurant—"

Natalie held up her hand. "No. It's fine. This is your domain, Vivi. I was wrong to be so pushy about the contractors, and about the kitchen."

"Are you sure? Because I don't think my nerves can take it if every time you come in here, you want to change something."

Natalie reddened. "From now on, I promise I'll be perfectly happy to let you write the checks from the restaurant account."

"Good." Vivi returned her kiss on the cheek. "I guess we'll just wait for the DiDinatos to come back—"

"With their 'samwiches,'" Natalie sniffed. "Honestly, the way some of these people speak . . ."

"Natalie?"

"Yes?"

"Do me a favor."

"Yes?"

Vivi put her index finger to her lips. "Shhh."

Natalie covered her face and laughed. "As you wish."

"C'mon, Little Ant! Hustle, hustle, hustle!"

Anthony and his sister-in-law Theresa exchanged worried glances as Michael Dante stood up with his hands cupped around his mouth, coaching his son from the stands. It was Little Ant's first hockey game, and as promised, Anthony was in attendance, not only to support the kid, but also to rein his brother in if he started acting like he was watching the Blades play rather than a midget hockey team. Little Ant had been on the ice less than a minute, and already Michael was shouting directives. Not good.

"Michael, sit down and shut up," Theresa admonished her husband. "He just hit the ice. Let him enjoy himself."

"I'm just making sure—"

"Michael." Theresa's voice was laced with warning.

"Fine." Michael reluctantly sat down, but his eyes remained glued to the ice. "Mother of God, this coach Plano doesn't know what the fuck he's doing . . ."

Theresa turned to Anthony, pointedly ignoring her husband. "It's so great that you're here. Little Ant was so excited."

"Hey, I couldn't miss his first game, could I?"

"Neither could I." Theresa's eyes nervously followed her son on the ice.

"How's work going?" Anthony asked, wincing as his nephew missed a cross-ice pass. He tensed, waiting for his brother to shout something. Michael managed to keep himself under control, but Anthony could see it was tough for him. Michael kept opening and closing his mouth like some sad fish out of water gasping for breath.

"Work's going great," said Theresa, giving her husband

a look. "It took me a while to get back into the swing of things, but I think I'm doing all right."

"Where's Dominica?" Anthony asked, referring to Michael and Theresa's older daughter.

"Over at my mom's." Theresa chuckled. "I asked her if she wanted to come and watch her brother play and she just looked at me as if the very thought was torture. She's turning into a real *principessa*, that one. She'd better watch her step."

"And the baby?"

"She's at my mom's, too, probably screaming her head off as we speak." She leaned close to Anthony and whispered, "How's Michael doing with the househusband stuff? Honestly."

"He's doing great," Anthony replied, wondering if it sounded like he was exaggerating.

"Good." Theresa looked relieved. "I have to confess, I was a little worried. He's used to the excitement of this"— she gestured at the ice—"not picking stale Cheerios off the carpet that the baby threw from her high chair, you know what I mean?"

"I think he's doing okay," Anthony reiterated, glancing at his brother, who looked on the verge of bursting a blood vessel in his temple. He was about to say as much when Michael sprang back to his feet.

"What the hell was that?" he yelled at the ref. "You bench my kid for boarding and you let that little *cretino* on the other team go scot-free? You did good, Little Ant," he called down to his son. "Hang tough. Remember what we talked about before the game."

"Michael," Theresa hissed, yanking him back down into his seat.

Anthony glanced around discreetly. Other parents were looking at them, most with displeasure. There were a few scattered whispers; Anthony caught the words "New York

Blades" more than once. He could just imagine what people were thinking.

"Mike, I really think you need to calm down," said Anthony under his breath.

Michael scowled at him. "I'm just trying to make sure Little Ant plays the best game he can."

"How about you let him have some fun?" Theresa snapped. She turned up her palms in disbelief. "Can you believe this?" she asked Anthony.

"Sadly, yes."

Anthony watched as his nephew returned to the ice with his line. All the kids, regardless of skill, looked gawky to him at this age, their helmeted heads making them look like lollipops on skates. Little Ant looked up into the stands, scouring the crowd for his parents. When he found them, he gave a tentative wave.

"Pay attention to what's happening on the ice!" his father shouted down to him. Little Ant dipped his head in shame and skated up the right side.

"So help me God, Michael," Theresa fumed, "if you don't stop it right now, I'm going to talk to the coach about having you banned. Seriously."

"You believe this?" Mike asked Anthony, gesturing at his wife. The same question Theresa had asked him not ten seconds before. *My hell is in stereo,* Anthony thought. But he couldn't lie to his brother.

"Theresa's right, Mikey. You're gonna turn the kid into a wreck. You should shut up."

Michael looked at his wife, then his brother, opened his mouth, closed it, and kept silent.

"Thank God you're here," Theresa murmured to Anthony. "If you weren't, I think I'd kill him."

"I heard that," said Michael, eyes following the puck.

"That means you've heard everything else I said," said Theresa. Michael muttered something under his breath, but he kept his opinion to himself.

"So," said Theresa with a friendly pat to Anthony's knee, "Michael tells me you have some very attractive competition."

"What?" It took him a second or two before he realized she was referring to Vivi. "Oh." His thoughts were further interrupted when a buzzer sounded, heralding that a goal had been scored.

"Yess!" Michael was pumping his fist in the air. "You see that?" he said to Theresa excitedly. "He got an assist! Keep the pressure on, Ant!" he called down to his son.

"Your competition?" Theresa said loudly to Anthony, trying to redirect attention to their conversation.

"What about her?"

"Michael says she makes a mean apple tart."

Anthony made a sour face. "It was good, not great."

Theresa's mention of the tart reminded him that he'd yet to carve out time to make the ricotta fritters that would reveal Vivi as the amateur she was. Maybe he'd make them Sunday morning, after visiting Ang. He'd see.

"Michael says she likes you," Theresa continued.

"*Likes* me? No offense, Ter, but I think Mikey took one too many pucks to the noggin. The woman doesn't like me at all, nor do I like her. She's a friggin' know-it-all."

"You worried she's going to cut into business?"

Jesus Christ, Anthony thought. Subtle, Theresa was not. "I'm sure *she* thinks she will," said Anthony. "She obviously doesn't know who she's up against."

"I'm kind of excited about a little French place opening in the neighborhood," Theresa confessed.

"Of course you are," said Anthony. "Anything to drive a stake through my heart."

Theresa jostled his shoulder. "Lighten up, Ant. No one's food compares to yours."

Anthony bowed his head in mock humility. "Thank you. That was the right thing to say." They both laughed.

Theresa glanced sideways at her husband with a look

laced with both exasperation and affection that Anthony
had seen many times before. Michael and Theresa might
argue with fervor, but their love for each other was never in
doubt. They were solid, the same way he and Ang once
were. Anthony felt envious.

As if reading his mind, Theresa said, "You still going to
the cemetery?"

"Yup."

For the first time since arriving at the arena, Michael
seemed to be listening to his wife and brother's conversation. "Who are you, Joe DiMaggio?" he sniggered.

"Mind your business, Mike," Anthony warned.

"I think Michael's right," Theresa said carefully. "We
just want to see you happy again, Anthony. You're such a
great guy. Maybe it's time to move on?"

Anthony stared down at the ice. "I have moved on."

"Visiting your wife's grave once a week isn't moving
on," Michael countered. "It's unhealthy."

Anthony turned to his brother angrily. "Tell you what,
Mike—when Theresa dies years before she's supposed
to, then you can tell me what's healthy or not. Until then,
zip it."

"Good morning, cara."

Anthony set up his small folding chair beside Angie's
headstone and sat down with a grimace. The day before,
he'd noticed as he emerged from the shower that he was
beginning to put on a little weight, always a hazard when
one works in a kitchen. Determined to drop a few pounds
before all the pasta he consumed started to do some serious
damage, he'd gone for an early morning run. Not only had
it left him winded, but it also felt as though someone had
taken a hammer to his kneecaps. He had no idea whether
standing for hours in the restaurant kitchen would make it
feel better or worse. He supposed he'd find out.

"Guess what, Ang? Little Anthony wants to learn to make the gravy! Mikey's going to drop him off at the house for a few hours. It'll be fun, don't you think? He's a good kid."

Anthony sipped his coffee, pleased that Al at the deli had remembered how he liked it. Inevitably, his thoughts turned to Vivi, and their coffee incident.

"Remember I told you about those two sisters who were opening the *bistro*"—he spat the word contemptuously—"across the street? Well, the one who's the cook is a real piece of work. Not only can she not make coffee to save her life, but she also showed up with an apple tart one day, and when I didn't bow down and tell Her Highness it was the greatest thing since sliced bread, she dared me to make something better! You believe that?"

He shook his head, imagining Angie's response. She'd agree with him that anyone thinking they could outcook Anthony was crazy. "Actually, you'd probably like this woman if you met her," Anthony continued after a pause. "She reminds me of that lieutenant friend of yours—you know, Maggie, the one with the long blonde hair and the sassy mouth?"

His voice seemed overly loud to his ears. He took a quick glance around, feeling conspicuous. He was the only one there, save for two guys, about fifty feet away, noisily digging a grave with a backhoe. A familiar heaviness settled on his chest and he found himself wondering, for the first time ever, whether coming here was such a great idea. Maybe Michael and Theresa were right; maybe his visits were proof he hadn't really "moved on." Confusion engulfed him—he who was usually so resolute, viewing the world in black and white. What was going on?

Chapter 6

Anthony stood on the sidewalk, staring at the crumpled piece of paper in his hand bearing Vivi's address. Leaving the cemetery, he'd headed straight for Dante's, where he'd whipped up a double batch of his mouthwatering ricotta fritters. They were best served hot, but still outstanding even when warm, which was why Anthony was glad he could still feel some heat emanating from the bottom of the plastic container. If Vivi failed to be impressed with the fritters, then she was just busting his balls for the sake of busting his balls. No other explanation was possible.

He knew these streets like the back of his hand, and Vivi's was no exception. It was right off Scarangella Park, where he and his dad used to throw a baseball around. Bensonhurst was still predominantly Italian, but there were lots of new immigrants coming in to fill up the two-family semidetached brick and stucco houses. Most of the newcomers were Chinese and Russian—and now French, too, he supposed, though as far as he could tell, Vivi was at the spearhead of that movement.

He'd called her cell number, but when it asked him to leave a message, he chickened out for some reason. He'd grown up in an atmosphere where it was okay for people to drop in on one another for a visit. Maybe it was that way in France, too, for all he knew. But the fritters were made, and he was determined she'd eat them today, even if it meant coming back later on.

He was surprised to find himself looking at an old five-floor walk-up, just like the one on Cropsey Avenue that his grandparents lived in before they saved up enough to buy a house. Anthony loved these old buildings, the feel of history behind them. You could almost see the generations of immigrants moving up and out as they made a life for themselves, making room for the next wave. It was comforting somehow.

He climbed the front steps and went to press the buzzer, then hesitated. Maybe just showing up was stupid. What if she wasn't there? Or worse, what if she was there and wasn't in the mood for a culinary showdown in the middle of the day? Well, she'd just have to deal with it. God knows she'd ambushed *him* more than once.

He shoved the paper into the back pocket of his jeans and rang her buzzer. Nothing. He waited a second or two, and then rang again. Nothing. "Figures," he muttered to himself, turning away. That's when Vivi's disembodied voice crackled over the intercom.

"Yes, who is it, please?"

"The best chef in Bensonhurst." Anthony heard her laugh. "I have a dessert here that's going to make you cry uncle."

"Uncle?" Vivi replied, puzzled.

"It's an expression. Never mind. You going to let me up or what?"

"Of course. You and your uncle can come right up."

He walked the four flights of stairs to her apartment. Vivi was waiting for him in the open doorway, her slim body swathed in a short, brightly patterned silk kimono.

Her damp hair was pinned up, her flushed face amused. Uncomfortable, Anthony looked away.

"I'm sorry. Did I drag you out of the shower?" he asked, wishing he *had* called ahead. This felt awkward, with her standing here in her robe.

"Bath."

Anthony tried to remember the last time he had had a bath. It had to be when he and Mikey were little kids. Their mother would throw them into a tub together, killing two birds with one stone. He could still remember her vigorously cleaning his ears with a washcloth, the way she impatiently manhandled the two of them. As soon as they were old enough, they started taking showers.

"Don't you have a shower?" Anthony asked as she ushered him inside.

"I do," said Vivi, motioning for him to sit down on the plump couch, "but I prefer to take baths when I can. They're much more relaxing."

"Understandable." Anthony knew if *he* took a bath on a Sunday morning, he'd wind up becoming so relaxed he'd crawl back into bed and sleep. Vivi sat down beside him, the faint hint of floral scent wafting from her body.

"What have we here?" she asked, tapping the top of the container.

"Ricotta fritters. Freshly made less than an hour ago." Anthony shook the small paper bag in his hand. "I brought honey, too. You have to drizzle them in honey."

"Interesting." Vivi glanced in the direction of the kitchen. "I'd offer you some coffee, but since you seem unable to appreciate a decently made cup of French roast, I don't see the point."

As a matter of fact, Anthony was dying for a cup of coffee. "I think I can manage to gag down a cup, as long as I can douse it in milk and plenty of sugar."

Vivi batted her eyelashes. "Has anyone ever told you you're a cow's ass?" she asked sweetly.

"Besides you? No. And the expression is 'a horse's ass,' by the way."

"Well, excuse *moi*." She rose. "I won't be a moment."

Vivi disappeared, giving Anthony a chance to check out her apartment. It was small and relatively spartan: a couch, a coffee table piled high with cookbooks, a small bistro table for two pushed up against a far window. But there were lots of plants, which gave it a homey feel—a feel his home used to have, before he let all the plants wither and die. He couldn't be bothered after Ang died.

Curious, he picked up a small black binder from the nearest pile of cookbooks and flicked it open. It contained page after page of handwritten recipes, some relatively new, some old and faded. Anthony knew from experience that those pages on the verge of tatters, covered in unidentifiable food stains, were her favorites. He didn't know much French, but he did know that *beurre* meant "butter," and that a helluva lot of the recipes in this book called for a helluva lot of *beurre*. Simple food my ass, he thought, recalling the conversation he and Vivi had that day in the candy store. French food thrived on butter; there were no two ways around it. If Vivi wanted to claim French cooking wasn't rich, that was her delusion.

"I see you've found my little black book," Vivi called out as she walked back into the living room, bamboo tray in hand upon which sat two coffee cups, a milk creamer, a sugar bowl, plates, and forks.

Anthony closed the binder. "Some of the recipes look pretty old."

"A lot of them were my grandmother's," Vivi said fondly.

"I have a book like that, too, full of recipes passed down from my grandparents. There are even a few from my great-grandparents in the old country," Anthony revealed, taking the liberty of clearing away some of the cookbooks to make space on the coffee table for the tray.

"It's good to keep tradition alive, don't you think?" Vivi sat down beside him. "Please, help yourself to some of my awful coffee."

Vivi's robe was tied loosely, and as she leaned forward to prepare a cup of coffee for herself, Anthony caught a fleeting glimpse of the top of one of her breasts. Flushed with embarrassment, he averted his eyes, waiting until she had leaned back before grabbing a coffee cup for himself. "So, where's your sister?"

"In the city."

"She doesn't live here with you?" Anthony asked, hoping she didn't notice him loading his small cup with five lumps of sugar.

Vivi erupted into peals of laughter. "Natalie wouldn't be caught dead in a place like this. It's too shabby."

"It's not shabby. It's just a little spartan right now, that's all."

Vivi gave a small nod of approval. "I like your attitude."

"As long as the kitchen's up to snuff, that's all that matters."

"Exactly. The kitchen here is small, but the stove is gas. Electric is horrible, no?"

"The worst."

"I actually chose this apartment precisely because of that," Vivi continued. "Imagine, trying to cook on an electric stove!"

"It's insane!" Anthony agreed.

Vivi's expression turned thoughtful. "When did you know?" she asked.

"What, that I wanted to be a chef?"

Vivi nodded.

"Always. From the time I watched my mother cooking."

"Me, too. The smells, the tastes . . ." She put her hand over her heart and sighed. "It was like heaven."

"A calling."

Vivi's eyes flashed with recognition. "Exactly! It's so nice to talk to someone who understands."

Anthony's eyes held Vivi's for a long moment before they both looked away. Anthony reached for the creamer, pleasantly surprised to find it indeed filled with cream, not the skim milk Ang used to insist he have in his coffee. So much for watching his waistline, he thought as he poured a smidgen into his coffee. He held his breath and took a sip. It was drinkable—just.

"You're not choking," Vivi observed wryly. "Perhaps you've seen the error of your ways."

"Let's not jump the gun here." He took another sip.

Vivi raised an eyebrow. "Well?"

"Still awful," Anthony said cheerfully.

Vivi sighed. "You're very predictable."

"Is that a bad thing?"

"It depends."

"We'll see how predictable I am. Break out the fritters."

Vivi opened the container, dishing three fritters onto each plate.

"Tell me they don't smell delicious," Anthony challenged, removing the honey he'd brought with him from the paper bag. "Tell me the mere scent of these fried beauties doesn't make you want to swoon."

Vivi passed her plate under her nose. "Lemon peel?"

"A little."

"I thought so."

Anthony passed her the small squeeze bottle of honey. "Drizzle them with this."

Vivi took the honey and proceeded to drown the fritters rather than drizzle them.

"You're doing it wrong," Anthony pointed out.

"I believe in seasoning liberally," was Vivi's retort.

Anthony held his tongue and watched as she cut into the first fritter with her fork and put the first bite into her mouth. A brief look of ecstasy streaked across her face before she squelched it.

"They're all right," she pronounced mildly.

"Oh, please!" Anthony snorted. "I saw your face! Your eyes wanted to roll up in your head from sheer bliss!"

Vivi blushed. "All right, you've got me. They are *tres magnifique*." She took another bite and this time, to Anthony's satisfaction, she did let her eyes roll back. The sight of it brought an unexpected flash of heat to his body. Swallowing, he helped himself to the honey, drizzling his own fritters before taking a lusty bite. Oh, yeah, baby, these weren't just good, they were great.

"Guess I outdid you," Anthony observed.

"Not quite," said Vivi, giving a small moan as she speared another piece of fritter and put it in her mouth. "You can't compare fritters to a tart. They're two different beasts."

"Hey, you didn't hear me moaning when I ate your tart, did you?"

"I didn't moan."

"Yeah, you did! Just now, when you put that piece into your mouth. You gave a small moan!"

Vivi shrugged. "Well, if I did, I was unaware of it." She finished the first fritter and began working on the second. The sight pleased Anthony immensely. He loved knowing his food gave others pleasure. It was also nice to see a woman who wasn't shy about enjoying eating. But then, he'd heard that about the French, how serious they were about their food.

"My brother and I used to eat them with our hands when we were kids," Anthony revealed.

"What fun!" Vivi enthused. She held her plate close to her chin, picking up a fritter with her free hand and biting into it lustily. A small trickle of honey ran down her chin.

"Oh!" she said with embarrassment, quickly licking honey from her fingers. "I'm such a slob."

"Not a big deal."

Without thinking, Anthony leaned over and tenderly wiped the honey from her chin with his thumb. Vivi glanced up at him shyly through her lashes as time seemed to hold its breath. Anthony knew he should take his thumb away, but some unseen force was keeping it there, the same force now whispering in his ear, urging him to kiss her. Slowly, Anthony put his lips to hers. Vivi put her plate down, returning his kiss as she closed her eyes.

The sweet taste of her mouth conspired with the enticing scent of her perfume to make Anthony's senses tumble. For the first time in over a year, he was aware of himself as a man. The realization quickly transformed itself into apprehension. Who was this guy, kissing a French woman in her robe on a cloudy Sunday afternoon? And who was she, her mouth pressing against his with equal pressure, her hands lightly anchoring themselves on his shoulders?

Anthony stood up. "I should go," he said gruffly.

"Good idea," Vivi agreed quickly. She rose, tightening her robe, not quite looking at him. "I have a lot of things to do today."

"Me, too."

She escorted him to the door. "*Au revoir.* Thank you for stopping by," Vivi said stiffly.

"Yeah, *au revoir* to you, too. I guess I'll see you around the neighborhood."

"Yes."

She closed the door, leaving Anthony standing in the hallway. He checked his watch; his nephew would be at his house in an hour for the first of his "cooking lessons." Anthony bounded down the apartment house steps and back outside into the murky sunshine, grateful for something to do.

Chapter 7

"You listening?"

Anthony gently tapped the side of the saucepan with a wooden spoon to get Little Ant's attention. They were in Anthony's home kitchen, and he had just finished chopping all the vegetables and herbs needed for the gravy while Little Ant looked on. He dumped them into the saucepan, where they now sizzled, sending up a mouthwatering aroma. Little Ant stood on a step stool beside his uncle, listening avidly as Anthony explained why heating the olive oil to just the right temperature was crucial. But somewhere between explaining the difference between browning onions and merely letting them wilt, Little Ant's attention seemed to wander.

"You hear me?" said Anthony.

"Sorry." Little Ant snapped back to attention. "Can I stir?"

"Of course." Anthony handed him the spoon. "You bored?"

"No."

"Because we don't have to do this if you're bored."

"I'm not bored," Little Ant insisted. His expression turned pouty. "Hockey is what's boring. Not this."

Anthony looked away with a grimace, unsure of how to respond. When Theresa had swung by to drop Little Ant off, she'd made a point of telling her son *to have fun*, as if it were something the kid had forgotten how to do. The second Little Ant was out of earshot, Theresa had turned to Anthony with pleading eyes. "You have to talk to Michael. He's insane. The other night after Little Ant finished his homework, Michael sat down at the kitchen table with him to go over 'strategy.' "

"Can't you talk to him?" Anthony asked. Going mano a mano with his brother was not one of Anthony's favorite activities, especially since it tended to feature yelling as well as the occasional piece of dinnerware going airborne.

"He won't listen to me," Theresa insisted, her expression mirroring the distress in her voice.

"He doesn't listen to me, either, Theresa. But I'll see what I can do."

"Thank you." Theresa gave Anthony's shoulder a heartfelt squeeze before leaving.

"Why do you say hockey's boring?" Anthony asked casually, pleased to see how intently Little Ant was studying the ingredients in the saucepan.

"Because it is," Little Ant insisted, sounding like the seven-year-old he was. "It's stupid."

"Tell me why."

"It sucks." Little Ant swallowed. "I suck."

Anthony jostled his shoulder. "You don't suck! I saw your first game, remember? You were awesome!"

"You're just saying that because you're my uncle," Little Ant muttered.

"No, I'm saying that because you were awesome." He stilled Little Ant's hand. "Don't stir *too* much, okay?"

"Okay." Little Ant slowed the wooden spoon's momentum. "Is that okay?"

"Perfect."

Anthony leaned over the saucepan and took a deep breath. "Smells good, don't you think?"

"When do we dump in the wine and stuff?" Little Ant asked eagerly.

"Soon. How many times have I told you: Being a chef is all about being patient."

"I know," Little Ant murmured, glancing around the kitchen. "Uncle Anthony, can I ask you a question?"

"You can ask me anything."

"Do you ever get lonely, living here without Aunt Ang?"

"Sometimes." He thought about the question. Right after she died, it was close to unbearable. But now he was used to it.

"Do you ever, like, feel her ghost?"

Anthony felt his chest tighten. "Not in the way you think." He tousled the boy's hair, trying to divert him. "What are you talking about ghosts for? You're going to scare yourself."

"Dad says there's no such thing."

"Well, there you go." Anthony glanced around the kitchen, really *seeing* it for the first time in a long time. One of the first things Angie had done when she'd moved in was to redecorate the house completely, ridding the kitchen of the drab olive green and gold tones of the 1970s. She'd replaced the linoleum on the floor with beautiful handmade tiles. The nicked green Formica countertop was just a memory thanks to the pristine white Corian, which perfectly offset the cornflower blue of the cabinets she'd painted. Anthony had balked at first, but in the end, even he had to concede it looked great. The whole house looked great—not that he'd noticed much over the past year. But now, viewing it with a fresh eye, he knew it was a home any man would be proud of.

"Do you believe in ghosts?" Little Ant pressed.

"Nah."

Little Ant seemed to consider this. "Me, neither," he said eventually.

"Great minds think alike," Anthony teased.

"Do you ever get mad at God for taking Aunt Angie away?"

Anthony swallowed. "Sad stuff happens sometimes. You can't blame God."

Little Ant nodded thoughtfully. Please, let the kid be done with the questions. It was kicking up a lot of emotion, much of it confusing. That kiss with Vivi . . . what the hell was that about? If ever there was a testament to how lonely he felt sometimes, it was that. Or maybe it was testament to their mutual love of food. Start discussing gas stoves versus electric and the next thing you know, you're in a lip lock. Talk about scary.

"Do you think you'll ever get married again?"

Anthony coughed into his balled fist. He should have seen that one coming. "I don't know," he said, sounding curter than he meant to be. "I haven't really thought about it." He wondered if Little Ant was driven to ask by his own curiosity, or if he'd overheard his parents talking about how it was time for Anthony to move on. "Why do you ask?"

Little Ant shrugged. "I dunno. I just think it would be cool to have a new aunt and stuff."

"Uh-huh." Anthony turned down the heat under the saucepan. "You ready to add the vino?"

Vivi hurried down Twentieth Avenue, intent on one thing and one thing only: dropping off Anthony's plastic container at Dante's undetected. Ever since his visit to her apartment a week earlier, her emotions had been in an uproar. No matter how many times she reminded herself that he was arrogant, was less than thrilled to have her as a neighbor, and had insulted her more than once, her mind could not let go of the kiss. She couldn't lie to herself; she'd enjoyed it. But so what? She didn't have time for a romance. More importantly, he was the last man on earth she wanted to have a romance *with.*

They'd been avoiding each other all week, that much was clear. She'd seen him on the street a number of times, but not once had his head turned in the direction of the candy store, even with the DiDinatos finally beginning construction. That was fine with Vivi. She wasn't exactly breaking her neck to scurry across the street to his place, either.

She knew from observing Anthony that he usually left Dante's around eight a.m. to pick up a newspaper and chat with the men up at Cuccio's Pork Store, who were obviously longtime friends. He usually returned to the restaurant around eight thirty or so. Vivi checked her watch—ten minutes after eight. Perfect. She'd drop off the container with the kitchen staff and be out and back across the street before he even knew she was there.

She shouldn't have been surprised when she tried the front door to the restaurant and found it locked. Undeterred, she walked around to the back. The kitchen door would probably be unlocked, and even if it wasn't, she was certain there'd be staff in the kitchen who'd let her in if she knocked.

She was gratified to see the kitchen door was indeed open. She could see people moving around through the screen door as the sounds of voices and laughter rose above the tinny sound of a radio. She was in luck.

The door gave a small squeak as she opened it, popping her head inside. "Hello?" she called out tentatively. "It's Vivi from across the street."

"Vivi." Anthony's brother came toward her, a pleasant but puzzled look on his face.

"Hello, Michael. Is Anthony here?" *What a fraud you are,* Vivi thought to herself. *You know damn well he isn't.*

"Actually, he just ran up to the deli to pick up the paper. What's up?"

Vivi thrust the container at him. "Can you give this back to him?"

"Sure." Michael took the container, but the puzzled expression remained on his face. "You borrow it?"

"No. He made me fritters and I'm just returning it."

Michael's eyes widened with surprise. "Anthony made you fritters?"

"Yes."

"And he brought them to your house?"

Vivi hesitated, confused by the excited look in Michael's eyes. "Yes."

Michael's excitement was now elation. "Oh my God, that's great! Do you know how great that is?"

"It's not what you think."

"What do you think I think?"

"You think your brother and I are romantically involved. It's not so," Vivi said very quietly. She knew the kitchen staff was listening to every word being said, restaurant kitchens being a hive of gossip. She wanted to think the radio might be muffling some of the sound of her and Michael's voices, but you never knew.

Michael regarded her skeptically. "You made him an apple tart just for the hell of it?"

Vivi was taken aback. "How do you know about that?"

"Because I devoured half the damn thing!" Michael's eyes shone with admiration. "That was the best apple tart I ever tasted in my life, Vivi. Seriously."

"Thank you," Vivi murmured, blushing with pleasure. Maybe Michael wasn't so pushy after all.

"What did you think of the fritters?"

"I thought they were wonderful," Vivi confessed, "though comparing a tart with a fritter is like comparing apples and oranges."

"I agree completely. I think you two need to keep your dessert Olympics going, appointing me as the main judge."

"Do you cook, too?"

"No. I'm a hockey player. Former hockey player." His voice sounded strained. Had she said something wrong? The light in Michael Dante's eyes seemed to have flamed out. Time to leave, Vivi thought.

"Well, thank you for your time," she said politely, edging in the direction of the kitchen door.

"You can go out the front," Michael said. "I unlocked it just before you came in."

"Are you sure?"

"Of course."

Vivi nodded appreciatively and headed through the swinging doors of the kitchen, stopping short at the sight of a small, portable playpen set up in the middle of the dining room. An adorable, apple-cheeked baby girl with lustrous black curls was gurgling happily to herself. Michael Dante's daughter? Or maybe—no, it couldn't be. The thought disturbed her, so she pushed it away. The baby was looking at her now, smiling. Vivi put her hands over her face then pulled them away, saying "Peek-a-boo," sending the child into a cascade of giggles. It was a lovely, mellifluous sound.

"Au revoir, ange," Vivi said, blowing a kiss to the baby. Then she pulled open the restaurant door, coming face-to-face with Anthony.

"What are you doing here?"

Anthony knew he sounded abrupt, maybe even rude, but the last thing he expected to find when he opened the door to his restaurant was Vivi.

"I came to return your container."

"Thank you." Anthony shoved his copy of the *Post* under his arm and folded his arms across his chest. "Actually, I'm kind of glad you're here. There's something I want to talk to you about."

Vivi crossed *her* arms across *her* chest. "Yes?"

"What happened last week? That kiss? Pure aberration."

"Oh, I'm so glad you said that," said Vivi, relieved. "You were simply carried away by all that ecstatic talk about cooking, yes? As was I."

"Exactly," Anthony agreed, though he could have done without the happy look on her face. What, kissing him was such a horror show?

"It's funny how those things happen sometimes, isn't it?" Vivi continued with a nervous little laugh. "How talking about food can make you so passionate you do things that seem crazy to you afterward?"

"Absolutely," Anthony agreed with a forced chortle. "If anyone knows about the bizarre effects food can have on some people, it's we chefs, right?"

"*Oui*," said Vivi, nodding her head vigorously. "I'm so delighted to know we're in agreement about this." She edged closer to the door. "I have to go now. I need to speak with the DiDinato brothers about something before they start today."

"Yeah, about that." Anthony gave a small grimace. "Do you know what time they plan on wrapping up each day?"

"No. Why?"

"Here's the thing: we have an early bird special. Starts around five p.m. I would hate for any of my customers to have their meals disturbed by the sounds of saws and hammers and all that good stuff."

"That's not my problem," Vivi said briskly.

Anthony raised an eyebrow. "*Au contraire*, missy. If I start losing business because of you, it very much *is* your problem."

Vivi pressed her lips together into a thin, hard line. "What are you saying?"

"I'm simply asking you, as a neighboring business, to please take into account the effect it could have. If you could ask the DiDinatos to start work earlier in the day so that they finish up earlier, I would appreciate it."

Vivi tilted up her chin. "Why don't you ask them?"

Anthony shrugged. "Fine. I will. I'm sure they'll accommodate me. We go way back."

"Typical," Vivi hissed under her breath.

"Typical what?"

"Typical male chef! Thinks he can just snap his fingers
and everyone will jump!"

"You mean they won't?"

"*Connard!*" Vivi growled in frustration. "Excuse me,
please. I don't have time for this."

Anthony smirked as he held the door open for her. "Be
my guest."

Vivi stormed out of the restaurant. She was halfway
across the parking lot when she abruptly turned back to
him. "Just so you know, those fritters were soggy, and so
was your kiss!"

"You wouldn't know a soggy fritter if you fell into the
Seine," Anthony replied. "As for my kiss, you simply didn't
inspire me, *mademoiselle*." He headed toward the kitchen
smiling, feeling more alive than he had in days.

Chapter 8

"*Newsflash, Mikey: This* is a restaurant, not a day care center."

Anthony leaned over the portable crib set up in the middle of Dante's dining room, glowering at his brother. He couldn't decide whether to yell (that might scare the baby), demand Michael leave immediately (Michael might yell and scare the baby), or turn around and leave himself (that might scare the kitchen staff). Bad enough that Marie Antoinette had to hurl insults at him across the parking lot; now he had to deal with his pain-in-the-ass brother. He glanced down at baby Angelica, a broad smile plastered on her cherubic little face as she held out her sock monkey to him. "It's not your fault your daddy's a loser, *cara*," Anthony said with a sigh. He took the sock monkey, made a show of kissing it, and returned it to the baby.

"What's the big deal with us being here?" Michael asked.

"Jesus Christ, Mike." Anthony pinched the bridge of his nose. "You said you'd keep out of my hair, remember?"

"I am."

"You don't get it. Your just being here is getting in my hair, okay? I've got a business to run, and you've got a household to run. Or am I wrong?"

Michael looked guilty. "I'm lonely at home. There's no one to talk to but the baby."

"Then take her to the park. Or join one of those play groups. Watch *The View*. I don't care what you do—just quit showing up here."

"I don't see what the big deal is," Michael repeated stubbornly.

"Yeah?" Anthony pulled his cell phone out of his back pocket. "Let's call Theresa and see what she thinks." He started dialing. Michael yanked the phone from his hands.

"Fine," Michael muttered, a sulky expression on his face. "I'll leave in a minute."

"Good." Anthony stuffed the phone back in his pocket. He never thought the day would come, but he actually felt sorry for his brother. Michael was a lost soul now that he'd retired, spending the hours between getting the kids off in the morning and chauffeuring them after school in a kind of twilight zone.

"Mike," Anthony said gently, "if this stay-at-home dad stuff isn't your cup of tea, that's okay. Not everyone—"

"It's fine," Michael snapped. "It's just taking me a little while to adjust, okay?"

"Not for nothing, but if you ask me, spending your spare time here isn't going to help. Can't you clean the house or something to help you kill time?"

"We have a housecleaner," Michael said glumly.

"Why don't you get a nanny so you're free to do stuff during the day?"

"I can't leave the baby with a nanny!"

"Why the hell not? You've got enough money!"

"It's not about money," Michael insisted. "It's about bonding."

"Yeah, I can see that. Nothing says bonding like sticking her in a playpen in the middle of an empty dining room."

"Don't bust my balls, Ant. You'll understand when you're a father."

Anthony felt a judder of pain go through his body as he looked away. It was as if gravity singled him out, rendering him immobile.

"Sorry," Michael mumbled apologetically.

"Don't sweat it." Anthony studied his brother. "I really think you need to figure something out, bro. You look terrible."

"Raising kids is hard work! By the time Theresa gets home, she's too exhausted to do anything besides grab a quick bite to eat and put them to bed. It's all falling on me."

"That's rough."

"You're damn right it is. So if I seek a little relief during the day by coming down here to hang with you, the least you could do is cut me some slack."

"Does Theresa know you're serving the kids restaurant leftovers for dinner every night?"

"No, and she's not going to find out."

Anthony chuckled softly. "I can't believe the kids haven't ratted you out yet."

"Give kids money and they'll clam up pretty fast."

"Don't take this the wrong way, Mike, okay? But you're pathetic."

Michael snorted derisively. "Look who's talking, Pepé Le Pew."

Anthony raised his eyebrows. "Excuse me?"

"Vivi told me all about your little tart versus fritters debate. I can't believe you didn't tell me—your own brother—what's going on."

"Nothing's going on."

"Funny, she said the same thing—proof positive something *is* going on!"

"Yeah, that's right. You're a regular Inspector Clouseau," Anthony mocked.

Michael was undeterred. "I think it's great, Ant. Vivi's really nice."

"Nothing's going on!"

His raised voice startled the baby, but she soon enough returned to contentedly gumming her sock monkey's nose.

"If nothing is going on," Michael persisted, "then why did you conveniently forget to tell me why you wanted to know which was better, your fritters or your olive oil cake?"

"Because I knew you'd try to make something out of nothing!"

"I've said it before and I'll say it again, Ant: It's time to move on. It's been over a year."

"Oh my God." Anthony closed his eyes, rubbing his forehead. "Read my lips: I'm not interested. Not because of Ang, but because I'm just not interested."

"You're a bad liar. Always have been."

"And you're a pain in the ass, Mike. Always have been." Anthony tried changing the subject. "Did Little Ant have anything to say about our cooking lesson last week?"

"He seemed to have a good time," Michael answered distractedly. "Speaking of which, I'm bringing him to a Blades game next Monday night to see if I can't get him a little more pumped up about hockey. You wanna come?"

Anthony hesitated. When Angie was alive, she was always nudging him to do more on his one day off. But even at home, he couldn't leave the restaurant behind. Being a head chef was a twenty-four-hour job whether you were in the kitchen or not. However, going to the hockey game might be a good idea. He could act as a buffer between Little Ant and his father if he needed to, and the game was in the beginning of the week, when business tended to be slow. "Sure, I'll come."

"Great. Little Ant will be thrilled. Speaking of which, I've got some news you'll be thrilled about, too."

"Yeah, what's that?"

"I took the liberty of hiring a hostess for the front of the house," said Michael, looking pleased with himself.

Anthony stared at him. Damned if blood didn't make a sound; he could hear his own in his ears, a pulsing torrent fighting to drown out the voice in his head, the one telling him to throttle his brother within an inch of his life.

"You did *what*?"

"Hired a hostess. Admit it, Ant, we need one. You can't expect Aldo to pinch hit."

"This is my restaurant, Mike. *My* restaurant. *My* domain. How many times, in how many different ways, do I have to say it?" The more he thought about his brother's unilateral decision, the angrier he became. "How dare you hire someone without talking to me first! How dare you hire someone, period?"

"I'm helping you out here, you jackass!" Michael yelled.

"I don't need your help!" Anthony yelled back.

Angelica's lip quivered. Then she began to cry.

"Good one," Michael hissed, picking up his daughter and bouncing her on his shoulder.

"Call whoever it is you hired and tell them you made a mistake," Anthony commanded. *"Now."*

"Anthony." Michael's tone was cajoling. "Try and think clearly for a moment. This is something we need."

Anthony bit down on his tongue.

"I can't unhire her. It's someone from the neighborhood. Someone who desperately needs the work."

"Who?"

"Lorraine Fabiano. Remember her?"

Anthony drove the heels of his palms against his eye sockets. "You better be shitting me."

"Why?"

"Do you remember her nickname from high school, Mike?" Anthony asked as he tore his hands from his eyes, staring his little brother down. "Do you?"

Michael looked uneasy. "No."

"Let me remind you, then: it was Insane Lorraine." Anthony took a step toward his brother, who clutched his baby daughter tighter. "Is it coming back to you now?"

Michael swallowed. "Kind of."

"Kind of. Maybe this will help. She had a crush on me, remember? Used to hang around in front of the house, leave love notes for me in the hands of Mom's Saint Francis statue? Is it coming back to you now?'

Michael's face fell. "Fuck."

"Fuck is right. So put Angelica down and get on the horn right now. Tell Insane Lorraine that you're very sorry, but you made a mistake and the position is filled."

"Anthony." Michael's voice was gently admonishing. "Don't be so friggin' hard-hearted. Her pop died a couple of months ago and she came back to Bensonhurst to help out her mother."

"Oh, you mean Insane Lorraine Senior?" Michael ignored him. "Let me ask you something—did you ask her where she's been the past ten years?"

Michael looked uncomfortable. "No."

"So how do you know she wasn't, oh, spending time in a mental hospital for burying cats up to their necks and chopping off their heads with a lawnmower?"

"Did she do that?" Michael spluttered.

"I have no idea. The point is, you know nothing about her apart from the fact she's 'from the neighborhood.' "

"She needs a job. I was trying to do a good deed."

"Then hire her as your nanny. Or better yet, your cook."

"Let's just give her a chance, Anthony. Okay? It could end up helping us—you—out."

"Or, we could end up losing customers when she strips off all her clothes and does the hokey pokey on top of the bar."

Michael looked apprehensive. "Did she—?"

"Yeah, she did, Mike. Mr. Leotardo's tenth grade geometry class."

"I was still in junior high," Michael mumbled, hanging his head.

"Convenient. You want to play Good Samaritan? You train her."

Michael's head snapped up. "What?"

"You heard me. You hired her, you train her. And if we need to, you fire her. We clear?"

"Ant—"

"We clear?"

Michael was sullen as he balanced Angelica on his hip and started folding up the playpen with his free hand. "We're clear."

Vivi was unhappy. Not only had her conversation with Anthony put her in a sour mood, but the DiDinato brothers were well over an hour late, as was Natalie. Natalie had promised to be on hand when the work started so that everyone would be on the same page. But in typical Natalie fashion, the appointed time came and went. Vivi knew she would be here eventually, but the DiDinato brothers were another story. She hoped their tardiness wasn't symptomatic of a lackadaisical attitude toward work in general. They were paying them a small fortune. The least they could do was *try* to be punctual.

She peered out the window of the candy store, watching pedestrians hurry down the wide concrete sidewalks, while in the street, a large panel truck sat idling at a red light, its exhaust belching sooty smoke. She felt homesick. She missed Paris's small winding streets, and the way the sunshine caressed the Seine, making it shimmer like a mirage. She longed to tarry in the open-air markets, squeezing fruit, selecting the freshest ingredients for that night's meal.

Paris wasn't her hometown, it was true, but she'd grown to love it almost as much as Avignon. Strolling briskly from her apartment that morning, she'd noticed a cyber café on Seventh Avenue. Perhaps when she was done here, she would go there and e-mail friends back home, filling them in on her progress. Then, later in the day, she would treat herself and call *maman*.

"Bonjour!" Natalie's voice was cheerful as she entered the candy store, clutching two cups from Starbuck's in one hand and a large shopping bag in the other. "I thought we'd see what the fuss was all about with this coffee."

Vivi took the paper cup proffered by Natalie, trying not to feel injured, or worse, paranoid. Suppose her coffee *was* substandard, and Natalie had purchased this coffee so she wouldn't have to drink Vivi's?

Natalie put the shopping bag down and raised her own coffee cup to her lips for a good long taste. "Nowhere near as good as yours."

Vivi gave a small curtsy. "Thank you."

As always, Natalie was stylishly dressed in an outfit Vivi had never seen before: tailored black trousers, a lovely gray silk blouse, a red scarf knotted expertly at her throat. "You look lovely," Vivi murmured.

"All Tahari," Natalie confided.

The name meant nothing to Vivi, but she guessed it was a big-name designer. Not for the first time, Vivi found herself wondering what Natalie did all day in Manhattan. Shop?

Natalie dipped into the large shopping bag at her feet, pulling out a box from Saks Fifth Avenue. "I have a surprise for you."

"Natalie!"

"Oh, Natalie, nothing," Natalie pooh-poohed, handing Vivi the box. "As far as I can tell, you haven't bought yourself one new thing to wear since we've been here. What kind of French woman are you? Don't you know we have an image to uphold?"

Do I look that bad? Vivi wondered, feeling inadequate for the second time. Like most French women, Vivi was careful with her appearance. She might not dress fancily, but the pieces in her small but simple wardrobe were well tailored, and she never, ever left her apartment without putting on at least one coating of mascara and a touch of lipstick. The American women she saw who went out in public in sweatpants—or worse, sneakers—stunned her. That was one of the easiest ways to spot a tourist in Paris: Their sensible shoes gave them away every time!

"Open it," Natalie urged.

Vivi tore the lid off the box, pulling out a beautiful, velvet blazer in chocolate brown.

"Now you can enter the fall in style," Natalie declared.

Vivi held the jacket up against her, stunned. "How much did this cost?"

"That's not your concern. Do you like it?"

"I love it, but—"

"Non," said Natalie, wagging a warning finger in her face. "Not another word, apart from 'thank you' if you're so inclined."

"Thank you," said Vivi, carefully folding up the jacket and putting it back in the box. It was beautiful, not a piece of clothing she would ever dare buy for herself. She glanced uneasily at Natalie, with her scarf, alligator purse, and pearl earrings, and again a small jab of pain came to her. Did Papa love Natalie so much more that he flooded her with riches?

Natalie glanced around the empty store with a frown. "Where are those thieves we hired?"

"Late, just as you were," Vivi teased.

"Yes, but I'm not being paid an exorbitant fee for 'quality craftsmanship.' "

"True." Vivi took a sip of the store-bought coffee. Tahari, the present from Saks—it was beginning to gnaw at her, the mystery of Natalie's days. "Are you enjoying living in the city?"

"Oh, God, yes. There's so much to see and do. When are you going to come join me for a weekend? I'm getting tired of calling you!"

Vivi glanced away guiltily. Natalie had called her a number of times to come into Manhattan to see this film or that Broadway show, or go to this or that art exhibit, but Vivi always turned her down. Not because she didn't want to spend time with Natalie but there always seemed to be something demanding her time. Plan out her menus. Call distributors to see what they charged. Apply for a liquor license. There were so many facets to preparing to open a restaurant that sometimes Vivi felt overwhelmed. She supposed she could ask Natalie for help, but part of her resisted, since she wanted to do as much as she could on her own. Their agreement was that Natalie would front the money, and Vivi would take care of the details. She didn't want to change the rules now and risk inducing another "maybe we made a big mistake" attack in Natalie.

Still, how hard was it to spare a night or two to join Natalie in Manhattan? "You know what I would love to do?" Vivi mused aloud. "Check out different restaurants." That interested her much more than going to see a play or a film.

Natalie looked noncommittal. "We could do that."

"Good. It will be fun. Why don't you pick a restaurant, and I'll come into the city once a week to join you?"

"Only once a week? What do you do at night, Vivi? If you don't mind my asking?"

"I cook," Vivi said simply. Every night she cooked dinner for herself, and sometimes, afterward, she would experiment with different dishes, whether it be a new dessert or a twist on one of her standards. She was an alchemist, transforming simple elements into culinary gold. The kitchen was where she was her happiest. Why wouldn't she want to spend as much time as possible there?

She had a brainstorm. "Why don't you come out here a

few nights a week and let me cook for *you*?" Cooking for herself was fun, but really, the joy of it was in cooking for other people.

Natalie hesitated. "I suppose I could do that."

Vivi deflated. "You don't sound very enthused."

"It's not that I don't think you're a fantastic chef," Natalie hastily assured her. "It's just, well, after we eat, what is there to *do* in Bensonhurst?"

"Why do we have to *do* anything? Why can't we just sit and talk, catch up on lost time?" There was so much she still didn't know about Natalie, so many gaps in her imagination she wanted filled. Hours of conversation could fix that.

Natalie laughed softly. "If there's one thing you should know about me by now, it's that I like to be out doing, doing, doing. Papa always called me his Little Sparrow—always flitting here and there, never still."

"Did he?" Vivi could imagine him saying it. Their father loved to tease. Ironically, he teased Vivi about the opposite, calling her his little House Mouse, thoroughly amused by what a homebody she was.

"Did he ever say anything like that to you?" Natalie asked shyly.

Vivi told Natalie the nickname their father had given her. Natalie clapped her hands in delight. "Perfect! It suits you, you know."

"And Little Sparrow suits you!" Vivi took another sip of her coffee. "So, will you come for dinner? At least once? We could take a nice walk afterward."

That was another thing Vivi enjoyed—strolling around Bensonhurst every chance she could. She was a firm believer that the best way to get know a place was to walk it. She loved walking different neighborhoods, wondering what was going on in the lives of the people in their small brick homes. All the homes had tiny front yards, many of them boasting a religious statue or some carefully sculpted topiary. There was a real sense of community here, a close-knit feeling that seemed to come from people remaining true to their roots.

Vivi also enjoyed that people were getting to know her. Both Cuccio brothers greeted her when they saw her on the street, and she was on chatting terms with the butchers at Santoro's. Even her neighbors in the apartment building were becoming a little more friendly, one woman on her floor stopping her one morning to ask about the mouthwatering smell coming from Vivi's apartment the night before. It was hazelnut cake, and Vivi brought a piece to her neighbor, whose name was Roberta, later that night. Slowly but surely, her new life was beginning to take shape.

Natalie still seemed to be considering the dinner offer. "I'll come and go for a walk *if* you promise to come into the city and spend a night out on the town with me."

"Done. We can also explore some restaurants here in Brooklyn."

"Perhaps we should pay a visit to the widower's establishment across the street," Natalie suggested slyly. Vivi clicked her tongue disparagingly, an action that wasn't lost on Natalie. "What? Did he say something about your coffee again?"

Vivi considered whether to tell Natalie about the apple tart, the fritters, and the kiss. She decided to skip the kiss and stick strictly to dessert. Natalie seemed suspicious.

"You're cooking for each other?"

Vivi blinked. "It was only once."

"I don't like this, Vivi. There's a certain animation in your voice when you talk about him that I've never heard before."

"Oh, please," Vivi scoffed. "He's a baboon. Do you know he actually had the nerve to say he'd be irked if the construction we're doing here impacts the traffic at his restaurant?"

"When was this?"

"Earlier. I ran into him on the street." She did not want to tell Natalie the dessert competition had extended beyond Dante's.

"Who cooked for whom first?"

"I did," Vivi admitted reluctantly. "I felt bad for blind-siding him about his wife, remember?"

Natalie looked alarmed. "Don't go down this road, Vivi. I beg you."

Vivi checked her watch. If the DiDinatos didn't show up soon, she would . . . what should she do? Perhaps this was what people meant when they talked about being held hostage by their contractor. *Merde*.

"Did you hear me?" Natalie pressed. "He's damaged goods. You'll always be second to the dead wife, no matter how hard you try to make it otherwise. You can't fix him, nor do you have time to."

"I don't want to fix him. I don't want to do anything with him, apart from trying to figure out a way to peace-fully coexist as neighbors."

"Your mouth says one thing, but believe me, your eyes say another."

What do *my eyes say?* Vivi wondered uneasily. Natalie had pursed her lips expectantly, clearly waiting for Vivi to mount a defense.

"You read too many romance novels," Vivi said to Natalie in a brisk voice. "You needn't worry about me and Anthony Dante. We share a common love of food, that's all. Nothing is going to change that."

Chapter 9

"*What do you* think is in this?"

Anthony dragged his attention away from the on-ice action to see Little Ant holding aloft a hot dog. As promised, Anthony had accompanied his brother and nephew to Met Gar to watch the Blades play Boston. It was clear Little Ant cared more about the ingredients in the frank than the game, and that Michael was oblivious to his son's lack of interest.

"You don't want to know, trust me," said Anthony.

Though Anthony preferred football, a lifetime of watching his brother play had led to an appreciation of hockey. He shot a quick, sidelong glance at Michael, who was watching his former teammates with unabashed longing. *Madonn'*, talk about masochism. The nonstop cavalcade of fans stopping by to say hi to "Mikey D" didn't help, either.

It sometimes embarrassed Anthony to think back on how resentful he'd been of his brother's pro athlete status. Growing up, Michael had been the one who'd been marked as having a unique talent. It wasn't until Anthony was much older that he began shining in the kitchen, but by then, it was too late. He and Mikey were frozen in their roles as jock and chef, each envious in some way of the other. Michael envied the special closeness Anthony had with their parents, the result of his cooking side by side with them for years. Anthony envied Michael his fame and adulation. Even now, with people still asking for his brother's autograph, Anthony was capable of feeling the slightest prick of resentment.

Little Ant gobbled down his last piece of hot dog, eyeing Anthony eagerly. "Can I have another?"

"Ask your father," said Anthony. "I don't want to be the one responsible for you puking all over the car on the way home."

"Dad, can I have another hot dog?"

"What?" Michael seemed annoyed. "No." He pointed at the ice. "Okay, now watch the left winger, Jason Mitchell. Watch how when the puck is dropped, he rushes ahead to where he thinks the puck is *going* to be."

Little Ant dutifully did as he was told. It was as if Jason Mitchell knew he was being watched; the puck flipped to him and he snapped it off his stick, scoring. The crowd went crazy.

"You see that?" Michael bumped his shoulder against his son's affectionately. "You could do that if you tried. You're good enough."

Little Ant nodded mutely, but his agonized eyes sought Anthony's. Anthony winked at him, hoping to alleviate the kid's obvious stress. It seemed to work. Little Ant winked back, his mouth curving into the smallest hint of a smile.

"Hey, Mike, how come we're not up in a skybox?" Anthony wondered aloud.

"Too high up," said Michael. "Center ice, halfway up, is where you get the best view."

Anthony rolled his eyes, passing his soda to his nephew. The kid was back to looking forlorn. Was his brother oblivious or what? "When are you coming over to cook with me again, Little Ant?" Maybe the prospect of another cooking lesson could revive his nephew's spirits for the remainder of the game.

Little Ant tugged excitedly on his father's sleeve. "Dad, when can I—"

Michael waved his hand away. "Shhh, one minute, Ant, okay?"

Little Ant slumped in his seat. "Fine."

All of Met Gar watched as Boston's first line center, Bickie White, broke away and started racing toward Blades goalie David Hewson. Bickie deked and tried to go wide to his backhand, but Hewson stacked his pads and made a sliding stop.

"Yes!" Michael was on his feet with the rest of the roaring crowd. "Way to go, Hewsie!"

"Their nicknames are sooo dumb," Little Ant said to Anthony.

"Tell me about it."

Michael sat back down, finally focusing on his son. "Now, what did you want to ask me?"

"When can I go over to Uncle Anthony's to cook?"

"That's up to you and Uncle Ant. Like I've said before, as long as it doesn't interfere with hockey, you can go whenever you want."

Anthony held his tongue, dumbstruck by his brother's priorities. Weren't there more important things than hockey—like Little Ant's studies, for example?

"How're you doing in school?" Anthony asked.

"Good," said Little Ant.

"Good," Anthony echoed, nodding approvingly. "That's the most important thing," he whispered into Little Ant's ear. "Don't let anyone tell you otherwise."

"I think cooking's more important," Little Ant whispered back, delighted that he and his uncle were sharing a secret.

"Nope, you're wrong. One of my biggest regrets is

goofing off in school. You can get good grades and still cook. Okay?"

Little Ant looked disappointed. "Okay."

Poor kid, Anthony thought. He's got his father on one side shoving hockey down his throat, and me on the other telling him that the one thing he loves to do should come second. No wonder kids think adults are nuts, or worse, confusingly inconsistent. Most adults had their heads so far up their asses they didn't know what the hell they were saying half the time.

Boston was whistled for icing. During the break in the action, Anthony found his attention wandering. Looking around at the crowd, he marveled that some of these fans had been coming here for years, decades even, himself included. He was scanning the nosebleed section directly across the arena when he gave a start. Three rows down from the top—was that Vivi? He thrust his head forward, squinting. Couldn't be. No way. Grabbing the binoculars Little Ant had insisted on bringing, Anthony raised them to his eyes. It wasn't her. This woman had a long blonde braid like Vivi's, but her face was kind of pink, nothing at all like Vivi's pale, delicate skin. She was medium height, too, not willowy like a ballerina the way Vivi was. Surprisingly disappointed, Anthony lowered the binoculars.

"What ya lookin' at?" Little Ant chirped.

"Nothing," said Anthony, handing back the binoculars. "Here, drink some soda."

"**So, Little Ant,** what was your favorite part of the game?"

The jauntiness in his brother's voice made Anthony cringe as he, Mikey, and Little Ant drove back to Brooklyn following the New York Blades' 4–0 rout of Boston. Michael had spent the third period dissecting every on-ice move for his son, who looked so bored he wanted to cry. Anthony wondered, do all parents see only what they want to see? If he and Ang had had a kid, would he have bought the kid a little chef's hat and insisted he learn to make the gravy? Anthony liked to think otherwise, but his brother's behavior was giving him serious pause. Michael was no dummy—except, apparently, when it came to reading his own kid's emotions.

Anthony's eyes shot to the rearview mirror. His nephew was squirming in the backseat.

"My favorite part was the hot dogs," said Little Ant after a long pause.

Anthony stifled a laugh. *Out of the mouths of babes*, he thought. Michael, however, seemed less amused.

"That's all you can think of?"

"Leave the kid alone, Mike," Anthony chided good-humoredly. "Maybe he got the Dante cooking genes rather than the Dante hockey genes."

"Yeah!" Little Ant chimed in from the back.

"I'd like to think he's got both," Michael grumbled.

Anthony shrugged. "Maybe he does, maybe he doesn't. Does it matter?"

Michael didn't answer.

"*Please tell me* we're here to check out the competition, and not because of your unhealthy fixation on the brooding widower."

"You're the one who suggested we try dining here," said Vivi to Natalie as Aldo led them to their table at Dante's.

She was gratified the distinguished old waiter recognized her when she walked in, just as she was warmed by the hearty hello Anthony's brother, Michael, gave her, though he did seem mostly distracted as he taught a nervous-looking woman with deep circles under her eyes how to work the phone system.

Vivi quickly sized up her surroundings. Six p.m., and not an empty table in the place. The clientele ranged from families with children to young couples making eyes at each other over a bottle of wine. The latter made her realize there *could* be some crossover between Dante's and Vivi's. The thought sparked her competitive side.

Persuading Natalie to come out to Bensonhurst for a meal, Vivi's first instinct had been to cook something for the two of them. But then she thought, why not take up Natalie's suggestion and see if Anthony Dante's arrogance was justified? Obviously he could make wonderful fritters. But did his talents extend beyond that?

"The head chef will be out soon to tell you of our specials," said Aldo, pulling out their chairs for them before handing them their menus with a flourish.

Natalie raised an eyebrow. "Perhaps he *can* do more than make 'gravy.'"

Vivi smiled nervously, her eyes magnetically drawn to the swinging doors of the kitchen. She'd had no doubt she might catch a fleeting glimpse of Anthony over the course of the evening, but she hadn't counted on actually having to interact with him. She had to admit, she was impressed by the personal touch of presenting the specials himself. It made good business sense. She decided she would do the same at Vivi's. If he wanted to accuse her of copying him, let him.

The busboy had just finished filling their glasses with ice water when the kitchen doors swung open and Anthony stepped out into the dining room. Had she not known what a jackass he actually was, Vivi would have been impressed by his stature and handsome face. Anthony's eyes locked on hers, and for a split second, she thought he might turn right back. But Anthony was a professional; he squared his shoulders, and by the time he reached their table, there was a charming smile on his face. Vivi was impressed once again.

"Ladies." Anthony gave a small bow. "What a pleasant surprise."

Natalie looked him over. "Is it?"

Vivi shot a look of warning across the table. She was not here to antagonize; why did Natalie always seem to turn disagreeable around Anthony, when all the man did was greet them?

To his credit, Anthony ignored her. "Would you like to hear tonight's specials?"

"Of course," said Vivi, finding it hard to hold his gaze. Each time their eyes met, one or both of them would look away.

"Our appetizer special tonight is crisp fried zucchini blossoms."

"Only the male blossoms, correct?" Vivi questioned.

Anthony looked insulted. "Of course."

Natalie looked at both of them in alarm. "There are male and female zucchini blossoms?"

"Yes," Vivi and Anthony answered simultaneously.

"Please," Anthony said to Vivi with the faintest tone of condescension in his voice, "feel free to explain the difference to your sister."

"I'm confident you could do a better job."

"As you wish," said Anthony with exaggerated politeness. He regarded Natalie. "Only the male blossoms, which are found on the stem, are edible. The female, attached to the zucchini itself, are mushy and bitter."

"Fascinating," Natalie drawled sarcastically. "Next?"

Anthony leveled her with an irritated stare before continuing. "Our pasta special tonight is tortellini with fish stuffing."

Natalie wrinkled her nose. "That doesn't sound very enticing."

"Then don't order it," Anthony said under his breath.

"I would very much like to hear what's in it," Vivi piped up, giving Natalie a small kick beneath the table.

Anthony actually looked appreciative of her interest. "The tortellini is, of course, homemade, while the filling is sea bass mixed with fresh spices, wine vinegar, and heavy cream."

"Sounds very interesting," Vivi murmured.

"I recommend it highly."

"It's not soggy, is it?"

"Sogginess is in the mouth of the beholder," Anthony replied coolly.

Vivi looked down at the table to hide her smile. She had to admit, she enjoyed their verbal sparring just a little bit. She could see he did, too. The hardness in his eyes when he spoke with Natalie disappeared, replaced by a look guarded but a little more sportive.

"Our other special is chicken breast with pork and rosemary filling," Anthony continued.

"You don't need to hear what's in that, do you, Vivi?" Natalie clucked impatiently.

Anthony and Vivi exchanged looks. Natalie just didn't understand, did she?

"Aldo will return shortly to take your orders." Anthony disappeared back into the kitchen.

"What on earth is going on?" Natalie demanded as soon as Anthony was gone.

Vivi sipped her ice water. "I don't understand."

"The energy between the two of you was almost embarrassing."

"It's called antagonism, Natalie."

"We'll see," said Natalie, unfolding her napkin with a snap.

"Excuse me." A handsome man with dancing blue eyes and thick, lustrous salt-and-pepper hair sitting at the next table leaned toward Vivi and Natalie. "I couldn't help but noticing your accents. You're French?"

"*Oui,*" said Vivi.

"Paris is one of my favorite places." The man extended his hand. "Quinn O'Brien."

"I'm Vivi Robitaille, and this is my . . . sister, Natalie Bocuse."

"Pleased to meet you. You here on vacation?"

"No, we moved here," Vivi explained, shooting a look at Natalie, whose face was frozen in disapproval. Vivi was baffled; the man was being very nice and friendly, what was wrong with that?

Quinn looked impressed. "For work?"

"Yes," said Vivi. "I'm opening a restaurant across the street shortly."

"Yeah?" Vivi loved the man's accent; it was real "New Yawk," like the accent she'd heard on so many TV shows and movies. "I'll have to check it out. This is my turf."

"You're a policeman?" Vivi asked politely.

"God, no." Quinn seemed to find the notion amusing. "I'm a reporter for the *New York Sentinel.* But a lot of my beat is here in Brooklyn." He turned to Natalie. "What about you? You opening the restaurant with her?"

"I'm an investor, yes," Natalie said primly.

"Professional?"

Natalie peered down her nose at him. "I don't believe that's any of your concern."

Quinn chuckled softly. "*Now* I remember the one thing I didn't like about Paris."

Natalie's lips pursed in disapproval. "What's that?"

"Parisians."

Vivi giggled, prompting Natalie to fix her with a glare. Perhaps the wisecrack didn't bother Vivi because she wasn't actually from Paris. Or maybe it was that she could see Quinn was just teasing Natalie, trying to get her to relax a little. Unfortunately, it didn't seem to be working.

"How terribly rude you are!" Natalie hissed.

Quinn flashed a devilish smile. "I wanted you to feel at home."

"Parisians might be rude, but at least we aren't overweight like most of you Americans," Natalie retorted.

"That's because you burn so many extra calories dodging the dog shit on the sidewalks."

Vivi snorted and covered her mouth. *Oh my,* she thought, *this Quinn O'Brien is very sharp and very funny.* She liked him immediately. Natalie raised her menu so it was in front of her face.

Quinn turned to Vivi apologetically. "I'm sorry. I didn't mean to intrude on your meal."

"Au contraire," said Vivi, "it was very nice meeting you. We love the American sense of humor, don't we, Natalie?"

Natalie said nothing. Quinn tipped the menu forward. "Sorry to bug ya, Nat. Hope to see you around."

"Oh!" Natalie looked scandalized as she pulled the menu back to her face.

"I'm going to check out your restaurant when it opens, Vivi. And that's a promise," said Quinn.

"Please do."

Quinn returned to reading his book. This time it was Vivi who pulled Natalie's menu from her face—pulled it completely from her hands, as a matter of fact.

"You can come out now," Vivi whispered. "The big, bad American man is gone."

"I don't believe you!" Natalie hissed. "How could you laugh when he said those things to me?"

"He was teasing you, Natalie. He didn't mean it. He was just trying to get you to lighten up, as they say here."

"What is it with these Americans, asking one's name, what one does—"

"Natalie." Vivi's voice was low and placating. "Those questions are not considered rude here. You should know that by now."

"A journalist," Natalie continued disdainfully as if she hadn't heard. "The lowest of the low."

Vivi ignored the criticism. "He's very handsome, don't you think?"

"For a swine."

Sometimes there was no talking to Natalie. Once she got an idea fixed in her head, it was etched in stone. Vivi supposed she could understand Natalie's aversion to anyone in the press; it was the French media, after all, who revealed her affair with the cabinet minister, in effect destroying both her personal and professional life. But Natalie really needed to accept that when it came to social mores, Americans were different. Not better, not worse, just different. Vivi opened her own menu with a sigh. Hopefully, Natalie would relax once dinner was ordered and a bottle of wine brought to the table.

"Garcon—I mean, waiter—can we have the check, please?"

Vivi's smile was polite as she hailed the faithful Aldo. She and Natalie had had a wonderful meal. The rosemary and pork–filled chicken cutlets were a *little* heavy on the rosemary, but other than that, she had no real complaints, which bothered her a little bit.

"What did you think?" she asked her sister.

"Good," Natalie allowed reluctantly. "You're better."

Vivi laughed. "Of course."

Aldo's expression was solemn as he appeared at the table. "The meal is compliments of the chef."

Vivi couldn't hide her surprise. "Excuse me?"

"A professional courtesy."

"Oh." Vivi perked up in her seat. "How lovely." So, Anthony did think of her as a professional. How gratifying.

"Thank him for us," Natalie told Aldo.

"Actually," said Vivi, "would it be possible to thank him in person?"

Natalie heaved a put-upon sigh. "Do we have to? The last thing I want to do is be stuck here while you two get all excited over chicken breasts and Lord knows what else."

"It will only take a minute," Vivi assured her as she rose. "In fact, you stay here and finish your coffee. I'll go back and extend my compliments."

"Okay, what didn't you like?"

Vivi tried to hold on to the goodwill she was feeling as she approached Anthony where he sat outside on the kitchen steps, puffing on a cigarette. Here she'd come to compliment him—to the degree she could—and immediately he had to put her on the defensive. She'd prove to him she was a bigger person than that by not stooping to his level.

"Actually, I'm here to thank you for the free meal."

"You're very welcome," said Anthony, throwing his cigarette to the ground and stamping it underfoot. "Nasty habit," he muttered, more to himself than her. "I only do it occasionally."

"I used to do it all the time," Vivi confessed.

"No more?"

"They crucify you in America if you smoke, yes?"

"Pretty much. You saying you stopped when you came here?"

Vivi hesitated. "Yes. To save money. Plus, like you said, it's a nasty habit."

"Who wants to smell like an ashtray, right?"

"Right."

Anthony folded his arms across his chest. Vivi was struck by how tan and muscled his forearms were. Alain, the last man she had dated back in Paris, over seven months ago, had been thin and pale, in no way robust. Odd, to think of Alain at this moment.

Anthony was eyeing her with disbelief. "You expect me to believe that as another chef, you've got absolutely no criticism of the meal?"

"Well . . ."

Anthony shook his head, laughing to himself. "Man, I knew it. Hit me. Go ahead."

Vivi blinked, alarmed. "You want me to hit you?" Perhaps Natalie was right, and Americans *were* rude in a way Vivi was just now experiencing.

Anthony ran his hand over his mouth. " 'Hit me' is an American expression. It means, let me hear it, don't hold anything back. Understand?"

"Yes, yes," Vivi said enthusiastically. *Hit me.* She liked that. It sounded tough, swaggering. Perfect for the braggart standing before her. "Shall I hit you?"

"Yeah, I bet you'd love to. Go on."

"I think there was a little too much rosemary in the chicken. A *soupcon* would have been better. *Soupcon* means—"

"I know what a *soupcon* is. And I disagree."

"It overpowered the pork filling."

"It helped accentuate the pork's natural flavors," Anthony maintained.

"Well, I beg to differ, but of course, you'll never admit I'm right."

"You think you could do better?"

"Of course." Vivi put a hand on her cocked hip. "Are you challenging me to another cooking contest?"

Anthony held up a hand. "Whoa, let's get our facts straight here, lady. You challenged me last time around, remember?"

"Yes, you're right. You thought you could do better than my tart. And you were wrong."

Anthony shook his head. "Sad, the way you twist reality

to make yourself feel better." He turned around, taking a quick look to make sure everything was okay in the kitchen. "You game?" he asked Vivi as he turned back to her.

Vivi looked at him blankly.

"See if you can figure that one out," Anthony urged.

"Does it mean, am I willing to meet your challenge?" Vivi asked uncertainly.

"Exactly."

"Of course I am," said Vivi.

An uncomfortable moment passed between them. Vivi wondered if he, like she, was thinking of the kiss they had shared at her apartment.

"Shall we have it here?" Vivi said tentatively.

Anthony looked reluctant. "I guess."

"You don't seem very enthusiastic."

"It's just a pain in the ass—" He stopped, looking apologetic. "Pardon my F— Never mind."

"No. What were you going to say?"

"I was going to say, 'pardon my French,' which is another American expression. It's something we say when we curse."

Vivi scowled. "Why? Because we French are so foul-mouthed?"

"Hey, don't blame me! I didn't come up with it."

"It's a very derogatory phrase."

"Try being called a guinea or a wop or a dago. Then you'll know derogatory." Anthony glanced back at the kitchen, obviously itching to get back inside. "You really want to have it here?"

"I would love it," Vivi said longingly.

"My house might be better."

Vivi narrowed her eyes. "You don't want me in your precious restaurant kitchen, do you?"

"Would you want me in yours?"

"Only if I had to," Vivi admitted, glancing behind her.

Anthony sighed. "All right, look: I can see you're dying

to be let loose inside. Why don't you meet me here Sunday morning and you can cook your little heart out."

"That would be wonderful—if you promise not to breathe down my neck."

"This is my kitchen, Vivi. I can do what I want."

Vivi shrugged. "Fine. Sunday it is, then."

"By the way," said Anthony, giving a small stretch as he yawned, "I'm expecting to be dazzled. Think you can manage it?"

"In my sleep," Vivi shot back at him, using one of the few American expressions she'd learned. "See you on Sunday."

Chapter 10

Anthony was always the last one to leave Dante's and lock up for the night. He loved standing alone in the silent kitchen after the staff had left, admiring the rows of gleaming pots and pans, knowing tomorrow would bring another day of joyous chaos. From there he'd move on to the dining room, where just a few hours before, the tables had been full of customers stuffing themselves with his delicious food. A sentimental man, Anthony never ceased to marvel at how his parents had built this place up from the ground, first as a pizzeria serving by the slice, then gradually expanding to a well-respected restaurant. He and Mikey had taken it a step further a few years back, enlarging the space and updating the menu, but deep down, Anthony still thought of Dante's as a humble Italian joint serving "good gravy and macaroni," as his old man liked to say. Anthony had always hoped that one day he'd be able to keep tradition going by handing over the reins to his own son or daughter, but Angie's death had forced him to reconfigure his dreams. Little Ant was his next best hope.

Not that he'd ever force the kid to follow in his footsteps, unlike someone else in his family.

"Anthony?"

Startled, Anthony paused in the darkened dining room, trying to place the voice calling out to him. "Who's there?"

"Lorraine."

King of heaven and all the damn saints, thought Anthony. He should have known this was coming.

"What are you doing sitting in the dark, Lorraine?" asked Anthony as he moved to flick on the lights.

"I was waiting for you."

"You could have waited with the lights on."

"I wanted to surprise you."

"Well, you succeeded on that score."

Lorraine was sitting at a table for two near the kitchen door, her hands folded primly in her lap. She looked much the same as she did in high school—same chin-length black hair, same dark circles beneath the hangdog eyes. Anthony could picture her sleepwalking. He could also picture her in her underwear, doing the hokey pokey in front of Mr. Leotardo's blackboard. Insane Lorraine. Goddamned Michael.

"What can I do for you, Lorraine?"

"I just wanted to thank you for hiring me, Anthony. I really, really, really appreciate it."

"No problem." Anthony swallowed, feeling guilty since God knows he'd only done so under duress. Maybe Mikey was right; maybe he was being a little hard-hearted. People like Lorraine needed compassion. He felt bad about making fun of her in high school along with everyone else, but then again, that's what kids did; they preyed on the weak to make themselves feel better. He had been on the receiving end of a few jokes back in the day, some guys calling him a "fag" because he liked to cook. Of course, the difference between them was that when Lorraine was taunted, she would snap like a strand of uncooked spaghetti, whereas Anthony could crush a tormentor's head like a walnut if he so chose.

Lorraine's gaze traveled anxiously around the empty dining room. "I think I did good tonight." Her voice was flat, a tin can that had been repeatedly run over in the road.

Anthony masked a grimace. "Did Mike talk to you about perking up your voice a bit? Smiling at the customers when they come in and all that stuff?"

"Uh-huh," Lorraine said flatly. "I'm pretty sure I can do it."

"Good, good."

Lorraine abruptly turned to Anthony in wonder. "Whoever thought Michael would have so many kids,'huh?"

"Yeah, well, you meet the right woman . . ."

Fuck! Why did he say that?

"I heard about your wife," Lorraine droned. "You have my sympathy."

"Thank you. I was sorry to hear about your dad."

"What can you do? When it's your time, it's your time."

Anthony didn't agree, but he held his tongue. "Whatcha been up to, Lorraine? You kind of . . . just disappeared after high school, you know?"

Lorraine shrugged, looking down at her raggedy nails, bitten down to the quick. "This and that. You know."

No, I don't know, thought Anthony, *nor do I really want to. I'm just trying to be nice and make conversation.*

Lorraine twisted her hands in her lap. "Look, Anthony, I need to talk to you about something."

Shit, Anthony thought, bracing himself. *Here comes the part where she confesses there are five bodies buried beneath an old house upstate.*

"Ma and I would love it if you could come over for dinner one night. Nothing formal, just a nice way to thank you for hiring me."

"You don't have to do that, Lorraine. Your mother must have a lot on her plate right now with, uh, her grieving and all."

"Not really. All she does is light novena candles and watch *Judge Judy*."

Sounds like a great time. "It's tough for me to get away from the restaurant, you know?"

"It's just one night," Lorraine said accusingly.

Anthony sighed. He looked at her sitting there, thought of the courage it must have taken her to ask him, and felt more pity than annoyance. Would it kill him to break bread with her and her mother one night, just to get her off his back?

"Let me see what I can do," Anthony said.

Lorraine's expression turned eager. "How about Sunday?"

"I gotta cook on Sunday, remember? The restaurant's open."

"Sunday lunch, maybe."

"I *can't*," Anthony said gently but firmly.

"What, you got a brunch date or something?" Lorraine snapped.

Perhaps compassion was something Anthony needed to work up to, since his first instinct was to bark, "It's none of your business." But that sounded like he was covering something up, so he just said, "No, family stuff, that's all."

This seemed to pacify Lorraine, who abruptly stood up. "I need a ride home," she announced.

"Of course you do," Anthony muttered under his breath. He rattled the keys in his pocket. "C'mon, I'll run you home."

"You always were sweet, Ant."

"Yeah, I'm a living doll. Let's go."

"*I thought we* were going to a restaurant, Natalie."

"They serve food here."

Vivi smiled tersely as Natalie gulped down the remainder

of her third cocktail, a sky blue concoction that looked like glass cleaner. After their positive dining experience at Dante's a few nights before, the sisters agreed it was Vivi's turn to come into the city to eat. Knowing Natalie to have refined tastes, Vivi assumed they'd be dining at a fine restaurant recommended via word of mouth or through the trusted Zagat guide. Instead, Vivi found herself in a futuristic-looking bar called Plutonium.

The warehouse-sized space was illuminated entirely by dim blue neon, the white plastic furniture inflatable and squishy. The spacey music being pumped through the sound system made Vivi feel like nodding off—an impossible feat since their waitress, a young woman clad in a silver cat suit, kept stopping by their table every two minutes to ask if Natalie needed another refill on her "Jupiter Juice." If she came by one more time, Vivi was prepared to politely ask her to find another solar system to inhabit.

"Let's pay the bill and find somewhere real to eat," Vivi urged.

"Nooo," Natalie whined. "We can eat here. C'mon, Vivi! Don't be such a bore."

"Fine," Vivi capitulated with a sigh. There seemed little point in reminding Natalie that their agreement was to get together to dine, not drink themselves into oblivion. Vivi, always careful about alcohol consumption, had ordered one glass of chardonnay that she'd been nursing for the past hour, despite Natalie's exhortations to do otherwise.

Vivi looked around at the studiedly bored faces of her fellow patrons. Never in a million years would she come to a place like this on her own. It was all surface, no substance; a place where people yearned to be seen. She opened up her rocket-shaped menu and perused the food offerings. In the end she decided on a cheese platter, the only item that didn't have a space name attached to it.

"So," said Natalie, swaying slightly, "when are you going to admit your crush on Chef Dante?"

"Never," said Vivi. She checked her watch; it was close to eleven. Her plan had been to have a nice meal with Natalie, then head back out to Bensonhurst to get a good night's sleep. She wanted to be at her absolute best when she cooked for Anthony tomorrow. But judging from Natalie's motioning to the waitress for another drink, it was going to take a crane to lift her out of her seat.

"I *know* you like him," Natalie continued, not seeming to acknowledge Vivi's answer. "And I know he likes you, too. I just wish someone liked me," Natalie said, the last word transforming itself into a sob.

"Oh, *cherie*." Vivi put her arm around her sister. "You'll find love again. You will."

"Will I?" Natalie wept. "Here? In America?"

"Of course, of course," Vivi soothed. "Didn't you see the way that journalist we met the other night was looking at you?"

"Yes, like I was a bitch!"

"Well, you weren't very polite to him," Vivi pointed out.

"I know!" Natalie lamented. "But I don't mean to be like that! It just happens. I wish you'd known me before, when we were girls." Natalie sniffled. "You would have really liked me. I was nice."

"I like you now," Vivi said.

"Men are such brutes, aren't they?"

"Some can be, yes."

"Thierry was," Natalie continued bitterly. She put her head in her hands. "God, the idiocy . . ." Her purse fell to the floor, spilling its contents. "Damn!"

"I'll get it." Vivi crouched down to pick up Natalie's bag. That's when she saw the credit card receipt from Saks for three thousand dollars. Stifling a gasp, she shoved the receipt back into Natalie's purse, along with her keys, a tube of lipstick, and a crumpled wad of one-hundred-dollar bills.

"Here you go." Vivi's voice was brittle as she handed

Natalie her bag. Any sympathy she'd felt mere seconds ago for Natalie and her wounded heart was rapidly being swallowed up by anxiety. What on earth was Natalie doing, spending that kind of money? What on earth was Natalie *doing*, period?

"Natalie, what do you do all day?"

"What do you mean?" Natalie wiped a tear from her cheek.

"I mean, what do you do all day?" Vivi prodded. "Tell me. I'm curious."

Natalie seemed perplexed by the question, so much so that it took her a while to speak. "I shop. Sometimes I meet old friends from Paris who are here on business. I oversee the cleaning woman who comes to the apartment because, really, she does an awful job. I watch TV. I go out at night and—"

"Go to horrible places like this and drink too much?"

Tears began seeping from Natalie's eyes. "You don't understand, Vivi. It wasn't only my heart that was destroyed by Thierry, it was my career, as well. I'm trying to do what I can to pull myself back together, but it's very, very hard."

"Well, drowning your sorrows in drink and shopping isn't going to help. If anything, it's making things worse. You need to work, Natalie."

"Work?"

"Yes. You need a purpose, something to give shape to your days," Vivi said firmly. "Why don't you help me? We could work together on getting everything ready for the restaurant. I need to start finding out about publicity. Maybe that's something you could take care of."

"Hmm." Natalie seemed taken by the idea. "Maybe I could." She appeared to cheer up a bit. "What if I come out tomorrow and we sit down and make up a plan?"

"I can't tomorrow," Vivi said evasively.

"Why not?"

"I'm going to be busy."

"Cooking?"

"Yes."

"For yourself, or for whatshisname?"

"As it so happens," Vivi said, trying not to sound defensive, "when I went into the kitchen to speak with him after our meal, I took the liberty of giving him some advice on how he might improve his pork and rosemary stuffed chicken."

"And . . . ?"

"And in typical, arrogant male chef fashion, he dared me to do better. So tomorrow, I'm going to do just that."

Natalie snorted. "In *your* poky little kitchen?"

"No," said Vivi, ignoring her jibe, "in the kitchen at his restaurant."

Natalie's mouth fell open. "You're not serious."

"I am."

Natalie's face arranged itself into a scowl. "I don't understand how you can insist there's nothing going on when, clearly, there is."

"Yes, a shared passion for food," said Vivi, tired at having to once again explain the obvious.

"Yes, and what if that passion spills over from the stove to the two of you lying on top of one of the tables in the dining room? What then?"

"That isn't going to happen," Vivi scoffed, though that very image flashed in her mind, bringing an unanticipated rush of heat to her body.

Natalie wagged a warning finger in Vivi's face. "He's damaged goods, Vivi."

"We're all damaged goods!" said Vivi, pushing her sister's hand away. "You, me, Anthony, Thierry—anyone who has ever loved and lost is damaged goods!"

Natalie considered this. "I suppose you're right."

"I am right, but that's beside the point. I just want to *cook*," said Vivi, struck by the yearning in her own voice.

"And until my own place opens, I have to grab my chances when and where I can find them. Tomorrow's chance just happens to be in Anthony Dante's kitchen, and I'm taking it. Now finish up your Jupiter Juice so we can find a proper place to eat."

Chapter 11

Prepare to be dazzled.

Anthony's expectation echoed in Vivi's head as she followed him through the Dante's dining room into the silent, silver kitchen. Though she'd barely slept a wink thanks to Natalie, adrenaline was beginning to pump inside her, giving her more than enough energy for the culinary challenge ahead. Dazzling Anthony Dante would be easy; the hard part would be making sure he didn't interfere.

"Coffee?" Anthony proffered a foam cup, which Vivi accepted gratefully. She would have brought her own thermos, but she didn't want to be teased.

"Where do you get coffee so early in the morning?" asked Vivi.

"There's a deli up the street. They open at five."

Vivi shook her head in silent amazement. No one could ever accuse Americans of being lazy. Open for business at five a.m. on a Sunday morning? Only the occasional *boulangerie* did that in France.

"Have you been up since five?" she asked.

Anthony nodded.

"To be here for the deliveries?" That was the one aspect of owning her own place Vivi was not looking forward to: the pre-dawn deliveries from suppliers.

"Something like that," Anthony mumbled.

Vivi gave him a puzzled look. How he spent his Sunday mornings was certainly none of her business, though her curiosity was piqued.

Vivi moved to one of the kitchen's long stainless steel tables and began unpacking her groceries. She wasn't surprised when Anthony came to stand right beside her, rubbing his hands together like an eager child. "What are you making?"

"*Poulet Basquaise*, or chicken with onions, ham, tomatoes, and peppers. The famous French gourmet Brillat-Savarin once said, 'Poultry is for the cook what the canvas is for the painter,' so prepare for the culinary equivalent of a Picasso, my friend."

"Mmm, nothing like eating dinner first thing in the morning."

Vivi laughed. "Tell me you've never eaten your own leftovers the next day."

"You don't want to know how many times I've had lasagna for breakfast, okay?"

"Exactly."

Vivi could feel the pull the recipe's ingredients were exerting over Anthony as he casually asked, "Need help with the prep work?"

Vivi looked at him stonily.

"Well, you have to give me something to do. I can't just stand here in my own kitchen and watch you cook."

Vivi brusquely rolled two heads of garlic toward him. "I need twelve cloves, cut paper thin." She knew this was going to happen; she should have made him come over to her place. Her kitchen might be "poky" as Natalie so bluntly put it, but at least it was hers.

Anthony began working on the garlic, while Vivi reached for a large stockpot, filling it with water before setting it atop a high flame on one of the burners.

"What's that for?" Anthony asked.

"To prep the two pounds of tomatoes that need to be peeled." She took hold of the apron he handed her, tying the strings briskly around her waist. "Listen to me: If you're going to question every little thing I do, I'm going to go mad, do you hear?"

Anthony looked offended. "Pardon *moi*, but it's just curiosity, not criticism."

Vivi stood her ground. "Just let me cook, all right?"

"Fine," said Anthony with displeasure. "I'll chop the garlic and keep my lip buttoned."

"Yes, please." His dramatic streak amused Vivi. All chefs had a penchant for the melodramatic—herself included, according to her mother.

Anthony brooded silently over the garlic while Vivi set about slicing the onions. As she and Anthony worked side by side, she thought she felt a certain sense of camaraderie. They weren't adversaries, they were two soldiers together in the trenches, united toward a common goal: culinary perfection.

"I never minded doing prep work," Vivi confided.

"Me either, though sometimes my old man could be a pain in the neck about it."

Vivi glanced sideways at him with interest. "I forgot you've been in this kitchen since you were a small boy."

"Yup." Anthony's fingers flew, slicing the first clove of garlic in seconds. "You grow up in the biz?"

Vivi shook her head. "My mother ran a small grocery store. But she always loved to cook."

"She still alive?"

Vivi nodded.

"Your dad?"

Vivi swallowed hard. "He passed away a little over a

year and a half ago." Even now, just saying it made her feel as if there were sand in her blood, dragging her down. Did grief feel that way for everyone?

"So, you grew up with your mom and Natalie grew up with your dad?"

"Mmm," said Vivi noncommittally, reaching for another onion. To her surprise, Anthony's hand shot out to still hers.

"Why so mysterious?" he asked, his expression serious as he studied her face.

Vivi gently pushed his hand away. "It's complicated." She began chopping the next onion, grateful for the busy-work.

"We've got time."

Vivi chopped faster. "You're very pushy."

"In some things. C'mon, Vivi. Spill."

Vivi put down her knife, wiping her hands on the front of her apron. The truth was, she wanted to tell him. She'd been longing to tell someone about it for a long time.

"I'm my father's illegimate child," she said softly. "Natalie is the child of his marriage."

Anthony looked like he didn't know what to say. "And you—the two of you—you're friends? I mean—"

"I'll explain," said Vivi, picking up her knife to briskly resume her chopping. It would be so much easier to talk about if she could concentrate on work as she spoke and didn't have to see Anthony's face. She was afraid she would see pity there. Or worse, disapproval.

"I grew up in Avignon with my mother. Ever since I could remember, my father would only be with us intermittently. I didn't understand why he was always coming and going, until one day my mother explained that he worked in Paris, and it was easier for him to stay there for work, coming to see us on the occasional weekend. I accepted this.

"Then one day, I turned on the TV and there was my father on the news, accompanied by another woman and a little girl." Vivi's face felt hot. "Needless to say, I was very confused."

"No shit," Anthony blurted. Vivi scowled at him. "Let me rephrase that: wow."

"That's when my mother explained to me—she was my father's mistress, and the woman and the girl on the TV were his wife and daughter."

Anthony's mouth fell open. "Your mother knew about them?"

"Oh, yes," Vivi replied matter-of-factly. "At first, I was upset. I remember asking my *maman*, 'Why doesn't Papa divorce that woman and come marry you?' But my mother just laughed. She liked her freedom! Besides, my father was a very well-respected politician. Breaking up his family for his mistress would have been frowned upon."

"And having an illegitimate kid wasn't?"

Vivi's brows knitted in frustration. "You don't understand. In my country, extramarital affairs are considered private. It's no one's business how someone conducts their personal life; it has nothing to do with the professional sphere unless it affects work somehow, like in Natalie's case. The nuclear family is considered sacred, which is why a divorce would have been frowned upon, but I wasn't. When my father died, my mother and I were both at the funeral, and no one blinked an eye."

Anthony's gaze shifted uneasily. "What about Natalie's mother?"

"She knew about my mother."

"Did her mother know about *you*?"

Vivi hesitated. "Not at first. But when I was accepted at Le Cordon Bleu and went to Paris, I made contact with Natalie." She smiled sadly. "I'd always wanted a sister, so I reached out. My father was furious; at that time, Natalie and her mother hadn't known about me, and they were quite shocked. But once things settled down, Natalie and I slowly got to know one another.

"I was hurt when Papa died and left Natalie much more money than me, but I understood; his wife would have been very upset if we'd received the same amount." Vivi put down the knife in her hand as tears welled up, blurring her vision. "Damn." She turned away from Anthony. "Excuse me a minute. These onions . . ." She clenched her jaw, but it didn't work; a tear broke free and trickled down her cheek.

"Vivi." Anthony's voice was kind as he turned her back to him, awkwardly enveloping her in his arms. "It's okay."

"It's ridiculous." Vivi sniffled against his large, warm chest. "I know my father loved me! But it still hurts, and with Natalie holding the purse strings for the restaurant, I feel as if I have to be careful about everything I say or do or she'll change her mind about the bistro." She squeezed her eyes shut. "Sometimes, I feel like I have to prove I even have a right to exist."

Anthony squeezed her tighter. "Of course you have a right to exist." He paused. "I'm glad you exist."

Vivi erupted into sobs. "I'm sorry. I—I'm getting your shirt wet."

"Big effin' deal," said Anthony. "Clothing doesn't matter. People do."

Vivi slowly lifted her eyes to his. "You're so kind," she whispered. She reached up, cupping her hand to his cheek and holding it there. A small flint of desire sparked in his eyes, and she wondered: is he seeing the same thing as he looks at me? The feeling took her by surprise. Worried his penetrating gaze meant he could read her thoughts, Vivi gently pulled away from their embrace, blotting her eyes with the hem of her apron.

"You okay?"

"Yes," Vivi said brusquely. She picked up her knife and resumed chopping onions. Anthony paused, then picked up

his own knife and resumed mincing garlic. Neither said a
word.

"Well?"

Anthony tried to ignore Vivi's nervous hovering as she
waited for him to taste her chicken dish. Ever since holding
her, it felt as if God had given him an extra sense, and he
didn't know what to do with it.

As Vivi held her breath, Anthony put a forkful of food
in his mouth, waiting until long after he'd swallowed to
make his pronouncement. "Pretty damn good."

Vivi looked pleased. "Thank you."

"You could use less garlic, though." Anthony laughed as
she stomped her foot in outrage. "I'm just kidding."

"You better be." Vivi wore a slight frown as she helped
herself to a plate of food. "I'm sorry about before," she said,
not quite looking at him. "About falling apart and all that."

"It's not a big deal."

"It is to me. Please, promise me you won't say anything
to anyone about what I told you."

"Who am I going to tell?"

"Your brother, perhaps?" Vivi took a taste of food, chewing slowly. "*Merde*, I think you're right. A little too much
garlic."

"The master is always right," Anthony boasted. "Don't
worry, I won't tell my brother anything."

"And you can't let Natalie know you know. And—"

"Anything else you want to tell me not to do?" Anthony
interrupted.

Vivi blushed. "I'm sorry."

"Does Natalie know how you feel?" Anthony asked,
dabbing his mouth with a napkin. "About you feeling like
she lords it over you?"

"No."

"Don't you think you should tell her?" He knew from

experience with his own brother that you shouldn't let things like this fester. Not only was it unhealthy, it was dangerous—likely to explode in a war of words that couldn't be taken back.

Vivi considered the question. "I don't know," she said carefully. "It's not as if we're outwardly battling. It's my issue."

"Yeah, but it's interfering with enjoying what you're trying to build here. I think you need to get it off your chest, or at some point you're going to pop your cork."

"Another wonderful expression," Vivi said with a soft laugh.

The sound of her laugh . . . Anthony immediately wanted to say something witty, just so he could hear it again. And yet, the mere recognition of that urge made him uncomfortable. He jumped up. "I really need to get my day started. The staff is going to start straggling in soon."

"Of course. Let me do the dishes and I'll be on my way."

"I'll take care of them. It's no sweat."

"That hardly seems right."

"Seriously, it's not a big deal." The sooner she left, the better. He desperately needed to get his head on straight before his day properly began.

"If you say so." Vivi rose slowly. "I was wondering," she said shyly, "if you would like to go to a new restaurant in New York with me."

Anthony peered at her apprehensively. "What kind of restaurant?" Was she asking him on a *date*?

"American *nouvelle*, I think."

"Huh." He hated these stupid labels that were put on cooking styles: American *nouvelle*, fusion, fill-in-the-blank. They were pretentious as well as limiting.

His lack of an immediate, enthusiastic response wasn't lost on Vivi as she quickly untied her apron, thrusting it at him. "I just thought it might be fun to go with another chef, that's all."

Anthony balled up her apron in his hand. "It could be interesting. Tell me what day you have in mind, and I'll talk to some people, see about getting someone to cover for me."

"Shall I call you?"

Anthony shrugged. "Just pop over when you get a chance."

"All right, then." Vivi edged toward the kitchen doors. "Thank you for letting me demonstrate which of us is truly the better cook. I must say, you accepted defeat very gracefully."

They both laughed.

"You ever hear the expression, 'It ain't over till it's over'?" Anthony asked as he held the kitchen door open for her.

"No."

He patted Vivi's shoulder. "Find out what it means; then we'll talk about defeat."

When Anthony told Vivi he'd "talk to some people," he saw no reason to mention that one of them happened to be his dead wife. For the first time since Ang had passed, he felt the need to go speak to her during the week.

He wasn't surprised to find the cemetery completely deserted. Most people were at home getting ready for their morning commute. Anthony had been up for hours, unable to sleep, unable to concentrate. It was only through a tremendous act of will, coupled with fear of being picked up by the cops as some kind of lunatic, that he hadn't come here in the middle of the night.

He stood in front of the grave, hands shoved deep in the front pockets of his jeans. He hadn't brought his folding chair with him because he hadn't planned on staying too long. He knew she'd understand; it was a workday, after all.

"I need to talk to you, Angie." How many times had he

said that to her, both in life and in death? She'd always been his guiding star, the angel who always knew the right thing to say to steer him in the right direction. Yet he doubted there'd be any advice forthcoming from beyond after what he had to say.

"There's this woman who's opening a restaurant across the street. Her name's Vivi." He pictured Angie nodding. Go on, she'd say, buttoning the front of her uniform. Some of their best conversations were had when they were both getting ready to start their day. "And she's . . . nice."

Nice. Christ, talk about lame. Nice explained nothing. He could do better than that. "What I mean is, she and I— there's this tension—*shit*." He pulled his hands from his pockets, slicking back his hair. "She came to Dante's to cook something for me yesterday morning, and in the course of talking, she told me something that was very upsetting to her, and she started to cry. Well, you know me; a woman starts to cry, it's like a knife in my heart. So I took her in my arms to comfort her, and I felt something, Ang. A stirring." He struggled to find the right words. "It was like my heart has been frozen in a chunk of ice and all of a sudden, it's beginning to thaw. Does that make any sense?"

A cold wind shook the trees, heralding fall. Anthony turned up the collar of his denim jacket, hunching his shoulders. "I'm not saying I'm in love with her or anything. But I do like her, even though she's kind of the enemy, you know, what with opening her place across the street.

"Anyway, she kind of asked me on this date. I think. And I think I want to go, but"—he swallowed—"it makes me feel kind of disloyal."

There. He'd said it. He fell silent, trying to imagine what Angie might say to him now, were she here to talk to him. She would say, *You gotta keep on living, Ant*. Wouldn't she? See, that was the thing: Was that just what he *wanted* her to say, or what she really would say?

Anthony began buttoning his jacket. "I need a sign, Ang. Anything you could give me would be great." He leaned over and patted the top of the headstone. "See you Sunday, *cara*."

"Anthony?"

He turned.

There stood Angie's mother.

Chapter 12

Anthony stood frozen in place, staring in astonishment at his mother-in-law. What the hell was Philomena doing here at this hour? Then he remembered: Angie's mom went to the early Mass at Saint Finbar's every weekday morning, the same one his late grandmother used to attend. Philomena must be on her way to church.

Anthony leaned over, awkwardly kissing the older woman's cheek. "Good to see you, Mrs. P."

Philomena Passaro had always been small, and age was making her even smaller. Anthony was shocked at how much she'd aged since Angie's death. It made him wonder: were there bags beneath his own eyes that he'd never noticed? Did he carry himself in a sad, stooped way? He'd like to think Michael would tell him if that was the case, but you never knew.

"It's good to see you, too, Anthony, though it would be even nicer if it wasn't at the cemetery, eh?" She looked tired.

Anthony nodded uncomfortably, unsure of what to say.

He watched as Angie's mother bowed her head in silence for a moment in front of the gravestone. Was she talking to God or to Angie? Anthony supposed it didn't matter, as long as she derived some peace and comfort from it. Mouthing a quiet "Amen," Philomena made the sign of the cross and turned back to him. "How often do you come here?"

"Every Sunday morning."

She looked baffled. "But it's Monday."

"I was convening an emergency meeting of the board," Anthony joked feebly.

Philomena smiled affectionately and reached out to squeeze Anthony's hand. "Anthony, Anthony. Don't you think it's time you stopped coming to the cemetery so often?"

Anthony blinked. "What?"

"You're a young man. You need to move on. It's not healthy." Before Anthony could protest she asked, "Tell me, Why do you come?"

Anthony paused. There wasn't one answer to that. In the beginning, it was because his grief was so unbearable, the only way he could cope was by being as physically close to Angie as possible. As his grief slowly became more livable, coming to visit Ang was a way of honoring her memory. But even that started to fade as time wore on. Now he came because it was what he did; it was part of his life.

"Truthfully? I come out of habit," he quietly admitted to Angie's mother. "Habit and guilt."

"What guilt? That you're alive?"

"I guess."

"She'd kick your ass if she heard you say that."

Anthony laughed.

"I'm serious," Philomena said sternly. "She worshipped you. The last thing she'd want would be for you to feel guilty. She died doing a job she loved. And she's still *here*." Philomena patted the spot over her heart. "And here." She patted the same spot on Anthony's chest. "God willing, you've still got years and years left to live. Promise me you won't waste them."

Anthony coughed to cover his discomfort. "I promise." He checked his watch, making an apologetic face. "I should run."

"You'll stop by one of these days for some coffee and *sfogliatelle*?"

"You got it." Anthony gave her another peck on the cheek. "Give my love to Mr. P?"

"Of course."

Walking back to his car, Anthony glanced skyward with a chuckle. "Real subtle sign, Ang."

"Do I look like crap?"

Anthony's question stunned Michael into a rare silence as he ushered Anthony inside. Unable to stop thinking about Mrs. P's perfectly timed appearance at the cemetery, Anthony decided to drop in unannounced on Michael, the way Michael so often dropped in on him. Anthony wasn't surprised Theresa had already left for work. But he hadn't expected to find Little Ant and Dominica lolling on the couch in their pajamas, both of them sneezing and coughing at what seemed like synchronized intervals.

"Hi, Uncle Anthony," Little Ant croaked, wiping his runny nose on his pajama sleeve.

"You're disgusting," Dominica pronounced in the phlegmy voice of an old woman with a five-pack-a-day cigarette habit. She'd no sooner gotten the words out than she erupted into a very unladylike coughing fit.

"Easy, easy," Michael urged, patting his daughter on the back until she stopped coughing. "Better?"

Dominica nodded, burrowing deeper beneath the comforter she was sharing with Little Ant. "Uncle Anthony said 'crap' when he walked in," she pointed out in a tattle-tale voice.

"Sorry 'bout that, sweetie," said Anthony. He looked at his brother. "You runnin' General Hospital here today or what?"

Michael shot him a look that said, *Don't even start.* "Head colds and coughs." Disappointment shadowed his tired face. "Little Ant here's gonna have to miss his hockey game this afternoon."

Anthony looked at his nephew, whose determined gaze was riveted to the cartoon on TV. Little Ant was refusing to make eye contact with him. The kid was probably thrilled not to have to play today, but there was no way he was going to let anyone see it, even Anthony.

"What the hell are you doing here?" Michael asked as he led Anthony out of the living room. "And at this hour?"

"What, you can drop in on me, but I can't drop in on you?" He noticed Angelica's playpen was empty. "Where's the *bambina*?"

"In her high chair in the kitchen, probably with a bowl of oatmeal over her head. I left her there when the doorbell rang. C'mon, follow me."

Anthony hated to be critical, but the house was a friggin' mess. There were piles of laundry waiting to be folded, toys strewn on the floor, and enough ground-up Cheerios crunching beneath his shoes to sustain a colony of ants for weeks. "I thought you had someone who comes to clean for you."

"I do. Wanda. She's got a cough and head cold, and has been out for over a week. Passed it on to the kids, obviously. Now shut up and get yourself a cup of coffee, and tell me why the first thing you said when I opened the door was, 'Do I look like crap?' "

"Do I?" Anthony grabbed himself a cup of coffee. That was one of the pluses of his brother's house, he always had a pot brewing, all day. And unlike Vivi, Michael knew how to make a decent cup of coffee.

"Define 'crap,' " said Michael, who looked profoundly

relieved to have found Angelica without food in her hair, babbling happily to herself in her high chair.

"Since Ang died," Anthony clarified, "have my looks, you know, dwindled?"

"Dwindled?"

"Don't bust my chops here, Mikey," Anthony said, yanking open the fridge door with a frustrated tug. "Just answer me."

"When Ang first died, yeah, you looked like total crap. Of course you did. Not eating, not sleeping . . ." Michael spooned some cereal into Angelica's mouth. "Now you look like your old self, pretty much."

"Which is?"

Michael shrugged. "Okay, I guess."

Anthony nodded. That was a good enough answer.

"Why you want to know?" Michael continued.

"I just ran into Angie's mom at the cemetery and she looked awful, Mike. Like someone attached a vacuum cleaner hose to the base of her skull and sucked all the life out of her face, you know?"

Michael winced. "You were afraid you might look like that?"

"Yeah."

"Well, you don't," Michael assured him, jaw tightening as Angelica playfully smacked away the oatmeal-filled spoon in his hand, sending it clattering to the floor.

"That's good."

"Is it?" Michael's eyes remained fixed on Anthony's even as he bent down to pick up the baby's spoon. "What were you doing at the cemetery this morning, Ant? I thought you went on Sundays."

Anthony hesitated. "I had something I needed to talk to Ang about."

"Vivi?" Michael asked delicately.

Anthony hesitated again. He was in no mood to be ragged on by his brother about talking to his dead wife, visiting her grave, Vivi Robitaille, any of it. Yet the way Michael had just said Vivi's name—so carefully, so respectfully, even—led him to think that maybe Mikey wouldn't give him such a hard time if he let him in on the latest development.

"She asked me to go with her to check out a new restaurant in the city," said Anthony.

"And you're going, *right*?" said Michael, poised to feed the baby another spoonful of cereal before Anthony intervened.

"Madonn'!" Anthony pulled the spoon from his brother's hands. "That was just on the floor! You can't put that in her mouth!"

"Don't change the subject," Michael shot back as he went to get another spoon. He sat down, made a show of waving the clean spoon in Anthony's face, and resumed feeding his daughter. "So? The restaurant? You're going?"

"I don't know. I want to, but . . ."

"But what?" Michael guided the spoon into his daughter's mouth. "Good job, *cara mia.*"

"I don't want her to think it's a date."

"Why not?"

"Because it's not."

"Why not?"

Anthony's shoulders tensed. "Because my dating days are behind me. Look, what Angie and I had only comes around once in a lifetime, okay? I met a woman, we fell in love, we got married, she died, and now, I live my life the way I did before she ever came into my life: working at my restaurant, spending time with family and friends. I'm fine with it. Lightning doesn't strike twice, Mikey."

"How the hell do you know?"

"Because I know."

"Fine. Then what's the harm in going to dinner with her, if you're so sure your heart's locked away all nice and tidy for the next fifty years of your life? Hmm?"

"I guess you're right," Anthony agreed uneasily.

"You don't sound so sure."

"No, I'm sure." He wasn't sure at all.

"How 'bout this?" Michael adopted his parental problem-solver voice as he wiped caked oatmeal off Angelica's face and lifted her out of her high chair. "What if Theresa and I go along with the two of you? That way, you won't *feel* like it's a date. There won't be all this pressure on you to talk and be witty and all that crap. We can help you out if conversation grinds to a screeching halt and both of you are silently thinking, 'I'm in hell.'"

Anthony was not amused. "You think you're funny, don't you?"

"I *know* I'm funny, pal," Michael chortled. "Talk to Vivi, and I'll talk to Theresa, and we'll figure out a night that's good." He balanced Angelica on his hip, bouncing her happily as he taunted his brother. "Daddy and Mommy are going to go out on a date with Uncle Anthony and his new girlfriend, *cara*. What do you think about that?"

"I love your jacket."

The admiration in Theresa Dante's voice made Vivi glad she'd chosen to wear the velvet blazer Natalie had given her. She'd been pleased when Anthony had agreed to accompany her into the city to try this new restaurant, Zusi's, though admittedly surprised when he added that his brother and sister-in-law would be joining them. Her immediate thought was, *He doesn't want to be alone with me.* Ever since cooking her *poulet basquaise* for him a week earlier, her mind kept circling back to the hug they'd shared. On the surface, it was simply a good-hearted man comforting a distressed woman. But the words he'd said ("I'm glad you exist, Vivi") and the tender look in his eye as he held her tight and made her feel wanted, led her to think it was more than sympathy. There *was* more; she'd felt it in her own bones when she'd looked at him. The question was what to do about it.

Getting involved with a widower was one thing. But a relationship with another chef—who happened to be right across the street? Would it distract her when she needed absolute focus on the bistro? One minute Vivi thought the attraction between them would only be a nuisance, the next she was ready to surrender to whatever Eros might have in store. The only thing she knew for certain was that despite his typical culinary egotism, she liked him.

Even though Zusi's was booked months in advance, as an established chef, all Anthony had to do was pick up the phone and a table for four was magically reserved. Walking into the restaurant, Vivi was struck by the subdued atmosphere. Sky blue fabric covered the walls and the cushions on the bentwood chairs, smooth jazz played softly in the background. It was a nice, relaxing space in which to eat. Vivi loved catching bits and pieces of people's conversations as they were led to their table: "I can't finish this"; "They're in Sardinia, I think"; "She's just starting chemo now." All these disparate souls, gathered in one place for one pure purpose: the sanctity of a wonderfully prepared meal. It never failed to leave Vivi humbled and renew her joy in being a chef.

Vivi smiled at Theresa as they were seated. "Thank you for your compliment. My sister bought me the jacket."

"She has good taste."

Expensive taste, Vivi thought. She felt a twinge of guilt about not inviting Natalie along to dine with them, but she wanted to be able to relax and not have Natalie dissecting every little thing she and Anthony said and did.

She glanced up into Anthony's handsome face with gratitude as he pulled out her chair for her. He looked very handsome tonight in his sports jacket and crisp, pressed white shirt. He smelled wonderful, too, very refreshing and woody. She liked men who wore cologne, men who took care with their appearance and toilette. It showed they cared about keeping themselves attractive.

"So, Vivi, are you enjoying Brooklyn life?" Theresa asked.

Vivi nodded. "*Oui*, very much." Though Vivi initially found Theresa's dark-haired beauty intimidating—the woman was truly stunning—it only took a few seconds for her to see Theresa was very down to earth.

"I can't wait for your restaurant to open," Theresa continued. "Bensonhurst needs some new culinary tricks, if you ask me." She winked playfully at Anthony, who rolled his eyes. Vivi could tell the two of them got along well and enjoyed needling one another.

"You know, Theresa does PR," Michael told Vivi. "She helped put Dante's on the map, so to speak."

"Dante's was already on the map, Mike," Anthony grumbled.

"You know what I mean," said Michael. "She helped us get to the next level," he clarified for Vivi. "Expand interest in us beyond Brooklyn."

"Do you have one of your cards with you?" Vivi asked Theresa politely.

"Yes, of course." Theresa dipped into her small beaded bag and pulled out a card, handing it to Vivi.

"Thank you." Here was a task she could pass on to Natalie, a project to help keep her occupied and involved.

Vivi glanced around eagerly. She couldn't wait to get hold of the menu so she could deconstruct it. She could tell Anthony was thinking the same thing; he seemed a little antsy and preoccupied. In fact, when their eyes met over the bread basket, they shared a knowing little smile, each perfectly attuned to the source of the restlessness in the other. She was glad she'd been bold and asked him to accompany her here. He *understood*. He—

"Do you have a boyfriend back in France, Vivi?"

Michael Dante's question punctured the carefree bubble

Vivi was trying to create for herself tonight. It seemed a deeply private question, and for a split second, she feared Natalie might be right after all about Americans being rude.

Vivi smiled politely. *"Non."*

"Michael." Theresa seemed deeply embarrassed. "You have to excuse my husband, Vivi. He can be a little rude sometimes." She flashed Michael a look that could split rock. Perhaps rudeness was a Dante issue, not an American issue.

"It's all right," said Vivi, stealing a glance at Anthony, who seemed distinctly ill at ease. When their waiter appeared with the menus, Vivi virtually snatched hers out of his hand. By the time they'd all ordered drinks, Anthony was already studying his menu with the intensity of an archaeologist trying to decipher the Rosetta stone.

"Black bass and sea urchin roe on a crisp potato pancake," Anthony read aloud. "Hmm." He looked at Vivi. "Thoughts?"

Vivi thought about the ingredients, their individual flavors, how they might meld or complement each other. "Could be interesting."

"Or a little too precious."

"True." Vivi's eyes scoured the menu. "Ooh! Spinach-stuffed veal chop with tomato polenta! That sounds like something worth trying."

"Or stealing," said Michael, nudging Anthony in the ribs playfully.

Vivi turned to him in offense at the same time Anthony did. "Good chefs don't steal."

"You took the words right out of my mouth, Vivi," said Anthony as he looked coldly at Michael.

"Geez." Michael cringed as he reached for his martini. "I was just making a *joke*."

"You mustn't joke about that," said Vivi. Anthony nodded in agreement.

Michael exhaled with exasperation as he cracked open his menu. "Yeah, this is gonna be a fun night."

"You are absolutely wrong about the chocolate glaze on these pears," Vivi insisted. "Shortening was used, not butter."

"I'm telling you, it's butter."

Anthony struggled to hold back the verbal torrent threatening to explode from his lips. All night long, he and Vivi had been disagreeing about the food at Zusi's. When he noted that the curried oysters didn't have enough curry, she said there was too much. When he observed that the marjoram sauce accompanying the baby pheasant wasn't really a reduction as the menu claimed, she insisted it was. More frustrating than her constant countering of his expert observations were her own off-base pronouncements. Vivi ordered leeks in creamy chive sauce, then declared they'd skimped on the chives. Wrong! The amount of chive used was perfect. Her first mouthful of grilled scallop in lobster sauce was accompanied by, "The sauce is too salty." Again she was wrong; just the right amount of salt had been used. They'd been passing plates around the table all night, and only once had they agreed, and that was on the cognac sugarplums Theresa has ordered for dessert.

Vivi was still shaking her head insistently. "I'm *telling* you, it's shortening."

"You two are scary," said Theresa.

"Anthony's been frightening all night," Michael added, flashing his brother a penetrating look that Anthony had no idea how to interpret.

What? Had he been talking too much? Not enough? Anthony rotated his palms upward, shrugging his shoulders in a gesture of confusion. Michael just rolled his eyes. Anthony fought a smile as he thought back to Michael's suggestion that he and Theresa come along in case he and

Vivi lapsed into silence. Vivi's mouth had been in motion from the minute they'd arrived. In fact, she wasn't letting the shortening versus butter issue go.

"Are you finally agreeing? It's shortening?"

"Butter," said Anthony with a small yawn.

Vivi took a spoonful of the sinfully delicious dessert and held it up to him. "Here. Taste again."

She guided the spoon between Anthony's lips. For a split second, he thought nothing of it, then he caught the look of significance that passed between Michael and Theresa. What was going on between him and Vivi was more intimate than he realized. He cleared his throat nervously and then swallowed, the creamy sweetness of the chocolate lingering long after it had left his mouth.

"Well?" Vivi prodded, the superior tilt of her head telling him she fully expected to be vindicated.

"I still say butter."

Vivi's expression was incredulous as she regarded Michael and Theresa. "Not only is he stubborn, he's wrong."

"Hey!" said Anthony. "Who copped to there being too much garlic in her chicken after *I* pointed it out, huh?"

"You've cooked for each other?" Theresa asked coyly.

Anthony and Vivi both nodded.

Theresa licked powdered sugar off her fingers. "And who's better?"

"I am," Anthony answered without hesitation.

Vivi's jaw dropped. "You are so rude!"

"No, I am so truthful." Anthony knew it was mean, but it was kind of fun getting her all riled up.

Vivi ignored him, concentrating her attention on Michael and Theresa. "Anthony is an excellent chef, but if I may use my own leaf blower—"

"Blow your own horn," Anthony corrected with a chuckle.

"I am better," Vivi concluded with a huff, dabbing her mouth with her napkin before settling back in her chair.

Mischief crept into Theresa's eyes. "Well, there's only one way to find out for sure who's better."

"What's that?" asked Anthony suspiciously.

"You have to have a cook-off and invite other people to judge."

"A cook-off!" Vivi's eyes lit up. "That's a wonderful idea!"

"It's a horrible idea." Anthony glared at his sister-in-law. "When in the name of hell am I supposed to find time to have a cook-off?"

Theresa looked unruffled. "We could set it up as a charity event, Anthony, except those invited would get to vote on the food. It'd be fun, and great publicity for both businesses."

"It'd be work," Anthony griped, but his mind was already beginning to put together possible menus.

"You could keep it simple," Theresa continued, her voice growing in enthusiasm. "You'd each be responsible for making an appetizer, a main dish, and a dessert."

"Oh, is that all?" Anthony asked. Theresa didn't get it. She'd never gotten it—how time-consuming and grueling being a chef was. He remembered all the cockamamie suggestions she'd come up with when she was initially doing PR for Dante's. Running certain specials during the Santa Rosalia Festival. Putting together summer picnic baskets. And now, just whip up some food for a cook-off. It ticked him off.

"C'mon, Ant." As usual, Michael's voice was cajoling. "It'll be fun. Think of it as Iron Chef Bensonhurst."

"You gonna help?" Anthony retorted.

"No, but Little Ant will," Theresa put in quickly. "He'd love it."

"That's true," Anthony agreed slowly. "Little Ant could be a big help." Seeing the look of perplexity on Vivi's face, he added, "Little Anthony is my nephew."

"Our son," Theresa clarified further in a proud voice.

"Ah," said Vivi. "It's good to start them young if they're serious about cooking."

"I agree," Theresa said, locking eyes with her husband.

"He can play hockey and cook," Michael said mildly. "No one ever said he couldn't."

Anthony took a sip of his espresso, trying to slow his thoughts. A cook-off. What a huge pain in the neck. Then again, if it was for a good cause . . . and it would give him the chance to try out some new dishes . . . and remind the locals why Dante's was *the* culinary landmark while generating some publicity, it could be worth it. He stole a surreptitious glance at Vivi, whose excitement as she chatted with Theresa lit up the subdued dining room. A cook-off meant Vivi would have to use *his* kitchen. Again. In fact, they'd more or less be cooking side by side. The thought made his teeth grind, but he supposed he could endure it, as long as certain ground rules were set.

"Are we going to do this thing or what?" Anthony asked grumpily.

"I'm willing," Vivi answered without hesitation. "Though I do worry about how you will save face when I best you in your own kitchen."

"Ouch!" said Michael with a stage cringe. "Cross check to the ego!"

Anthony gave a low chuckle and smiled. "You're a damn good cook, Vivi, but I can out-chef you with one hand tied behind my apron. And I intend to prove it."

Chapter 13

"*Where were you* last night, Vivi? I called and called."

Natalie looked mildly irritated as she joined Vivi on the small couch in Vivi's apartment. After coming home from the dinner at Zusi's, Vivi had spent the night jumping in and out of bed, jotting down her thoughts for the cook-off. Tired as well and slightly cranky, she was in no mood for Natalie's peremptory manner.

"I was out to dinner."

"With—?" Before Vivi could answer, Natalie groaned, "Oh, God."

"Oh, God nothing. It's not what you think."

Vivi calmly stirred her chamomile tea, trying to not to feel guilty at the accusation in Natalie's voice. She hadn't seen her half sister since their night at Plutonium, when the spilled contents of Natalie's purse revealed the bill from Saks Fifth Avenue. Determined to bring her up to date on things, Vivi filled Natalie in on cooking her *poulet basquaise* for Anthony, omitting the part where she cried in his arms. She told Natalie about going out to dinner with him and his brother and sister-in-law, then tried to change the subject by asking Natalie how her week had been.

Natalie didn't answer, peering at her in mystification instead. "You like him, don't you? Anthony Dante."

"Yes." Vivi saw no point in lying about it.

Natalie looked apprehensive. "What are you going to do about it?"

"Nothing." Vivi had never been one for active pursuit, and she'd decided there was no reason to change her ways now. She liked Anthony, but she was not going to go out of her way to make something happen. If the spark between them burst into flame, then she would *consider* embracing it, but only after she thought long and hard about whether being involved with another chef, who also happened to be widowed, was something she could handle. If the spark didn't catch, well then, at least she had made a friend in the neighborhood who understood her passion about food, even though he was so often wrong about it. She just hoped they could remain friends if her business wound up cutting into his.

"Did I tell you about the cook-off?" Vivi asked abruptly, in another effort to change the subject. She explained the idea behind it, how ostensibly it would put to rest forever the debate over who was a better cook, and how fun it might be. The idea seemed to intrigue Natalie momentarily.

"How many people will be invited? Or will you just be asking whatever diners come in to vote?"

"I don't know. I'll have to speak with Anthony about it."

"I can bring someone who will definitely vote for you," said Natalie.

"Who's that?"

"Papa's good friend, Bernard Rousseau?"

Vivi smiled tersely. "I don't know who that is, Natalie. I never knew any of Papa's friends, remember?"

"Of course." Natalie looked embarrassed. "But you did

meet him once. At the funeral. He's very nice. About forty, I think, and very elegant. He rang me when he got to New York a few days ago. He's going to be here for at least a year, working at the UN. I'll bring him to the cook-off."

"That's a good idea." Vivi took another sip of tea, wondering if their father had been a very social man, or if he was more of a homebody, the way he was with Vivi's mother. There were so many gaps in her knowledge about Papa she would love to have filled in. Butterflies in her stomach, she turned to Natalie.

"Did Papa have a lot of friends?" she asked hesitantly.

Natalie considered the question. "Yes. He and my mother used to entertain a lot." Natalie's expression turned pensive. "Did Papa and your mother entertain a lot?"

"Not at all. It was usually just the two of them. Or, if I was around, the three of us."

Natalie looked pained. "Did they fight a lot?"

"Not that I can recall."

Natalie looked away. "He and my mother fought all the time." There was a long pause. "I think, in the end, your mother was the one he loved." Natalie turned back to her. "I don't care, of course," she said breezily. "I mean, what is love, anyway? I would much rather have money than love any day."

Vivi didn't know what to say. Her impulse was to put her arm around Natalie's shoulders, tell her she needn't get defensive. Vivi *knew* that her parents had loved one another, and her, but that didn't mean Papa didn't love Natalie. She was struck by the irony that while Natalie was the one who grew up with every comfort, the child of a true two-parent household, she was the one who'd known a calm, loving atmosphere, despite her parents' unconventional arrangement.

"I have something for you," she told Natalie, hurrying to get Theresa's card from where she'd left it in her purse.

"I have something for you, too." Natalie dug into her

large leather shoulder bag and held out a small wrapped box to Vivi.

"Natalie." Vivi's voice was reproachful and she didn't care.

"I felt awful about the other night at Plutonium. Drinking too much and getting maudlin and all that. I wanted to apologize."

"The words 'I'm sorry' will suffice perfectly well. You didn't have to buy me a gift."

"But I wanted to," Natalie said softly. "You're my sister."

Tears filled Vivi's eyes. "Then you'll understand why I'm refusing." She took Natalie's hand. "You don't have to buy my affection. You already have it. Nor do you have to feel guilty about how I grew up. I turned out perfectly fine, didn't I? Please, Natalie."

Natalie was silent as she stuffed Vivi's gift back in her bag. *Oh, God, have I insulted her?* thought Vivi nervously. But when their eyes briefly caught, Vivi could see Natalie wasn't upset, she was moved. Vivi's words were the most honest they'd ever exchanged. It was a relief for her say them, and it seemed it was a relief for Natalie to hear them, too.

"What's your present for me?" Natalie asked, breaking into a smile. Vivi handed her Theresa's card. "What's this?"

"Anthony's sister-in-law runs a PR firm. They did publicity for Dante's a while back. Remember we chatted a bit about this at Plutonium? About you and I working together more closely on getting the restaurant ready?"

"I seem to remember something about that," Natalie said evasively.

"Good. Then perhaps you wouldn't mind calling her and finding out what they might be able to do for us?"

"Of course." Natalie regarded the card distastefully as she slipped it into her purse. "Anything else?"

"I was going to go down to the candy store to see how

the DiDinato brothers' work is coming along. Do you want to come?"

Natalie rose. "To be honest, Vivi, I'm not feeling very well. Would you mind terribly if I just went home?"

"Of course not," Vivi answered, concerned. "Is there anything I can do?"

"*Non, non.* I just feel a little cold coming on, is all." She kissed Vivi on each cheek. "I'll phone you later tonight; we can talk about 'coordinating our efforts' then, all right?"

"Of course."

Watching Natalie leave, Vivi couldn't shake a sense of unease. All was not well, that much was obvious. But until Vivi knew what the trouble was, there was nothing she could do to fix it.

"Vivi!"

Vivi had just rounded the corner of Twentieth Avenue and was walking toward her bistro-in-progress when she heard her name called. She glanced across the street. Michael Dante was standing behind a baby stroller, waving at her. Vivi hurriedly crossed to him, smiling down at the curly haired little cherub who seemed so content to just be sitting still, looking out at the world.

"Hello, Michael." Vivi kissed him on both cheeks, beaming down on the baby. "I thought this angel might be yours. I remember seeing her in the playpen in Dante's once."

Michael looked mildly embarrassed by her recollection. "I forgot about that." He smiled down at his daughter. "This is Angelica."

"Appropriate name," Vivi noted.

"Not last night it wasn't." They both chuckled.

"You are the one who stays home with the children?" Vivi asked curiously.

"Yeah," Michael said, almost sounding apologetic. "Like

I told you once before, I was a professional hockey player, but once your skills diminish to a certain point, it's best to retire."

"Athletes retire so young," Vivi observed. "I've always wondered about that. About them having to reinvent themselves."

"We wonder about it, too, believe me," Michael said ruefully. He jerked a thumb behind him at Dante's. "I'm half owner, you know. I plan on getting more involved in the day-to-day operation."

"Anthony will appreciate that, I'm sure." She felt envious that Michael actually wanted to help his brother out.

Michael gestured toward the candy store, where a symphony of saws and hammers colored the air. "They do good work, the DiDinatos."

"They did your expansion, yes?"

"Yeah. Anthony screamed about the money, but—" He stopped. "Don't get me wrong, he's not cheap, it's just—"

"Believe me, I understand," Vivi interrupted. "My sister was displeased because they were so much more expensive than the other bids. But your brother told me they were worth it, so . . ." She shrugged.

"Theresa and I had a good time with you and Anthony the other night."

"Yes, it was a wonderful time," Vivi agreed. "Your wife is lovely."

"She is. Works too hard, but what are you gonna do?" Michael looked upward, shielding his eyes from the sun with his hand. "So, you like my brother?"

Vivi puffed up her cheeks, exhaling softly. There it was again, that Dante rudeness. "He's very nice."

Michael looked down at her, his gaze unnervingly direct. "That's not what I'm asking."

"What you're asking is not appropriate, I think," Vivi replied politely.

"I'm being pushy, aren't I?"

"Yes, you are."

"I'm sorry." Michael looked contrite as he absently pushed the stroller forward and back over the same patch of sidewalk. "It's just that I think Anthony likes you, but he's not the most aggressive guy in the world when it comes to these things, you know?"

"He's certainly aggressive with his opinions," Vivi snorted.

Michael looked amused. "You both are."

"Yes, well, it comes with the territory, I suppose."

"If you like him, you might have to nudge a little, know what I'm saying?"

"Nudge," Vivi repeated to herself.

"Yeah. He's a little gun-shy." Michael groaned. "Ugh. Bad choice of words, *cafone*," he muttered to himself.

Vivi cocked her head questioningly. "I don't understand."

"Anthony's wife was a police officer. She was shot and killed," Michael explained quietly.

"How awful!"

"It was. A drug bust gone wrong." Michael's eyes began getting glassy. "She kissed him good-bye, went to work, and two hours later he gets a phone call she's been killed. Shouldn't have happened." Michael pulled a pair of gloves out of his coat pocket. "Ant was pretty much toast for about a year."

Vivi wrinkled her nose in confusion. "Making toast helped his grief?"

"No, no," said Michael, the sad look on his face lifting. "What I meant was, he was devastated by her death."

"Of course."

"But now, enough time has passed, and he seems ready to get back on the horse—I mean, get on with his life, not, you know, rent a horse and ride it around so he doesn't get sad."

"I see," said Vivi, even though she really didn't.

"I guess what I'm trying to say, Vivi, is that he's a great guy. Don't let his gruffness or bullheadedness put you off;

underneath, he's a pussycat. And like I said, I can tell he likes you."

Vivi nodded and said nothing, thinking back to Anthony holding her in his arms. She already knew he was "a pussycat." A pussycat whose wife was killed. Dear God, it was beyond awful. No wonder he was so tightlipped about it. Every time he thought of her death, his mind must have been in an agony of "What if?" Poor Anthony.

"How long has she been dead?" Vivi asked, just out of curiosity.

"A little over a year."

"Was she beautiful?"

"Um . . ." Michael seemed surprised by the question. "I'm not really sure how to answer that. She was earthy. Do you know what I mean by 'earthy'?" Vivi shook her head. "She was very strong. Big hips, big—you know. Big laugh. Maternal."

In other words, nothing like me, Vivi thought. "Could she cook?"

Michael laughed uproariously. "God, no, she sucked in the kitchen! I think that's one of the reasons Anthony enjoys talking shop with you, Vivi. For the first time in his life, he's spending time with a pretty, vivacious woman who actually *cares* as deeply as he does about the issue of butter versus shortening."

Vivi smiled with pleasure, more at Michael's description of her as pretty and vivacious than anything else. "That's an *important* question, Michael."

"Apparently." A breeze kicked up, and Michael leaned over to zip up his daughter's jacket. "Well, I should run along." He gave Vivi a friendly peck on the cheek. "We're glad you came to Bensonhurt, Vivi. All of us."

"*Let me guess,* the baby wants some leftover *scungilli* on top of her Cheerios."

Anthony knew Michael would turn up at Dante's at some point after the Zusi's dining experience. He just didn't expect it to be the next day. Yet there Michael stood in the dining room, grinning like a circus clown, with little Angelica in her stroller right next to him. Jesus, his brother was predictable.

"I just saw Vivi on the street," Michael informed him as he unstrapped Angelica from the stroller. Pulling up the nearest chair, Michael put her on his lap, unzipping her out of her jacket.

"Gee, that's surprising. She has no business in this part of town," Anthony said dryly.

"She said she had a good time last night."

"That's great, Mike."

"Theresa and I had a good time, too. We like her a lot."

"That's great."

"You had a good time last night, right, Ant?"

Anthony slowly ran a hand down his face. "Is this why you're here? To talk about last night?"

"Pretty much. And a few other things."

Anthony pulled up a chair for himself. "Let's get it over with."

"You can deny it all you want, but I'm sorry, last night the vibe between the two of you at the restaurant was intense. Just ask Theresa."

"We're both chefs, Mikey. Intensity is a given."

"Oh, so you'd let Lenny Dinuzzi from Lucatelli's in Sheepshead Bay feed you from his spoon? Is that a given?"

Anthony felt a deep heat flash to his face. "That didn't mean anything."

"Bullshit, Anthony. It shows how comfortable you are with each other."

"I don't need you explaining this stuff to me, okay? I know how it works," Anthony said gruffly. *Madonn'*.

"She likes you."

Anthony just shrugged.

"Look, you *cafone*, she's smart, she's sweet, she's pretty, she cooks, she's got a cool accent . . . How long do you think it will be before someone else figures out she's a catch? Go for it now, Ant."

"I'll think about it," Anthony grumbled. Michael made it sound like Vivi was a prize to be won. It didn't surprise him that a jock like his brother would think in those terms, but that wasn't Anthony's MO. Still, he had never thought about the possibility of someone else pursuing Vivi.

"What else did you want to talk about?" Anthony asked his brother. He was itching to get back into the kitchen, where he belonged.

"Do you have any ideas for the cook-off?" Michael asked eagerly.

"A few." Anthony didn't like the chirpiness in his brother's voice.

"Like what?"

Mother o' God, did his brother have concrete for brains or what? "Mike, I don't really have time to sit here and go over menu choices with you, all right? I have a restaurant to run."

"It'll take two minutes."

Knowing his relentless brother was not going to leave until he'd gotten what he'd come for, Anthony resigned himself to sitting in the empty dining room and being interrogated.

"Here's what I'm thinking," Anthony began. "For the appetizer? *Arrosticini abruzzesi*—marinated, skewered lamb tidbits."

Michael nodded slowly, a smile of approval spreading over his face. "Go on."

Surprisingly, Anthony found himself warming to the topic. "For dinner, stuffed flank steak with a side of mushroom *timballo*."

Michael licked his lips. "Is that the steak you make with the roasted red peppers and prosciutto inside?"

"Yup."

"Perfetto," Michael murmured dreamily. "And for the grand finale?"

"Hazelnut risotto pudding."

"That's the one Mom made, with the raisins, right?"

"Yes, it's Mom's. But I use dried currants, not raisins."

"Mom always used raisins."

Anthony felt his temper coming on. "It's better with dried currants."

"I hate to tell you this, Ant, but it's better with raisins."

Anthony glowered at him. "You're saying my pudding sucks?"

"No." Michael's voice was resolute. "I just think the way Mom made it was better."

"Excuse me, but who's the chef here?"

"That was the other thing I wanted to talk to you about."

Anthony just stared at him. His brother wanted to talk to him about *chef* stuff? Oh, this was gonna be good. He couldn't wait to hear this.

Anthony lifted his eyebrows expectantly. "Yes?"

"I'm gonna help you cook this sucker."

"Excuse me?" Anthony leaned forward so the baby could grab his nose, which she'd been reaching for. "Say that again?"

"I'm going to help you in the kitchen during the cook-off."

Anthony gently removed the baby's hand from his face. "Um, no."

"What do you mean, no?" Michael seemed offended. "My kid can help you out, but I can't?"

"Exactly. Your kid has an interest in cooking. You don't. It's gonna be bad enough sharing the kitchen with the competition. I don't want you in there, too, putting in your two cents where it doesn't belong. You're going to be out here in the dining room, doing what it is you do best: schmoozing the guests, encouraging them to vote for me. *Capisce*?"

"But—"

"This issue is closed, Mike."

"You know—"

"Zip it," Anthony warned with a glare. "And just so you know, there's no way Little Ant is going to be in the kitchen while dinner is in full swing. It's too dangerous. He can help me prep stuff, but that's it."

"I'm sure that'll be fine with him," Michael muttered.

"Anything else?"

"Do you have any idea what Vivi is planning to cook?" Michael asked uneasily.

"Nope." Anthony kissed Angelica on the top of the head. "But we'll find out soon enough, won't we?"

Chapter 14

Vivi stared into one of the mirrors in the ladies' room, trying to decide whether her wide-eyed "I'm shocked I won" face or her humble "This is a great honor" face would be better. In five minutes, she and Anthony would each begin their cook-off. Every table at Dante's was filled with eager patrons who had paid for the privilege to vote, the proceeds going to Loaves and Fishes, a charity responsible for feeding the poor. Vivi had no doubt her tomato and zucchini gratin appetizer would eviscerate Anthony's lamb kebabs, regardless of whatever fancy name he'd chosen to give them. From that point on, the issue of who was the superior chef would never be in doubt.

Vivi knew she'd made the right menu choices. After days of agonizing indecision, she'd settled on the gratin appetizer, turbot in cider vinegar sauce with a side of roasted red pepper for the entrée, and for a real dazzler of a finish, fresh pineapple flan. Vivi was annoyed when she learned Anthony was also making some kind of pudding for dessert, but then she realized this could actually work to her advantage; the similarity in concept and texture would make the superiority of her flan's flavor all the more obvious.

"Vivi?"

Startled, Vivi turned. Natalie had poked her head in the ladies' room door. "Are you all right?"

"I'm fine. I just needed to collect myself." She prayed Natalie hadn't seen her making faces at herself in the mirror.

"Bernard Rousseau is here. He would like to meet you. Do you have a moment?"

In truth, Vivi didn't. She really should get back to the kitchen. She was also mortified by the thought of meeting a friend of her father's in her already spattered chef's whites, no makeup on her face and a plain blue bandanna twisted around her head to keep her hair back. Still, she could tell from the hopefulness in Natalie's voice this was important to her.

"Yes, of course," said Vivi, following her sister out of the restroom as she tightened her apron, which had gone slack. "I would love to meet Bernard. But I can only stay for a moment."

"Vivi."

Now that she had Bernard Rousseau standing right in front of her, Vivi indeed recognized him from her father's funeral. He was tall, swarthy, and handsome enough to be egotistical about it, yet she got the sense he wasn't. His smile was warm as he embraced her, his delight in seeing her genuine.

"My God," he marveled in French. "I'd forgotten how much you resembled your father."

Vivi blushed. "People usually think I resemble my mother." She didn't dare look at Natalie for fear Bernard's observations somehow pained her.

"Well, perhaps you do," Bernard allowed, making Vivi

wonder if he'd ever met her mother. "But you also resemble your father, very much."

"Thank you so much for coming," Vivi said in a raised but sincere voice, wanting to make sure she was heard over the din of the restaurant crowd. Around her, the voices of the patrons seemed to swell and recede, like the tide. It was a sound she loved. Others might find ecstasy in silence, or in their favorite piece of music; Vivi found it in the bang and clatter of the kitchen, and in the cacophony of a full dining room.

"I cannot wait for your restaurant to open," Bernard told her.

"Nor can I."

When Theresa had first shown her the invitations she'd had printed up for the cook-off, Vivi had nearly fainted with pleasure at the line reading, "Dishes prepared by Chef Vivi Robitaille of Vivi's, coming to Bensonhurst in spring 2008." For some reason, the printed words made her dream feel real in a way it hadn't yet, despite the checks being written and the handiwork of the DiDinatos, who promised they'd be done with the interior by the New Year. It was really going to happen. She was really going to have her own restaurant.

She squeezed Natalie's arm. "I hate to be rude, but I really do need to get back into the kitchen."

"Of course. Just one more thing." Natalie pulled Vivi slightly away from Bernard. "Whoever arranged the seating has put Bernard and me with that oaf of a journalist, Quinn O'Brien," she hissed. "Can you see about getting our seats switched?"

"Natalie, I don't really have time to deal with this." Vivi's eyes scoured the crowd for Theresa. She pointed her out to Natalie. "That's who you should speak with. Have you phoned her yet about PR?"

"I will, I will."

Vivi frowned at her unhappily before turning back to

smile at Bernard Rousseau. "It's been very nice to see you, Bernard. I appreciate your coming, so much."

"Once Natalie told me about it, I wouldn't have dreamed of missing it." Bernard shook Vivi's hand warmly. "I will see both you and your sister soon, yes?"

What a nice man, Vivi thought. "Yes, of course."

Vivi was shocked when Natalie took her hands in her own, and held them tightly. "Relax," Natalie commanded. "You're going to win."

"Yes." Vivi hadn't realized the tension she was feeling showed on her face. She squared her shoulders and stood up tall. "I can knock their corpses over, no problem, right?"

Natalie looked too confused to disagree. "Er, yes. Of course. You're a wonderful cook. And it's really all just for fun, remember?"

Vivi snorted. Fun. She'd try to remember that as she made her way back to Anthony's kitchen.

"Let's go, let's go, let's go!"

Anthony's voice was a clap of thunder echoing off the kitchen's white tile walls, startling his staff into overdrive or cowering, depending on their personalities. As he watched the waitstaff carry plates of his glorious *arrosticini abbruzzesi* out to the waiting crowd alongside plates of Vivi's pedestrian gratin, he couldn't resist stealing a look at her. Her porcelain smooth face was glistening with a thin film of sweat. Her long blonde hair was twisted back in a braid. Michael was right, she was beautiful. Already feeling victorious with the departure of the appetizers, he couldn't resist the chance for a little fun.

"Your gratin looks a little burnt around the edges, if you don't mind my saying."

"I refuse to listen to you," Vivi sniffed. "You're just trying to upset me."

"Well, *I* wouldn't serve those pieces around the edge, that's for sure."

"What do you know?" Vivi retorted. "You expect people to be dazzled by lamb kebabs. Tell me: is this an Italian restaurant or a Greek taverna?"

Scowling, Anthony turned away just in time to see his brother and Little Ant stroll into the kitchen. "What the hell . . . ?" Anthony muttered to himself, hustling over to them. "I told you," he said to his brother in a controlled voice. "I don't want Little Ant in here while we're going crazy."

"Please, Uncle Anthony?" Little Ant pleaded. "I won't get in the way."

Jesus help me, Anthony thought. The kid was looking at him with such desperate puppy dog eyes, it was heartbreaking. "Fine," Anthony capitulated gruffly, pointing to the back door of the kitchen. "You can go stand there and don't you dare move. If anyone needs to use the door, you jump right out of the way. Got it?"

Little Ant's face lit up. "Thank you, Uncle Ant."

"As for you," Anthony said to Michael, "get out there and schmooze. Talk up the dishes I've prepared as if your life depended on it."

"What'll I get in return?"

"I won't kick your ass for constantly getting underfoot. Now go."

Desperate for a small breather, Vivi peeked her head out of the kitchen doors. Anthony was going from table to table, talking to patrons. *Merde*. She should do the same. He looked like he was running for office, so smooth was his smile. What if he won? He'd taunt her endlessly; she knew it.

Her gaze lit on Natalie, who motioned for her to come over. Vivi hesitated, then headed toward the table.

"How is everything?" Vivi asked the table at large.

"*Tres magnifique!*" Quinn O'Brien replied with gusto clearly designed to irk Natalie. It worked; Natalie made a disgusted face, as if she couldn't believe she was sitting next to such an idiot.

"It's wonderful," Bernard Rousseau assured her.

"Which?" Vivi couldn't resist asking. "The gratin or the lamb kebabs?"

"Both," said Bernard.

Well, which one is better? Vivi longed to ask, but knew she couldn't.

Seated to Bernard's left was a large, handsome man whispering in the ear of a curvy, red-haired woman. Vivi edged toward the couple. "Hello," she said. "I'm Vivi Robitaille. I'll be opening a bistro across the street in a few months."

The woman extended her hand. "I'm Gemma, Anthony and Michael's cousin. And this is my husband, Sean."

"Nice to meet you," said Vivi. Michael and Anthony's cousin, she thought. And her husband. That was two votes for Anthony right there.

Gemma's husband, Sean, jerked a thumb at Quinn. "I'm responsible for turning this guy on to Dante's."

"Don't worry, Vivi," Quinn assured her. "I can't wait for Vivi's to open so I can check that out, too. Natalie has promised to be my date the first night it opens, haven't you, Nat?"

Natalie gave a bored yawn, then turned her body away from him completely, which only made Quinn laugh.

Vivi's thoughts crept back to Anthony's cousin, Gemma. She wondered if Anthony knew how lucky he was to have so much family nearby. The woman didn't resemble either Anthony or Michael, but that didn't mean anything; Vivi and Natalie looked nothing alike. Vivi was disconcerted, though, by the appraising way Gemma was looking at her.

She excused herself to go back to the kitchen. On her way, she crossed paths with Anthony, their shoulders brushing. "If you'd like, I'll help you with your socializing skills as a consolation prize," he said with a smirk.

"Don't flatter yourself," Vivi huffed, steaming through the kitchen doors. Honestly, it was a pity such a handsome man was such an arrogant ass.

"How's everyone doing?"

Finishing up his rounds in the dining room, Anthony saved the Blades' table for last. Michael and Theresa sat there with the team's coach, Ty Gallagher, and his wife, Janna. With them was their latest hotshot player, Jason Mitchell, with his cute but meek-looking girlfriend.

Michael tapped his fork against his plate. "Vivi's gratin is exceptional."

"But so is your lamb," Theresa added.

"Which is better?" Anthony demanded.

Michael winced apologetically. "I'd have to say it's a tie."

"Tie," Theresa agreed.

Anthony frowned. "Thank you. That was very helpful." He pointed to his brother. "Ever think of luring this guy out of retirement?" he asked Ty Gallagher. "I don't think playing househusband is his forte."

"Judging by the number of take-out boxes in the fridge, I'd have to agree with you," said Theresa.

Ty regarded Michael with amusement. "You wanna be our stick boy?"

Michael twisted around in his seat, looking at Anthony like he wanted to pop him one. "I think I'll stick with diapers and dishes for just a little while longer, thank you."

Anthony decided to wrap up his visit to the table, not wanting to leave Vivi to her own devices in the kitchen for too long; the ruthless gleam in her eye was beginning to worry him. "Please, if there's anything I can do to make your dining experience more pleasant, let me know," he concluded with a small bow.

"What he really means is, vote for him," said Michael.

The table laughed.

Vivi stole a quick look out of the corner of her eye as Anthony, working not two feet away from her, put the finishing touches on his stuffed flank steak. It was an interesting dish, but she'd be damned if she'd ask for a preview. She didn't want to pump up his already oversized ego. Besides, he hadn't asked to taste anything of hers.

"Go!" Anthony barked to the kitchen's tournant, who hurried to bring the first of the dinner platters to the waiting waiters.

"You're being quite an ass tonight, you know," she informed him mildly.

"To you? Or in general?"

"To me."

Anthony wiped his hands down the front of his apron. "Competition is competition. If you can't stand the heat, get out of the kitchen. Literally."

"Another one of your American phrases, yes?"

"Yes."

She tensed as he came closer to her, watching as she spooned cider vinegar over the poached fish she'd prepared.

"Did Hugo warm the dinner plates for you as you requested?" asked Anthony.

"Do you really care?"

"When junior staff are asked to do something in this kitchen, I want to make sure they've done it."

"In that case," said Vivi, hating the thought of getting someone in trouble, but knowing she had to be honest, "the answer is no."

"Hugo!" Seconds later, a skinny, frazzled boy who

looked to be about twenty presented himself to Anthony. "Yes, chef?"

"Vivi asked you to warm these plates for her and you forgot."

Hugo looked stricken. "I meant to. It's just that I was helping Rocco—"

"Don't care," Anthony barked, cutting him off. "You'll be emptying the grease traps tonight. Got it?"

"Yes, chef," Hugo said glumly, skulking away.

Anthony turned back to Vivi. "Are the warmed plates crucial? Or is the quality of the dish sufficient to endure room temperature flatware?"

Bastard, Vivi thought. *Don't let him rattle you or make you doubt yourself. Be strong.*

"The plates could be fresh from the freezer and this turbot would be outstanding," Vivi informed him. She told the staff they could start serving the turbot. With that, she sashayed past him to begin preparing the flan.

Anthony couldn't believe how tense he felt as the votes were being counted. Dessert was done, the patrons were lingering over the coffee, and at the bar, two volunteer diners, both unknown to Anthony and Vivi personally, were tabulating the paper votes. He was dying for a glass of Sambuca to quell his nerves, but he didn't want to distract the vote counters.

Exhaustion had worked its way into every bone in his body, but it was the good kind that comes with working hard and completing a job well done. He looked at Vivi, sitting at her sister's table. The imperious manner she'd assumed all evening in the kitchen was gone, replaced by a mild anxiety that mirrored his own. His eyes caught his cousin Gemma's and she smiled, pointing discreetly to Vivi then giving him a subtle thumbs-up. Anthony scowled back at her in disbelief. His own cousin, the same one he'd given endless piggyback rides to as a kid, telling him she'd voted for the competition! Real nice.

The seconds seemed to crawl by. "What do you think?" Anthony asked Aldo, the ancient waiter hovering faithfully by his side.

"It could go either way," said Aldo noncommittally.

"Thank you for not quitting tonight."

Aldo just shrugged. There'd been a few nights over the past couple of weeks that Aldo hadn't torn off his apron and stormed outside to puff furiously on a cigarillo like some kind of sulky, wrinkled teenager. Perhaps the old man was mellowing as he entered his seventh decade.

Restless, Anthony's eyes scanned the dining room again. He did a double take; there was Insane Lorraine and her mother, Mrs. Insane Lorraine, sitting at a table with two of *his* aunts, Millie and Betty Anne. The twosome must have slipped in late, well after he'd made his rounds of the tables. The sight of Lorraine sitting with members of his family made his guts flip, though both Millie and Betty Anne were batshit crazy, so maybe they all had a lot to talk about.

"We've got a winner."

The dining room hummed with low, excited murmurs as Anthony leaned forward stiffly in his chair, awaiting the verdict. The man making the announcement, portly with a moustache so thick it looked like he'd glued a squirrel to his upper lip, waited for the room to quiet. "The winner of the cook-off—by one single vote!—is Miss Vivi Robitaille."

One vote. Anthony fought the urge to slump in his chair. He couldn't believe it. She was a great cook; just not as great as him. Vivi was hugging herself, crying. The win meant she had a ready-made crowd of admiring customers for her bistro when it opened in the spring. He tried not to think about it.

The crowd was chanting for a speech. Vivi turned to Natalie, looking dazed. Though it hurt to lose, Anthony found a small measure of comfort in being beaten by a worthy opponent. He'd been in cooking competitions before; there was nothing worse than losing to some slick jackass who dazzled with presentation but didn't know a crepe from a canapé. At least Vivi had talent.

Knowing it was the right thing to do, Anthony rose to go congratulate her. He just hoped she wouldn't gloat too much in public.

"Congratulations." He leaned over to kiss her cheek.

Vivi stood up and looked at him with wide eyes. "Thank you. I'm shocked I won."

"Bullshit," he whispered. "You thought you were going to win, just like I thought I was going to win."

Vivi laughed softly. "You're right." She indicated the diners. "They want me to say something, I think. But you and I will talk alone later, yes? After the kitchen is cleaned up?" She leaned toward him, putting a hand on his arm. "Do you have any cigarettes lying around? I would love one later, after everyone has gone."

"I think I may have an old pack somewhere in the kitchen. I'll try to find it. You give your speech."

Vivi nodded, clearing her throat. She thanked Anthony for giving her the opportunity to use his kitchen, as well as thanking everyone who voted. But Anthony was only half listening as he stopped by the bar to pour himself that much-needed Sambuca and gather the ballots so he could burn the evidence of his failure.

Chapter 15

"Benedict Dante! It was you, wasn't it?"

Anthony shook a handful of crumpled ballots in Michael's face as the two adjourned to the restaurant's un-heated back office for some privacy. He couldn't resist carefully tallying the votes himself before he burned them. He and Vivi had tied on the appetizer and the main dish, and it was the dessert vote that tipped the scale. That's when it dawned on him: Their mother's pudding. Raisins versus currants. His brother.

"It was me what?" Michael asked, his eyes shifting away guiltily.

"You know what! You voted for Vivi's flan over my pudding, didn't you?"

Michael looked caught. "I'm sorry, Ant. I told you, you should have made it the way Mom used to."

Anthony couldn't believe what he was hearing. "So, you had to vote against me? You couldn't just—"

"Lie?"

"Yeah."

"I didn't think it was right to do that, and if you're honest with yourself, you wouldn't have wanted me to lie, either."

"No, in this case it would have been okay."

Michael edged toward the office door. "Does it really matter who won? This was all in good fun, right?"

"I suppose," Anthony muttered. "You've created a monster, though. Did you see Vivi out there? Preening and so graciously accepting everyone's congrats?"

"Like you wouldn't do the same!"

"She's going to be unbearable now."

"What do you care? I thought you were just *friends*." Michael crossed his arms. "*Minghia*, you ever think of putting a space heater back here? When Dad ran things—"

"Did you let Insane Lorraine and her mother in?"

"They bought tickets like everyone else, Anthony." Michael smiled uneasily. "They seemed to be having a nice conversation with Aunt Millie and Aunt Betty Anne."

"Yeah, no kidding. I'm sure Lorraine was telling them about our imaginary upcoming nuptials."

"Cut her some slack. She's been doing better with the hostessing, hasn't she?"

"I guess."

To be honest, Anthony hadn't really noticed. When he was in the front of the house, it was usually to speak with patrons. He hadn't received any complaints about her, so he supposed she was doing all right.

"Can I go now?" Michael asked. "My nuts are about to freeze and crack off."

"For someone who spent so much time on the ice, you're certainly a wuss when it comes to the cold."

"Yeah, well, I'm not around the ice that much anymore, am I?" Michael said bitterly. "Except at my son's games."

Where the coaches wish they could put a gag in your mouth, Anthony thought to himself.

"I didn't appreciate that crack you made to Ty about letting me come back to the Blades," Michael continued.

"Sorry."

"I think I'm doing pretty well with the househusband stuff."

Anthony said nothing.

"I'm getting better," Michael insisted.

"Yeah, but are you enjoying it? People should do what they enjoy, Mike," said Anthony, thinking of Little Ant.

"Whatever," Michael mumbled. He went to leave, but Anthony put a hand on his shoulder.

"One more thing."

Michael's shoulders slumped.

"Did you say something to Gemma about Vivi?"

Michael coughed into his fist, looking away.

"You SOB. What did you say?"

"I just told her that you and Vivi had chemistry, and asked her to, you know, check out Vivi's aura."

Anthony bit the inside of his cheek. Sometimes his cousin Gemma's woo-woo witch stuff plucked on his nerves. Even so, he had to ask. "And . . . ?"

Michael grinned, then did his best impression of Gemma. "Predominantly red, meaning passion, vitality, force of will."

Anthony affected nonchalance as he opened the office door. "That's nice. Wanna stick around and help me clean the kitchen to make up for stabbing me in the back?" Anthony asked. Michael made a sour face. "Didn't think so. I'll catch you tomorrow."

"*You're right, this* is a filthy habit," Vivi said to Anthony as she took a small puff from her cigarette before passing it to him to share. They were leaning up against one of the long, steel tables in the kitchen. The restaurant patrons had long departed, their bellies filled, and the last of the kitchen staff had just bid them good night, all of them having worked together to leave the kitchen spotless and gleaming, ready for the next day. Vivi felt a twinge of remorse when she caught sight of poor Hugo emptying the grease traps, his punishment for failing to warm the plates for her as requested. But she knew Anthony was right in chiding him. That was how she had been treated when she was a young apprentice, and it was the way she'd have to treat her staff, as well.

"Happy about your win?" Anthony asked, a thin veneer of ill humor overlaying his voice.

"You're being an achy loser," said Vivi, taking the cigarette from him. She actually felt a bit guilty about besting him, even though a few hours ago, she would have hid his toque blanche if she thought it would give her an advantage. Yet here she was, contemplating apologizing.

Anthony corrected her gently. "The phrase is 'sore loser,' and if I'm being one, I don't mean to be." He tilted his head from side to side, stretching his neck. "It's just that my own brother voted against me."

"How do you know?"

"He admitted it. The dessert was the tiebreaker."

Vivi laughed. "I think it's wonderful that you two are so honest with each other, so close. It's really enviable."

"I was thinking more along the lines of, 'What a traitorous bastard.'"

Vivi thought of Natalie, the minor breakthrough they seemed to have had when Vivi told Natalie she didn't have to buy Vivi's affection. Perhaps one day she and Natalie would be as close as the Dante brothers. She hoped so.

Anthony took the cigarette from her fingers and inhaled deeply before handing it back to her. "That's enough for me."

"Me, too." Vivi walked to the sink to douse the butt under water, then threw it into the nearest trash can. She could feel Anthony's eyes on her, tracking her. Small frissons of heat corkscrewed up her spine.

"Do you really think your flan was better than my pudding?" he asked her as she walked back to him, his arms folded across his chest in a posture of defense more than defiance.

"Hard to say, since I didn't taste anything you made, just as you tasted nothing I made." She realized it wasn't just the patrons she'd wanted to impress that evening, but him, too. Him, most of all.

"I'm game for some tasting right now." Anthony walked over to one of the double-doored, stainless steel fridges and pulled out a bowl of his pudding and a small plate of her flan.

"Who goes first?" he asked, stopping to get two spoons.

"Me," said Vivi like an excited child. Pulling back the plastic wrap covering the flan, she dug her spoon in deep, relishing the tang of pineapple as it passed her lips. It was more than delicious; it was perfect. She was tempted to say so out loud, but thought it only fair to wait until she'd tasted his pudding.

She licked her spoon before digging into a bowl of Anthony's pudding. It was good—very, very good. But hers was better. She shrugged.

"Let me guess: yours is better," Anthony said stonily.

"Of course."

He sighed. "This was a stupid idea. Of course each of us would choose our own dishes."

"No," Vivi insisted. "If I really thought yours was better, I'd tell you." She put her hand on her hip. "Wouldn't you do the same?"

"I'm insulted you would even ask that." With great flourish, Anthony thrust his spoon into his own creation for a taste. "Mikey's insane," he muttered to himself. "The currants are what make it."

"Excuse me?"

"Nothing. Just talking to myself. Okay," he said, eyes fastened on Vivi. "Here goes. The true test."

He helped himself to a big spoonful of flan. Vivi held her breath, scanning his face for a glimmer, however small, of what he might be thinking. But Anthony revealed nothing. He took two more tastes of his pudding, and two more tastes of her flan. "Stop stalling!" Vivi said with exasperation.

"I'm not. I just want to be *sure*."

Another taste of pudding, another taste of flan. Then he put the spoon down.

"I concede defeat; yours is better."

Vivi was shocked. "You really think so?"

"I thought we agreed neither of us would stoop to lying."

Vivi found herself unexpectedly moved by his honesty. "Thank you," she said quietly. "It means a lot to me that you like it." An overwhelming feeling of gratitude welled up inside her. "Actually, I have many things to thank you for—recommending the DiDinatos, and letting me use your kitchen tonight."

"No problem."

"Thank you," Vivi repeated, rising up on tiptoes to kiss his cheek. The room seemed to hold its breath as Vivi found her lips sliding from his cheek to his mouth, lingering there. Anthony's arms came around her, pulling her into an embrace, his mouth crushing down on hers. Vivi felt herself swoon as a wildness grew inside her that she couldn't contain. She forced Anthony's burning lips apart with her tongue. This was no friendly kiss. This was a man and a woman, wanting each other, craving one another. Vivi's heart was going mad in her chest; she could picture it, red as a cartoon heart, pumping the desire now overwhelming her through her body. *Anthony,* she thought giddily. His hard mouth, his hard body, his wonderful, wonderful mouth doing magical things to her.

"Anthony! Oh my God!"

Startled, Vivi pulled away from him. They both turned at the same time; standing in the doorway of the kitchen was a haggard-looking woman with deep circles under her eyes. She stifled what sounded like a sob, then fled.

"Jesus H. Christ," Anthony muttered under his breath.

"I do not believe this." He tilted Vivi's chin up so her eyes were looking into his. "One minute. Just give me one minute, and I'll be right back."

Anthony disappeared though the kitchen doors.

By the time Anthony returned, Vivi's mood of ecstasy had transformed itself into one of puzzlement, even suspicion. Was it possible this woman was somehow involved with Anthony? If so, what was he doing kissing *her*?

"Who was that?" Vivi asked coolly as Anthony rejoined her.

"Insane Lorraine," Anthony replied, looking and sounding exhausted.

"Excuse me?"

"I went to high school with her," Anthony explained with a grimace. "She's a total fruit loop. My idiot brother hired her as a hostess for Dante's."

"She's in love with you, yes?"

Anthony scrubbed his hands over his face. "I don't know. I guess. It doesn't matter."

Vivi felt sorry for him. "Don't worry. It will all be fine."

"Will it? I'm afraid that one of these days, she's gonna pop out from behind the stove with a meat cleaver and mince me into Dante burgers."

"At least they'd be tasty," Vivi said without thinking, regretting it immediately. Anthony looked embarrassed. "I'm sorry. I didn't mean—"

"It's okay." Anthony ran a hand across the brushed steel of the tabletop. "Look, we need to talk."

"About the kiss?" Vivi asked nervously.

"Yeah, about the kiss, about everything." He paused. "It's not . . ." He stopped, seeming to cast around for the right words. "It's just . . ." He exhaled heavily, looking frustrated. Finally, after a silence that seemed to drag on interminably, he concluded with a miserable "Fuck."

"Listen to me." Vivi took his hand. "I'm sorry if my kissing you disturbed you. It just felt like the right thing to do at the time."

"It was."

"I know what happened to your wife," Vivi said, choosing her words carefully. "Your brother told me. I am so, so sorry. I can't even imagine how terrible that must have been."

Anthony squinted with disbelief. "My *brother* told you?"

"Yes." Vivi's hands knotted together. "He told me . . . how she died . . . and how hard it's been for you. He sensed, you and I, you know . . ." Vivi didn't know what else to say.

Anthony's touch was gentlemanly as he reached out to briefly caress her cheek. "I have some things I need to think about, Vivi, okay?"

Vivi looked at him uncertainly. "I understand."

"Please, I don't want you to think I'm blowing you off. I'm just really confused right now."

Vivi nodded. "So am I, Anthony." Suddenly exhausted, she slowly took off the apron she'd borrowed from him. "I should go."

"You're not walking home at this hour. I'll run you home."

"Thank you."

She waited for him by the back door of the kitchen, itchy to leave the scene of their mutual desire and bewilderment. Anthony quickly threw on his leather jacket, absently swinging his keys around the index finger of his left hand as he took one last look around the kitchen. That's when Vivi noticed—he'd slipped his wedding ring back on his finger.

"*I'm trying to* decide which would be more effective: sewing your lips permanently shut or throwing your body into the East River."

After driving Vivi home from their cook-off, Anthony had spent a largely sleepless night, fueled in equal parts by confusion, despair (What was he going to do about Insane Lorraine?), and anger at his brother for telling Vivi intimate facts of his life without his permission. By the time the sun rose over Bensonhurst, Anthony knew what he had to do: He had to grab Michael by the scruff of his meddling, muscled, hockey player neck and tell him to butt the hell out. So here he was, back at his brother's brownstone. This time, both Dominica and Little Ant were at school as expected. It was just him, Michael, and baby Angelica, all together on the couch while *Sesame Street* blared from the TV.

"Good morning to you, too," Michael said sarcastically. "We've got to stop meeting this way."

"Who the hell said you could tell Vivi about how Ang died?"

"Ah." Michael looked caught off guard. "She told you about that, huh?"

"Yeah, she did. How dare you? That's *my* info to share, not yours."

"I was just trying to help," Michael answered defensively.

"Help what?"

Michael started jostling Angelica up and down on his knee, a convenient prop, Anthony noticed, when his brother was under the gun. "Look, Ant. I know you like her, and I know she likes you. And I just thought—if she knew about what you went through, it would help give her some insight into your personality."

"She doesn't need insight into my personality! At least not from you! When are you going to stop sticking your nose in where it doesn't belong?"

"When you get your head out of your ass, that's when!" Michael stopped jiggling his daughter. "Do you think Angie would want you to be alone? Here's this wonderful, sexy woman right in front of your face, who's actually crazy enough to be attracted to you, and what are you doing about it? Nothing!"

"You don't understand." He'd thought about this all night—his desire, his ambivalence—and had finally figured out what, for the most part, was up with him. "I know Vivi's special, okay? I know that." He ran his hand through his hair. "Which is why I want to be *sure*. It's not fair to her if we get together and I can't give her everything she deserves, emotionally speaking. She deserves my full attention. I don't want to make promises I can't keep. Does that make any sense to you?"

Michael looked impressed. "Yeah." He patted Anthony's knee. "I hear ya, bro."

"So you'll butt out?"

"I was just trying to help, Ant. Honestly."

"I know you were coming from a good place. Just trust me on this, all right? I know what I'm doing here." He touched his nose to Angelica's. "Right, pumpkin?"

For the first time since coming in, Anthony took in the living room. The place was still, as his dear, departed mother would put it, "a sty." "Cleaning lady still out sick, huh?"

"Worse than that," Michael replied, glumly. "She's gone back to Poland."

"What the hell is there in Poland, besides Lech Walesa and bottled water?"

"Grandkids."

"Gotcha."

"Why don't you hire Insane Lorraine?" Anthony taunted.

"Yeah, right."

"Oh, but it's okay to inflict her on me."

Jesus, just thinking about having to tear himself from Vivi to calm down Insane Lorraine pissed him off all over again. There she was, tearful in the empty dining room, as if he owed her an explanation. He should have just let her go, but he was afraid she might do something, well, insane.

He'd been forced to state firmly and plainly that he was her boss and nothing but her boss. Lorraine kept sniffling and harping on how he'd promised to come to dinner at her house, and hadn't yet. Purely to get her off his ass, he agreed he'd come for brunch the following Saturday, regretting it immediately. But it was the only way he could think to mollify her.

He could tell from the look on Vivi's face when he rejoined her in the kitchen that she thought something might exist between him and Lorraine, which was kind of insulting, in his opinion. He might not be George Clooney, but *Madonn'*, he was a reasonably successful, good-looking guy. If Vivi thought that was his caliber of woman, then she was as crazy as Lorraine. Still, that pinched look around her mouth when she asked about Lorraine was kind of satisfying.

Anthony stood up. "Right. I gotta run."

"Not yet. I've got three words to say to you before you go: Blades Christmas Party."

"Yeah, what about it?"

"Corporate wants to switch the date to the twentieth. Can you do that?"

"This is pretty short notice, Mikey. That's what, two weeks away?"

"C'mon. Ant. This is tradition we're talking about here."

Anthony was adamant. "I have to check to make sure no one else has booked the banquet room. If not, then it's a go."

"Great. I can't wait."

Anthony couldn't hide his surprise. "You're going to go to the party?"

"I'm still a Blade," Michael maintained sharply. "And it is my"—he caught himself—"*half* my restaurant."

"Why don't you start taking care of the early morning half of the day, then?" Anthony needled. "You know, be there for the dawn deliveries."

"Can't," Michael said, deliberately not looking at him. "Gotta get the kids up and ready for school."

Anthony zipped up his jacket. "Convenient." He ruffled Angelica's hair. "See you, gorgeous." He pointed at his brother. "No more playing Cupid, you got it?"

Michael put up his hand as if taking an oath. "I swear on the heads of my children."

"Yeah," said Anthony, heading for the front door. "We'll see how long *that* lasts."

Chapter 16

"More olive loaf, Anthony?"

Anthony stared at the tower of luncheon meat Insane Lorraine's mother held out to him and tried not to gag. If coming to Insane Lorraine's house for brunch didn't earn him an E-ZPass through the Pearly Gates, then there was no God. Not only was the food revolting (olive loaf, Kraft singles, industrial rye bread, yellow mustard, horrible coffee), but the company was depressing. Insane Lorraine Senior, or Mrs. Fabiano, as most people knew her, was simply an older, mothball-scented version of her daughter: same dark circles under the eyes, same scary Prince Valiant haircut, though hers was shot through with gray. The setting didn't help, either. The heavy velvet curtains covering the living room windows remained perpetually closed, while the overwrought French provincial furniture looked like it had never been used, and was, of course, protected by clear plastic slipcovers. At least the dining room, where they were now seated, had some light coming in, even if it was muted by floor-length sheers covering the windows that had once been white, but were now dirty gray.

"No, thank you," Anthony said politely, helping himself to the rye bread. He vigorously shook the mustard (the mere concept offended his culinary sensibilities), and spurted some onto the bread before slapping on a slice of cheese, wishing himself luck, and biting into it. "Great," he lied. The bread was so squishy and artificial it stuck to the roof of his mouth, the same way Communion wafers had when he was a kid. As discreetly as he could, he tried using his tongue to dislodge it, but it remained firmly glued in place. He'd just have to wait for it to slowly dissolve.

Mrs. Fabiano sat down, beaming at him. "Lorraine tells me you two have picked up right where you left off in high school."

"Uh . . ." Anthony was speechless as he turned to Insane Lorraine for some kind of hint about what her mother was talking about, but she just smiled at him beatifically.

"She was telling me how closely you two are working at Dante's. It's wonderful when couples work together."

"Uh . . ."

Beneath the table, Lorraine's hand snaked its way to Anthony's knee. Anthony firmly pushed it away with a glare. Lorraine flashed him a wounded look before petulantly peeling off two slices of olive loaf for herself.

"We were very sorry when we heard about your wife, Anthony."

"Thank you, Mrs. Fabiano. I was sorry to hear about Mr. F's passing, myself. You're suing the construction company, I take it?"

Mrs. Fabiano stared at him blankly. "What?"

Shit, Anthony thought. *I hope I haven't opened a can of worms I don't want to get into.* Can of worms—now there was an expression for Vivi to mangle. "I thought some scaffolding collapsed on him," Anthony continued carefully.

"No." Mrs. Fabiano sighed. "It was an elk's head."

"Excuse me?"

"We were having dinner at the Elks Club—Roberto was a lifelong Elk, you know—and he was sitting beneath the mounted elk head on the wall when it fell. It killed him instantly."

"That's awful."

Mrs. Fabiano shuddered. "It was. Especially with the antlers and all."

Death by elk head . . . what a way to go. Anthony couldn't believe he hadn't heard about this; usually the gossip network in Bensonhurst was pretty strong. The Elks Club must have deliberately kept the actual circumstances of his death under wraps for fear of losing members.

"Some olive loaf, Anthony?" Mrs. Fabiano asked again.

"No, thanks, I'm fine."

He endured an hour of avoiding olive loaf and stilted conversation before making his excuses to leave—but not before cornering Insane Lorraine while her mother cleaned up in the kitchen.

"Thank you so, so much for coming, Anthony." The excessive nature of Lorraine's gratitude made him sad, even while irritating him. "It meant a lot to us."

"No problem. Look, we need to talk."

Lorraine perked up. "Yes?"

God help me, Anthony thought. "Did you tell your mother we were a couple?"

"Sort of," Lorraine mumbled as she hung her head, her pageboy fringe hanging in her eyes.

"It's not good to lie, Lorraine. You need to listen to me." He waited for her to lift her head, but when it became apparent that wasn't going to happen, he forged ahead. "I'm very flattered that you like me. But you and I have an employer-employee relationship, period. You've been doing a really good job at Dante's, and I'd like to keep you on. And that isn't going to happen unless you let go of this fantasy that you and I are involved, or are ever going to get involved. Okay?"

Lorraine lifted her head; her expression was bitter. "It's because of that French woman, isn't it? You think she's prettier than me."

"Lorraine." Anthony was beginning to feel powerless in the face of Lorraine's obvious aversion to reality. "I'm not discussing Vivi Robitaille with you. My personal life is none of your business. I told you, I'm your boss, you're my employee. Either accept that, or start looking for another job, all right?"

Lorraine said nothing. All righty, then. He'd said his piece, and it was time to go. "Thanks again for brunch, Mrs. F," Anthony called into the kitchen, where Insane Lorraine's mother was wrapping up the leftovers. Not surprisingly, there were a lot.

She hurried out into the living room/mausoleum to kiss his cheek. "It was so nice to see you, Anthony. You've made Lorraine so happy, you don't know. Next time, let's make it dinner."

Anthony managed a sickly smile. "Sure."

Shaken, he left the house without a further word.

"God, they're killin' me here."

Anthony studied the guest list for the Blades Christmas party, which seemed to grow longer every year. Luckily for the team, he was able to switch the dates as Michael had requested. But the number of people they expected him to cram into the banquet room was unreal. He'd need all the help he could get, both in the kitchen and with the front of the house. Aldo would bust his balls about having to work the party, but in the end would capitulate. Everyone else would be on board as long as Anthony paid them well, which he always did. He was a firm believer in paying people what they were worth; it showed respect and helped create loyalty. Between working the Blades party and their regular Christmas bonuses, his staff would have a very Merry Christmas indeed.

"Hello?"

He looked up to see Vivi peeking her head through the restaurant's front door. He hadn't seen her since the night of the cook-off. It surprised him how much lighter just seeing her face made him feel. It was as if she brought the sunshine into the room with her.

"Come on in."

Vivi approached the table, eyes bright. "I was hoping you'd be here."

"I'm always here. What's up?"

"The DiDinatos have finished installing my kitchen equipment. It's so beautiful! I want you to see it."

"I would love to." Anthony slid out of his chair and followed her across the street.

"Well?"

Vivi looked at Anthony expectantly. The equipment for the kitchen had indeed been installed. What surprised him was how small a space the kitchen was—long and narrow, like a galley. He couldn't imagine fitting more than a couple of people in there at a time.

"It's great," Anthony told her. "It's just—small."

Vivi frowned. "This is a small bistro, Anthony, remember? I don't need a kitchen your size."

"Yeah, but—" He clamped his mouth shut, determined not to dampen her enthusiasm.

"But what?" Vivi demanded. She was scowling at him like a Halloween witch.

"Nothing." Anthony held up his hands in surrender. "I'm sorry I said anything. Clearly, I'm talking out my ass."

Vivi's scowl turned into a look of mild offense. "My kitchen is somehow related to your ass?"

"No, no, no." Jesus, he really had to watch the colloquialisms. "It's an expression. 'Talking out my ass' means 'I don't know what I'm talking about.'"

Vivi considered this. "You *are* talking out your *derriere*," she declared.

"Exactly. It's a nice kitchen, Vivi. I mean it."

She sighed wistfully. "I just wish I didn't have to wait months to be able to use it. I'm dying to cook."

Anthony hesitated a moment, then jumped in. "Mikey's old hockey team is having their Christmas party at Dante's in a few weeks. Would you like to help me out?"

"Yes!" Vivi enthused, but then her face fell. "When is it? I'm going back to France for Christmas."

"Oh." Anthony felt a wave of disappointment. "The party is the twentieth."

"Perfect! Natalie and I are flying back the twenty-first."

"How long will you be gone for?"

"Just through the New Year. We'll be back on January second."

"I see." That disappointed him, too, though he wasn't sure why. It wasn't like he was a big New Year's Eve guy. Usually he was working; New Year's Eve at Dante's was one of his busiest nights of the year.

Vivi rubbed her hands together excitedly. "When do you want me here to help you cook? And what should I make? A *buche de noel*? That's a traditional French holiday dessert; it's in the shape of Yule log."

"I know what it is. Look, here's the thing, we'll be following my menu, and it's pretty basic: fried calamari, large trays of lasagna and eggplant parm, that type of thing. Nothing fancy. This is not a fancy crowd."

"But perhaps they'd like to try something new."

"Vivi." Anthony was keeping a leash on his mounting annoyance. "The foods I serve, they're kind of a tradition, you know? You know what it's like cooking for a large party or a wedding or something like that, right? They get

the choice of a few dishes, period, for both simplicity's
sake and expediency's sake."

Anthony could tell by the frustrated look on Vivi's face
that this wasn't what she wanted to hear. "What if I made
something on my own time and brought it in?" she whee-
dled. "Would that be all right?"

There was only one reason Anthony could think of for
why it wouldn't be: he didn't want her outdoing him, the
way she did at the cook-off. He knew it was petty, but he
couldn't help it. This was *his* gig.

"Let me think about it."

Vivi looked pouty. "Can I bring Natalie?"

"Sure, if she doesn't mind hanging around with a bunch
of hockey players—though there will be some corporate
types there as well."

"Natalie does very well with corporate types. She's
been feeling very low. I think being at a party will cheer
her up."

"You're a good sister, Vivi."

"Half sister. I try to be." She touched Anthony's forearm, her hand lingering there. "I promise I won't be too
much of a pain in the jaw—"

"Neck—"

"—in the kitchen. I'm so happy you asked me to help
you. It's the best Christmas present anyone could give me."

Anthony winked at her. "It'll be fun. You'll see."

"*These hockey players*—they're so loud."

Vivi nodded in agreement as she and Natalie stood in
the doorway to Dante's banquet room, looking out over the
crowd. Everyone seemed to be having a good time. Of
course, the never-ending flow of liquor helped. Many of
the players seemed well on their way to getting toasted, as
the Americans would say. Vivi liked that some of the
players had their families with them, too. There was a real

close-knit feeling to this group. Her eyes sought out Michael and Theresa, sitting with their three children, and two other couples Vivi assumed were related to the team. Vivi nudged Natalie.

"Why don't you go talk to Theresa? Tell her you want to discuss PR for Vivi's as soon as we get back from France."

"Stop pushing me, Vivi," Natalie said, irritated. "It will be taken care of." Natalie's eyes did a second circuit around the room. "Many of the men are handsome, though apparently, many of them lack their own teeth."

"Have you met anyone interesting?" Vivi asked coyly. She was hoping Natalie might meet someone nice. Frankly, she was nervous about Natalie returning to France for the Christmas holidays. For weeks, Natalie had been gripped by an unhealthy nostalgia. "At this time last year, Thierry and I were planning a weekend together." "At this time last year, Thierry bought me perfume for an early Christmas gift." Vivi feared that upon returning to Paris, Natalie's depression might deepen, and she wouldn't want to come back to America after the New Year.

Natalie considered the question with a snort. "No."

"Have you even tried speaking with any of them?"

"*Cherie*, listen to me." Natalie looked touched as she pushed some wisps of hair out of Vivi's eyes. "I know what you're up to, and I appreciate it. But you don't need to worry about me. I'm fine."

"You don't seem fine. You seem very melancholy to me."

"It will pass. Trust me."

"That Quinn O'Brien likes you," Vivi pointed out. "He likes to tease you."

"He's a barbarian. Besides, I would never go out with a journalist. Journalists ruined my life, as you might recall."

Vivi dropped the subject. She'd learned that when Natalie didn't want to discuss something, it wasn't discussed—unless Vivi pushed hard. Vivi decided to let it go for today. It was five days until Christmas, after all. She wanted goodwill to prevail.

"What are you and your *maman* doing for Christmas?" Vivi asked. She couldn't wait to see her mother, to go to Midnight Mass with her and her grandmother, then come home and drink hot chocolate together while they all opened their presents. She missed her mother so much it was a physical ache sometimes.

"I don't know," Natalie confessed. "When Papa was alive, we would always go to his brother's house. But now that he's gone, my mother doesn't want to. She could never stand his family, anyway."

Vivi nodded, a small lump forming in her throat. Never in her life had she spent Christmas Eve and Christmas Day with her father. He always came a few days after, when his other responsibilities were out of the way. Sometimes, she'd go to bed on Christmas Eve and pray that by some miracle he might be there in the morning when she awoke. But he never was.

"Will you celebrate at all?" Vivi asked.

"I'm sure we'll figure out something to do, even if it's to stare at each other over our brandies."

The image depressed Vivi immensely, even if Natalie was just being flippant.

"Would you like to come home with me for the holidays?" Vivi asked shyly. "I'm sure my mother wouldn't mind having you."

Natalie looked teary. "Thank you for the offer, but no, I'd prefer to stay in Paris. Perhaps you'll make a day trip up to see me, though? We could shop, maybe go to the Pompidou Center. I haven't been in a very long time."

"Yes, that might be nice."

Natalie checked her watch impatiently, one of her tics. "When will you be done here, do you think?"

"Oh, don't wait for me." Vivi had arranged to sleep at Natalie's tonight so they could taxi together to the airport early the next morning. "There's a few hours of the party left yet, and then I have to help clean up. I'll come later, when I'm done."

Natalie looked suspicious. Vivi wondered, did Natalie think she wanted to stick around because of Anthony? If so, that wasn't the case. Not really. Well, perhaps a little. She did have a small gift for him.

"All right." Seemingly mollified, Natalie lightly kissed both Vivi's cheeks. "Don't work too hard. I'll see you later this evening."

Vivi couldn't believe that all the food from the party was gone. When she had seen the trays and trays of lasagna Anthony was preparing, the pounds of squid being breaded and tipped into the deep fryer to make calamari, she was appalled; there was no way it would all be consumed! It was a waste. But she was wrong. Not only was every last bit gobbled up, but they'd actually *run out*, forcing Anthony to improvise. No one seemed to complain when steaming bowls of pasta and Dante's trademark sauce replaced the lasagna and the delicious, wafer-thin eggplant parmesan that was melt-in-the-mouth good. Yet the pasta and sauce disappeared, too, right along with the olive oil cake Anthony had made for dessert. Luckily, she'd ignored his request for her not to make anything and had baked trays of macaroons, which helped save the day when every last crumb of Anthony's cake had been devoured. He was annoyed at first, but then begrudgingly grateful to have something to serve. Vivi was convinced that if he kept bringing food out all afternoon, everyone would simply keep eating. She was actually glad when there was no more food to be served.

Afternoon affairs like this one always warped her sense of time. It felt like it should be very late at night when it was only eight p.m. She rejoined Anthony in the kitchen, where he was finishing up the last of the cleaning. The staff had long gone, but Anthony, being a perfectionist, couldn't lock up until he knew everything was exactly where it was supposed to be. Vivi understood completely. She had no doubt she'd be the same way once Vivi's opened.

Anthony looked surprised to see her. "What are you still doing here? I thought you'd left with everyone else."

Vivi feigned offense. "You think I'd leave without saying good-bye? Especially when I'll be gone for two weeks?"

Two weeks . . . Why did that suddenly feel like an eternity to be away? She'd been excited for months about going home to see her mother and grandmother. But now, standing with Anthony, it seemed bittersweet. In all her holiday planning, she hadn't counted on the possibility of missing him.

"Got any special plans for New Year's Eve?" he asked, picking up a damp rag to wipe down one of the stainless steel tables. The table was perfectly clean as far as Vivi could see. He was either more neurotic than she thought, or he was trying to keep occupied while they talked.

Vivi shook her head. "Not really. At midnight, *maman* and I usually go to the Saint Benezet Bridge and toss coins into the water, making a wish."

"In Paris?"

"In Avignon. Where we live."

"Yeah?" Anthony seemed to be concentrating very hard on the already-clean table. "What are you gonna wish for?"

Vivi flushed. "I don't know." She paused. "What are you doing on New Year's Eve?"

"Working. New Year's Eve is a big night at Dante's. We have three seatings, starting at five."

Vivi nodded. She could picture it—the patrons all dressed up, talking and laughing as the clock counted down, and the tinkling of bumping champagne glasses ringing through the room as people wished one another a joyous New Year. She almost wished she could be here, even if it were just to help. "I enjoyed today," she admitted.

"I'm sure you did."

"You're upset about the macaroons."

"I was at first, but then they wound up saving my bacon. So thank you," he concluded begrudgingly.

"It was nothing," Vivi said, waving a dismissive hand. She watched as he moved on to the next table, rubbing it down in broad circles. It was beginning to annoy her. "Why are you cleaning that again?" she asked, following him. "It looks fine."

"To you, maybe."

Vivi reached out, stilling his hand. "Stop," she commanded softly.

Anthony slid his hand out from under hers, pushing the rag away. "Better?"

"Better."

"I have a Christmas present for you," he said, looking almost shy. "I was going to stop by your place tonight to give it to you, but your sister told me you were spending the night in the city with her."

"Yes."

Anthony smirked as he asked, "Did she have a nice time at the party today?"

Vivi sighed. "I was hoping she might meet someone nice, but I guess it wasn't to be."

"Believe me, someone as highfalutin as your sister is *wayyy* out of the league of most of those bozos."

Vivi's eyes practically crossed with confusion. "Bozo? Highfalutin? Is that even *English*?"

Anthony grinned. "Let me get your present." He strode out of the kitchen, returning a few seconds later with a wrapped, rectangular square the size of a box of chocolates. Vivi hoped it wasn't; she'd eat herself sick on the plane home.

"Merry Christmas," he murmured, handing it to her.

"I have one for you, too, you know," she said, refraining from the impulse to shake the box.

"Yeah?"

"Of course I do. What do you think I am, a total looter?"

"Loser," Anthony corrected affectionately. He gestured at the package in her hand. "I really think you should open that."

Vivi excitedly tore away the wrapping, revealing two books: *The Dictionary of American Slang*, and *A Guide to American Colloquialisms and Expressions*. She laughed. "This is wonderful!"

"Yeah?" Anthony repeated uncertainly. "I thought you might be insulted, the way some women are when you buy them something practical for a present, instead of something . . ."

"Oh, no, I need this, very much so," Vivi said seriously. "Thank you." She rose up on tiptoes, planting a soft kiss on his lips.

"You're very welcome."

Vivi put her books down on the table. "Now, for *your* present."

She hustled to the restaurant's coat closet to fetch Anthony's present from the large shopping bag she'd brought with her. Usually she hated flying, but with the two books he'd gotten her, she had no doubt the flight back home would pass quickly. What a wonderful, considerate gift, even though she knew that on a certain level, he meant it to be somewhat tooth in cheek, as the Americans said.

Breathless, she scurried back to the kitchen, carefully laying the gift down on the table beside him. "Here you go. Be careful opening it. I don't want you hurting yourself."

Anthony peered at her quizzically, then opened the package. There was no mistaking the shock in his eyes as he took in the sight of the shiny new meat cleaver.

"Vivi." He picked it up, turning it over in his hands as he admired it. "You shouldn't have done this."

Vivi ignored him. "Isn't it beautiful?"

"Vivi," Anthony repeated more sternly. "You have to return this. I know how much this brand of cleaver costs."

Vivi's mouth hardened into an angry line. "When someone gives you a present, you're supposed to be gracious and accept it."

"Not when that person buys you something outrageously expensive you know they can't afford."

"I'm the judge of what I can and can't afford. Not you."

"I already have a cleaver, Vivi."

Vivi hesitated. "Yes, but it doesn't hold its edge any more. I was shocked when I cut up the chicken to make you my *poulet basquaise*. The cleaver was far too dull. I decided then and there that you needed a new one."

"That's very considerate of you," Anthony replied frostily, "but it's still too expensive."

Vivi could see she'd insulted him. "I'm sorry," she said. "I thought I was being helpful."

"I know you did." His face softened. "I'll accept it on one condition."

"What's that?"

"You promise never to use it on me."

Vivi laughed. "You'll have to behave, then."

It was the wrong thing to say. Or, perhaps, the right thing. A whisper of tension stole into the room, rendering them both still. Finally, Anthony put the cleaver down. When he turned back to look at her, there was longing in his eyes.

"Please kiss me," Vivi murmured, surprising herself.

She didn't care about their last conversation, when he said he needed to sort things out. All she could think about was the feeling of his mouth on hers, the way her skin warmed like honey in the sun when he touched her. There was no hesitation as Anthony put his mouth on hers. God, he always kissed perfectly, Vivi marveled. There was no awkwardness, no stabbing his tongue into her mouth like an impatient adolescent, the way so many men did. Vivi let herself fall into the moment and then, a moment later, into his arms.

Breaking their embrace, Vivi felt confused. She'd told herself not a month before that she would in no way actively pursue him; yet she'd asked him to kiss her. Still, given the sexual tension between them, it was possible he would have anyway. She'd stopped denying to herself that she liked him. Perhaps the next step was admitting that she actively wanted him?

It was usually men who made declarations first, wasn't it? Men who declared their hearts, who took it upon themselves to transform basic attraction into something deeper and lovelier. Vivi felt herself slipping into uncharted territory. She'd never been the first to tell a man her feelings, and now, standing here in front of the man who frustrated her but whom she was growing to adore, she wondered if she wasn't making a mistake. But she couldn't go back home for Christmas without a more solid grasp on how he felt.

So Vivi gave voice to the cliché: "We have to talk."

Anthony didn't seem put out or puzzled by her statement. In fact, Vivi thought he looked rather relieved. "Talk away," he said.

"I like you."

"I like you, too."

"No, you don't understand," she huffed. *"I like you."*

"And I like you," Anthony repeated back with a pleased smile. "But I just need a little time to sort things out in my mind."

"What things?" Vivi asked. She touched his shoulder. "Please, I need to know."

"Well, for one thing, you're another chef. Getting together could be dangerous."

"I agree."

"Then there's, you know, my emotional state."

"Are you still in love with your dead wife?"

She regretted saying it immediately. The words sounded so harsh in the silent kitchen.

"I'll always love her," Anthony said carefully. "But I'm pretty sure I'm ready to move on."

"Then why have you been hesitating so?"

Anthony rubbed his forehead, pained. Vivi could see this was a struggle for him. She got the sense he wanted to state things just right so that there was no misunderstanding.

"I don't want to start a relationship with you until I'm absolutely sure I can be there for you. I don't want us to get something started, and then halfway into it, realize I'm not ready for it, and hurt you. You're a special woman, Vivi, and you deserve to be treated that way, always. Can you give me just a few more weeks to straighten my head out?" He shook his head in disgust. "Christ. I sound like such a wimp."

"No, you don't."

"Do you even know what a wimp is?"

"Yes, it's someone who's weak. Indecisive."

"That about sums it up." He reached out to touch her cheek. "I promise: I'll have this all worked out by the time you come back in the new year. Okay?"

Vivi bowed her head for moment. "Okay. But if you start seeing someone else while I'm away," she said as she looked back up at him, "I *will* use that cleaver on you, and it won't be pleasant."

"I'm not gonna start seeing someone else. Don't worry." Anthony looked sad. "I'm really gonna miss you."

"Me, too," Vivi said, tears springing to her eyes. *"Merde,"* she said, looking away from him in embarrassment. "It takes nothing to make me cry."

"Read the books I gave you, and you'll learn how to say that in American."

"Tell me now."

"The American expression is, 'I cry at the drop of a hat.' "

"I don't understand."

"Neither do I. But it's catchy, isn't it?"

"It is," Vivi agreed. Her eyes crept to the clock on the wall. "I have to go. A cab is picking me up at my apartment in about forty minutes to bring me to Natalie's."

"Cancel it. I'll drive you into the city."

"Don't be silly." The truth was, she wanted to take the cab. It would give her a chance to ruminate over all that had been said.

Anthony shrugged. "Whatever you want. I'm gonna head out soon myself." He opened his arms. "Farewell hug?"

"Farewell hug," Vivi agreed, stepping into his arms. They held each other tightly. Vivi felt she could stay there forever. But she knew the longer she stood there like this, the more she'd be tempted to push for more: more kisses, more passion, more everything. She pulled away gently.

"*Joyeux Noel*, Anthony."

Anthony pressed his lips to her forehead. "Merry Christmas to you, too, Vivi. I'll see you in two weeks."

Chapter 17

"Anthony?"

Anthony felt his stomach heave at the sound of Insane Lorraine's voice. Vivi had left Dante's, but he had deliberately remained behind to think about what had just passed between them. The kitchen was where he thought best. It was his home, the place where he felt most alive. He'd been deep in thought when the drone of Lorraine's voice broke the silence. *Mother of God, is there no escaping this woman?*

"Lorraine, how did you get in here?"

She was standing by the kitchen doors wrapped in a long camel hair coat, her eyes nervously shifting to and fro. Never mind Vivi and the cleaver, Anthony thought tensely, Lorraine is about to pull a Squeaky Fromme.

"I've been here since the party."

The hair stood up on the back of his neck. "You were at the party?"

Lorraine nodded. "Hiding in the bathroom. I told

Michael I left something here after work on Friday, and he let me in."

"Great." Michael was going to pay for this. "Well, what can I do for you?"

"I wanted to give you your Christmas present."

"I don't accept presents from my employees," said Anthony, discreetly slipping Vivi's cleaver into the nearest utensil drawer, "though I appreciate the gesture."

Lorraine took two steps towards him. "Please, Anthony? You've done so much for me."

Anthony sighed. He was trapped, and he knew it. The only way he was going to get her out of here was by capitulating. "Fine. Give me your present."

He held out his hand to receive it. Instead, Insane Lorraine opened her coat, revealing her naked body beneath. "I love you, Anthony," she declared breathlessly. "Fill me with your man seed. Let me bear your children."

"Jesus Christ!" Anthony roared, his hands flying up to cover his eyes. "Close your coat, Lorraine! *Now!*"

"Think of how beautiful our children would be," Lorraine continued unfazed. "I want—"

"Close your coat or I'm calling the cops!" He turned his back to her.

"But—"

"No buts! *Do it!*"

He had been half-prepared for her to attempt to stab him. But he'd never expected her to flash her boobs and everything else God gave her. And to do it in the kitchen at Dante's! Talk about a desecration of sacred space. She was finished. Fired. Done. Mikey was a dead man.

"You decent?" Anthony called over his shoulder.

"Yes."

"You swear on your mother's eyes?"

"Yes," Lorraine said in a defeated voice.

Anthony cautiously turned around, peering at her through

the screen of his fingers. She'd closed her coat, and wrapped it tight. She wouldn't look at him.

Compassion, he said to himself. *Christmas, peace on earth, kindness to your fellow men. Be nice.*

"Lorraine, I think you need to talk with someone. Your memory doesn't seem to be very good. Remember what I told you at your house? I'm your *boss.*"

"But I love you, Anthony. I always have. Remember in high school . . . those anonymous notes stuck in the hands of your mother's statue of Saint Francis? Those were from me."

No shit. "Lorraine." He tried to keep his voice kind; it wasn't easy. "I'm sure you can find someone just right for you, if you just try. Please, this situation is making me very uncomfortable. Go home right now, before I get angry."

"I need a ride," she said pitifully.

Anthony fought the temptation to pull his new cleaver out of the drawer and whack himself in the skull with it. "No problem. Just—keep your coat closed, okay?"

"No way in hell am I firing her right before Christmas." There was no mistaking Michael's vehemence as he glared at Anthony from his perch three steps above on a Macy's escalator. Two days until Christmas, and of course his brother had yet to shop for anything for Theresa or the kids. Anthony supposed it could be worse; he could have waited until Christmas Eve. But this was pretty bad. The store was packed wall-to-wall with shoppers whose nerves were frayed as they searched for the perfect gift. *Goodwill toward men my ass,* thought Anthony. It was every man for himself in the department store jungle.

Anthony was resolute as he followed his brother off the escalator. "You hired Lorraine. You fire her. It's that simple."

"I've never fired anyone in my life," Michael protested,

making a beeline for a low-cut blouse that a woman in a fur coat plucked from the rack just as he was reaching for it, her expression victorious. "*Minghia*, these people are like animals."

"Ever hear of the Internet?"

"I'll try that tonight if we don't find anything here." Michael looked around desperately. "Shit. Maybe I should just get her a gift certificate."

"Then she'll know you left it until the last minute."

"She already knows. When I told her I was hanging out with you today, she gave this weird little smile and said, 'Have fun.'"

Anthony shrugged. "So she knows. So what?"

"Easy for you to say, Mr. Anal Retentive."

Anthony just chuckled. It was true, he tended to get his holiday shopping done way ahead of the curve, mainly to avoid the chaos they now found themselves in. Angie had been even worse; she used to complete her holiday shopping by Thanksgiving.

Inevitably, his thoughts turned to Vivi. What was she doing right now? France was five hours ahead, making it seven p.m. in Avignon. Was she cooking for her mother? Seeing old friends? He couldn't believe how joyless everything felt since she left. Hopefully, watching Mikey's kids open up their gifts on Christmas morning would help cheer him up. He wouldn't be able to stand feeling this gloomy for the next two weeks.

Michael sprinted toward the lingerie section, grabbing the first bra he set eyes on. "What about this?"

"It's a nursing bra, Mikey."

Michael looked at it. "You're right." He put the bra back on the rack.

"C'mon, man, you can do better than this," Anthony cajoled. "Where's that hopeless romantic Theresa always says she fell in love with?"

"Tickle Me Elmo killed him."

"Maybe it's time to give the stay-at-home dad gig a second thought, then," Anthony said delicately.

Michael glared at him. "This isn't the time."

"With you, it's never the time. I have an idea: you could take over for Insane Lorraine."

Michael didn't smile. "You're really expecting me to fire her, aren't you?"

"You're goddamn right I am! You made this mess, you're going to fix it!"

"Okay, okay, how about this," Michael said, plunging blindly into a sea of women's lace and silk. "How about I find her another job?"

"Fine. But fire her first."

"That's pretty hard-assed, Ant. Especially since she's working off the books. We fire her, we can't even say she was laid off so she can collect unemployment. She gets nothing."

"Not my problem," Anthony growled.

"Let her work until I find her something else."

"Yeah? And what if she flashes me again? What if she does something nutty in the middle of the dining room? What then?"

"I'll talk to her. I'll tell her she's got to keep her shit together, or else."

Anthony snorted. "Like she'll listen to you."

"She'll listen to me. I got her this job. I'm like a God to her."

"Whereas I'm just a potential stud."

"Speaking of studs," Michael said, holding up a beautiful, sky blue kimono for Anthony's input, "did you and Vivi have a tearful good-bye? I was surprised to see her at the Blades party."

"I was surprised to see you at the Blades party," Anthony shot back. "You were the only ex-player there."

"I own half the restaurant, remember?" Michael snapped. "I wanted to make sure everyone was having a good time."

"Sure, fine, whatever. Thumbs-up on the kimono."

Michael threw the kimono over his arm with a glare. "You never answered my question about Vivi."

"We're gonna talk again when she gets back."

"Screw talking. Don't you think it's time to 'do'?"

"I think that's between me and Vivi. Now let's get the hell out of here before I start verbally abusing the elves."

"Uncle Anthony! Look!"

Anthony yawned and rubbed his bleary eyes as his niece Dominica held up some kind of doll with an emaciated body and giant head. It was six a.m. Christmas morning, still dark outside, and Michael's kids were already up and opening their presents. It was tradition for Anthony to be there. He wouldn't have missed it for the world. Still, he wished the kids had slept in for a little bit. When his phone rang at five thirty and it was his brother telling him the little ones were already champing at the bit to get to their toys, he couldn't believe it. He'd barely gotten three hours of sleep.

Part of his exhaustion stemmed from how hard he'd worked the night before. The extended family always had the traditional Italian "Seven Fishes of Christmas Eve" dinner late at night, before Midnight Mass but after Anthony had finished up at the restaurant. When his mother had been alive, she'd been the primary cook. But since her death, the responsibility had fallen to Anthony, a task he accepted gladly. None of his dotty old aunts could cook worth a damn.

Dominica shook the doll in his face, impatient for an answer. "The doll's nice, honey," Anthony managed. Satisfied, she moved on to her next gift, tearing the wrapping paper with gusto.

Anthony stole a glance at his brother and Theresa, both of whom looked as tired as he imagined himself to look.

Baby Angelica was sitting on Theresa's lap in the rocking chair, looking bright eyed and adorable in a little Santa's hat. Little Ant was on the floor with his sister and father, his gift-opening much more deliberate than Dominica's. So far, Dominica had opened three gifts to Little Ant's one. Anthony could foresee her running out of presents to open before Little Ant was even halfway done with his, a scenario guaranteed to generate some resentment. He hoped his brother or sister-in-law would tell her to slow down.

"Here, open this." Michael stretched forward to pluck a gift from the far recesses beneath the tree, turning to wink at Anthony before handing it to his son. There was excitement on Little Ant's face as his fingers tore at the wrapping, but his face fell when he opened the box.

"New skates." Michael was beaming as he tousled his son's hair. "Whaddaya think, huh, kiddo? You'll be lightning on the ice in those babies."

"Thanks, Dad," Little Ant replied glumly as he returned the skates to their box, pushing the gift far back under the tree. Theresa caught Anthony's eye, shaking her head in silent disbelief at her husband's utter cluelessness.

Anthony decided to rescue the moment. "My turn," he said, handing Little Ant one of the gifts he'd bought him.

"What about me?" Dominica pouted.

"I'll give you yours in a minute," Anthony promised, perching expectantly on the edge of the couch as Little Ant slowly opened his present. It was sad; thanks to his father, the kid seemed almost afraid to discover what was inside.

"Look!" Little Ant gasped when all the paper had been torn away. "Cookbooks!" He held them up for his parents to see before jumping up to give Anthony a hug. "This is the best, Uncle Ant! Thank you."

"You're very welcome," said Anthony, pleased to have done well. Last year he'd gotten Little Ant some stupid talking robot that fell apart after ten minutes. This year he'd scored ten out of ten, both with Little Ant and Vivi. Not bad.

He turned to ask Michael a question and was taken aback. The look of resentment on his brother's face was unmistakable. "I need to talk to you when we're done here," Michael murmured under his breath. Anthony nodded curtly. He could guess what was coming.

"*Look, you have* to lay off with the cooking stuff."

Anthony watched as his brother halted in the middle of the kitchen floor, sloshing coffee over the rim of his mug. Theresa was still out in the living room with the kids, helping Dominica dress her new doll while listening to Little Ant read aloud the recipes he wanted to try. Baby Angelica sat on the floor beside her mother, shredding wrapping paper to her heart's delight.

"He liked the gift, Mike. He likes to cook. Those cookbooks are geared specifically to kids."

"*I don't care.*" Michael's expression was momentarily hostile; then he backed off. "I didn't mean that. What I mean is, with school and all, Little Ant really only has time for one extracurricular activity, not two."

"And you want that activity to be hockey."

"Right."

"Have you ever thought of consulting Little Ant about that? Seems to me he'd rather be in the kitchen than on the ice." Anthony went to the refrigerator and pulled out a carton of eggs. He'd scramble some up for everyone for breakfast.

"He just needs a little more time to warm to it," Michael insisted.

"He's been playing for what, four months now?" asked Anthony, grabbing a frying pan and throwing a healthy-sized chunk of butter into it.

"Yeah? So?"

"Don't you think he knows by now whether he likes it?"

"He's a kid, Anthony. He changes his mind every thirty seconds."

"Except when it comes to wanting to cook," Anthony pointed out, reveling in the aroma of the sizzling butter.

"I want him to be part of a tradition," Michael continued, seeming not to hear.

"He is," Anthony said sharply. "The cooking tradition. Dad, me, and now him. What, it has to be hockey?" He glared over his shoulder at his brother. "Cooking isn't macho enough?"

"You know that's not it."

"Then what's your problem?" Anthony broke six eggs into a bowl and began whisking them with a fork. "Why can't you just let him be who he wants?"

"You sound like Theresa."

"Yeah, well, maybe we're on to something here. Go put up some toast."

"You think I'm being an asshole, don't you?"

"Pretty much, yeah." Anthony poured the eggs into the pan, pausing as they hissed and sputtered in the pool of melted butter.

Michael put four slices of bread in the toaster and sank down in a kitchen chair. For a few seconds, the only sound filling the kitchen was that of the eggs frying. "All right, I'll see how it goes. If he seems totally miserable playing the second half of the year, then maybe—*maybe*—I'll let him drop out. I just hate the thought of my kid being a quitter."

"There's a difference between being a quitter and giving up an activity that makes you completely miserable!"

Anthony sensed movement in the kitchen doorway. He looked. Little Ant was standing there, holding both the cookbooks he'd given him, a big smile on his face.

"What's up, sport?" Michael asked in a strained voice.

"Can Uncle Anthony and I pick out a recipe for me to cook sometime during the Christmas vacation?"

Anthony's eyes shot to his brother's. *You gonna break his heart on Christmas morning or what?*

"Sure," said Michael. "I'm going to go help Mommy with stuff in the living room. You two chefs work it out."

He picked up his coffee mug and walked out of the kitchen.

Chapter 18

"*A Euro for* your thoughts, Vivi."

Vivi lifted her head from the book she was pretending to read, surprised to hear Natalie try to use this foreign idiom. Over the holidays, she'd devoured the books Anthony had given her and now felt she had a firmer grasp on American slang, finding it fascinating. She especially loved the phrases "hit the sack" and "open a can of whoop-ass," though she couldn't imagine a situation where she'd ever get to use the latter, which made her sad.

"It's penny, not Euro, but how do you know that expression?"

"I know lots of things," said Natalie. "Like the fact that you're extremely distracted. You've been reading the same page for at least an hour."

Vivi sighed, closing her book. Ever since their flight left Paris earlier in the day, alternating moods of melancholy, trepidation, and anticipation had plagued Vivi. She was sad at having to say good-bye to her mother. They'd had a wonderful two weeks together cooking, laughing, and gossiping like two old friends. But she couldn't wait to see Anthony. He'd been on her mind day and night. She was like some lovesick schoolgirl, wondering what he was doing at any given moment of any given day. She almost telephoned him Christmas Day, but decided not to. She'd agreed to give him two weeks to sort his feelings out; calling might make her look desperate.

Her newfound certainty made Vivi even more anxious to get back to Bensonhurst to discover what he'd decided. Suppose he thought it better they stay friends? Or that he needed still more time to sort things out? Vivi tried to block out anything other than the outcome she wanted—the one with the two of them together.

She turned to Natalie, who'd insisted on the window seat as soon as they'd entered the plane. Vivi was sad they hadn't managed to get together over the holidays, but at least it enabled her to spend lots of time with her mother. Now that they'd be back in the States, she and Natalie could see each other anytime. Theoretically.

"I was daydreaming," Vivi admitted. She was surprised Natalie had noticed; she'd spent most of the flight listening to music on her iPod, lost in her own world.

"The bistro?"

"Yes." She was tempted to again remind Natalie of the importance of contacting Theresa Dante about PR as soon as they got back to New York, but refrained. Better for both of them to reacclimate for a few days, and then get down to business.

"Is that all?"

"No." Vivi saw no point in lying. "I was thinking about Anthony Dante."

Natalie shook her head, drawing the flimsy airplane blanket tighter around her legs. "I worry about you, Vivi. I don't want to see you get hurt."

Vivi thought Natalie's worry had more to do with Natalie's own doomed romance of the year before than it did with Anthony. Vivi decided to gently probe the issue. "Did you see Thierry when you were in Paris?"

"No." Natalie looked sad, but resolute. "I wanted to, but it was too masochistic a thing to do. Better to move on."

Vivi squeezed her hand. "I'm so relieved to hear you say that."

"Why? So you can keep pushing me toward that Quinn character?"

Vivi rolled her eyes. "He's a nice man, Natalie."

"You've met him twice in your life, Vivi, for five minutes each. He could be a monster for all you know."

"Well, he seems nice," Vivi insisted.

"Hitler loved dogs. Just remember that."

Vivi laughed. "Papa used to say that, didn't he?"

Natalie smiled. "Yes." She seemed to relax for just a moment before sadness overtook her face again. "It felt strange, not having him around for the holidays."

Vivi clutched the book on her lap. "Yes."

"How is your mother?" Natalie asked politely.

"Very well. And yours?"

"The usual: a pain in the neck."

"Was your Christmas awful?" Vivi asked, semidreading the answer.

"Awful. I should have accepted your invitation and come to Avignon."

Vivi squeezed her hand, touched. "Next year, perhaps."

"Perhaps. If we're not bankrupt by then."

Vivi knew Natalie meant it as a joke, but her flippancy made Vivi uneasy. Still holding Natalie's hand, she said, "Promise me something."

"Yes?"

"Promise that you'll always tell me the truth."

"Of course," Natalie murmured, glancing out the window. "What an odd thing to request."

"Not really. You're my only family in America, Natalie. I need to know I can count on you."

"If you don't know that by now, then I don't know what," Natalie replied huffily, pulling her hand away from Vivi's.

Vivi recoiled, confused. "I'm sorry. I didn't mean to upset you or imply—"

"You didn't." Natalie briskly wound the cord of her earphones around her index finger and shoved it into the carry-on bag between her feet. "It's me. I had a very stressful time with my mother, and I'm just feeling a little fraught. I didn't mean to take it out on you." She cupped Vivi's cheek. "Go back to your daydreams, *cherie*. And whatever they are, I hope they come true."

A new year, a new lease on life. That's how Anthony saw it, anyway. He'd had two weeks to think about Vivi, two weeks to miss her, and since he wasn't a complete *idiota*, he had to conclude that he was ready for a relationship. Vivi could be a royal pain in the ass in the kitchen, but that just meant she was spirited, with brains and balls and a steely determination to succeed that sometimes left him speechless with admiration. Plus, she was gorgeous. And that accent—Jesus, talk about sexy. Just imagining her whispering in his ear in French made the heat rise in his body.

He knew she was back in Brooklyn. Driving to his brother's for a Mikey-sanctioned cooking date with Little Ant, he'd seen a light burning in her apartment window. He sensed she was going to come see him tonight when the restaurant closed, which was why he remained there, waiting. It was a feeling he'd had all day, an intuition. His cousin Gemma, the *stregh*, claimed all the Dantes had inherited some of "the sight" from their late grandmother, Nonna Maria. Anthony usually thought the idea was nuts. But today was different. The air around him felt charged the way it did before an impending storm. So when Vivi finally did walk through the swinging doors of the kitchen, he could have sworn he heard a crack of thunder overhead.

"Hello," she said softly, walking toward him. "I had a feeling you'd be here."

I had a feeling you'd come. She was so much more beautiful in person than the image he'd been holding of her in his mind's eye. Her long gold hair was loose around her shoulders, not braided behind her head as usual. She was smiling at him beguilingly.

Without any hesitation, she kissed him hard on the mouth. Anthony fought the urge to crush her roughly to him and claim her on the spot. Instead he returned the kiss.

"It's good to see you," he murmured, priding himself on being a master of understatement.

"You, too." Vivi put her hands on her hips. "So, have you decided?"

Anthony looked at her, then burst out laughing. "You don't believe in beating around the bush, do you?"

Vivi's eyes lit up. "That expression was in one of the books you gave me! I know what it means!"

"Yeah? Do you know what this means?"

Eyes pinpointing hers, Anthony stepped into the small space separating them and took her in his arms. Her scent, her soft skin, the surprised intake of breath when his mouth greedily sought hers—all conspired to rob him of coherence. He could feel Vivi's heart beating against his chest, a captive bird longing to break free of its cage and soar. He would be her liberator. Her liberator and captor both.

Vivi dragged her mouth from his. "Say it," she commanded. "Tell me your decision."

"I want you, Vivi."

It was what she wanted to hear. She kissed him, nipping at his lips with her teeth like a hungry animal.

"C'mon," Anthony murmured in her ear, wrapping an arm around her waist. "Let's go back to my house."

"No." Vivi's voice was resolute, the blue of her eyes

glinting like sapphires. "Right here." Her hands reached
for the front of his shirt, her fingers nimbly undoing the
buttons. "Have you ever made love in your kitchen before?" she asked mischievously.

"What—no."

Vivi smiled at him saucily. Shirt now open, her hands
slid up and down the skin of his chest. A low moan escaped
Anthony's lips. Just who was the captive here? He put his
hands firmly on her small, slim hips to steady himself, then
dipped down to savage her throat and mouth, greed for her
pumping through him. Aroused, Vivi groaned. It was a
sound Anthony could almost taste, sweet and drugging. He
wanted more.

"Since we're in a kitchen, let's make use of what's
available to us," he murmured into her ear, nipping at her
lobe before breaking away and walking over to one of the
kitchen's industrial-sized refrigerators. He pulled out some
chocolate syrup he used to drizzle over profiteroles, as well
as a small bowl of caramel left over from tonight's crème
caramel.

Vivi's eyes were glued to the bowls in his hands as he
detoured to a microwave to heat them up. By the time he
came back to her and put the bowls down on the table,
there was no denying the longing in her eyes, the hot flush
of desire on her cheeks.

He watched to see her reaction as he placed his hands at
the neck of her blouse and violently tore, the small white
buttons clattering to the tile floor like scattered pearls. Vivi
swallowed and swooned, her hand coming up to softly
touch the skin of her own throat, as if checking to see if she
were still alive. "Yes," he heard her whisper. Need reared
up in him, unrelenting and strong. He grabbed her by her
shoulders and pushed her roughly up against the long,
stainless steel table.

Vivi gasped in surprise, but the fire in her eyes belied the shock of his action. She was as hungry as he was. Tugging off her shirt, Anthony pushed her bra up and then dipped his fingers into the bowl of deliciously warm caramel. Vivi's breath held, shuddered, as he spread the caramel on her nipples with the care of an artist before he carefully began licking it off. God, the sweetness, the firmness of her breasts. He wanted to gorge himself on her.

"Anthony . . . Anthony . . ."

Vivi was breathlessly chanting his name, her body trembling as he continued to use teeth and tongue to pleasure her. Fevered, he lifted her hips slightly so she sat on the lip of the table, dark lightning crashing through him. He lifted his head to look at her. The sweat blooming on her face added to the feeling of delirium rising within him. He returned to suckling her, Vivi's hands fisting in his hair as she breathed hard, the staccato rise and fall of her rib cage the metronome counting out the beats of her desire. She was arching against him, her body daring him to take her here, now. Anthony's eyes stole back to hers. Vivi looked back at him, bold yet needy at the same time, pausing for only a second before reaching down to rub her hand back and forth against the front of his jeans, bringing him to fullness.

The pleasure of it was too much. Blood spinning through his veins, Anthony reached for the zipper of her pants, tugging madly. Vivi gave a small, teasing laugh, but didn't hesitate in accommodating him, shedding her jeans and panties with surprising quickness. She lay back on the table, wrapping her legs around him. But Anthony wasn't ready for the plunge. He wanted to play some more. Tease some more.

"Patience, *mademoiselle*," he whispered to her with a devilish chuckle. Lifting his lips from her body, he reached for the bowl of chocolate syrup, and holding it above her bare belly, began pouring it in a slow, steady stream from her rib cage to her slightly opened legs.

Vivi looked stunned, her expression ecstatic as Anthony began streaking a chocolate trail down her body, the flicks of his tongue long, delicious, and slow.

"Oh, God . . ." Vivi moaned.

Her naked desire had Anthony's heart thundering, his pulse pounding out one word over and over again: *Now. Now. Now.*

And yet.

Her moaning turned to gasping as he lapped at the warmed chocolate trickling between her legs. She began rocking her hips, panting, opening herself wider and wider to him, begging, whimpering. Anthony couldn't refuse her any longer.

There was a shared madness between them, tangible and real. Vivi saw it in his eyes as he pulled her up from her prone position, slid her feet back down to the floor, and drove himself into her right there against the table. The rough pleasure of it was more arousing than she could ever hope to give voice to. Anthony's hands, the strong, scarred hands she loved, were anchoring her firmly to him from behind, while his mouth continued to play across the curves and plains of her body, one minute caressing, the next demanding and ravenous as a beast. Dazed, Vivi closed her eyes and gave herself over to each dazzling ray of joy streaking through her body, each more intense than the next. When the final burst of sun came, she gave a laughing gasp, feeling as free and uninhibited as a child discovering the world for the first time.

Anthony covered her face in kisses, delighted to have been the architect of her pleasure. All his senses were firing at once as he moved in and out of her, the building rhythm like the pounding of drums, heralding triumph. To feel this alive again, to know again the heady pleasure of a woman's soft, silky body moving beneath his, was overwhelming. It was as if he'd finally come in from the cold after a long banishment in the wilderness. Drawn to Vivi's life-giving flame, he had no choice but to plunge directly into the fire, and let it incinerate him.

"Well," *Vivi said* breathlessly.

She and Anthony were resting, sated and half naked, against the long steel table that had just served them well, the kitchen silent except for their hard breathing.

Anthony looked dazed. "That was . . ."

"Delicious?"

"In more ways than one."

"It certainly was, *chere*." Vivi looked up at him in surprise. "You've really never had sex in here before?"

"Nope. First time." He drew her in close. "But it won't be the last."

Vivi smiled contentedly, resting her cheek against his chest. "I'm so happy," she admitted. "I was so afraid I would come back to America and you would tell me you just wanted to be friends."

"We are friends. And now we're lovers. It's good to be both, don't you think?"

"Yes." It was what she needed to hear, that their bond was emotional as well as physical.

She lifted her head, looking around the pristine industrial kitchen. There was no place for them to lie in one another's arms unless they hopped back up on the table or sank down on the floor. Given the hardness of both surfaces, neither was an appealing option.

"I guess we should go," she said, not really wanting to.

Anthony planted a long, lingering kiss on her forehead and slowly began gathering up his clothes. Vivi did the same, frowning a little when she put on her blouse, which he'd divested of half its buttons when he tore it off her. "I liked this blouse," she pouted.

Anthony stooped to pick up the buttons lying on the floor. "Can't you sew them back on?"

"I suppose."

"I can buy you a new one," he offered, stepping into his jeans.

Vivi smiled. "I might let you." She decided she'd show off her newfound idiom skills, in the hopes of impressing him. "Shall we go back to my place and hit the sack?"

Anthony sighed, wrapping his arms around her. "I would love to, but as you know, I have to get up really, really early in the morning."

"So?" She nuzzled his neck. "I can get up with you. It will be good practice for when Vivi's opens."

Anthony pulled back slightly so he could look down into her face. "Let's sleep solo, just for tonight." He kissed her softly. "I can feel you fretting. Don't. I'm just exhausted, Vivi. If I have you next to me tonight, I know I won't get any sleep, if you catch my drift."

Vivi's tilted her head, puzzled. "That one wasn't in the book."

"It's a way of saying if you spend the night, we'll spend the whole night having sex and not sleeping."

"How about this," said Vivi. "Why don't we make a date for next Monday night, when you're off. You can come over to my place. I'll fix you dinner, and then for dessert . . ." She nibbled his ear.

"I'd be a fool to pass up an offer that good. You've got to let me make something, though. Dessert, maybe."

To her surprise, Vivi found herself bristling a bit. "I'll make it all. Besides, I'm better at desserts than you, remember?"

"It was one vote, and it was cast by my traitorous brother. I wouldn't take it too seriously if I were you."

"You just can't admit it, can you? That I'm better."

"I'll admit you make better pineapple flan. But on everything else, I'd say it's a draw."

Vivi rubbed her nose against his affectionately. "Stubborn man." She was pleased when he took her hand as they began walking toward the kitchen door. "So, we're on the same page, then, about Monday night?" She smiled proudly at another successful use of an English idiom.

"It's a date, babe," Anthony assured her, holding open the door for her. Hand in hand, they left Dante's and went out into the perfect night.

Chapter 19

Anthony poured himself a glass of wine and sat down in front of the TV, just as he did every night on returning home from the restaurant. When he found himself drifting off he'd go to bed, where he slept so soundly a bulldozer wreaking havoc in the next room couldn't have awakened him. Tonight he'd hit the pillow with an added sense of contentment; Vivi was his. He had returned to the land of the living.

He kept the lights in the living room off, the flickering light from the TV bathing the room in a faint, eerie glow. For a second, he heard Angie's voice in his head—"You're going to ruin your eyes doing that"—and smiled. It was the same thing his mother had said to him and Michael when they were kids. It hadn't affected their eyesight one bit.

He surfed, more restless than he thought. Perhaps he should have gone back with Vivi to her place. They could have just cuddled, not done anything else too, er, taxing. Yeah, right. Anthony laughed out loud.

He settled on the local news. The reporters, a graying

man with a flushed face flanked by a grim looking Hispanic woman, stood by a fire truck. Beneath them were the words, "Live from Brooklyn." Anthony turned up the volume, worried.

"Good evening. We're reporting to you tonight from Bensonhurst, Brooklyn, where a small plane has crashed into a five-story apartment building near Scarangella Park . . ."

Anthony leaned forward. Scarangella Park. Vivi. Hypnotized, he stared at the TV. Behind the newscasters, a fire was roaring out of control. As if he were at the scene himself, he craned his neck, trying to see past them, while deep in his guts, the contentment he'd felt just moments before was quickly curdling into something different.

"Get the hell out of the way!" Anthony roared at the talking heads on TV, who were spewing out endless streams of words: "Accident . . . terrorism . . . number of dead unconfirmed . . ."

As if they heard him, the camera zoomed in for a closeup of the building. Anthony recognized it immediately. It was Vivi's. He fell to his knees slowly, the wineglass in his hand falling and shattering into a million little pieces. Not happening. No. Impossible. He crawled toward the TV. No. NO.

The man and woman kept talking. Behind them, the sound of sirens, firefighters talking on walkie-talkies. He heard the word "tragedy." Saw flames. Smoke. Vivi was dead. Like Angie. Dead.

He covered his face with his hands and let out an ungodly howl.

"Jesus."

Anthony jerked awake and looked around wildly, his body coated in sweat. He was still sitting on the couch. On the TV screen was an old sitcom from the seventies. His wineglass sat atop the nearest end table, empty. He was still dressed. Breathing hard, he told himself to calm down, to think straight. It was some minutes before the feelings of dread and panic left him, before he was able to put two fingers to the artery in his neck and feel that his pulse had returned to normal.

He dialed Vivi's number, not caring that it was two a.m.

"Hello?" Her voice was groggy.

Anthony held back from shouting with joy. "Vivi? It's Anthony."

"Anthony?" She sounded alarmed. "Is everything all right?"

"Yeah," he said, relief washing over him. "I just wanted to hear your voice before I went to sleep."

She laughed. "So you're still awake! Maybe you should have come home with me."

"I was thinking the same thing."

"Are you sure everything is all right?" she asked with a little yawn.

"It's fine. I'm sorry to have woken you."

"You can wake me anytime," Vivi assured him in a sexy voice.

"Talk to you tomorrow, honey."

"Yes, *aime*. Sleep well."

Anthony hung up the phone, fighting the urge to weep tears of gratitude. She was alive. She was okay.

But he wasn't. The next night, he had the dream again.

"*Mon dieu, are* you trying to squeeze the life out of me?"

Vivi's laugh was affectionate as she wiggled her way out of Anthony's bone-crushing embrace. They'd just finished making love, and were now wrapped around each other amidst the tousled sheets. Such a night! Champagne and dark bitter chocolate . . . feeding him Brie and strawberries while she sat on his lap . . . the sweet tang of their kisses after she put some orange blossom honey to both their lips. So heavenly, so delicious.

Anthony looked apologetic. "I'm sorry. I just love holding you, is all."

"And I love being held," said Vivi, snuggling back into his arms. "But not so tightly I can't breathe."

They lay together quietly for a while, perfectly content, or so Vivi thought. But it soon became apparent that Anthony's mind was elsewhere.

"I know you like to take walks," he said, "but you don't walk around alone late at night, do you?"

"Of course not!"

Anthony's eyes interrogated hers. "You don't go on the subway late at night, either, do you?"

Vivi propped herself up on one elbow and looked at him. "Anthony, what is going on?"

"Nothing," he insisted, caressing her face. "It's just if anything ever happened to you . . ."

"What on earth could happen to me?" Vivi scoffed.

"You're right," said Anthony, but there was a troubled look in his eyes that belied his agreeing with her.

"You're being silly," she said, taking a playful bite of his shoulder. "I'm going to get some more chocolate and feed it to you, if only to hush you up."

"No more chocolate," Anthony groaned.

"And no more worrying, either."

"I promise."

She lay back down with a contented sigh, nestling against him again. She knew it was unfair to compare, but her last boyfriend had been so thin, so slight, that Vivi sometimes thought, "This must be what it feels like to hold a woman." But Anthony was all man—broad and muscular, with lovely stubble on his face at the end of the day to rub her cheek against, and hard muscles to push against. She had to be careful; she could easily become obsessed with his body, giving herself over to endless sexual daydreams when she should be concentrating on the bistro. She reached down, twining her fingers through his. That's when she felt it: his wedding ring.

"*Chere?*" Her voice was gentle.

"Mmm?"

"Are you ever going to remove your ring?"

"My . . . ?" Anthony replied, puzzled. Then he realized. "Oh." Untangling it from hers, he held up his left hand for examination. "I hadn't really given it much thought, to be honest."

"I see." Vivi felt her heartbeat begin to pick up the pace. "Do you think, perhaps, you could take it off now?" It was a bold request, but she didn't care. He was hers now. He was in her bed.

Anthony lifted her hand to his mouth, kissing her knuckles. "I promise I'll take it off, but not right now."

Vivi couldn't help herself. "Then when?"

"When I can do it in private, okay?" He sounded aggrieved. "I'd like to put it in with a bunch of other stuff of Angie's that I'm keeping."

"I'm sorry," said Vivi, embarrassed by her own insensitivity. "I didn't mean to pressure you. I just need to know that you're all mine."

"I'm all yours, believe me—which is why I want you safe."

Vivi rolled her eyes. "Back to that again, are we?"

"Yup." He began stroking her hair, a sensation she loved. "Better deal with it." He lifted his head to peer at the clock on her nightstand. "We should get to sleep so I'm not late when the predawn delivery comes." He kissed her tenderly, then turned her onto her side so they were spooning. "'Night, *cara*."

"Good night, my love."

Vivi tried to concentrate on the lovely way their bodies fit, and the pleasure of having a man in her bed, keeping her warm, keeping her safe. Anthony fell quickly to sleep. Vivi envied him. All she could think about was the ring.

"What do you think of this?"

Vivi was sitting on Natalie's couch, perusing a catalog of restaurant furniture with her half sister. She'd already selected simple black wrought iron bistro chairs with cushioned seats, and had moved on to tabletops and bases. Vivi wanted white marble tabletops, but Natalie didn't agree.

"What about these fiberglass tabletops?" Natalie pointed to the catalog. "They're less than a third of the price of the ones you're looking at, and seem a lot more functional, in my opinion."

"Mmm." Vivi neither agreed nor disagreed, though she was disappointed by Natalie's selection. They looked cheap, and not at all right for her cozy little bistro. As she had so many other times over the past six months, Vivi couldn't escape the feeling Natalie was trying to cut corners when it came to the restaurant, and it made her uneasy.

"What are you thinking of for the floor?" Natalie asked, reaching for her espresso.

"Wood. Or black and white tile. I haven't decided."

"Tile might be cheaper. And the walls?"

"You've seen the walls—exposed brick."

"And the artwork?" Natalie asked. She sounded like an impatient schoolteacher standing at the blackboard, awaiting an answer.

"I don't know," Vivi said, brows knitting together in frustration. "Framed black-and-white posters of famous Parisian scenes? Reproductions of paintings by famous French artists?"

"I like the latter better, though posters would probably cost less. I suppose you'll play lots of Piaf?" There was a slight tone of condescension in her voice that wounded Vivi.

"Maybe. Maybe not. It's something I need to investigate further." Vivi rolled up the catalog, putting it into her shoulder bag. "How much have you budgeted for the advertising, if you don't mind my asking?"

"I haven't come up with a solid figure yet," Natalie murmured, slipping off the couch to stand before the bank of floor-to-ceiling windows. The sky was gray and cloudy, giving the city a melancholy look. "And before you even ask," she continued, turning back to Vivi, "I'm waiting for FM PR to call me back."

"Good." That, at least, was a relief. But Vivi still had other concerns, most of them fueled by Natalie's on-again-off-again penny pinching. "Don't forget, we still have to buy tableware, cutlery, napkins, glasses. We need to have menus printed up—"

"Yes, I know all that, Vivi," Natalie cut in impatiently. She came away from the windows, rejoining Vivi on the couch. "I saw Bernard Rousseau for dinner last night. He was asking about you."

"How nice," said Vivi, pleased. He seemed like such a nice man. "Send him my regards if you see him again, will you?"

"Of course." Natalie's expression was philosophical as she took another sip from the tiny espresso cup before her. "Being with him reminded me how French men are so much more refined and sophisticated than American men." She gave a small shudder. "I could never go out with an American. Never."

"Well, I could," Vivi replied happily, "and I am."

Natalie's eyes held Vivi's. "Anthony Dante?"

"Anthony Dante," Vivi said with a big smile.

Natalie raised an eyebrow. "Have you . . . ?"

Vivi blushed. "Yes."

"Well, I hope he brings you happiness."

"Me, too."

"So now that the two of you are together," Natalie asked,

finishing off the last of her espresso, "has he taken off his wedding ring?"

Vivi froze. So, Natalie had noticed the ring, too. She wasn't surprised. Inspector Natalie noticed everything. Maybe, because they were half sisters, they were somehow telepathically linked. All Vivi knew was that Natalie had just mentioned the one thing she'd been obsessing on.

"Not yet," said Vivi, trying to sound confident, "but he's planning to."

"Well, until it's off, he's not really yours," said Natalie. The expert on romance was back.

Vivi blinked. "Why do you say such hurtful things to me? Do you do it on purpose?"

Natalie went wide-eyed with shock. "Of course not! I just don't want to see you get hurt, Vivi, that's all. Widowers can be problematic."

"Have you ever dated one?"

Natalie's face turned bright red. "No."

"Then button your lip." She stifled a laugh as Natalie's mouth fell open. God, she loved the new idioms at her disposal. They were so pithy and evocative, and in this case, the perfect cover for the uncertainty Natalie had just unleashed within her. Vivi promised herself she'd put the wedding ring issue out of her mind . . . until Friday night.

Chapter 20

Vivi was anxious as Anthony's black Pathfinder rolled to a stop in front of his house. The first thing she'd noticed when Anthony had come to pick her up was that his wedding ring was gone. But his home was new territory.

His block was nice, the house typical for Bensonhurst—small, brick, with a wrought iron front gate and a tiny front yard. Some of the homes had paved front yards used as parking spaces. Anthony's, however, had a statue of the Virgin Mary on the front lawn.

Seeing Vivi stare at the statue, Anthony explained, "It belonged to my mom." He closed the car door behind her. "In fact, I grew up in this house. I just haven't had the heart to get rid of it." Sweet, Vivi thought, and wonderful the house was still in the family.

Anthony thrust his head forward with a squint, then walked over to the statue, plucking what looked like a piece of paper from the plaster hands pressed together in prayer. "Holy Hanna," he muttered to himself as he shoved it into his coat pocket. "Can I catch a break here?"

"Is everything all right?"

"Fine." His mouth twisted into a frown. "There's a disturbed person nearby who likes to leave notes of, uh, petition, in the statue's hand. She's been doing it for years. It's not a biggie."

Not a biggie. That was a good phrase to add to her growing vocabulary list.

"Entres vous."

Vivi smiled appreciatively at Anthony's French as he ushered her through his front door and flicked on the lights. They were standing in a small entry hall, a flight of stairs directly in front of them, a closet to the left.

"Here, let me take your jacket." Anthony helped her off with her coat. Vivi rubbed her arms vigorously to ward off cold. Obviously he kept the thermostat down since he wasn't home during the day, or most of the night, either. He opened the closet, first hanging Vivi's coat, then his own. Vivi glanced absently at the closet and away, but then something caught her eye, and she looked back. Hanging alongside Anthony's many jackets was a policewoman's jacket.

"I'm sure you want to see the kitchen first," Anthony teased.

"Guilty."

Anthony paused to raise the temperature on the thermostat, and then took Vivi's hand, leading her toward the back of the house. Along the way, Vivi caught fleeting glimpses of the many framed photos gracing the walls. Pictures of a large extended family. Pictures of two little boys who clearly were Anthony and his brother. And then, Anthony and Angie's wedding picture, the bride looking radiant and more attractive than Vivi had imagined, Anthony's face transformed by joy. Vivi found herself burning with curiosity; she wanted to stand in front of the wedding picture studying it, trying to get a sense of who this woman was, but Anthony was eagerly steering her into the kitchen.

"What do you think?" Anthony asked as he turned on the lights and the marble and glass kitchen shimmered to life. It was a beautiful space, with state-of-the-art appliances and more counter space than one cook could ever hope for.

"It's beautiful," Vivi marveled.

"Yeah, I fixed it up pretty good," Anthony said proudly. "My parents had kept it the same for years, but when I got married, I redid it. For me, mostly. Angie couldn't even fry an egg."

"Well, that's exactly what I'm going to do for you tomorrow morning—fry you some eggs," Vivi declared, picturing herself in front of the stove. "And some bacon, if you have it."

"Of course I have bacon."

"You never know. Americans have such a terror of fat."

"I'm a chef, remember? I love fat. I adore it."

Vivi laughed.

"Can I get you a glass of wine?"

"*Oui.* That would be wonderful." A glass of wine was just what she needed. It would take the edge off her nerves, help her relax.

Anthony strode toward the fridge and pulled out a bottle of Beaujolais, holding it up to her. "Is this okay?"

"More than okay. You have good taste in wine for an Italian," she teased.

Anthony laughed as he fetched two glasses from the cabinet and poured.

"Here you go."

He handed Vivi her wine, and with his hand at the small of her back, guided her out into the living room. The room was small but cheery, with a big, plump couch just like hers, a lovely, shiny hardwood floor, and one entire wall lined from floor to ceiling with books, many of them cookbooks. Vivi immediately went for the right-hand corner of the couch, her favorite place to nestle, patting the empty space beside her for Anthony to come sit.

"Should I put on some music?" asked Anthony, leaning over to kiss her cheek.

Vivi smiled up at him contentedly. "Some music would be lovely." She watched his broad strong back as he walked across the room to put on a CD. A smile spread across her face as she heard the opening notes of Nat King Cole's "Unforgettable," one of her father's favorite tunes. Perhaps this was a good omen.

"You like the old classics?" Anthony asked, coming to sit beside her.

"Yes." Vivi's voice dropped seductively. "They're very romantic, don't you think?"

"Very," Anthony agreed, putting his arm around her. He leaned into her, lifting a strand of her hair and kissing it. "I love when you wear your hair down, *bella*," he murmured.

Bella. He was telling her she was beautiful. Vivi reached for her wine, taking a small sip. "You really have a lovely home."

"Thanks, but I really can't take credit for it. It was frozen in time until Angie moved in."

"Frozen in what time?"

"The seventies. It was like walking into an Italian version of *The Brady Bunch*."

Vivi cocked her head quizzically. "The . . . ?"

"It was a popular TV show. It was the story of a lovely lady who was bringing up three very lovely girls. All of them had hair of gold, like their mother, the youngest one in curls."

Vivi nodded. "It sounds very nice, actually." Her eyes traveled the room. "Angie had good taste, both in decor and men."

Anthony kissed her, a loving kiss full of tenderness and affection. She had his full attention. Vivi put down her wine on the end table, taking her hands in his. "Thank you for removing your wedding band, *chere*. I know that couldn't have been easy for you."

"It was time," Anthony said quietly.

Vivi nodded, curiosity still nibbling away at her. Suddenly she felt she wanted to know more about the woman who had once occupied Anthony's heart—not because she was jealous of there being someone before her, but because she wanted to know everything about Anthony, and Angie was a big piece of the puzzle.

"I noticed her police jacket in the coat closet."

Anthony looked stricken. "Shit. I didn't even think to—"

"Don't fret." Vivi put her hand on his arm. "It didn't bother me."

"You sure?"

"Of course."

Anthony shook his head ruefully. "You know, it's the only article of her clothing I saved. Everything else went to the Salvation Army. I gave her jewelry to her sisters. But her uniform, I don't know . . ." He rolled his wineglass between his palms. "She loved being a cop so much. I just couldn't let it go."

"She must have been very brave," Vivi ventured.

"Oh, she was brave, all right. A real tough little cookie. She hated those goddamn drug dealers peddling shit to kids. She couldn't rest until she helped put as many of them as she could away." He paused. "That's what got her killed, you know. Some crackhead shot her."

"Yes, I know," Vivi said quietly. "Michael told me, remember?"

"That was always my big fear, her dying in the line of duty, but what can you do?" He shrugged with resignation. "When someone does a job they love, you can't stand in their way, no matter how dangerous it is or how afraid you are of something happening to them."

"I agree," Vivi murmured, smoothing his hair. She was glad he was opening up to her like this. It was true intimacy, the sharing of one's past. "How did you meet her?"

Anthony smiled sadly. "She and her partner came into Dante's one night after their shift. She ate a whole bowl of pasta and they ordered seconds on garlic bread. I thought, a girl who's not afraid to eat is the one for me! Kinda like someone else I know," he said, lifting her hand to his mouth and kissing it.

"And how soon after that were you married?"

Anthony looked up at the ceiling, clicking his tongue, trying to remember. "A year and a half, I think."

"Where did you go on your honeymoon?"

"What's with the twenty questions, Vivi?"

Vivi felt rebuked. "I'm just curious, that's all. I want to know everything there is to know about you."

"You will, over time," he promised. "But for now, can we concentrate on the present?"

"Of course." She snuggled closer to him, satisfied. She loved these first heady days of a relationship, when they couldn't get enough of each other physically and emotionally. Looking at his handsome face, at the strong, hard body that fit so easily with her own, Vivi felt a small hum in the pit of her belly, the first stirrings of excitement. Anthony was obviously feeling the same way.

"C'mere," he said, pulling her onto his lap. Vivi's mouth curled into a feline smile as she wrapped her arms around his neck and crushed her mouth to his. There was fervor as he kissed her back, a hungriness that begged to be sated. Her desire rising, Vivi gave a deep, swooning sigh, which seemed to inflame Anthony even more. With an ease that surprised her, he shifted their bodies so he was lying atop her on the couch, taking her face in his hands as he kissed her passionately, almost brutally. He was staking claim to her body, and Vivi was more than willing to surrender as their long, drugging kiss continued.

Shifting his body weight slightly, he moved to tug up her shirt. Vivi arched up to meet him, wanting his mouth

on her. He read her body language perfectly, impatiently
shoving her shirt and bra out of the way with a groan and
filling his mouth with her breasts.

Joy, pure joy. Feverish, Vivi pushed herself hard against
him, throwing her head back in complete abandon. He was
doing such amazing things with his lips and tongue that
she had no doubt that if he wished he could bring her to
orgasm here and now. But she wanted more. Was in fact
aching for more. Taking hold of one of his hands, she
moved it the length of her body, so he was cupping her between the legs. When he began moving his hand against
her, tiny fault lines began appearing over the terrain of her
body. When the explosion came, she knew she would crack
apart, only to be put back together again so they could do it
all again . . .

"*Chere.*" Her voice was guttural, rough with need as she
lifted her head to look at him. "The bedroom, please.
Please." She wanted to be able to do this for hours, roll
around with him, sprawl their bodies across one another
and dip in and out of fevered sleep. Couches were fun, but
they could be confining. She wanted freedom.

Anthony paused. For a split second Vivi thought he was
going to protest, but then he pushed himself off her, pulling
Vivi to her feet and lifting her up into his arms as if she
were light as a cloud. Vivi was enchanted. No man had ever
carried her off this way, like a knight rescuing a damsel. It
was romantic. Intoxicating.

"*Hurry,*" she urged before crushing her mouth to his
once again, her body quivering with the effort to contain
herself. Such was his strength that she barely jolted in his
arms as he took the steps two at a time, his stride forceful
as he moved across the upstairs landing toward a closed
door.

And then he put his hand on the doorknob, and it all
stopped.

Vivi held her breath, waiting. Perhaps he was out of

breath, needing to pause a moment before plunging inside. But agonizing seconds passed, and still nothing. "Anthony?" Vivi looked at him, alarmed. "What is it?"

Anthony shook his head, too overcome to speak. The passionate look in his eyes had faded; in its place was doubt. Vivi tensed as he sadly, slowly lowered her to her feet. "Jesus Christ," he muttered to himself. He pressed his forehead against the closed door, shutting his eyes.

Vivi's heart was pounding as she stared at him, unsure of what to do. He looked tormented. He wanted to focus on the present, or so he said. In the back of her mind, a voice was telling her to be patient and understanding, that maybe she had brought this on herself by asking him all those questions. But there was another voice, firmer and louder, that she couldn't ignore—the one reminding her how humiliated she felt standing here right now, rejected by the man she loved.

"It's her, isn't it?"

The sharpness in her voice sounded like a slap. Anthony turned his head away.

"Angie," Vivi continued, spitting out her name like a curse. "You say you've moved on, but that's just self-deception!"

"No, it's not." Anthony looked at her with anguished eyes. "I don't know why I can't do this. I don't. It's like . . . this invisible barrier just sprang up. Christ . . ."

A dark silence fell as Vivi waited and waited for more of an explanation. Finally, she couldn't take it anymore.

"Say something!"

The fury in her voice was completely justified. Seeing him give a slight wince should have provided some satisfaction, but it didn't. Instead, her humiliation over being rejected just kept growing.

"Vivi." Hearing the pain in his voice, she tried not to give him a poisonous look, but it was hard. "I don't know what to say, except that I'm completely embarrassed, baffled, and Christ knows what else." He scrubbed his hands slowly over his face, his gaze tortured as he finally looked into her eyes. "If I thought this was going to happen, do you think I would have carried you up here?"

Vivi crossed her arms and looked down at the floor. Her heartbeat had returned to normal. In fact, it felt rather slow, a dull thud . . . thud . . . thud, reflecting her newly demoralized state.

"Let's go downstairs and talk about this," he suggested.

"I don't want to talk. I want to go home."

"Vivi—"

"Just take me home, Anthony, please. I need to get out of this—this—*haunted house*. I need to think."

"It's not a haunted house."

"Oh, no? Then why do I feel the presence of a ghost?" In her mind, the subject was closed.

"Promise me we'll talk about this." Anthony moved to touch her hand and she jerked out of reach.

"What is there to say?"

"Everything!" he snapped.

The anger in his voice got her attention. "Fine, we'll talk," Vivi said in a pinched voice. "Now excuse me while I go call a cab."

"Don't be ridiculous," Anthony scoffed. "I'll run you home."

"There's no need."

"Yeah, there is." He licked his lips nervously. "Cabdrivers around here can be nuts. I want to make sure you get home safe and sound."

"You're being ridiculous."

"Big deal. I'm taking you home."

"Fine," Vivi repeated. "But I do not want to talk about all this in the car. Agreed?"

"Agreed," Anthony muttered reluctantly. He took a step toward her, looking wounded when she again stepped back and out of reach. "Vivi, I'm really, really sorry about this."

Vivi was too distraught to look at him as she started down the stairs. "So am I."

"Holy shit! If this is what happens when you have insomnia, I hope you never sleep again!"

Anthony was silent as he finished unloading the bags of food he'd brought with him to Michael's. After driving Vivi home—a drive made in stone cold, torturous silence—he was too wound up to sleep. Rather than pace, tear at his hair, or finish the open bottle of wine in a quest for temporary oblivion, he decided to put his restless energy into something more productive: cooking. He drove to Dante's, and over the remainder of the long dark night, made two pans of lasagna and an olive oil cake, finishing up with a batch of almond cookies just as the sun started to peek over Brooklyn's rooftops. After dealing with the early morning deliveries and sundry other tasks, he packed up the food and drove over to his brother's. Theresa was at work, Dominica and Little Ant were at school, and baby Angelica was in her playpen, hypnotized by *Teletubbies*. It was just him, Michael, and a boatload of food in the kitchen.

Michael was still exulting over the tin trays spread out on the table. "This is fantastic. I won't have to worry about making dinner for the kids for over a week."

"You can't give them lasagna every night. They'll get sick of it."

"Not my kids. Especially if I pay them to eat it."

"Great parenting skills." Anthony pulled out a kitchen chair and sat down. His lack of sleep was finally catching up with him; he felt as though he'd been lightly pummeled, his brain muzzy. "You got a beer or anything?"

"Anthony, it's eight o'clock in the morning."

"Oh. Right." He grabbed an almond cookie, still warm, and popped it in his mouth.

Michael pulled up the chair next to him. "What's going on?"

"I blew it with Vivi."

"Whoa, hold on. You and Vivi finally . . . ?"Anthony nodded glumly as Michael gave him a thumbs up. "Way to go, stud!"

Anthony made a disgusted face. "Do you always have to reduce everything to locker room clichés?"

"Excuse *me*. Perhaps if my only sibling bothered to tell me what was going on in his life, I wouldn't blurt out the first thing that comes to my head. And P.S., I haven't had my second cup of coffee yet, so I beg your friggin' indulgence." Michael reached for a cookie. "What happened, Ant?"

"Things were going fine, right? We had this passionate reunion when she got back from France, great sex, yadda yadda yadda. Then she wants to know when I'm going to take off my ring, which was okay, because it was time, you know?"

"Makes sense," Michael agreed, hand snaking toward the plate of cookies for another.

"So I have her over to my place last night. We're drinking wine, talking, having a nice time. We start fooling around on the couch, and decide to move the action upstairs. No problem. I scoop her up, we go upstairs. Except when we get there"—Anthony felt his guts knot— "I can't do it."

Michael chuckled knowingly. "It happens to all of us from time to time. Get some Viagra."

"Let me finish, *cidrule*. I couldn't even open the bedroom door. It was like there was this invisible forcefield preventing me from going in there." Anthony shook his head in remembered humiliation.

Michael pondered this. "Were you . . . was it . . . did you feel like you were being disloyal to Ang or something?"

"No." Anthony was resolute. "It's nothing to do with

that." He struggled to find the right words. "It was fear. If I love her, I can lose her. Something could happen to her, and I don't know, I just couldn't go there. I was totally paralyzed." He rubbed his forehead. "I've been having these dreams."

"What dreams?"

"I'm watching the news, and there's a building on fire. And it turns out to be a plane that's crashed into Vivi's apartment building."

Michael recoiled. "Jesus, Ant. That's horrible."

"No shit. I've been obsessed with something happening to Vivi. I insisted on driving her home because all I could think was that some crazy cabbie could lose control of the car and she could be killed. I know it sounds nuts."

Michael's gaze was reassuring. "Nothing's going to happen to Vivi, Anthony."

"How the hell do you know?"

"I don't know!" Michael threw up his hands in despair. "What was it Ma used to say? 'I could get killed by a bus crossing the street'? She was right! What are you gonna do, not love Vivi because you're afraid she might die on you like Angie?"

Anthony put his head in his hands. "I know. I know it's crazy."

"It is crazy. Angie worked a dangerous job, Anthony. There was always a chance of her getting killed. Vivi's job doesn't carry the same danger. She's no more at risk than the rest of us."

"I know," Anthony repeated. Everything his brother was saying was true. But the fear of loss still haunted him.

"What did Vivi do when you couldn't take her into the bedroom?" Michael prodded gently.

Feeling miserable, Anthony lifted his head. "What do you think she did? She totally freaked out! She thinks I haven't gotten over Ang. She called it 'a haunted house.' "

"Have you told her about your dreams?"

"No," Anthony muttered.

"Well, then go tell her, you *gavone*. What's the big deal? You talk about it, you fix it, you roll merrily along."

"She was pretty upset, Mike. She wouldn't even talk to me in the car."

"She was hurt, that's all. Go talk to her and it'll all be fine."

"And what if it's not? What if she tells me to take a hike? What if I keep having those dreams?"

"If the dreams keep up, then go talk to a shrink. If she tells you to take a hike, then, I don't know what to say." Michael shrugged apologetically.

"I knew I shouldn't have let this happen! I stood right in this kitchen and told you that lightning couldn't strike twice, that I was perfectly fine with my life as it was. But no! You encouraged me to go for Vivi! And now look where I am! I take a second chance and it blows up in my face!"

"Oh, so now it's my fault you're a mental case?" Michael bellowed.

"I don't need this shit." Anthony went to stand up but Michael gripped his arm.

"I'm sorry. I didn't mean it that way."

Anthony glared at him. "How did you mean it?"

"Look," said Michael, dipping into a half-eaten bowl of Cap'n Crunch, "I know how difficult this stuff can be. Remember what happened to Theresa? The assault?"

"Kind of."

"Well, it messed her up good. And she wanted a relationship with me, but she was afraid. Every time we'd come close to getting something going, this fear of hers would raise its ugly head and *badaboom*! It was back to a broken heart and blue balls for Mikey D."

"What finally happened?" asked Anthony, impatient for the punch line.

"I was patient, and she worked it all out, and now here

we are—three kids, a messy house, but happy as hell. It's not rocket science, Ant. Tell her your fears, ask her to be patient, and I guarantee you, things are going to be fine."

"You really think?" Anthony wanted to believe him, but he couldn't seem to make the leap of faith.

"I *know*."

"Okay." Anthony stood up. "I'll take your word for it."

"Where you going? The restaurant?"

"Where do you think?"

"Hang on a minute." Michael jumped up from his chair. "I'll just get Angel dressed and we'll come with you."

"To do what? Mike, I don't want you hanging around. How many times do I have to tell you that?"

Michael scowled, but he didn't protest.

"How's that job hunt for Insane Lorraine going, by the way? You find anything for her yet?"

"Very funny."

Anthony folded his arms across his chest. "I wasn't kidding. Either you find her another job or she's out on her crazy ass."

"Yeah, yeah, yeah," Michael muttered, loading the lasagna trays into the fridge. His expression was unhappy as he glanced back over his shoulder at Anthony. "You really don't want me to come with you?"

Anthony just stared at him.

"Suit yourself," Michael said with a frown. He closed the fridge. "Thanks for the chow."

"Reheat it for an hour at three fifty." Anthony hugged his brother. "Thanks for the advice."

"Spill your guts and ask for patience," Michael repeated with a hearty pat on the back. "That's all you've got to do."

Chapter 21

Vivi wasn't surprised when her buzzer sounded in the late afternoon and it was Anthony asking if he could come upstairs. She knew he'd come to see her eventually.

Vivi buzzed him up, her eyes doing a quick sweep of her small flat. The place was tidy, but there were no mouth-watering smells coming from her kitchen to smooth what she anticipated would be an awkward conversation, no coffee percolating on the stove. For the past three days, Vivi had found herself unable to cook a thing. She'd spent her time brooding, sometimes crying, and deciding whether or not to confide in Natalie. It turned out to be a moot point; for three days she'd been leaving messages for Natalie to discuss business, but to no avail.

The knock on her door was so quiet she almost missed it. She felt strangely calm. Even so, she found herself fumbling to open the locks. Seeing Anthony's face, a surge of heat came to her cheeks as the scene of her rejection replayed in her mind. She'd turned the incident over and over so many times, viewing it through the prism of her complicated, sometimes conflicting emotions. Standing here now, she felt as confused as ever.

"Come in," she said, ushering Anthony inside.

He looked as though he hadn't been sleeping. Dark circles ringed his big brown eyes, and there was a washed-out look to his face. Still, he exuded an odd confidence that bordered on the resolute.

Vivi gestured toward the couch. "Please, sit."

"Do you mind if I take off my coat?"

"Of course. How stupid of me." Embarrassed by her lack of hospitality, she took his jacket. It smelled of impending snow mixed with the scent of his cologne. A lump formed in Vivi's throat. How could she feel a flash of humiliation just a second before, only to have it followed by this, a welling up of sentimentality? Tamping down her emotions, she hung up his coat, following him over to the couch.

"How did you know I'd be here?"

"Wild guess." Anthony craned his neck, looking behind him toward the kitchen. "Any chance of getting a cup of coffee?"

Vivi looked at him with disbelief. "You're a real piece of wood, aren't you? I thought you hated my coffee."

"I'll endure it for now. And it's 'piece of work,' not 'piece of wood.' " His voice was affectionate.

"Fine," Vivi harrumphed, "I'll make coffee. I'll be right back."

She made her way to the kitchen, relieved when he didn't follow her. She needed a few seconds alone to try to sort her feelings out. When she returned with their coffee, she found him leafing through her notebook filled with handwritten recipes, as he'd done the first time he was ever here.

"There it is, the famous pineapple flan recipe," he noted ruefully, closing the book.

Vivi handed him his coffee and sat down on the couch a small distance from him. Anthony noticed.

"Need a buffer zone, huh?"

Vivi pushed a stray, ticklish hair off her face. "I guess. I don't know."

"We need to talk."

"What's there to say?" Unwelcome tears sprang to Vivi's eyes. "You're still in love with your dead wife."

Anthony's gaze was unwavering. "You're wrong. I'm in love with you."

"I gave myself to you and you humiliated me."

"Don't you think I was humiliated?"

Vivi said nothing.

"Please, let me explain."

Vivi nodded reluctantly.

"I never would have brought you home if I was still pining for Ang. I never would have brought you upstairs to make love to you if I was still pining for Ang. What happened *was* related to her, but not in the way you think."

"I'm not an idiot," Vivi replied, her voice cracking. "You couldn't bear to bring another woman into the sacred bedroom the two of you shared."

"*No.* I couldn't bear to take that final step of making you completely mine, because if I did, if we were really, truly together, that would mean"—pain clouded his tired eyes—"I could lose you the same way I lost Angie."

"So it was better to get my hopes up and then change your mind?"

"You're not hearing me." Anthony scratched at the pale band of skin where his wedding ring used to be. "I had no idea that was going to happen. I got to the doorway, and one minute, all I could think about was the two of us laughing, making love in my bed; the next, I'm imagining getting a phone call telling me something has happened to you and that you're dead. And I just couldn't go there."

Vivi remained silent.

There was an embarrassed hunch to his shoulders as he clasped his coffee mug between his hands. "I've been having these nightmares about you dying, Vivi. About a plane crashing into this building. Is it rational? No. But feelings never are, are they?"

Vivi peered down into her mug. It all seemed to make sense. Yet there was something inside that kept her from murmuring, "My poor darling, your nightmares, if only I knew . . ." or even just "Yes, I understand." What had seemed so easy now seemed complicated.

"Say something," Anthony urged, a subtext of despair in his voice.

"I don't know what to say. To you this all makes sense, but in my heart, it still feels very confusing. I was so certain, and now . . ." She shook her head, words failing her.

He moved closer to her on the couch. "I need your patience and understanding, Vivi. That's all. We hit a bump, and now we're talking it out like two rational adults—or rather, one rational adult and one irrational French woman."

"You're not funny."

"*Bella*," Anthony pleaded, "we're just getting started. Don't pull the plug before we've even begun."

Vivi twisted away from him. "I need time to think, Anthony."

She heard him put down his mug of coffee on the table, feeling the shift of weight as he rose from the couch. She turned back to him. "Anthony?"

His gaze was loving. "Take as long as you need, Vivi. You were patient with me, now it's my turn to be patient with you. Just know I love you."

Tears returned to her eyes. "Thank you. Please don't think I'm being deliberately difficult or coy."

"I would never think that." He leaned over, planting a soft kiss on her forehead. "Enjoy the rest of your day. You know where to find me."

"*Vivi!*"

The sound of a female voice coming from behind startled

Vivi until she turned to see Anthony's sister-in-law, Theresa, hurrying toward her in a beautiful fur coat, a big, friendly smile on her face. Vivi was seized with the fear Theresa might want to discuss Anthony. "Hello, Theresa." Vivi kissed each of her cheeks. "It's wonderful to see you."

"You, too." Theresa gestured up the street toward Vivi's. "Things seem to be coming along nicely."

"Yes."

"That's why I'm glad I caught you. I don't mean to be pushy or anything, but you really need to start thinking about the publicity campaign."

"Well, what have you and Natalie talked about?" Vivi asked, relieved not to be discussing Anthony. She bundled her silk scarf tighter around her neck. It was much colder out than she had thought.

Theresa looked perplexed. "What?"

"Natalie has been in touch with you, yes?"

"Vivi, I haven't heard from your sister at all."

Vivi stared back at her. "Are you certain? She said she called."

"Our receptionist would have passed the message on to me."

Vivi felt the sidewalk beneath her feet beginning to splinter. "Is it possible the message was passed on to your partner?"

"No, Janna would have told me. We discuss everything."

"Merde," Vivi hissed under her breath. As soon as Vivi was done with Theresa, she needed to take the subway into New York and pay a visit to her half sister. She didn't care if she had to yank her out of bed by her hair, or sit in the lobby all day waiting for her, she needed to know what was going on *now*.

Theresa was gazing at her with concern. "Vivi?"

"I'm sorry," Vivi apologized, trying to corral her thoughts. "It's just that Natalie told me she'd been in touch with you, and now I'm confused. I must have misunderstood."

"Don't look so distressed; we still have time." Theresa pulled a BlackBerry out of her coat pocket. "You and I could set up a meeting right now, if you'd like."

Vivi's mind was like a Tilt-A-Whirl, thoughts spinning within thoughts. "Let me talk to my sister first and try to clear up this confusion, if you don't mind."

"Of course I don't mind."

Vivi forced herself to ask the question she wasn't sure she wanted the answer to. "How much do you charge a month for publicity?"

"Our normal retainer is three thousand dollars a month," said Theresa, pocketing her BlackBerry, "but since you're a friend"—Theresa smiled broadly—"I'll only charge you twenty five hundred."

Vivi did the math. It was January, Vivi's opened in May, five months, a little over twelve thousand dollars. That seemed affordable. Then again, what did she know about what was reasonable or not? She was dancing blind.

Theresa pressed her card into Vivi's hand. "I know I already gave you one of these, but just in case." She stamped her feet. "*Madonn'*, it's cold. I should get going."

"It was nice to see you, Theresa." Actually, it had just ruined her morning, but that wasn't Theresa's fault.

"You, too. Michael and I were talking about having you and Anthony over for dinner soon. I'll call."

Vivi forced a smile. "That would be nice." She relaxed a little; Theresa knew nothing of her and Anthony's spoiled evening.

Theresa pointed up the street. "I'm actually on my way to Dante's to drop something off for Anthony before work. Want to come along?"

"I can't. I'm on my way to see my sister." *To confront her. Possibly to pummel her and beg her to tell me the damn truth once and for all.*

"Give her my regards," said Theresa with a cheery wave,

setting off in the direction of the restaurant. She stopped and turned. "Call soon to set something up."

"We will," Vivi promised, hoping the queasy feeling in her stomach didn't show on her face.

She watched Theresa recede into the distance, wondering if she should have walked with her just to be sociable. Ah, well. The determined set of Theresa's shoulders coupled with her brisk walk told Vivi this wasn't a social visit she was paying to Anthony. Besides, Vivi had something to deal with that couldn't be put off any longer.

"*I'm so sorry* I haven't called, Vivi. Things happened so fast."

Seeing Natalie's exhausted face, Vivi felt a twinge of guilt over her original plan to ambush her at home, demanding to know the truth about contacting FM PR. Vivi had spent the entire subway ride into the city sparring with Natalie in her mind. By the time she actually arrived at Natalie's apartment, she was afraid Natalie would open the front door and Vivi, unable to control herself, would spring at her like a wild animal. But one look at Natalie's pale, drawn face—a face Vivi had never, ever seen without makeup—burned off all the anger Vivi had been harboring.

Natalie had been called back to Paris because her mother was ill.

"A small heart attack." Natalie sighed, rubbing the back of her neck. "I didn't know they came in sizes."

"You look exhausted. Why don't you sit down and I'll fix you something to eat?"

"I'm not hungry, but I would love a cup of tea. Hot, with lots of milk and sugar." She sat, then bounced back up again. "I can't sit still. I'm coming to the kitchen with you."

"Suit yourself."

Vivi prepared the tea, shocked when she opened the refrigerator to fetch some milk, only to find the small carton hidden amongst tins of caviar and bottles of Veuve Clic-quot. Anger bubbled up in her again, her fingers curling tightly around the refrigerator handle as she remembered Natalie trying to talk her into inexpensive furniture and decor for the bistro.

She pulled out the milk, tipping it into Natalie's cup. She longed to yell at her, but how could she? The poor woman's mother had just had a heart attack. What kind of a bitch would yell at someone in that situation? No; they would make small talk, gossip about this and that, and then, when Natalie seemed a bit more relaxed, Vivi would casually slip in a question about contacting Theresa.

"I'm surprised you're back," Vivi said, noticing how spotlessly clean the kitchen was. She wondered how much Natalie was paying her cleaning lady to mop these floors, or polish these marble counters to such a high sheen. Money was just pouring out . . .

"I wanted to stay longer," Natalie was saying, "but my mother put up such a fuss that, in the end, I did what she wanted. My aunt came up from Toulouse to look after her. That'll be a comedy! My aunt will try to tell my mother what to do, and my mother will tell her to go straight to hell." Natalie sighed, looking at Vivi worriedly. "Are all families this mad?"

"It certainly seems that way." Vivi sipped from the tall glass of the water she'd poured for herself. "Do the doctors know what caused the heart attack?"

"Bitterness, if you ask me." She looked uncomfortable. "My mother claims it's a broken heart."

"Perhaps so," Vivi said stiffly. Though if that were the case, her own mother would have died hours after her father.

"She's just being dramatic," said Natalie. "As always."

Vivi didn't know what to say. She didn't know Natalie's mother; perhaps she truly was cold and critical the way Na-talie was always making her out to be. Even so, Natalie's lack of sympathy baffled her; that is, until it dawned on Vivi that, once again, Natalie was doing her "devil may care" act to cover up her feelings.

"You must have been terrified of losing her," said Vivi.

Natalie tucked her hair behind her ear, staring down at the floor for a long moment. "Yes."

"Is there anything I can do?"

Natalie lifted her head. "Raise Papa from the dead?"

"I would if I could, believe me." Pain wrapped itself around Vivi's heart like a pair of murderous hands and squeezed. What she wouldn't give for one more day, one more hour, in her father's presence.

She followed Natalie back out into the sumptuous living room, momentarily enchanted by the sight of the tiny snowflakes twirling past the solid wall of windows. How bad could life be, really, when a quiet snow was falling?

"How is Anthony?" Natalie asked. The interest in her voice drew Vivi's eyes away from the window. She fought her impulse to spill her guts simply because there was another woman present to confide in, and with restraint answered, "Wonderful."

"I'm glad. It's nice one of us is having a romance."

"Maybe you will soon, too. I'm going to invite Quinn O'Brien to the opening of Vivi's."

"Not if you ever want me to speak to you again, you're not!"

"We need as many people there as possible, people who will give us good reviews and spread the word. Speaking of which"—Vivi took another small sip of water to steady herself—"I ran into Theresa Dante this morning."

"Oh, yes?" Natalie replied distractedly.

"She said she hasn't heard from you at all about doing PR for Vivi's. Not a word."

"Yes, I meant to speak with you about that." Natalie dabbed delicately at her mouth with the back of her hand.

"I was speaking with Bernard Rousseau about it, and he thought we should go with a bigger-name firm."

Vivi blinked, confused. "When did you discuss this with Bernard?"

"A while back," said Natalie. "I can't remember the exact date."

"And you're just telling me now?"

Natalie looked at her crossly. "I've had a lot on my mind, Vivi, in case you haven't noticed!"

"I know that, but this is something we discussed before your mother got ill."

"I'm sorry. It slipped my mind."

"I'm sorry, too," Vivi said curtly. Any idiot could see things were not right. "Is there something you're not telling me, *cherie*? Something I need to know?"

"Of course not," Natalie scoffed. "Honestly, you're going to add wrinkles to your face with all this worrying!"

That's because I'm worrying for two, Vivi thought. "Natalie, this puts me in a very awkward position. Theresa thinks her firm is going to be doing the PR, and frankly, I want them to do it. She did the PR for Dante's. She knows the area. She knows the New York food world."

"So does the firm Bernard recommended," Natalie said haughtily.

Vivi was back to feeling incredulous. "How could you speak with him without consulting me first?"

"It was a casual conversation, Vivi. I mentioned you were hounding me about the PR and he asked whom we were planning to use. When I told him, he recommended someone else."

"Well, who are they? What's their name? How much do they charge? Do they specialize in restaurant PR? Have you bothered to call *them*?"

Natalie was staring at her like she was raving. "Vivi, calm down."

"No! I'm sorry, but something isn't adding up here. I feel it in my bones. I see it, too. You try to talk me into cheaper goods for the store, and then I open your fridge and see stacks and stacks of caviar!"

"So what?" Natalie challenged. "As long as there's enough money to cover anything, what business is it of yours what I spend the rest on?"

"*Is* there enough?"

Natalie's face began turning red. "Of course there is! Are you calling me a liar?"

"No, of course not! I just—"

"What? You just what? Want me to account for every dollar I spend? Let's remember who's putting up most of the money here, shall we?"

"How could I possibly forget? You remind me at every turn," Vivi snapped. "I thought we were partners. I guess I was wrong."

"We are partners!" Natalie insisted.

"Then keep me abreast of what you're doing in regard to the bistro!" Vivi practically yelled. "Theresa said we should be putting the PR together *now*! Did you know that?"

"I'll call the firm Bernard recommended right away," Natalie promised.

"Now. Call them now, right here, right in front of me."

Natalie's lips pressed together primly. "I don't have the information with me just now. But I can assure you—"

"Enough." Vivi finished her water and stood up. "I can't listen to this right now. I don't have the energy."

"Vivi?" Natalie sounded nervous.

"Now that, then this," Vivi muttered to herself. "I should have stayed in Avignon. I never should have come to Paris. Or come here. Everyone around me—*foufou*!"

"Vivi." Natalie rose from the couch, following at a safe distance as Vivi strode toward the door. "Are you mad at me?"

"Mad at you?" Vivi repeated with an incredulous laugh.

"I don't know what the word is for what I'm feeling. Truly."

Natalie wrung her hands. "Please don't be mad at me. I don't think I could bear it." She opened her mouth as if to speak then quickly closed it.

"What?"

"Nothing." Natalie seemed to shrink as her voice got small. "Just promise you're not mad at me. Please."

"I'm through with making promises," said Vivi, walking out the door.

Chapter 22

"Quit lickin' the spatula, Little Ant."

Anthony tried not to sound like too much of a scold. Three days earlier, Theresa had come bursting into the restaurant in a tizzy on her way to work, a flyer for the hockey team's bake sale in her hand. She didn't have time to bake, and Little Ant, a purist after Anthony's own heart, balked at the idea of getting store-bought cupcakes and passing them off as homemade. Little Ant wanted to bake them himself, but his father vehemently nixed the idea. That's when Theresa came up with the idea of begging Anthony to do it on his day off. In reality, having Little Ant do it while Anthony "supervised." In other words, deceive Michael. Speaking of whom . . .

"Where does your dad think you are?" Anthony asked Little Ant.

"At my friend Julio's soccer game."

Anthony pulled another batch of cupcakes out of the oven. Little Ant had insisted on baking five trays of twelve. Anthony thought that was way too much, but he indulged the kid anyway. If they all sold, great. If they didn't, Little Ant would go home with a ton of leftovers that Anthony *knew* his brother would devour, even if it meant Michael was initially clueless that his son baked them.

Out of the corner of his eye, Anthony saw Little Ant moving to take another lick of frosting off the spatula, but he halted when he felt Anthony watching him. Pouting, he pressed the spatula to a naked cupcake instead.

Anthony addressed his nephew. "It's not good that we're lying to him, you know. He's gonna be really pissed if he finds out."

Little Ant lowered his eyes. "I know. But he wouldn't let me bake! He said the adults are supposed to make the stuff for the bake sale, not the kids."

Anthony snorted. "So why isn't he baking them?" The thought of Michael in the kitchen amused him immensely. The guy could barely turn on the stove without setting the house on fire.

"He said you'd do a better job."

Lazy bastard, Anthony thought.

"He's not home today, anyway," Little Ant continued, frosting the next cupcake with the precision and care of an artist. That was one thing Anthony had already inculcated in him: never rush. Never do a half-assed job.

"No? Where is he?"

"In the city. At Met Gar." Little Ant swiped a taste of frosting when he thought his uncle wasn't looking, but Anthony let it go. "He's been going in a lot."

"Yeah? What for?"

Little Ant shrugged. "I dunno. Nana Falconetti watches us. She says we live in a sty."

Anthony chuckled, tipping the most recent batch of cupcakes from the baking tin onto the cooling rack. It figured Theresa's mother would say that; the woman had never met a vacuum cleaner she didn't like. He pondered Mikey spending time at Met Gar. It wasn't good. Anthony had this pathetic image of him hovering around the locker room, boring rookies with tales of his glory days in the NHL, driving the new assistant captain, Jason Mitchell, crazy. He wondered if Theresa knew.

Still watching Little Ant out of the corner of his eye, Anthony put the final tray of cupcakes in the oven. "You had a chance to test out any of those recipes in those cookbooks I gave you?"

"I haven't had time," Little Ant mumbled, head down. "With homework and hockey and stuff."

"How's hockey going?"

"It blows," Little Ant confessed miserably. "But Dad won't let me quit. He says I have to finish the season."

"Jesus, Mary, and Saint Joseph," Anthony muttered under his breath. Michael was a great father, but Little Ant and hockey was his blind spot, the one area where Mikey put his own needs ahead of that of his kid. Anthony didn't know what else he could do to help. He'd talked to him. Theresa had talked to him. But the stubborn SOB wouldn't budge.

"Your dad doesn't mean to be a hard-ass, you know," said Anthony, hating the idea of Little Ant resenting his father. "He just loves hockey so much, he wants you to love it, too. He wants it to be something you guys can share."

Little Ant huffed with frustration. "I'd rather cook." He frosted the last cupcake before him, then reached for another on the cooling rack. Anthony gently nudged his hand away.

"Still too warm. Wait until they're room temperature. Otherwise, the frosting will melt right off."

Little Ant nodded solemnly as if Anthony had just imparted the wisdom of the ages to him. Sometimes the kid reminded him so much of himself it made him laugh. So unnecessarily solemn. So intense, too, though that was something both he and Michael shared, a trait inherited from their father.

"Anthony?"

He glanced behind him. Vivi's head was peeking around the back door of the kitchen, her expression tentative. "Can I come in?"

"Of course," he said in his best neutral voice, not wanting to sound anxious, or anticipatory, or hopeful, even though he was all those things and then some. "You can meet my nephew, Little Ant."

Vivi smiled warmly at the boy as she entered the kitchen and approached the cupcake assembly table. Anthony's heart was in his throat. Not a minute had gone by since they'd last spoken that he didn't fantasize about her coming to him and sweetly cupping his cheek, telling him she understood everything and was more than willing to be patient. That she was smiling was a good omen.

"Hello." Vivi extended a friendly hand to Little Ant. "I'm Vivi."

Little Ant, ever the gentleman, wiped his hands on his apron before taking Vivi's hand, prompting an approving nod from his uncle. "I'm Anthony Dante," he said.

"Two Anthony Dantes!" Vivi exclaimed. "I'm not sure the world is ready for that!"

"Are you Uncle Ant's girlfriend?"

Vivi's smile turned uncertain. "Little Ant," Anthony rebuked in a low voice, "that's personal stuff."

Vivi reached for the large silver bowl of frosting and tipped it toward her, inspecting the contents. "This looks a little runny," she said to Anthony. "Too much milk, maybe?"

"It's fine, Vivi." He rolled his eyes at Little Ant as if to say, "Women!" then stifled a laugh when Little Ant nodded knowingly.

"Vivi and I are going to talk in the dining room," Anthony told his nephew. "You keep frosting. Call me when that last batch in the oven is done so I can take it out. I don't want you burning yourself." He glanced surreptitiously at Vivi, trying to read her face as he escorted her out

into the empty dining room. Her expression was impassive,
almost blank. So much for omens.

Vivi knew it was silly, but she hated that Anthony picked
a table beneath an autographed picture of a stern looking
cardinal. The holy man's gaze was disapproving and harsh,
and she found it hard not to take it personally. She was already feeling exposed, and the empty dining room didn't
help. They'd sat alone in here like this before, but today it
felt different. Today it *was* different.

Vivi saw no point in delaying what she'd come to say. "I
think we should just be friends," she told Anthony quietly.
How was it that hours of agonizing could be distilled into
one devastating sentence? She was ashamed of the way her
eyes were darting to and fro, but she couldn't help it. She
couldn't bear to look at the face of a man upon whom she
was inflicting pain.

At first Anthony said nothing. But then Vivi saw the hard
look that came to his face, an expression designed to cam-
ouflage anger, and she knew he wasn't going to meekly accept her decision. Whatever made her expect he would?

"Care to explain?" Anthony asked caustically.

"I can't do it," said Vivi, still not quite looking at him.
"You're a wonderful man. A good man. But I must have
been mad, thinking I could have a relationship while trying
to get a new life for myself off the ground. I can't, especially when the other person thinks he has released his
past, but he really hasn't."

Anthony's stare grew more intense. She could feel it
on her face, needle sharp. "You know what? Up until now, I
found your stubbornness admirable, even adorable. But I'm
beginning to realize what a liability it can be. Did you listen to *anything* I said the other day, Vivi?"

"Of course I did!"

"Then what do I need to do to convince you that I love *you*? I took off my wedding ring. I explained why I've been so obsessed with your safety. I asked for your patience. Saying you can't open the restaurant and have a relationship at the same time is bullshit. It's just an excuse."

"You don't understand." Vivi half hoped his nephew would emerge from the kitchen to interrupt them so she didn't have to continue. "I don't have the time to help you wrestle your demons while making sure my restaurant is a success."

"You mean you don't want to make the time."

Vivi sat very still. "Yes," she admitted. "I don't want to make the time."

"Well, that's a whole different issue, then, isn't it?"

"Anthony, listen to me." She moved to take his hand, but his cold stare froze her and she retreated. "Do you remember, before Christmas, when you told me you didn't want to commit until you were sure you could give me the attention I deserved? Well, this is what I'm telling you now: that I can't give you the attention *you* deserve. I wish with all my heart that I had figured this out before we got intimate. But I didn't, and for that I'm very, very sorry. I hate that I'm hurting you. But isn't it better that I had this realization now, before we became more deeply involved?"

Anthony was glaring at her. "Can I ask you a question?"

"Certainly."

"Would we even be having this conversation if we'd gone into my bedroom and made love?"

Vivi swallowed. "I don't know."

"Yeah? Well, I do. The answer is no, we wouldn't. Everything would be great."

"You don't know that. There were many obstacles we were ignoring." She hesitated. "My sister pointed this out to me early on. She said not to get involved with a widower, especially one who happens to be my competition.

She said a relationship would divert my attention from the thing I should be devoting my every waking hour to: Vivi's. And she was right."

"Your sister?" Anthony exploded. "You're taking advice from your goddamn sister? What the hell does she know about you, me, or even having a decent relationship? She's a snooty bitch who was banging her boss!"

Heat swam to Vivi's face.

"Uncle Ant? The cupcakes are done."

Vivi breathed a sigh of relief as Anthony whipped his head around to look at his nephew, who was hovering now by the kitchen doors.

"I'll be there in a minute," Anthony barked, turning back around to face Vivi. "I'm sorry for what I said about your sister," he said, though his expression indicated otherwise.

"I should go," Vivi said, rising from her chair. Anthony stood, too. The cardinal on the wall stared at her with disapproval.

"Yeah, you probably should."

Vivi stood on the sidewalk outside Dante's, breathing hard, waiting for the churning feeling in her stomach to pass.

The sound of loud voices cut into her trance. She looked across the street. The DiDinato brothers had the door to Vivi's propped open with a brick and were breezing inside as if they owned the place, each carrying a large bag of tools.

"What are you doing?" Vivi shouted at them as she darted across the street, nearly colliding with a car in the process.

"What do you think we're doing?" Joey DiDinato replied with a sneer. "We're dismantling the place. You don't pay us, we tear it down."

"What?"

"You heard him," said Ricky, putting down his tool bag and lighting up a cigarette.

Vivi put her hand to the nearest wall to steady herself. "But we signed a contract. We gave you a deposit."

"That's right," said Joey, "and the contract said the balance would be paid when we were done with the work. Well, we finished up two months ago, and you haven't given us jack shit. So wave bye-bye to your pretty brick walls and the rest of it."

Vivi felt her knees buckling. "My sister—my sister said she paid you—"

"Your sister is a liar."

"Maybe you misplaced the check?"

Joey stared at her in disbelief. "We're businessmen, lady, not morons. Okay?"

Vivi's head was swimming. "I'm sorry, I didn't mean to insult you, I'm just"—she swallowed hard—"very confused."

"No need to be confused," Joey said in a saccharine voice. "It's simple: no money, no bistro. We'd take you to court, but experience has taught us that this is a bit more effective when it comes to recovering payment."

Vivi couldn't suppress a glare. "Threatening people, you mean?"

"Yeah."

"You can't do this," said Vivi, panic rising.

Ricky puffed hard on his cigarette. "You gonna stop us?"

"Wait, please, just wait a minute," she pleaded. Ricky ignored her, taking a pry bar out of his bag with which he pointed to a section of wooden wainscoting. "Start with this, Joe?"

"Yeah."

"Please." Vivi darted toward him, desperation mounting. "Can't we work out some kind of compromise?"

"We want our money," said Ricky, tossing the cigarette from his mouth and crushing it beneath the toe of his work boot.

"You'll get it. I promise."

Joey shook his head. "Do you know how many times in my life I've heard that?" Suddenly he changed moods, actually looking sorry for her. "Look, you seem like a really nice person, but business is business, you know what I mean?"

Vivi looked around wildly. "What if I got someone to tell you I was good for the money? Someone you know and trust?"

"Who?" Joey asked.

"Anthony Dante."

Ricky peered at her suspiciously but said nothing.

"If I get Anthony to come here and tell you I'm good for the money, will you give me a few more days to pay you? Please?"

The brothers exchanged wary glances. "Maybe," said Joey.

"Oh, God." Vivi put her hand to her chest, breathless with relief. "Oh, thank you. Thank you. I'll be right back."

"You're rushing," *Anthony* said sharply to Little Ant as they finished frosting the last of the cupcakes. What had started out as a day of spending quality time with his nephew had turned into one of those days where he felt like punching a wall.

He couldn't believe Vivi had short-circuited on him like that. All those months of them flirting, dancing around one another, taking their time, making sure—and for *what*? So she could schiz out on him and decide that she had to throw everything she had into Vivi's? It didn't make sense. And all that crap about him not being over Angie? Total smoke-screen. She knew he was over Ang. She knew he would never play with her heart that way, would never have proceeded if there was even any question of him not being ready for a relationship. The damn sister was behind this somehow. He knew it.

He watched his nephew frost the last cupcake before the kid threw him an imploring look about licking the remaining frosting from the bowl. "Go ahead." The plan was to leave the cupcakes here, and Theresa would swing by and pick them up tomorrow before Little Ant's game. He was walking to one of the sinks to wash the last of the cupcake tins when out of the corner of his eye, at the back door, he saw Vivi.

"I need your help." There was true desperation in her voice as she hurried toward him.

Anthony was immediately concerned. "What's wrong?"

"It's the DiDinato brothers." Her bottom lip was quivering as she held back tears. "They're threatening to take everything away. They said Natalie hasn't paid them. They said if you come and stand up for me, they'll give me a few days to write a check. Will you come with me?"

He pointed a warning finger at his nephew. "I know exactly how many cupcakes we frosted, so don't even think about stuffing your face while I'm gone, my man."

Little Ant's face fell. "But . . ."

"You can have *one*."

Little Ant's face brightened. "Cool."

Vivi was practically charging toward the back door. "Slow down," Anthony called after her. "Nothing's going to happen, apart from you maybe getting hit by a car."

Vivi slowed, waiting for him to catch up. "I can't believe Natalie did this to me. She said she paid." She glanced up at Anthony guiltily. "I know this is asking a lot of you, especially after—"

"Save it, okay? Later, after everything is straightened out, I'll make you feel bad. But for now, let's just get this put right."

Vivi nodded gratefully, her expression still anxious as they crossed the street. Anthony had grown up with the DiDinatos; there was no way they'd be so quick to destroy work they'd busted their balls to complete. This was their time-tested money extracting technique. It was thuggish, but it usually worked.

"Hey, guys." Anthony's smile was broad and friendly as he stepped over the threshold to Vivi's, greeting the two brothers with whom he'd spent hours shooting hoops in his youth.

"Hey, Ant." Shovel-faced Joey gave him a hug. "Long time, no see."

"Whose fault is that? You know where the restaurant is."

Both Joey and Ricky chuckled. Because of Vivi, who had her arms locked tight around her waist and was rocking back and forth on her feet expectantly, the atmosphere felt slightly strained. Anthony wished she'd stand still; she was making him feel jittery. He tried to convey that to her with a look, but it didn't register. Vivi kept rocking away, waiting for him to say something. To save her.

"I hear there's a problem?" Anthony asked casually.

"She and the sister owe us some money," said Joey. "They're two months overdue."

"How much?"

The brothers exchanged looks, as if uncertain whether to reveal the sum. Anthony was puzzled. They couldn't think *that* was unethical when they were standing here ready to dismantle Vivi's like two thugs, could they? That would be too hilarious.

"Fifteen K," Joey finally volunteered.

Vivi inhaled sharply, whimpering under her breath. The color was draining from her face so quickly Anthony was afraid she might faint. Without blinking an eye, he pulled out his wallet, extracting the one blank check from his business account that he always kept with him in case of emergencies.

"You got a pen?" he asked Ricky.

Vivi flew at him, pulling on his arm. "You can't do this! I can't let you do this!"

Anthony put his hands on her shoulders and looked

directly into her eyes. "This gets it over with here and now, all right? Suppose your sister gives you the runaround? What are you going to do then? Who would you rather worry about paying back? Them or me? I know you're good for it, Vivi." He took the pen from Joey. "DiDinato Brothers Construction, right?"

Joey nodded. Anthony wrote the check and handed it over to them.

Vivi began to cry. "I don't know what to say."

" 'Thank you' might be good for a start," Anthony said gently. But Vivi didn't move. Her eyes were frantically combing his face, searching, waiting for some hitch, some catch, some rider he would attach to his largesse. When it became clear none was forthcoming, she lapsed into complete incredulity and asked, "Why did you do this?"

"This is what friends do for each other, Vivi. They help each other out." Shamefaced, Vivi looked away from him. "I'm gonna go back across the street now. But if I were you, I'd find your sister, pronto, and find out what the hell is going on."

Chapter 23

"*Have you been* waiting long?"

Vivi said nothing as Natalie stopped short at the sight of her sitting in the lobby. As a matter of fact, Vivi *had* been waiting a long time—three and a half hours to be exact. Over that time, Vivi had gone to get coffee, read the *New York Times* from front to back, and gracefully ignored the occasional disapproving glances from the doorman, who clearly doubted she was in any way related to, or waiting for, Miss Natalie Bocuse, the same Miss Bocuse who had just breezed through the door laden with designer shopping bags of all shapes and sizes. Seeing Natalie's bags, imagining what might be inside and how much things might have cost, Vivi had a fantasy of setting them on fire and just walking away. Instead she focused all her attention on being civil toward her sister, at least until they were behind closed doors.

Natalie came closer, lowering the larger bags to the foyer's marble floor. "Vivi? Is something wrong? Why didn't you call my cell?"

"What we have to talk about can't be discussed on the phone."

Vivi watched with interest the rapid transformation taking place on Natalie's face, from rich girl returned from doing some fabulous shopping to "Oh, *merde*" alarm.

"Would you like me to help you with those?" Vivi offered, gesturing to the larger bags. Chanel, Louis Vuitton, Michael Kors—clearly Natalie hadn't been shopping for place settings for the bistro.

"You don't have to." Natalie picked up all the bags herself, gesturing for Vivi to follow her to the elevator. Vivi was glad when Natalie pushed the up button and the doors slid back immediately. Tension was mounting with each passing moment. Vivi noticed her sister's hand trembling slightly as she rummaged through her purse for her keys. Opening the door to her apartment, Natalie seemed to momentarily relax, perhaps thinking that now that she'd reached the shelter of her home, things would be fine. Vivi pitied her.

She followed Natalie inside, but when Natalie gestured for her to sit, Vivi refused. She pointed to the small village of bags Natalie had constructed on the floor by the door.

"Have fun?"

Natalie swallowed. "I bought you something."

"You're taking it back. You're taking it *all* back."

Her eyes tracked Natalie as she gingerly moved toward the sofa. "I know what you're thinking," Natalie began nervously.

"No, you do not. But we'll get to that in due time. For now, the only thing I want from you is the truth, Natalie. Can you handle that? Or do you need to dash out and buy some with the money we're supposed to be spending on the restaurant?"

Natalie flinched as her eyes began filling. "Vivi, please."

"Please, nothing," said Vivi, exasperated. "Would you like to hear about the morning I had, while you were shopping?" She folded her arms across her chest. "First, I broke

up with my boyfriend." Natalie's lips parted in surprise.
"That's right, it's already over. That should make you
happy, eh, to know you were right in advising me to be cautious about him? At least now I can dedicate myself totally
to Vivi's, just the way you've been, right?"

"Vivi—"

"Let me speak." Vivi stood in front of her, strangely
gratified when Natalie pressed herself hard against the
back of the couch as if she thought Vivi might strike her. *I
wish I could,* Vivi thought. *I wish I was one of those people
capable of such things.* But she wasn't, and so she'd have
to make her point using the only weapon she had: words.
"After wounding Anthony, I left Dante's, and guess who I
saw? The DiDinato brothers. They'd broken into Vivi's and
were about to begin tearing the place apart. Do you know
why?" Natalie moved to cover her face with her hands, but
Vivi slapped them away. "*No!* You look at me when I'm
talking!"

Natalie's breath hitched. "I—I'm sorry."

"Answer my question. Why do you think the DiDinatos
were there?"

"I don't know."

"Stop lying!" Vivi shouted. "Please, please, stop lying!"

"I don't know how!" Natalie shouted back. "I swear,
Vivi, I don't." She covered her face with her hands and began to cry.

"Oh, dear God." Vivi eyes traveled to the high cathedral
ceiling as she let out a disgusted breath. "Do you want to
know what a fool I am? I'm actually feeling sorry for you
right now. Can you believe that?"

Natalie uncovered her face. "Vivi, please. I'll tell you
everything you want to know. I swear."

"You lied about paying the DiDinatos, didn't you?"

Natalie nodded fearfully.

"And you never contacted Theresa."

"No," Natalie whispered.

"How about the restaurant furniture? The artwork? The flatware? Linens? The flooring? Did you take care of *any* of that?"

"No."

"No." Vivi felt as though an invisible strap were tightening around her body, biting into her flesh. "So what you're saying is, you've been spending *all* the money we were to use for Vivi's on yourself."

"Yes."

"How much is left, Natalie?" Vivi demanded. "And don't you dare lie!"

Natalie looked at Vivi with watery eyes. "None. We're in debt." She broke down in sobs.

The room fell into such a profound silence that Vivi swore she could hear both their hearts pounding. *We're in debt.* Vivi had the image of herself standing on a castle rampart, the structure slowly crumbling beneath her. She leaned over, hands on her knees, head hanging down a moment as she breathed deeply. When she lifted her head, she couldn't stop staring at the shopping bags by the door.

"If we're in debt, then explain how you could be so selfish—or maybe the word I'm looking for is stupid—as to keep shopping"

"I have a problem with money, Vivi." Natalie reached for a tissue on the coffee table, winding it round and round her index finger until it began to disintegrate. "I thought I'd be able to control it this time."

"This time? You've done this before?" The strap was tightening. Vivi's flesh was going to begin bleeding at any second.

"Yes." Natalie couldn't look at her. "In the past, when I'd run into trouble, Papa would always bail me out."

"Oh, God." Vivi felt her legs go rubbery. Fearful she might collapse—or worse, faint—she made her way to the couch to sit down.

"Papa would help me," Natalie repeated, "but this

time"—tears began coursing down Natalie's cheeks again—"he isn't here."

"What about your mother?" Vivi asked tersely. "Did she even have a heart attack? Or did you just fly home to ask her for money?"

"She had a heart attack!" Natalie cried. "Of course she did!"

"Why should I believe you? Why should I believe one word that comes out of your mouth?" Vivi cradled her head in her hands. "You can't imagine how much I hate you right now," she said through gritted teeth.

"Don't say that!"

Vivi's head snapped up. "How could you do this to me, Natalie? I've been dreaming my whole life of owning my own restaurant, and what do you do? You throw away the money from Papa as if it's nothing!" Tears began blurring her eyes. "You know what your problem is? You've never had to worry about money in your life, so you treat it carelessly, as if worrying about how much one is spending is just so bourgeois!

"I trusted you. You're my half sister. I told myself it was all right that you held the money because you knew more about it than I did, and all would be well. I allowed you to treat me as if I were lesser sometimes because I'm not the 'legitimate' daughter! But you know what, *cherie*? Papa loved me and my *maman* more than he ever loved you and your miserable mother!"

"You think I don't know that?" Natalie choked out. "Momma and I, we were Papa's 'show' family, the ones he trotted out in public to make him look good. At first I hated it, but then I grew to accept it—even like it—because it meant I would at least get to spend time with him. He was always working, Vivi. Do you understand that? He was *always working*, and when he did take time off to relax, he went to see you and your mother!"

Natalie swiped a hand across her eyes to stem her

swelling tears. "Do you know how desperate I was for his attention? As a politician's daughter, I was always expected to look good. It was the only thing he ever complimented me on. Not what I could *do,* but how I *looked.* Because it reflected back on him.

"Don't you see? Each time I got myself into trouble, I got his attention. And every time he made the problem go away, it showed he loved me." Natalie's face crumpled with shame. "I never wanted to hurt you. I could feel myself getting deeper in trouble, but I just couldn't stop, and the deeper I fell, the more frantic I became to hide it from you. Because I knew, eventually, we'd reach this moment when you'd tell me you hate me and I'd have to face the fact that this time I'd wrecked not only my life, but yours, and there's no Papa to help us out!"

She began to wail, an eerie keening sound that made Vivi's hair stand up on end. It was the sound of someone in pure anguish. Vivi froze, unsure of what to do. But then she slid across the couch, taking Natalie in her arms. She was still angry, but Natalie needed to be reassured that she was still loved. Vivi held on to Natalie for dear life, and together they wept until there was no pain left to extinguish, and no tears left to cry.

"N-now what?" Natalie asked, hiccupping to a stop.

Vivi dragged her eyes to her sister's face. She was exhausted. All talked out. All cried out. Please, she longed to say, just let me curl up on your couch and sleep, waking months from now when this is all behind us. But that would be postponing the inevitable, and if there was anything Vivi hated, it was prolonging agony—not only her own but someone else's. It was better they face their problem here and now.

"I still have some questions," she said.

Natalie timidly nodded her acquiescence.

"When did you plan to tell me what was going on?"

"I don't know." Natalie looked desperate. "I kept thinking, 'I'll find a way out of this, I know I will.' But I haven't."

Vivi shook her head. "I don't understand. Overspending as a way to get Papa's attention and help made sense when he was alive. But he's gone, Natalie."

Natalie flushed with shame, her voice dropping low. "It's an addiction, Vivi. It doesn't matter whether he's gone or not. I reach a tipping point in my brain and I just can't stop. Half the time I'm buying things I don't even need or want."

"You shouldn't tell me things like that," Vivi replied coolly, "unless you want me to go back to hating you." Natalie looked stricken until Vivi rolled her eyes. "That was a *joke*."

Vivi rose slowly, testing her legs. They felt solid now, able to bear the weight of her continuing conversation with Natalie. "You need to get help."

"I know that."

"I'm serious, Natalie. We're going to take care of this as soon as we can." Though how they would pay for it was something Vivi hadn't figured out yet.

She touched Natalie's arm. "What I said before? About Papa not loving you and your mother? I didn't mean it. I was just angry."

"I know that." Natalie was saying one thing, but Vivi could tell she was glad Vivi had apologized. Vivi wouldn't be able to live with herself if she hadn't. It was a terrible thing to say to someone.

"Are you hungry?" Natalie asked meekly.

"Starving."

"I'll fix us something to eat." Natalie jumped off the couch, scampering toward the kitchen. But halfway there, she halted. "Vivi?"

"Yes?"

Natalie ducked her head. "All I have is champagne and caviar."

Vivi stared at her a moment, then burst out laughing. No

money, in debt, but they'd come up with plan B over champagne and caviar. It was perfect.

"I love champagne," she said with a sigh.

Natalie returned with a tray of champagne, caviar, and crackers. Vivi had never been a big fan of caviar. When she was younger, she thought it proof of her lack of sophistication, but over the years she'd made peace with the realization that it just wasn't for her. Even so, she spread some on a cracker and bit into it, hunger trumping taste buds. She followed it with a sip of Veuve Clicquot, which tasted gorgeous, the way she imagined the perfect spring day might taste if you could bottle it. Her spirits revived a little. She would figure a way out of this. She knew she would.

Natalie took a sip of champagne and sighed. A look of peace had returned to her features, something Vivi hadn't seen in a long time. "I'm so relieved to have finally confessed to you. But at the same time—"

"Don't," Vivi cut in gently. "Let's just try to focus on salvaging things." She had one last question to ask her sister, an important one. She steeled herself with another sip of champagne. "How much in debt are we?"

Natalie swallowed. "I spent all the hundred thousand that Papa gave me, and twenty thousand more that—that we don't have—using credit cards."

"Oh, Christ." Vivi's pressed a hand against her chest. She used to think her *grandmaman* was being melodramatic when she'd get bad news and her hand would immediately fly to the space over her heart, or when she'd start fanning herself as if she might topple over. But now Vivi understood that it was instinct; shock really *could* induce a galloping heartbeat that made you feel as if you might have a coronary. Vivi breathed deep and tried to calm down. One hundred twenty thousand plus Anthony's fifteen thousand meant they were one hundred and thirty-five thousand dollars in debt. Oh, God. Her heartbeat surged again, and she took a gulp of champagne to ease it. There, that was better.

"Vivi?"

"I'm all right. I was just doing figures in my head. We owe more than that—Anthony loaned us fifteen thousand dollars this morning to pay off the DiDinatos."

"Thugs," Natalie sniffed.

Vivi's jaw dropped. "We owed them money, Natalie! They are not 'thugs' for wanting to be paid for their hard work!"

Natalie hung her head. "You're right." She reached for her champagne flute and took a tiny sip. "May I ask you a question?"

"Of course."

"Why did you break up with Anthony Dante? I thought"—she seemed to be searching for the right word—"he was what you wanted."

"I decided I couldn't handle the complication right now." A dry shard of cracker stuck painfully to the back of Vivi's throat, and she swallowed hard, struck by how close she was to fighting back tears. "I need to focus on the restaurant."

"It's the dead wife, isn't it?" Natalie asked with a knowing expression.

"Yes," Vivi admitted, feeling a sharp jab to her heart, "but it's also me. I realized I can't have it all, Natalie, at least not at once. Maybe later, once the bistro is up and running, I can learn to juggle, and by then, Anthony will have sorted his feelings out. But for now, I have to concentrate solely on Vivi's." *If there's even going to be a Vivi's,* she thought but didn't say.

Natalie looked surprised. "He lent you money even though you broke up with him?"

"Yes." A sense of shame washed over Vivi as she recalled it. "He's a good person. A much better person than I am, clearly."

"I don't know about that," Natalie replied with a loving squeeze to Vivi's shoulder. The peaceful expression on her face faded, replaced by a more appropriate look of unease. "So what are we going to do?"

Vivi briskly wiped cracker crumbs off her lap and turned to her. "We're going to call Bernard Rousseau."

Vivi hadn't seen Bernard Rousseau since the cook-off at Dante's, and she'd forgotten how handsome he was: tall, with regal bearing and thick black hair graying slightly at the temples, contributing to his wise and sophisticated look. He seemed delighted that Vivi and Natalie had asked him to meet them for dinner, though the choice of where to eat had been agonizing. Vivi wanted someplace quiet yet not too expensive, with delicious food and good service. She settled upon Zusi's, where she and Anthony had dined with Michael and Theresa.

Walking into the restaurant, she felt a small sting of melancholy as she remembered that night and how close she felt to Anthony, the laughter the four of them shared still ringing in her ears. It seemed so long ago, when in reality it was only a matter of months. Funny how quickly things could change. She sent the melancholia packing, since she was its author. If she was missing Anthony, she had no one to blame but herself.

Natalie had looked horrified when Vivi told her they were taking the subway to the restaurant, but in the end she complied, knowing she had no room for complaint. Vivi wondered if bringing Natalie with her was a bad idea, but she had no choice—Natalie knew Bernard well, and she didn't. As long as Natalie didn't break down and admit that she'd thrown away their inheritance and then some, all would be well, or so Vivi hoped. She had no problem securing a restaurant reservation: all she had to say was that it was for one of the French ambassadors to the UN, and—*voila!*—a free table magically appeared at the exact time Vivi had asked for. Position indeed had its privileges.

Bernard rose as Vivi and Natalie approached the table, his expression warm and open. *"Bonjour,"* he said, kissing each of them on both cheeks. "It's not often I get to dine with two beautiful women."

Vivi and her sister accepted the compliment with graceful smiles, though inside, doubts were jockeying for position in Vivi's mind. What if he turned them down? Was this the right action to take? Would he be insulted that the first time they socialized together, she'd be making a loan request?

Bernard was taking in the restaurant as he pulled their chairs out for them, head bobbing with approving nods. "Very nice. I've heard about this place. It's new, yes?"

"Yes," said Vivi. "The food is very good."

Natalie looked at her, surprised. "You've eaten here?"

"Yes."

"When?"

What does it matter? Vivi wanted to snap. "With our neighbor, Anthony."

"Huh," said Natalie. She seemed insulted. Vivi ignored it.

Bernard insisted on ordering the wine. *God forbid a man doesn't order the wine,* Vivi thought, but both he and Natalie let Vivi order the food, since she'd been here before. Their meal was pleasant as they discussed life in America, life back in Paris, and the plans for the restaurant. Vivi found herself slightly envious of Natalie's easy rapport with Bernard, especially since it was Vivi who was going to be asking for the loan. Were she here alone with Bernard, she had no doubt he would think her a pest as she plied him with questions about her father: How long did you know him? What was he like at work? When did you know about my mother and me? Did he talk about us to you? Have you ever met my mother? What is Natalie's mother really like? Did she love him?

Eventually, dessert was ordered: apples braised in butter orange sauce for Vivi (too much butter, not enough sauce), chocolate mousse for Bernard, a slice of apple pie for Natalie. Vivi had watched Natalie with amazement the entire evening. She didn't seem in the least nervous or worried. In fact, at several points over the course of their meal, she had flashed Vivi a small enigmatic smile, which Vivi wasn't sure how to interpret. Did it mean, "Don't worry, there won't be any problem"? Or "Ask now, *now*, while he's laughing at my joke or interested in your cooking"? Vivi hadn't a clue.

They lingered over dessert, Bernard ordering some port as a final digestif. Vivi could understand how he and her father could be friends; both were witty, warm, and solicitous. She wondered if he had ever married, or if he was divorced. She would ask Natalie after dinner.

"This has been wonderful," Bernard sighed, looking with affection at both of them. "I'm so glad you invited me out this evening."

Vivi looked down, brushing her fingertips back and forth against the lip of the table. "I hope you still feel that way after you hear what I have to say."

She felt Natalie stiffen beside her, and looked up. Bernard's head was cocked quizzically to one side as he asked, "What is it, Vivi?"

Vivi took a deep breath. "Natalie and I need your help. The expense of opening up the bistro is far more than we anticipated. I know this is very sudden, and most certainly unexpected, but we wanted to ask if we might borrow two hundred thousand dollars from you." The floodgates in her brain opened. "Before you say anything, know this: I'm not talking about doing business on a handshake. I'm talking about a real loan, with signatures and a monthly payment schedule. I'm hoping that within a year—"

"Vivi." Bernard's voice was almost chastising. "Don't get yourself all worked up. Of course I will give you the loan."

Vivi fought the urge to vault over the table and kiss him.

"I don't know how to thank you, Bernard." She blinked back tears. "If you'd said no—"

"But I didn't." He topped off her glass of port.

Natalie reached for Vivi's hand beneath the starched white tablecloth, clutching it hard. "Are you certain?" Vivi asked.

"Of course. I owe my diplomatic career to your father. We can go to my attorney and make the arrangements tomorrow if you'd like."

Vivi swallowed. "That would be wonderful."

Dinner finished on a quiet note. Bernard insisted on paying, but Vivi refused. She and Natalie had asked him to dinner, not the other way around. So what if she had to put it on her credit card? Vivi still had some pride. She was not going to let this man save her dream *and* foot the bill for the meal where they'd asked him for money.

They took their time strolling out of the restaurant, Natalie slightly ahead of them, talking to someone on her cell phone.

"You know," said Bernard as he held the restaurant door open for them to leave, "there is a way you can thank me."

"What's that?"

"Have dinner with me Friday night. You're a chef, Vivi. You must know which restaurants in the city are best. Pick one, and we'll go."

Vivi glanced quickly at Natalie. She seemed not to have heard. She looked back at Bernard. Was he asking her on a date? She couldn't tell. He was wearing the same confident expression he'd worn all evening. She thought it over. Accepting his invitation would give her a chance to prove to him she was serious about Vivi's, and she could ask him about her father without worrying about possibly offending Natalie.

She said yes.

Chapter 24

"Feel free to kiss my feet. I got Lorraine a job."

Anthony glared at Michael and continued chopping fresh basil for that day's batch of gravy. Michael had just breezed into the restaurant with little Angelica in tow, despite Anthony's repeated requests he not do that anymore.

Michael sighed, readjusting Angelica in her baby seat, which was perched on one of the long, stainless steel tables in the kitchen. "Don't you want to know where she'll be working?"

"You can tell me right after you fire her."

Michael frowned. "Can't you—"

"No way," Anthony cut in. "You hired her, you fire her."

"But you're her boss."

"You're her boss, too, Mister 'Half Owner.'"

Michael scowled, sidling up to Anthony at the cutting board. "I got her a job at one of the concession stands at Met Gar."

"I guess that explains why you've been going there all the time."

Michael narrowed his eyes. "What?"

Idiota, Anthony cursed himself. He wasn't supposed to know that little nugget of info that had come his way courtesy of Little Ant.

"What?" Anthony asked back innocently.

"How do you know I've been going in to Met Gar?" Michael asked, popping a sprig of basil in his mouth.

Anthony played it cool. "Little Ant told me on the phone the other day."

"You talk to Little Ant on the phone?"

"Yeah. Sometimes we e-mail, too. What are you, in the FBI?"

"No." Michael looked peevish. "I just didn't know, that's all."

"Is that why you've been going into the city?" Anthony tried again. "Trying to rustle something up for Lorraine?"

"Yeah," Michael said evasively, picking up another sprig and studying it as he rolled it between his fingers. His eyes cut to Anthony's, then looked away. *Madonn'*, thought Anthony, *he really is hanging at Met Gar with his ex-teammates, strolling endlessly up and down Memory Lane.*

Anthony plucked the sole remaining basil sprig from his brother's hand, chopped it, then tipped the whole cutting board of chopped basil into the stockpot bubbling on the stove. "Suppose Lorraine doesn't want to jackass into the city for work?"

"Why wouldn't she? People do it all the time."

"Some people don't like it. And she's, um, what's the word I'm looking for here?" Anthony snapped his fingers as if trying to recall something. "Oh yeah, *insane*."

"She'll take it," Michael replied in an overconfident voice that really grated Anthony's cheese. "I got her a full-time job without her even having to be interviewed. She'll be so grateful she won't be able to turn me down."

"You better be right," Anthony warned, "because if I lock up here one night and she comes flying out of the shadows at me wanting to play Adam and Eve, you're a dead man."

"Have a little faith."

Anthony frowned. "I'm not too big on that word these days." He leaned over to kiss the tip of his niece's nose on his way to fetch some onions to chop. He could feel Michael watching him.

"What? Vivi?"

"Oh yeah."

Michael looked concerned as Anthony walked back toward him. "It didn't go well? Your talk?"

"It didn't go at all. I did just what you advised: laid it on the line, was honest with her, asked her to be patient, told her I loved her, told her about the dreams, yadda yadda yadda."

Michael picked up a wooden spoon nearby and began stirring the sauce. "And—?"

"She thinks I'm not over Ang. Also, she can't handle a relationship right now while she's trying to get ready to open the restaurant. It was like, 'Oops! Sorry to fuck up your life, but I've changed my mind! *Au revoir*, Pasta Boy!'" Anthony peeled the spoon from his brother's fingers, putting it down on the steel counter with a resounding *clap*. "I told you I never should have gone for it, Mike. My life was perfectly fine as it was."

"No, it wasn't. You were a moody, pain-in-the-ass workaholic, just like you were before Angie entered the picture and showed you there was more to life."

Anthony wasn't listening. "I should have known this would happen. All chefs are fucking nuts. I of all people should know."

"Listen to me." Michael's voice was firm. "Maybe she's just feeling overwhelmed right now, okay? Why don't you wait until Vivi's opens, and then see what happens?"

"And what?" Anthony snapped. "Go crawling across the street and say, 'Think you can handle a relationship now?' No way. She doesn't want me? Fine. Whatever. Have a nice life, *Mademoiselle* Nutball."

"You don't really mean that. You're just pissed right now."

"You're damn right I'm pissed," said Anthony, slicing through an onion with unusual vehemence. He shook the knife in his hand at his brother. "The sister's got something to do with this, I'm telling you right now."

"What do you mean?"

"I don't know. It's just a feeling I have. I've always gotten the sense the sister thought she was better than us, you know?" Michael frowned, but nodded in agreement. "Maybe she talked Vivi out of seeing me."

"Vivi doesn't strike me as the type who can be talked out of things."

Anthony gave a dry little laugh. "That's true." He shook his head. "I don't get it. I really don't." He reached for another onion, not sure whom he was speaking to—himself, his brother, or both. "Maybe it's better this way, who knows? God knows she's got an opinion about everything. It probably would have driven me up the wall after a while."

"Just wait until her restaurant opens and see what happens," Michael repeated.

If it opens, Anthony thought to himself. Should he tell his brother about his impromptu loan to Vivi? Probably not. His brother was the biggest gossip this side of Rush and Molloy.

Ever since he'd written the check for Vivi, he'd been plagued with worry. What the hell was going on? First rule of business: never get behind in your payments. How could Vivi and her sister not know that? What would have happened if he hadn't been there to give her the money, or vouch for her? Would Joey and Ricky really have wrecked the place?

At least he'd been able to help out. It gave him the

chance to prove to her, in a very concrete way, that he wasn't just your average, run-of-the-mill guy. What other man would lend fifteen thousand dollars to the woman who'd just trampled on his heart? Either he was extraordinarily kind or he was a total patsy. Shaking his head one final time, he concentrated on chopping onions. Maybe his generosity would shock some sense back into her. You never knew.

More wine?

Vivi smiled politely at Bernard Rousseau's question and shook her head no, fearful a third glass would make her tipsy. At his request, she had selected what she knew to be one of the finest French restaurants in the city: Rene's, named after its famous chef, Rene Bruel, a culinary superstar in France. Vivi had never had the privilege of cooking under him, but her friend Marcelle from Le Cordon Bleu had, and he said it was grueling yet rewarding, as was the case with all great chefs. Vivi had been in some beautiful, expensive restaurants in her day, but Rene's, with its soaring ceilings, luxurious tapestries, and intimate, individual dining niches, took her breath away. The china, glassware, and flatware were delicate and exquisite. She wasn't surprised to learn they were custom designed for the restaurant.

She'd almost choked on her wine when the famous Rene himself stopped by the table, and Bernard told him that Vivi, too, was a chef who was opening a restaurant. "Is that so?" Rene asked politely, eyes narrowed in competition. Vivi hastily pointed out that it was a small bistro in Brooklyn, nothing like the magnificent Rene's. She then invoked the name Marcelle. Rene's expression softened, and together the three of them spoke volubly about fine food, fine wine, the importance of setting, and atmosphere. By the time Rene said his *adieus* and moved on to greet the diners at the next table, Vivi was surprised to find herself feeling a little homesick after speaking in her native tongue of the things she loved.

For the first time in she didn't know how long—years, perhaps—Vivi couldn't come up with a single critique of the meal she'd been served. Her appetizer, tomato tarte tatin, had been delicious enough to make her swoon; her entrée, pancetta-wrapped tuna with potato puree, filled her with envy. By the time dessert rolled around and she took her first bite of spiced Bosc pear with Vietnamese cinnamon, she wasn't sure if her ego could take the beating. Everything was flawless.

"He's amazing," Vivi sighed with a touch of envy as Chef Rene moved out of sight. She looked at Bernard. "Wasn't the food incredible?"

Bernard smiled companionably. "Fantastic. We'll have to come here again."

Vivi hesitated. "Yes," she said faintly, not sure how else to respond. She finished her last few drops of wine, more than certain that she'd had enough. "Bernard, I don't want to sound like a broken record, but I can't thank you enough for the loan."

"*Pffttt,*" he said with a dismissive wave of the hand. "Enough about that. It's the least I could do for Stephan Bocuse's daughter."

"Daughters," Vivi corrected.

"No, daughter." Bernard's gaze was unnervingly direct. "I know Natalie got you into this mess, Vivi. I know because I remember her doing the same thing in Paris."

Vivi blinked hard. "Papa told you about Natalie?"

"Oh, yes. It was his heartache. That, and not being able to see you and your mother enough."

Vivi's head was spinning. "Bernard . . . you have to excuse my ignorance . . . but there's so much I don't know about my father."

"Perhaps I can help you out. What would you like to know?"

Vivi's hands twisted in her lap. "Was he easy to work with?"

"Very easy," Bernard assured her.

Vivi swallowed hard, trying to keep at bay all the questions on her tongue competing for voice. "And you knew about my mother and me?" she continued.

"Of course."

"What—what did he say about my mother?"

"That he loved her, of course." He paused, thinking hard. "He said she was very free-spirited. Unconventional, if you will. He liked that."

Vivi laughed in recognition. "She is!" Tell me more, she wanted to beg, like a child clamoring for the fairy tale being told them to never end. "Can you remember anything he said about me?"

Bernard's smile was gentle. "He was very proud of you, Vivi. He used to talk about you all the time, what a wonderful cook you were. What a wonderful young woman you were."

"He did?" Vivi looked away, trying to stay tears. "Thank you for telling me that. It means a lot to me to know he said that to other people, not just me."

"What else can I tell you?" Bernard teased. "His shoe size? How many *Gauloises* he smoked a day?"

Vivi affected pique. "I already know the answers to those questions, thank you very much." She hesitated, unsure whether she really wanted to hear the answer to her next question. But she had to know. "Do you know if he loved Natalie's mother?"

Bernard began fiddling with his teaspoon. "He did love her," he said carefully, "but that does not mean he was in love with her. He was in love with your mother, Vivi."

Vivi inhaled raggedly as a tear splashed onto the tablecloth. "Then why didn't he leave his wife? Why didn't—"

"Shhh." Bernard came around to her side of the table and sat down beside her, patting her shoulder. "You know why. You know how important appearances are for a man of his station. You know leaving his wife for his mistress would have been frowned upon. Besides, both your parents were perfectly happy with their arrangement, so don't fret."

"Well, no one bothered to ask me if *I* was happy with it, did they?" Her chest ached from holding back a cry of frustration. "I would have given anything for him to be there full time, not part time! Didn't he know that?"

"It was what it was, Vivi. Would it comfort you to know that Natalie and her mother only had him part time, too, since his work was so demanding?"

"That's what Natalie said."

"There, you see? It's the truth. He loved both you girls very much, Vivi. More importantly, he loved both of you the same."

"Natalie's mother." Interesting, wasn't it, how she could never bring herself to refer to her as her papa's "wife"? "Is she mean and horrible? Natalie always says she is."

Bernard furrowed his brows. "She's . . . dramatic."

"Very diplomatically put," Vivi said with a sniffle.

"Appropriate, is it not, since I'm a diplomat?"

"Yes." She turned away, blowing her nose discreetly into a tissue. "I'm sorry about this. There are just so many things about my father I don't know. So many things about Natalie I don't know."

"You can ask me anything you want about your father anytime. As for Natalie, I can tell you she was thrilled when she found out she had a half sister—after the shock died down, of course. She loves you, Vivi. But she's troubled. This money problem . . ." He shook his head.

"She's getting help."

"Yes, I know, but I still think it was unfair of her not to tell you about her history."

Vivi paused thoughtfully. "Shame can make people

keep secrets about all sorts of things. When I was young, I used to lie and tell people my father was a traveling salesman, always on the road. It was better than 'I was born out of wedlock and my father has a wife and child in Paris.'" She thought about Natalie. "No, I can see why she hid it from me. I'm not pleased about it, but I understand it."

Bernard gave a small whistle of admiration. "You're very generous, Vivi. Someone else might want nothing to do with her."

"She's my half sister, Bernard. And she's the only person I have in this country."

"That's not true. You have me." He leaned over, softly kissing her lips. Vivi stiffened. "You're a very attractive woman, Vivi," he murmured, touching a hand to her cheek.

"I'm flattered you think so." Vivi could feel herself bristling. "Is this why you loaned me the money?"

"I can assure you, *mademoiselle*, I meant nothing untoward," he declared. "I have no expectations of you beyond paying back the loan."

Vivi regarded him fiercely. "I swear we will repay the loan, Bernard."

"I know that." Bernard looked contrite. "I'm very, very sorry if I offended you, Vivi. You have my solemn promise that I will never make a pass at you again, okay?" Vivi nodded in relief as Bernard extended a hand for her to shake. "Friends?"

"Friends," Vivi agreed. She could not tell Natalie about this. Natalie would think she was insane. After all, Bernard was smart, rich, good-looking, powerful, and *French*—all the necessary ingredients for Natalie's dream man. She wondered if Natalie had ever pursued him, or vice versa. It was not a question she could ever imagine asking either one of them.

Bernard returned to his seat across the table from her, his mouth tilted into a sentimental little grin.

"What?" Vivi asked suspiciously.

"Nothing. You just remind me of your father, that's all."

"How's that?"

"Painfully blunt."

Vivi lifted a brow. "Not rude?"

"Perhaps a little," Bernard allowed with a small chuckle. "But we're French, aren't we supposed to be rude?"

Vivi laughed, slightly giddy over being compared to her father. Her mother always told her they shared many of the same traits, but she herself had a hard time seeing it when they were all together. Plus, she assumed *maman* was simply biased. To have the similarities confirmed by someone impartial was wonderful.

Vivi put her elbow on the table, resting her chin in her palm. "So, what else do my father and I have in common?" She had to keep an eye on herself; she could easily keep Bernard here for hours, asking him questions.

"I may not know you as well as I'd like, but I can already see that you share his drive and determination. That's why I didn't think twice about loaning you the money. I know your bistro is going to succeed."

Vivi removed her chin from her palm and sat up a little straighter. "Thank you so much, Bernard. I promise, I won't take your generosity for granted. I'll give you an account of where every single penny is being spent."

"There's no need. We'll set up a payment schedule, and that's enough." Vivi moved to pick up the bill, but he snatched it up before she got the chance. "*I* asked you to dinner, *I* pay. Agreed?"

Vivi sighed, seeing no alternative. "Agreed."

"I hope I'll see you and your sister again before the restaurant's official opening."

"You will." She promised herself that no matter how busy things became, she would make time for the man who had come to the rescue—but only when she was with Natalie, never alone, like tonight. Life was complicated enough without having to worry about fending off an amorous, handsome, wealthy suitor. She felt flattered, but there was still a soft core within her that no man could touch—except one.

Chapter 25

There were any number of things he could be doing on his day off, Anthony thought. He could be jogging, trying to take off a few pasta-related pounds accruing around his midsection. He could be catching up on back issues of *Bon Appétit*. He could be checking out the new farmer's market that had opened in Park Slope. Instead, he was sitting in the empty dining room at Dante's, poring over menus and recipes, wondering whether it might be time to shake things up a bit. Pitiful.

The urge for change was driven by walking past Vivi's yesterday and noticing an artist had started the preliminary stenciling of what would become the bistro's logo on the front window. For the first time in months, it dawned on him that Vivi's wasn't just an abstract idea. An actual restaurant was going to be opening right across from his. Somehow, in the midst of falling in love with her, he'd forgotten that. Now that he remembered, a sense of unease rose up within him. He loved her, so of course he wanted her to succeed—but not too much. Certainly not at his expense.

There was a rap on the front door of Dante's, and he sighed heavily. It felt impossible to catch a moment's peace these days. There was a sign outside the restaurant clearly posting the hours—how hard was it for someone to realize they were closed? He decided to ignore the knock, returning instead to the debate he was having over whether it was time to drop the eggplant patties from the appetizer menu and reintroduce his mother's Italian wedding soup. It had been a big favorite a couple of years back, though Michael thought it "boring." Anthony frowned to himself. Why he took into account anything Mikey said relating to the restaurant was beyond him.

The knock sounded again, louder this time. Whoever was on the other side of the door knew he was in there. Seeing no other option, he reluctantly went to answer the door. He had a sick feeling it might be Insane Lorraine. If it was, no way was he going to let her inside. God only knows what might, or might not, be lurking beneath her coat.

He was surprised to find Vivi standing there, looking radiant, her nose and cheeks pink from the cold, her long blonde hair loose and topped with a bright ski cap. Her loveliness filled him with a hollow feeling. Seeing her was like seeing a ghost of happiness, something once solid but now spectral, here to haunt him. He ran through a catalog in his mind of all her contradictory behavior, her lame reasons for dumping him, and told himself that she was unstable. Not on the level of Insane Lorraine, but definitely a frontrunner in the category of "women who don't know what the hell they want, and don't care if they kill your spirit." So how come he wanted to beg her to give him a second chance?

"Hello," said Vivi. She pointed behind her at his SUV, the sole car in the parking lot. "Isn't today your day off?"

"You know chefs never really have a day off." He ushered her inside, watching as she stomped her snow-caked boots on the doormat, then peeled off her cap, shaking her hair free. The hollow feeling inside him took deeper root. To be this close to her and not be able to touch her was torment. Restless, he removed the pencil he'd stuck behind his ear when he went to open the door, tapping it against his open palm. "What's up?"

Vivi smiled proudly, reached into the oversized leather bag on her shoulder she called a purse, and pulled out a check, handing it to him. "The money I owe you," she said, as if it might need explaining. Her face was a mask of perfect humility. "I don't know how to thank you."

Surprised, Anthony studied the check a moment before folding it into the back pocket of his jeans. "That was fast."

It wasn't the response Vivi expected. Looking momentarily flustered, she said, "I didn't think it was right not to pay you back right away."

"What happened? With Natalie and the DiDinatos, I mean?" He contemplated inviting her to sit down, but didn't. He didn't want her to see that he was reassessing the menu. Knowing Vivi, she'd guess that it might have to do with her bistro, and he was in no mood to deal with an episode of culinary gloating.

Vivi shrugged. "She forgot to pay them. That's all."

"That's all?"

Vivi pressed her lips together. "Yes."

"Gimme a break, Vivi," said Anthony skeptically. "Only a idiot would forget to pay someone they contracted for major work, and Natalie is no idiot. What's the deal?"

The cheerful light in Vivi's eyes dimmed a little. "Not that it's any of your business, but Natalie wasn't managing our money very well."

"And now?"

"Now it's all fine."

"Meaning . . . ?"

"I don't think you need to know the details," Vivi huffed in exasperation.

"Really? Even after I saved your ass?"

Vivi's mouth folded into a small frown. "If you must know, Natalie got us into a bit of debt. But it's all solved now."

"Solved how?" Anthony smirked. "Did she hock some jewels or something?"

Vivi shot him a look of warning. "That's not nice."

"Neither was not paying the DiDinatos. You're lucky I was here to vouch for you."

"I know," she said humbly, her face softening. "The money problem is solved because a friend of our father's was generous enough to give us a loan."

"Who?" Anthony asked, even though he knew he sounded like an old biddy digging for gossip. But he couldn't help his curiosity. Vivi had never mentioned anything about a friend of her father's before.

"A lovely man named Bernard Rousseau. I don't know what we would have done without him."

Anthony felt a bite of jealousy. He didn't like her use of the word "lovely," or her seeming belief that if it weren't for this guy, they would have been screwed.

"How come you never mentioned him before?"

Vivi shrugged. "There was never any need to."

"Who is he, exactly?"

"He used to work with my father. They were old friends."

"And you know him well?"

"Well enough," Vivi said with a hint of defensiveness. "Natalie knows him better."

"Huh," Anthony grunted, wondering if she was telling the truth. He didn't trust the way this guy had just appeared on the scene to rescue Vivi and her sister. He was obviously French. Probably loaded, too.

Anthony put the pencil back behind his ear. "What does he do now?"

"He's a diplomat."

Definitely rich, definitely French, thought Anthony.

The glow returned to Vivi's face. "He was telling me the

other night how much I remind him of my father. It was wonderful."

"That's nice," Anthony forced himself to say, trying not to sound like a total curmudgeon.

Maybe something was up between Vivi and this guy. It would certainly explain her pulling a one eighty on him. Maybe she had to decide between the two of them, and Jacques Cousteau won.

"I gotta go," Anthony said abruptly.

"Oh." Vivi seemed taken aback. "All right, then." She put her hat back on her head. "Did you see across the street?" she asked eagerly. "They're going to be painting 'Vivi's' on the window soon."

"Yeah, I saw," said Anthony with a yawn. "What color is it going to be?"

"White."

"I hate to tell you, but that's not going to pop."

"Pop?"

"Stand out. Draw people's eye. No offense, but white's totally ho-hum." Which was fine with him, not that he'd ever tell her so.

Vivi scowled. "What would you suggest?"

"Red."

"Red?" she snorted. "It's a bistro, not a bordello."

"You know best," Anthony murmured under his breath sarcastically. He put the pencil back behind his ear. Vivi was glaring at him.

"You're just saying white is boring to upset me. Here we were, having a perfectly nice conversation, and you had to ruin it."

"How? By telling the truth? You asked what I thought and I told you. End of story."

Vivi's movements were tense as she buttoned up her coat and swung her leather satchel back up onto her shoulder. "You think you know everything! But you don't."

"Neither do you," Anthony said pointedly.

"I'm leaving now."

"You want a medal?"

"God, you're maddening!" Vivi spat. "Here I've been feeling badly about hurting you, and all along I'd forgotten what an arrogant jackass you are! I'm very grateful to you for helping to save my ham—"

"Bacon—"

"—but perhaps we should try to steer clear of each other as much as possible from now on."

"Whatever you want," Anthony said, affecting a bored voice. "You know your way out. See you around."

He walked away and heard the door slam behind him. For a moment, he actually felt a twinge of regret at being so sarcastic. He also felt mildly provoked by the casual yet oh-so-timely appearance of Bernard Rousseau. He didn't like the reverence in her voice when she talked about this guy, whoever he was. He intended to find out.

Anthony had never before set foot in the office of FM PR. He was impressed at how big and spare the space was, with three walls so white they blinded him. Entering the suite, he immediately felt himself being sized up by the small, prim man behind the reception desk, peering at him over the top of his frameless spectacles.

"Good morning," the man said, looking annoyed at having to close the issue of *GQ* in front of him. "I'm Terrence. May I help you?"

"I'm Theresa's brother-in-law, Anthony."

"Michael's brother." The man's mood seemed to lighten, though his stare was as coolly appraising as ever. "I can see the resemblance—though it looks to me like you should have been the hockey player, you're so . . . big." The man smiled coyly, and Anthony frowned. He'd never had a man flirt with him, and it disturbed him.

"Is Lady Dante expecting you?"

"No."

"An early morning surprise, then. That's nice. Let me buzz her."

While Terrence buzzed Theresa, Anthony studied one whole wall lined with photographs of some of Theresa and Janna's more famous clients: actors, athletes, businessmen, musicians, even a few politicians. Mikey was damn proud of the work Theresa did, and Anthony could see why. She and Janna had quite a client base, all of it hard earned.

Terrence hung up the phone with a sigh. "Her highness says to come on back to her office. It's the first door on the left. Be forewarned: they were out of cinnamon bagels at the deli this morning, so she's a bit cranky."

"I think I can handle it. Thanks."

Theresa was waiting for him behind her cluttered desk. He was surprised to see she hadn't put on any makeup yet. Her expression wasn't cranky; it was worried.

"Is something wrong?" she asked as Anthony closed the door behind him. "With Michael? With the kids?"

Anthony blinked. "No."

"Oh, thank God." Theresa heaved a sigh of relief as she pulled her long, curling hair behind her into a ponytail. "What brings you into the wilds of Manhattan, then?"

"I need your help with something."

"That works out well," said Theresa, "because I need your help with something, too."

She reached into the briefcase sitting on her desk and pulled out an elementary school worksheet, which she handed to him. "Write about your hero," the worksheet instructed across the top. Then, below it, in childish scrawl:

My hero, by Anthony Dante.

My hero is my uncle Anthony. He runs a restaurant and is a chef. I want to be a chef when I grow up. He shows me how to cook things and even the right way to frost cupcakes. His wife is dead but he's nice anyway. When I grow up I want to run the restaurant with him and be a good cook just like he is. The End.

"Shit," Anthony murmured, even though he was immensely moved.

"I found it when I was tidying up his room. He didn't show it to me or Michael."

Anthony unzipped his jacket. It was hotter than a sauna in there.

"I need you to talk to Michael," Theresa implored.

Anthony opened his mouth to protest but Theresa silenced him with pleading eyes. "He won't listen to me. It's 'a guy thing,' he says, this insane need of his to make Little Ant continue to play hockey. Last night he was talking about sending him to hockey camp over Easter break. Little Ant looked like he was going to burst into tears."

"Theresa, I've tried talking to him—"

"Try again," Theresa begged, looking like she was going to burst into tears herself. "He respects you, Anthony. You're his big brother. You can make him see reason. Pound it into him if you have to. Whatever it takes."

"Did you ever think of showing him the worksheet?"

"I think it might be more effective coming from you." There was a hiccup of emotion in her voice as she said, "I'm worried it would really hurt him. I'm really concerned about him. He's been hanging out at Met Gar."

"I know," said Anthony quietly.

She looked anguished. "Do you think he's having a nervous breakdown?"

"Nah, he was always nuts."

Theresa ignored the joke. "He won't talk to me about it." She began to weep. "Do you think he's having an affair?"

"With who? The girl who drives the Zamboni? Are you *insane*? He worships you, Theresa. He would never do that."

"Then why is he acting so furtive?" she lamented, reaching for a tissue with which to blow her nose.

"I don't know. I mean, I know some of the time at Met Gar was spent securing a job for that hostess we had working at the restaurant for a while."

"Thank God. What the hell were you thinking when you hired her, Anthony? I mean, honestly."

"What the hell was *I* thinking?" Anthony retorted. "Mikey's the one responsible for that brilliant idea! That's why I made him find her another job."

Theresa blew her nose again. "Wasn't she your high school girlfriend or something?" she asked vaguely.

Anthony drew himself up to his full height, insulted. "Excuse me? You think that's the best I could do in high school? You've got your facts mixed up, lady; she *wanted* to be my girlfriend."

"Speaking of which," Theresa ventured with a small, sympathetic wince, "I was really sorry to hear about you and Vivi."

"Yeah, well, that's why I'm here." Anthony rubbed his chin thoughtfully, trying to think of the best way to put what he wanted to say. "I need you to go on a fact-finding mission for me, since you've got a gazillion connections all over this city."

Theresa looked intrigued. "What?"

"I want you to find out about Bernard Rousseau. Apparently, he's some French diplomat or something."

"And I'm doing this because . . . ?"

"Because I think Vivi might have a thing going with him. The guy just appeared out of nowhere to help her and her sister out of a jam, and the way she talks about him, you'd think he was Napoleon."

"Maybe it's just gratitude, Ant," said Theresa, opening up a small mirror on her desk. She pulled one of her eyelids taut and began to line it.

"Or maybe something's up," Anthony grumbled, watching Theresa's careful ministrations to her face. He remembered the few times he'd watched Angie put on makeup. It seemed awfully complicated to him, all those creams and powders and colors. Unnecessary, too. Angie had looked gorgeous without her makeup. So did Vivi. In fact, so did Theresa. Did women really think makeup made them more attractive to men?

"What kind of money jam were they in?" Theresa asked, lining her other lid.

"I don't know all the details. I just know it was the sister's fault, until this guy showed up and—*voila!*—everything's back on track."

"Well, at least I know why Vivi looked at me like I was nuts when she asked about Natalie setting up a meeting, and I told her Natalie never even called here."

"She's a piece of work, the sister. Believe me."

"Not too much of one, I hope," said Theresa, picking up her lipstick. "She and Vivi are meeting with me on Friday to start discussing a PR campaign."

"Traitor."

Theresa looked up sharply. "Hey. Business is business."

"Yeah? And what happens if her business cuts into my business? Blood is thicker than water. Dante's could be Little Ant's one day. Don't forget that."

Theresa clucked her tongue. "I've said it before and I'll say it again: it'll be nice to have a little French bistro to go to. You're crazy to feel threatened. If anyone should be sweating a bit, it's Vivi. As you of all people should know"—she gave him a penetrating look—"people in Bensonhurst don't like things to change too much. But with the right PR, she should be able to flourish." She winked at him.

"Anyway," Anthony said, changing the subject, "if you're going to be meeting Vivi, find out what you can about

Rousseau. Use your intuition to get a sense of whether she's interested in this guy or not. Or seeing him."

Theresa frowned. "And what if she is? What will have been accomplished?"

"Then at least I'll have someone to blame."

Theresa put away her lipstick. "Can I give you a word of advice?"

Anthony squirmed in irritation. "Shoot."

"Just let it go for now. If her sister is really a whack like you said, then that must be sucking up a tremendous amount of Vivi's energy. Couple with that the stress of opening a new restaurant, and it's easy to understand why she feels a relationship might be too much right now."

"That's all fine and dandy, but her reasons for breaking up had less to do with Vivi's and more to do with some idea she pulled out of thin air that I'm not over Ang."

Theresa raised a perfectly penciled eyebrow. "Are you?"

"Jesus Christ." Anthony rubbed his hands over his face. *"Yes."*

"Are you still going to the cemetery?"

"No. I haven't been in months—only to lay a wreath at Christmas."

"Michael told me you were having dreams," Theresa said with concern.

"Yeah," Anthony admitted reluctantly, swearing he'd never speak to Mikey again as long as they both lived.

"Well, don't you think you should go talk to someone about that? It's not going to fix itself, you know."

Anthony's eyes grazed the carpet uncomfortably. Mikey had told him a shrink had helped Theresa immensely in the aftermath of her sexual assault by one of his former team-mates. Maybe he should talk to someone, and make sure he told Vivi about it. Where he was supposed to find the time for it, God only knows. But if it gave him something he could bring back to Vivi, something that said, "Look, I'm working to get over this crap you think I need to get over, because it's you that I want," it might impress her and make her reconsider her abrupt (and in his opinion, insane) decision to end things.

Fully made up now, Theresa stuffed her mirror and makeup bag into one of her desk drawers and switched on her computer. "I hate to be rude, but—"

"You've got an empire to run," Anthony finished for her with a smile. He pointed at the worksheet. "May I?"

"Please do."

Anthony folded the ditto and put it in his back pocket, then zipped up his coat. "I promise I'll try to finally get through to Mikey."

"And I promise I'll try to find out about Bernard Rousseau. Now hurry back to Brooklyn before you turn into a pumpkin."

Chapter 26

Perhaps it was underhanded, but Anthony's way of luring Michael into a chat about Little Anthony was to ask him to come to Dante's to discuss menu changes. At first he thought he'd tag along with Michael to a Blades game, but then he realized a rink was the wrong place to discuss letting Little Ant ditch hockey. Next he thought of asking Mikey if he wanted to go grab a beer on Anthony's night off, or even bring in some Chinese food and watch *Monday Night Football*, but both seemed too contrived. He and Mikey had never been big on going out drinking, and they had a hard time watching football together. Anthony liked to concentrate on the game, while Michael yakked from the opening kickoff to the final whistle.

Michael had made overtures about becoming more involved now that he was retired, but so far, apart from the Insane Lorraine debacle and showing up unannounced, he'd pretty much obeyed Anthony's "hands off" edict. Asking for input would definitely lure him in.

"Hey, big guy." Michael seemed cheerful as he breezed through the back door of the kitchen, no Angelica in tow.

"Where's the *bambina*?" Anthony asked.

"With Nana Falconetti." Michael greeted the kitchen staff, pausing at each station to ask after everyone personally. He was as smooth as a politician, but Anthony knew his interest was genuine. Anthony had seen Michael in action at enough Blades parties held at the restaurant over the years to know his brother couldn't rest until he'd talked to everyone, making sure they were happy. It was just his way.

Even so, Anthony couldn't help but grit his teeth when Michael tipped open one of the oven doors where focaccia was baking. "How many times have I told you not to do that, Mike?" he snapped.

Michael hastily closed the oven, looking embarrassed. "You're right. It just smells so good."

"C'mon," said Anthony, picking up menus and recipes, new and old, as he walked toward the swinging doors of the kitchen. "We'll talk in the dining room."

Michael followed him out of the kitchen, pointing to a four-seater in the corner where he, Theresa, and the kids always sat. "Let's sit there." He glanced around nostalgically. "Jesus, Ant. Remember when it was just Dad and Mom selling ices and slices to go on wax paper?" He shook his head in wonder. "We've sure come a long way."

"We sure have," Anthony agreed. "A lot of blood and sweat went into making this place what it is."

"A labor of love, though, right?"

"Why do it if you don't love it?"

Michael seemed to ponder this as he sat down while Anthony detoured to the bar to get them some bottled water. His brother looked so thrilled to be here and somehow be part of things that Anthony felt bad that he was about to, in effect, bludgeon him.

"You see they painted Vivi's logo on the window?"

Michael said, twisting in his chair to look at him. "It looks great."

Anthony scowled. "Why don't you just drive a stake through my heart?"

"What, you two are back to being feuding chefs now?" Michael chuckled, taking a sip from his bottle of water.

"Kinda." Anthony rubbed his forehead worriedly as he sat down opposite his brother. "I don't know."

Michael seemed not to hear, or care, as he spread out the menus and recipe cards, perusing them eagerly. "So what are we doing here?"

"I'm thinking of changing things up a little. Not too much!" Anthony warned, in case Michael had any ideas about going totally upscale. "Just shake things up a bit, you know."

"Well, give me some idea of what you're talking about."

"I'm thinking of ditching the eggplant patties and reintroducing the wedding soup."

Michael made a sour face. "Boring."

"To you. The last time it was on the menu, we couldn't keep up with the demand."

"What else?"

Anthony glanced down at his notes. "Ditch the risotto with zucchini—go with sautéed scallops with garlic and parsley on the appy menu."

"Seafood is always a good choice," Michael said authoritatively.

What the hell do you know? Anthony almost said, until he reminded himself he was the one who sought his brother's input.

"What else?" Michael asked.

"More basic pasta dishes, in keeping with our rep as a homestyle family restaurant that serves comfort food. Cut out the fancy schmancy."

"You mean, make it more basic than it already is? Like a *bistro* might be?"

Anthony stared at him stonily. "You trying to insinuate something?"

"Nope," said Michael, but Anthony could see he was fighting a smirk.

"I also think we should do away with the holiday specials," Anthony continued. "You know I hate doing Christmas Eve and Easter Sunday dinner here, too. Those are times for family, and I want to be with mine."

"Let's think about that," Michael said cautiously.

Anthony grimaced. "Come on, Mike. Wouldn't you rather be at my house this year scarfing down lamb chops *scottodito* and stuffing yourself with coffee custard?"

"Well, yeah," Michael admitted. "But there are lots of people who come for those holiday specials every year. We could be creating an opening for someone else." He wiggled his eyebrows significantly.

"She's not gonna be able to fit more than thirty people in there at a time," Anthony snapped. "And I'd keep doing New Year's Eve." It was time to broach the topic of Little Ant. He feigned looking off into space distractedly. "When is Easter this year? Do you know?"

"April, I think." Michael took another sip of water. "Why?"

"The kids get a week off, don't they? Maybe Little Ant could do some cooking with me."

"He's going to be at hockey camp."

"Yeah?" said Anthony. "You think that's a good idea?"

Michael looked annoyed. "Don't start with me, Anthony."

"I just want to point one thing out to you."

Michael frowned. "What?"

"Remember when we were growing up, and Dad was always on our asses to play bocce ball but we hated it, because we thought it was stupid and boring?"

"It is stupid and boring," Michael snorted.

"Well, what if Dad had forced us? What if he said you

couldn't play hockey, and made you go to bocce camp instead? You would have been pissed, right? You would have been resentful about him making you do something *he* wanted you to do, not something *you* wanted to do."

Michael was silent.

"Well, that's what you're doing to Little Ant."

"You don't understand. If he'd just give it a chance—"

"He hates it, Mike. Period. He thinks it's stupid and boring, like we thought about bocce. Here, I want to show you something." He pulled the worksheet out of his back pocket and handed it to his brother, careful not to watch him read it, because he didn't want to see the pain on Michael's face. Michael silently folded up the worksheet, putting it in his own back pocket.

"Where did you get this?" he asked quietly.

"Theresa. She asked me to talk to you about this. She said you wouldn't listen to her. Dad let us be ourselves even though what he wanted was for us to be bocce boys! He let me cook, and he encouraged you in hockey. Don't you want to do the same for Little Ant?"

"Yes. No." Michael looked pained. "God, I miss it so much, Anthony."

"I know that, bro." Anthony reached across the table to give his brother's arm a consoling pat. "But it's not right to try to live vicariously through him. You know?"

Michael pulled his face from his hands. "Can I confess something to you?"

Anthony shrugged. "Sure."

"This stay-at-home dad stuff? It's not for me. I'm going nuts."

"So what are you going to do?"

"Something might be going on at Met Gar that could change things. But I'm not at liberty to talk about it right now."

"Not even to your wife? She's worried sick about you, Mike. She thinks you're losing your mind. She's even worried that you're having an affair, with you creeping into the city all the time."

Michael laughed. "*Me?* She's got to be kidding!"

"Well, set her straight." Anthony paused. "What's the big mystery?"

"I can't tell you, Ant. Seriously. I don't want to say anything to anyone until I know for sure."

"Well, whatever it is, I hope it comes through for you, because Christ knows you've been a pain in my ass since you've been Mister Mom."

Michael looked contrite. "Yeah, sorry about that. I just suck at not being around lots of people, you know?"

"Mike, if you let Little Ant be who he wants to be, he'll love you for it." He gestured at the four walls surrounding him. "He loves it here, Mike. Dante's could all be his one day, if he wanted. We'd be able to keep it in the family. Hockey isn't the only Dante legacy."

Michael hesitated. "I'm just afraid of him getting picked on at school. Being called a 'fag' because he likes to cook."

"He'll survive. Believe me, I know. They won't be calling him a 'fag' twenty years from now when he's got his own successful restaurant. He could be a great chef, Mike. If you let him."

Michael tilted back in his chair, staring up at the ceiling. "I feel like an asshole."

"You are an asshole. Now go home and tell your wife you're not cheating on her, and let me finish these menus."

All Theresa's talk of press kits, "generating buzz," and getting reviews was making Vivi's head spin as she sat opposite Theresa in her office, watching her get more and more enthusiastic as she herself got more and more anxious.

Yesterday the artist had finished the sign on the front window. It looked gorgeous, the swirling script very romantic.

Anthony was wrong, wrong, wrong about the color. The white looked classy, not boring. As if he were the arbiter of good taste—his restaurant filled with fading pictures of priests and amateur paintings of gondolas.

Vivi liked railing against him in her head. It helped her not to miss him. Sometimes she felt sad when she looked across the street at Dante's and realized there would be no more cooking contests, no more passionate exchanges about food—no more passionate exchanges, period. But whose fault was that?

"One of the things we need to do," Theresa was saying, "is make sure we invite some French people to the opening, just to give it that extra dash of authenticity and panache. I'll come up with a list, but off the top of your head, can you think of anyone French besides you and Natalie?"

"Bernard Rousseau."

"Bernard Rousseau," Theresa repeated back thoughtfully. "That name sounds vaguely familiar."

"He's an ambassador to the UN."

"Wow." Theresa looked impressed. "How do you know him?"

"He worked with my father." *Were it not for Bernard, I'd be back in Avignon, a heartbroken failure, soaking my mother's blouse with tears.*

"You sound fond of him," Theresa noted.

"I am. My father adored him. I don't know him as well as my sister does, but he's a very nice man. Very generous. I definitely want him at the opening."

"Will he have a plus-one?"

Vivi looked at her in confusion. "A . . . ?"

"Does he have a wife or girlfriend he might want to bring?"

"I don't think so." Her mind flashed back to his lips on hers at the restaurant. "No."

Theresa gave her an oddly satisfied look. "Then we'll put him on the list as a solo." She paused. "Obviously, as your publicist, I'll be at the opening, and Michael wants to come, as well. I was wondering, how do you feel about inviting Anthony?"

"Anthony?" Vivi hadn't really thought about it.

"Whatever else may have happened, you two are neighbors. It would be a show of goodwill."

"Of course he can come, then."

"You're sure?"

"Yes, of course, of course," said Vivi, even though the more she thought about it, the more fluttery her stomach felt. No, she told herself, it would be good for him to be there. She wanted him to walk into her beautiful little bistro and hear people raving about her cooking; she wanted him to see her in her *own* restaurant kitchen.

"Terrific." Theresa scribbled something on the notepad on her lap. "You know," she murmured casually, head still bent over her writing, "he's made an appointment to go talk to someone about those dreams he was having."

"I see." So, his whole family knew the details of their breakup. She wondered if they knew about the "incident at the bedroom door," as she referred to it in her mind.

Theresa looked up at her. "He loves you, Vivi. He really does. You were so good together."

"We were terrible together," Vivi scoffed. "Bicker, bicker, bicker over spices and sauces and this and that."

"That was foreplay, or haven't you figured that out yet?"

Vivi blushed. She wondered if it would be inappropriate to ask Theresa a question about Angie. Well, why not? They were supposedly having a business meeting and Theresa had ventured into personal territory. Why couldn't she do the same?

"Do you think Anthony is over Angie?"

"Yes, I do," Theresa answered without hesitation. "If you'd asked me that six months ago, I might have hesitated. But you gave him back his spark. I would really hate to think of the two of you never working things out."

Vivi studied the beautiful woman before her. "You're very pushy, aren't you?"

Theresa laughed appreciatively. "Yes, I am. That's why I'm so good at my job."

Vivi laughed back. "I can identify with that."

"Think about what I said. About Anthony." Perhaps sensing Vivi's discomfort, Theresa's gaze turned sympathetic. "Shall we go back to discussing business?"

"Yes, please," said Vivi. Business was always better. Business was safe.

"What do you think?"

Vivi could barely keep from bouncing off the walls as she ushered Natalie over the threshold into Vivi's. The window sign was painted, the floor had been redone in wide, rugged planks of pine, and the bistro tables had arrived, though Vivi had yet to figure out which would go where. Just to annoy Anthony, she'd put a large sheet across the front window so he couldn't look inside. She wanted him to be as surprised as everyone else when Vivi's finally opened.

Natalie slowly walked the perimeter, nodding her head. "It's going to look fantastic."

"I know." Vivi grabbed Natalie's hand and pulled her toward a small table for two. "Sit down. No more folding chairs!"

Natalie's gaze continued sweeping the walls as she took a seat. "This place is going to be a success. I *know* it."

"I think I can get by with just two assistants in the kitchen and two wait persons on the floor. Maybe even one."

"Yes, I wanted to talk to you about that." Natalie's head was bent in a posture of submission as she looked up at Vivi through her lashes. "I want you to hire me as a waitress, Vivi."

Vivi gaped at her. "Are you serious?"

"Yes," Natalie said earnestly. "It's not right that you should do all the work. I want to help make Vivi's a success, too, by working just as hard as you in what way I can. My waitressing would be cheaper than hiring someone from outside—*and* we'd be able to pay off Bernard that much faster."

Natalie was right, of course. But Natalie as a waitress? Since she'd been going for "retail therapy" and had joined Shopaholics Anonymous, Natalie had been a lot more even tempered and relaxed. But Vivi could still imagine someone asking her for some more bread and Natalie dumping the breadbasket on their head and huffing off. Not exactly good for business.

"*Cherie*, don't you think it would be better if you looked for a job in your chosen field?" Vivi asked carefully.

"Yes, of course. But until I find one, I desperately need to bring money in. You *know* that."

Vivi fell silent. After the great debt debacle, the time for awkwardness between them should have been past. And yet, Vivi found herself unable to say what was on her mind, which was that Natalie was a bit too *haute* for the bistro. Then again, waitressing might be good for her newly burgeoning humility.

"Natalie, have you ever waited tables before?"

"Believe it or not, yes." There was a proud cast in her eye. "When I was at university. Papa insisted. He didn't want me to be completely spoiled, he said. And"—Natalie glanced away uncomfortably—"I was in debt, just like I am now. He made me work it off."

"I see." Vivi ran her index finger back and forth slowly across her lower lip, contemplating what to do. "Were you any good?"

"I was. I made so much in tips I was able to pay Papa off much faster than anticipated."

"Hmm."

Vivi noticed her sister was sans jewelry, and was more

simply dressed than usual in jeans, boots, and a low-neck sweater. Natalie hadn't said as much, but Vivi deduced she must have sold off a great deal of her designer wardrobe. "If I say yes, do you promise you won't turn around and quit on me after a few weeks?"

"I promise." Natalie looked at her imploringly. "I want to do this, Vivi. I want to make it up to you. I want us to work together to make the restaurant a success."

"All right," Vivi agreed. How could she say no? Natalie was really trying to make amends. Everyone deserved a second chance—maybe even a third or a fourth if they wanted it badly enough. Vivi believed Natalie did.

"Thank you." Natalie appeared relieved as she pulled a cigarette out of her purse and lit it. *Cigarettes are expensive!* Vivi thought, but held her tongue. It was a small pleasure compared to Natalie's past indulgences.

"I need to ask you one more favor," Natalie continued, looking nervous.

"What's that?"

Natalie hesitated. "Can I move in with you? Just temporarily," she added quickly, "until I find my own place. I can't afford the rent on the apartment in the city anymore."

Vivi pictured herself and Natalie. They'd be at each other's throats like crazed cats after two days. Living together, working together—it would be too much. Still, it if was just temporary . . .

"Of course you can stay," said Vivi. "But I'll give you an advance on your waitressing salary, so you can start looking right away."

"Can't stand the thought of living with me, eh?" Natalie joked quietly.

"No. Not in an apartment that small. As it is you'll have to share my double bed with me."

"That's all right," Natalie assured her. "As long as you don't kick in your sleep."

"No one has ever said so."

"You know, when I was little, I used to pray for a sister to share my room with," Natalie revealed shyly. "I used to imagine us in twin beds close enough for us to reach out and hold hands, exchanging secrets and giggles in the darkness. Sometimes I hated being an only child."

"Me, too. But we've got each other now, don't we?"

"Yes," Natalie whispered, getting teary. "And we have this." She gestured at the four walls surrounding them. "It's more than enough."

Chapter 27

"*If you three* stoogettes don't leave my kitchen, so help me God, I'm going to send you home without a morsel to eat."

Anthony knew he was bellowing, but he couldn't help it. For the past half hour, his Aunts Connie, Millie, and Betty Anne had been hovering in his kitchen offering unsolicited advice while he prepared Easter dinner. Millie was the worst. Always had been. Sometimes he wondered if they were really his mother's sisters; his mom had been very gentle and relatively sane.

Millie pointed to the oven with the cigarette that was permanently soldered to her hand. "You put too much marjoram on the lamb. Your mother always used it sparingly," she noted in her gravelly voice.

"I'm not my mother," Anthony pointed out, amazed a woman who subsisted on Parliaments and hot dogs had the *coglioni* to say anything to him about cooking. He must have been glaring, because Aunt Betty Anne, timid in the best of circumstances, was backing toward the kitchen doorway. Aunt Connie, like her bossy, tobacco-addicted sister, was still sticking her nose where it didn't belong.

"We're just saying," she sniffed defensively.

"Saying what?" Anthony retorted. "I run a restaurant, remember? I know what I'm doing."

Millie rolled her rheumy eyes and tapped Connie on the arm. "C'mon, let's go out into the living room and leave Mister Touchy alone."

"Thank you," Anthony said in an exaggerated voice. "And put that damn cigarette out! I told you, no smoking in the house!"

Millie pretended not to hear him.

He sighed and wondered what the hell he'd been thinking when he'd decided to close Dante's for Easter Sunday and cook dinner for his family instead. When he had brought it up to his brother months ago, it seemed like a good idea. He loved to cook, they loved to eat, and it had been years since he'd been able to sit at a table with everyone and just relax. But now that they were all here under his roof, making more noise than a Met Gar crowd and invading his kitchen uninvited, he was beginning to doubt the soundness of his decision.

He stood in the center of the kitchen, savoring the scents swirling around him and admiring his own handiwork. There was still a hint of the rosemary lingering in the air from the *Pan di Ranerino* rolls he'd made earlier that morning, and the succulent smell of the lamb basted in herbs wafting from the oven smelled *exactly* the same as his mother used to make, if not better. Christ only knows what Millie was talking about with the marjoram. He couldn't smell the coffee custard cooling in the fridge, obviously, but the orange cake sitting on the counter was spongy to the touch, just as it should be, and smelled as fragrant as an orange grove. If one more person opened their mouth to question or criticize, he'd show them the front door.

If anyone would understand his wanting to banish relatives from the kitchen, it would be Vivi. He wondered what she was doing today. Probably putting the finishing touches on the bistro, due to open in a week. It had annoyed him when, a few months back, she'd put a sheet up across the bistro's window so no one could see what was going on. Michael told him he was paranoid thinking she'd done it specifically to keep him from seeing inside, but he knew the truth. As if he cared. As Theresa had said, if anyone needed to be worried, it was Vivi. Bensonhurst was his turf, solidly Italian. She was going to have to blow everyone away if she expected to garner one tenth of the following he had.

"Anthony?"

He instinctively tensed before turning to see his cousin Gemma tread lightly into the kitchen, as if she were sneaking inside. She was the most well-balanced person Anthony knew, despite being into that witch stuff.

"Hey." He leaned down to kiss her. "How ya' feelin', chooch?"

"I needed to take a break from the mayhem," she said, tilting her head toward the living room. "Plus Aunt Millie is smoking."

"Apparently, smoking can cause deafness. I asked her to put it out and she ignored me."

"That's Aunt Millie," said Gemma, rubbing her lower back. There was a ravenous look in her eye as she fixated on the stove. "Everything smells great. I'm starving." She smiled apologetically. "I'm always starving."

Anthony raised an eyebrow. "A new *bambino* on the way, maybe?"

"Bite your tongue!"

"Well, dinner won't be too much longer, I promise."

"I told you we can't stay for dessert, right? Sean's family will freak out if we don't put in an appearance."

"Not a problem. I'll send you home with some orange cake that you can have later."

"Great." For a split second, Gemma's face remained lit up, but then she slowly narrowed her eyes, fixing Anthony with a penetrating gaze. Anthony felt hair on the back of his neck rise up. She was doing her witch thing, which always creeped him out.

"You're depressed."

"No, I'm not!"

"Yes, you are. I can see it in your aura. It's murky green. You miss her, don't you?"

Anthony sighed, seeing no point in denying it. "Yeah."

Every time he'd run into Vivi over the past three months, things had felt awkward. Conversation was stilted. Perhaps it was the presence of Natalie, who was always glued to Vivi's side. In Natalie's eyes, Anthony could feel himself being evaluated, judged, assessed, the same way he had been the first time they met. *Lo, how the mighty have fallen* is what he always thought whenever he found himself on the receiving end of those cool, appraising stares. It was obvious what the deal was. Natalie was Cinderella in reverse, having given up her luxurious life in the city to move to Brooklyn instead. Poor Vivi. Poor Brooklyn.

Gemma reached her hand up high, gently brushing his cheek. Their height difference had always been a source of amusement between them. "Don't worry so much. There are big changes coming. Nonna Maria told me."

"That's great, Gem. Anyone else from the Great Beyond have an opinion? Maybe you could try dialing up Angie on the heaven hotline and see what she has to say."

"Fine, don't believe me," Gemma said crossly. "But I know what I know."

" 'Big changes are coming' could mean anything. It could mean my restaurant is going to burn down. Who the hell knows?"

"Good changes, Anthony. That's what she meant."

"Yeah? Maybe she was referring to your mother, Aunt Millie, and Aunt Betty Anne getting off my ass. That would be a big change, don't you think?" He ruffled her mop of red hair affectionately, eager to get off the subject of Vivi and finish up his cooking. "Go back inside and sit down. Dinner will be done in a minute."

"*Listen up, everyone!* I have a couple of toasts to make."

The living room fell quiet, or as quiet as a living room full of Italians could be, at the sound of Michael's announcement. The family was seated around the long foldout table Anthony had borrowed from his Aunt Connie, with Mikey's children seated at a smaller "kids' table," which Little Ant seemed to resent bitterly, if the piercing stare he kept locked on Anthony was any indication. Aunt Millie had put out her cigarette. Gemma was practically salivating as she stared at the lamb in the center of the table. Anthony tried not to think about how fast the food might be cooling. All he could think was, *This had better be quick, Mikey.*

"First, a toast to the family." Beaming, Michael looked around the table. "I'm so happy we're all together tonight."

Everyone raised their wineglasses and touched them together, murmuring their agreement.

"Next, a toast my brother, Anthony, the best chef in all of Brooklyn, who cooked this fantastic meal we're about to eat."

Anthony stood up and took a bow as his relatives applauded.

"Next—"

"Is this gonna take a long time?" Aunt Millie interrupted with a growl. "Because if you're gonna go on the way you usually do, I'll just step outside for a quick cigarette."

Anthony glanced down, suppressing a laugh as he shook open his napkin. Looking back up, he was glad to see his brother looked on the verge of laughter, too. "It'll only be a few more seconds, I swear," said Michael.

"You ever think of getting remarried, Aunt Millie?" asked Anthony. "I hear Joe Camel's available."

Aunt Millie seemed not to appreciate the joke as the family laughed. She gave Anthony a dismissive back-handed wave, sinking deeper in her chair with a scowl.

Michael's attention was turned toward the kids' table, his eyes blazing with pride as he looked at his son. "I want to toast my son, Little Anthony, who helped his uncle prepare this meal. Your mother and I are so proud of what a great cook you're becoming." He turned back to Anthony. "You better watch it, bro. You've got some serious competition coming your way in a few years."

Anthony looked down at his lap to cover the mist forming in his eyes and then glanced at Little Ant. The kid looked elated.

"Can we eat now?" Dominica whined from the kids' table. "I'm, like, starving."

"One more thing," said Michael.

Everyone groaned.

"You all know I've been playing Mister Mom for the past year or so while my beautiful wife"—Michael raised his glass in salute to Theresa, who blushed—"went out to work and patiently put up with a mopey, depressed *cidrule* who couldn't manage the household if his life depended on it. My brother put up with a lot from me, too, and saved my butt on too many occasions to count when I was too scatterbrained to cook.

"I'm pleased to announce that as of June, I'm going to be out of everyone's hair. Kidco Corporation has asked me to come back to be the Blades assistant coach, and I've accepted the job."

The table erupted with cheers of "Congratulations!" and a frenzied clinking of glasses. Anthony looked across the table at Theresa. "Thank God," she mouthed to him. "No kidding," Anthony mouthed back. It was turning out to

be a good day. Only one other thing could have made it
perfect.

A week later, Anthony strolled into Al's Deli for his
usual six a.m. cup of coffee and ham and egg on a roll, and
Vivi was there. The sight of her without Natalie in tow took
him aback. Then he remembered, Vivi's grand opening was
in just a few days. She was up to receive early morning deliveries from suppliers just like he was.

"The usual, Al," he called over the counter. The deli
owner nodded and scurried off to make Anthony's sandwich.

"Hello," said Vivi. It was spring, but early mornings
were still cold, and she was wearing an oversized fisher-
man's sweater over baggy jeans that made her look like a
waif. For a split second Anthony entertained the thought
that the sweater might belong to Bernard Napoleon, but he
purged it from his mind. He'd seen her in the sweater this
past winter, her hair tied behind her back just the way it
was now, her pale skin without blemish. *Jesus,* Anthony
thought. *Why couldn't she at least look like crap in the
morning like everyone else?*

"How are you?' Vivi ventured. She was holding a tall
foam cup that he assumed to be full of coffee.

"Fine," said Anthony. *Where's your sister, Mademoiselle
Hyde?* He was tempted to ask, but refrained. Somehow, it
seemed wrong to be combative before the sun was even up.
"How are you?"

"Very well." She took a sip of coffee, gasping as she
pulled it away from her mouth. "It's boiling!"

"Al always makes it too hot," Anthony said under his
breath. "Take off the lid for a couple of minutes and blow
on it. It should be fine."

Vivi looked dubious, but she did as he advised.

"Up for deliveries?" he asked.

"Yes. You?"

"Yes."

She carefully ventured another sip of coffee, wincing. "Still too hot."

"I told you a couple of minutes. It's only been five seconds."

"Were you counting?"

Anthony rolled his eyes and kept silent. He didn't want to think about how alive this was making him feel.

Al passed him his own cup of coffee, and with great exaggeration, Anthony took off the lid and began blowing onto the cup, counting under his breath just to see how she'd react. "One . . . two . . . three . . ."

"Did you get the invitation to my opening?"

"Four . . . five . . . six . . ."

"Anthony—"

"Seven . . . eight . . . nine . . ."

"Fine, I get your point!" Vivi huffed with a small stamp of the foot he found adorable. "I'll let my coffee cool some more."

"Always listen to the master," said Anthony with a suave smile. He took the sandwich from Al and paid for it, moving toward the door. "Want to walk back with me? Or—"

"That would be fine."

They left the deli together, walking in the gray dark toward their respective restaurants. Anthony hated the idea of her out walking alone at this hour, but knew if he said so, he'd be giving her ammunition to use against him. He kept his instincts under control . . . for about ten seconds.

"No offense, Vivi, but you shouldn't be out alone at this hour."

"I know," she said, which shocked the hell out of him. "That's why I'm picking up my new car later today. Actually, it's not new, it's used, but it's new to me."

"Glad to hear it," said Anthony, relieved. "What kind did you get?"

"A Honda Civic."

"Good car."

"That's what I'm told."

By who? Anthony thought. *Bernard Parlezvouz?* They were walking slowly, both of them trying not to let their scalding, filled-to-the-brim coffees splash over the sides as they continued blowing onto the hot liquid.

"You never answered my question," said Vivi. "About the opening."

"I got the invite."

"And?"

He could feel her studying him as he kept his eyes fixed on the sidewalk in front of him. "And what?"

"Are you going to come?" she asked with a slight hint of impatience in her voice.

"Do you want me to come?" Anthony paused to take a sip from his coffee. He still wasn't looking at her. A garbage truck passed by, the driver turning to look at them as he rumbled down the street. Anthony wondered what he thought, seeing a man and a woman stopped in the middle of an empty sidewalk at six in the morning, drinking coffee. Who was he kidding? The guy didn't think anything. This was New York.

His question hung in the dark quiet between them. Anthony took another sip of coffee, waiting.

"Yes, I want you to come," Vivi eventually murmured. "Of course I do."

"Then I'll come."

They resumed walking. Anthony pulled his ham and egg sandwich out of the bag, handing her half.

"What is this?" Vivi asked, looking at the sandwich distrustfully.

"Just eat it. Trust me."

He watched as Vivi took a bite. She always ate so delicately, so carefully, fully appreciating every bite. "Delicious," she concluded. "But the roll is a bit soggy."

"It's supposed to be soggy."

"If you say." She took another careful bite, nodding appreciatively. "Mmm. Not good."

"Not bad," Anthony corrected.

Vivi gave an embarrassed little laugh. "I'm sorry. I'm still learning."

"It takes time. You need to be patient."

The use of the word "patience" made the molecules in the air around them freeze. Anthony wondered if Vivi thought he was sending her some kind of veiled message. That wasn't his intent, but if she took it that way, maybe it wasn't such a bad thing.

"I'm low on patience," she confessed with a weary sigh. "Natalie is living with me, and with Vivi's opening . . ." She shook her head apologetically. "I'm sorry. I'm very distracted these days."

"You'll feel better once the bistro opens. Don't worry."

"I hope you're right."

This time he looked at her as she searched his face. A thin band of dawn was creeping over the rooftops, enough light for him to really look into her eyes. What he saw there gave him hope. There was concern. Genuine care, even.

Vivi lightly touched his wrist. "How are you feeling these days?"

"I'm feeling okay," he said, which for the most part was true, though the tingling spot on his wrist where she'd just touched him was somewhat distracting.

"The dreams . . . ?"

"Gone," he said curtly.

Vivi blew out a breath. "That's good. I'm glad."

Glad enough to reconsider your decision? Anthony wondered as a lukewarm breeze swept the street, sending an empty soda can rolling into the gutter. *Glad enough to realize you still care about me?* They lingered there on the sidewalk, both at a seeming loss for words. He knew he couldn't touch her the way he longed to. Yet he couldn't escape the feeling that here was his chance to say something. *Do* something, even if it made him look like a fool. The next time he saw her, she'd be surrounded by admirers at her bistro's opening. This was his shot—here, in the midst of the mundane, where real life happened, the two of them drinking too-hot coffee and splitting a runny egg sandwich.

"I miss you, Vivi." The words came out hoarse, as if his lips didn't want to surrender them.

Vivi looked down at the sidewalk. Long, agonizing seconds passed before she finally tilted her face to his. "I should go," she said softly.

He watched as she walked across the street and opened the door to her restaurant, silently slipping inside. Did she go because she felt the same way but couldn't tell him? Or because she didn't feel the same way but didn't want to hurt him? He'd lost his ability to read her. Maybe he'd never really had it.

He made a vow to himself right there on the sidewalk: never again. Screw Gemma and her woo-woo predictions. Screw his brother and sister-in-law telling him to be patient. From now until the day he was too old to clutch a sauce ladle in his hand, Dante's would be his life.

Chapter 28

Vivi's lack of response set the tone for Anthony's day. The seafood delivery was late. Worse, the produce wasn't up to par. This was getting to be a pattern. Today it was droopy lettuce, last week it was bruised tomatoes. He sent the driver back with a blistering note and the lettuce to boot, making a mental note to call the offices of the distributor later in the day. Dante's had contracted with them for years, but contracts could be broken.

At ten thirty, his sous chef, Sam, called to tell him he had the flu and couldn't come in. Though it left him short-handed, Anthony preferred Sam take the sick time rather than come into work and risk infecting the rest of the staff, not to mention the customers.

Finally, Aldo walked in hours before his shift, puffing on his trademark off-hours cigarillo. Anthony worried that he might be going senile.

"What's up, old man?" Anthony boomed over the chatter of the kitchen staff, who were already working away.

"I want a raise," Aldo declared loudly.

The kitchen fell silent. Anthony put down the mezza-luna he was using to chop hazelnuts and, taking the old man gently by the elbow, steered him out into the dining room.

"What are you talking about? You just got a raise six months ago. You're probably pulling down more than Mayor Bloomberg at this point."

Aldo looked petulant. "I need more. Or I'll quit. For real."

Anthony peered at him with concern. "You in some kind of trouble? You're not in bed with those bookies again, are you?"

Anthony had bailed Aldo out once, and he knew for a fact his own father had bailed him out a couple of times. If Aldo was into the Murphy brothers again for a fat sum of dough, Anthony would kill him.

"Of course not." Aldo's nostrils flared with insult. "I was talking to Pietro." Pietro was Aldo's oldest friend, an-other waiter who worked for a restaurant called Michael's in Sheepshead Bay. "He's been working two years less than me and he gets two dollars an hour more than me! You think that's right?"

"I'm sure you get more in tips."

"A man has to eat, Anthony!"

Anthony squeezed the bridge of his nose between his thumb and forefinger. He needed this today like he needed a hole in the head. "Let me think about it, okay?"

Aldo pointed a bony finger at him. "Don't you forget how long I've worked here. I helped build this place with your father."

"Broke his balls is more like it."

Aldo took a long, deep drawl on his cigarillo, blowing the smoke out the side of his mouth like a gangster. "I want an answer now or I quit."

Since Aldo quit at least once, if not twice, a month, An-thony called his bluff.

"Okay, quit," he told him, heading back toward the kitchen. "Just don't be late for your shift tonight."

But Aldo didn't show.

The next morning, Anthony tried calling him, but he got no answer. He'd managed to get another one of his waiters, Tommy, to fill in for the ornery old bastard, but it wasn't the same. While competent, Tommy didn't have the same panache as Aldo, nor was he a Bensonhurst legend the way Aldo was. Since Aldo had always had a soft spot for Michael, Anthony decided it might be best if his brother tried to cajole the old fool back to work.

When Michael asked Anthony on the phone if he was okay, Anthony became suspicious. "Why wouldn't I be?" he replied.

There was an uncomfortable silence. "Why don't you meet me in the schoolyard behind Saint Vincent's in about fifteen minutes? I'm taking Angel there to play."

"No offense, Michael, but I don't have time to go traipsing around the playgrounds of Brooklyn."

"You told me you don't want me hanging around Dante's, and I'm trying to respect your wishes," Michael snapped.

Anthony reluctantly agreed to meet him.

The playground was within walking distance of the restaurant; it was a small square of green, a quarter acre in size, if that. Anthony was shocked—gone were the metal monkey bars and sturdy jungle gyms of his childhood. Today's kids had colorful plastic forts atop soft rubber padding to play on, no chance of anyone falling and cracking their skull on the open blacktop the way it had been when he was a kid. Only the rubber-seated, chain metal swings of his childhood remained, and those were now anchored in sand.

Benches lined three sides of the park, empty strollers

lined up before each like parked cars. Michael was the only man there amongst seven women, most of them foreign. Nannies, Anthony assumed. Michael caught sight of Anthony and waved, crouching down to Angelica to point her uncle out to her. She looked up, waving in imitation of her father, the sight of her small, chubby hand slicing the air making Anthony smile.

"It's good for you to get out, get some fresh air once in a while," said Michael as he hugged Anthony in greeting.

"I get fresh air all the time, *gavone*. I've just started running again."

Michael looked at him enviously. "I wish I could join you, but as you know, my knees are shot."

"Likely excuse."

Michael gave Angelica some giant, red furry creature to grapple with, placing her at his feet to play with it as he sat on the nearest bench. Anthony sat down beside him, in no mood to exchange pleasantries.

"Why did you ask on the phone if I was okay?"

"I thought you might have seen this already." Michael leaned forward, pulling out a copy of today's *Sentinel* from the mesh pocket in the back of Angelica's stroller. Anthony noticed the corner of one page was bent down, the page Michael opened to as he handed Anthony the paper and suddenly became very interested in his daughter playing at his feet.

The paper was open to the "Fine Dining" page. Among reviews of two other restaurants—one in the meatpacking district, one in Queens—there was a review of Dante's. The headline said, "Mama Mia! Some Things Never Change."

Anthony sighed deeply and plunged into the review. It said his meals were "deliciously predictable," that Dante's was like "a faithful friend you could count on always to be there, even if they're not as exciting as your newer pals," that the restaurant was becoming "a victim of its own nostalgia." It concluded with the backhanded compliment that if you were seeking basic Italian food, Dante's was the place to go, but more adventurous palates might want to explore any number of little bistros beginning to spring up in the outer boroughs instead.

Anthony folded the paper and thrust it back at his brother. "Fuck him. I don't get it. Wasn't 'basic Italian food' the whole point of the PR campaign when we renovated? To make it the place you go to when you *want* comfort food?"

Michael scratched his head. "Yeah. But I think the reviewer is also saying, uh, that we're getting kind of stale." He flipped open the paper and skimmed the review. "It's really not that bad of a review, Ant, if you think about it."

"Then why were you worried I wouldn't be okay?"

"Because I know how hard you take this stuff to heart."

"You shouldn't have even shown it to me."

"You would have seen it eventually, or someone would have mentioned it to you."

"Oh, yeah, don't I know it," Anthony snorted. "Vivi probably cut it out and has it hanging on her kitchen wall as we speak." He shook his head. "I can't win. I've been doing gourmet crap for years, Mikey, in addition to the old favorites."

"Yeah, and then you retooled the menu a few months ago and went completely basic, remember?"

Anthony said nothing, preferring not to reflect back on the menu changes he'd made that were driven by a sense of competition against a restaurant that didn't even exist yet. "If it ain't broke, don't fix it," his father always used to say. He should have listened, rather than letting his ego get in the way.

The happy cries of children pierced the air, an ironic counterpoint to the shame he was feeling inside. Dante's was his life. It was his pride and joy. The idea that anyone could find it subpar or mundane mortified him. Anxiety was taking root, but he couldn't give in to it, lest he really shoot himself in the foot. He needed to think things out. Slowly. Carefully.

As if reading his mind, Michael said, "We can fix this."

"First things first. We need to get Aldo back."

"I've called twice, still no answer. I'll shoot over to his place tonight before Vivi's opening."

Vivi's opening. Fuck a duck. Anthony glanced skyward. *Why don't you just hit me with a bus and get it over with?* he silently asked God. Anything would be better than this slow failing by degrees.

"You're going, right?" Michael asked uneasily.

"Sure, why not? It's always been my dream to go to a restaurant opening the same day my own establishment gets a mediocre review. It'll be fun—especially when I open the Sunday paper and see *her* place get a glowing review."

"Maybe it won't."

"It will," Anthony muttered. "She's a fantastic cook."

"Well, so are you. Look, it's one review. We'll add a few items back to the menu, and we'll be back on top."

For the first time in a long time, Anthony didn't begrudge his brother the use of the word "we." The success of Dante's meant as much to Michael as it did to him. Keeping it going, making sure it remained excellent, was a point of pride for both of them. They owed it to their parents' memory.

Anthony glanced down at his niece, playing in her own world at her father's feet. Her world was simple and uncomplicated. His life used to be that way, too, or at least it felt that way, until Angie died, and Vivi came along to reawaken him, only to snatch the light back from him.

He stared into the distance. "You're right. We can fix it."
At least there was something in his life he could fix.

"This food is fantastic!"

Vivi smiled nervously at Michael Dante's compliment as her eyes slowly scoured the bistro, reading people's faces. After almost a year of hard work, her day had finally arrived: Vivi's was open. Theresa had told her there were a few food critics on hand, but Vivi begged her not to point them out, as it would make her too nervous.

She watched as Natalie and their other waiter circled the room, taking orders and delivering food. Vivi had wanted to hire someone else to work the opening so that Natalie could help her mingle and talk the bistro up, but Natalie insisted it was only right that she should be waiting tables since Vivi was going to be working so hard in the kitchen. Perhaps it was just wishful thinking, but Natalie actually seemed to be enjoying herself. She had a big smile on her face as she handed Vivi the latest order.

"They're loving it, *cherie*." Her eyes glistened with happy tears as she squeezed Vivi's hand tightly. "The food, the atmosphere—I heard one woman say she felt like she was in Paris!"

Vivi put her hand to her chest. "Oh, thank God."

"Please don't tell me the chef is having a heart attack."

Quinn O'Brien smiled roguishly as he approached Vivi and Natalie, his blue eyes flashing with friendliness. "How's it going, ladies? Thanks so much for inviting me."

"It was her idea, not mine," Natalie grumbled.

"I had to come over here and give you my compliments," Quinn continued. "The food is outrageously good, Vivi. You'll be seeing me in here a lot."

"God help us," Natalie muttered under her breath.

"*Mademoiselle* Natalie." Quinn gave a small bow as Vivi

suppressed a smile of amusement. "I notice you're helping to serve tonight. Can I assume your role in the restaurant now extends beyond mere investor?"

Natalie scowled, then walked away.

"Look how she loves me," Quinn said to Vivi with a lovesick sigh.

"Must you tease her so?"

"I can't help it," Quinn answered with a shrug. "She's such an easy target—and way too pretty to be that uptight."

"Perhaps you can cure her of that."

"Curing cancer might be easier." He gave her shoulder a convivial pat. "I'm under deadline, so I have to run."

Vivi swallowed. "You're not one of the reviewers, are you?"

Quinn laughed. "Me? No. But trust me, the one critic I know is here is gushing to her companions, and she usually hates everything. I don't think you have anything to worry about."

"Thank you. See you soon," Vivi called after him as he threaded his way through the densely packed room. Not only was every table filled, but people were also standing, balancing small plates filled with hors d'oeuvres in their hands as they clustered in small groups. Theresa was "working the room," as she put it, talking to this one and that. She seemed to be lingering a particularly long time with Bernard Rousseau. Their heads were close together, and when they turned simultaneously to look at Vivi with admiration, she blushed deeply. She could tell what they were thinking—Vivi's was going to be a success. Perhaps not overnight (success never really happened overnight, despite what people said), but in good time. Thank God for Bernard, for his loan and for his willingness to accept that she wanted nothing more than a platonic relationship. It would have complicated things immensely had he lobbied for more.

She walked back into the kitchen—*her* kitchen, she

thought with mild shock—and checked to see if the leek tart had finally started to brown, its lovely, oniony aroma tickling her nostrils as she tipped open the oven to peek inside. Everything she'd worked for her whole life was within these four walls. All those years of cooking for those she loved, of sweating her way through the fierce competition of Le Cordon Bleu, of apprenticing in kitchens under demanding sexist chefs . . . it had all paid off. She was the head chef and proprietor of Vivi's. It was a stunning achievement.

And yet, she felt a tiny tug of melancholy. She wished her father were still alive to see the success she'd become. She wished her mother had come over from Avignon to share in her big moment. Vivi had invited her, but *maman*'s back was acting up again and she didn't want to exacerbate it by flying, and Vivi was not about to force her. She wished Anthony were here. Whatever else had happened between them, he was the one person she knew who could appreciate the sweat and toil that had gone into this labor of love. His absence bothered her. In fact, it bothered her more than her mother not being present, which was unsettling. He said he would come. So why wasn't he here?

"You got everything under control?"

Anthony's staff nodded, which was not the answer he wanted. He wanted to be told that they couldn't afford for him to step out for even a few minutes, thus giving him an excuse not to go to Vivi's opening. They were on night two sans Aldo. Anthony wondered if Michael had gotten the chance to stop by Aldo's as promised. He hoped so. He also hoped the old man was just trying to bust his chops about the raise. Anthony's fear was that he *was* into the bookies in a big way, and that right now, Aldo's body was lying at the bottom of Jamaica Bay, weighed down by chains.

He took off his apron, tossing it into the laundry hamper in the staff locker room before heading to the restroom to change out of his chef whites and clean up a bit. His heart was heavy with guilt and dread. Even though he knew it was the right thing to do, he did not want to go across the street and congratulate Vivi. All he could imagine was walking through the door and people whispering behind their hands as they stared at him in pity. *There's Anthony Dante. Did you read that awful review of his restaurant in the* Sentinel? *It sounds like it's really going downhill. He should give it up.*

Then there was Vivi herself. She wouldn't bring up the review to his face, but he knew she'd know about it, and she'd be gloating inside. What chef didn't when their competition slipped a little? Worse, seeing her would lead to a chain reaction in his heart. Longing would lead to depression that he could easily turn into anger if he didn't watch himself. Christ, if only he could just stay put and cook.

Five minutes, he promised himself as he splashed cologne on his face and neck. He'd pop in, he'd congratulate her, and leave.

He grabbed his jacket, heading out through the back door and onto the street. He could see through Vivi's front window; the place was packed. He was about to step off the curb when he paused mid-stride to slap himself on the forehead, and turn back.

Chapter 29

"You traitorous old bastard."

The minute Anthony clapped eyes on Aldo waiting tables at Vivi's, the temptation to strangle his skinny neck was strong. How could he? No, wait, how could *she*? He could forgive Vivi a lot of things, but stealing his longtime headwaiter wasn't one of them.

Aldo breezed past him, his noble Roman nose in the air, pretending not to hear as he deposited four bowls of French onion soup at a table of lively older women. But when the old man started back in the direction of the kitchen, Anthony and Michael zeroed in on him from opposite sides, forcing him to stop in his tracks.

"Yes?" Aldo sniffed imperiously.

Michael was goggle-eyed. "What the hell are you doing here, Aldo? You work for us!"

"Not anymore." Aldo folded his arms smugly across his chest, accusing eyes pinning Anthony. "I told you I quit, but you didn't believe me. Maybe now you'll believe."

Anthony's hands curled into fists. "You quit at least

twice a month, Aldo. How the hell was I supposed to know you meant it this time?"

"You gotta come back," Michael pleaded. "Dante's isn't Dante's without you. You know that."

Aldo raised an eyebrow, his eyes still burrowing into Anthony's. "Well?"

"Fine!" Anthony said loudly. A woman sitting nearby gave him a dirty look. "Shit," he muttered to himself. He felt as if everyone's eyes were on him, including his brother's.

"You okay?" Michael asked Anthony pointedly.

"Yeah."

"He's come to kill me," Aldo stated matter of factly. He pointed at the paper bag Anthony was holding in his left hand. "What have you got in there? A gun?"

Anthony snorted. "You really think I'd waste a bullet on you, old man?" Aldo scowled as Anthony tried to ignore the delectable scents wafting his way from the nearest table, that of perfectly cooked tomato and zucchini gratin, and soft, chewy French bread piping hot from the oven. Damn Vivi to hell.

Michael, meanwhile, was still looking at him with concern. "You sure you're okay, big guy?"

Anthony gritted his teeth. "Yes."

"My raise?" Aldo prompted, smoothing the front of his white waiter's jacket with care.

"You can have your raise," Anthony grumbled. "But you have to come back to work tomorrow. *Capisce?*"

"Capisce," Aldo agreed, the faintest smile of triumph on his face.

"Ballbuster," Anthony growled as his eyes followed Aldo into the kitchen.

"Smart ballbuster," Michael said with a touch of admiration. His eyes fell to the bag Anthony was holding. "Whatcha got there?"

"An opening night gift for Vivi." When his brother began to grin, Anthony growled, "I'm just being polite."

"So you're not planning on shooting anyone?" Michael double-checked.

Anthony scowled. "Apart from you? No."

"Glad to hear it." He patted Anthony on the back, and then went to join Theresa, who was hovering over a table of well-known, hand-selected foodies. Speaking of whom . . . Anthony went to join his brother and sister-in-law, tapping Theresa on the shoulder to get her attention. "Which one is Bernie boy?"

Theresa discreetly cocked her head in the direction of a dapper, handsome man speaking Italian to Aldo. *Show-off,* Anthony thought. "Over there," Theresa said. "And you don't have to worry, he and Vivi aren't romantically involved at all. But you don't care anymore about that, right?" she needled.

"That's right." He moved, turning when he heard someone growl, "Excuse me," behind him.

Vivi's pinch-faced sister was glaring at him. He'd never met someone who frowned so much. It was too bad, because she was a good-looking woman.

"What are you playing at?" she hissed. "How dare you show up here?"

"Your sister invited me," Anthony answered smugly, trying not to bare his teeth at her.

She jerked her head at the bag in his hand. "What's in there?"

Jesus Christ, hadn't anyone here ever seen a paper bag before? "It's an opening night gift. For your sister."

Natalie held out her hand. "I'll give it to her."

"My ass you will."

Natalie looked appalled at what he said, which pleased Anthony immensely. "I'm going into the kitchen now to say hello."

"*Aldo tells me* you've come to shoot him."

Vivi couldn't resist a barb as Anthony strolled toward

her, his entire body tense. Perhaps it was because Natalie
was right behind him, smug and officious as if she couldn't
wait for him to make some kind of mistake. When the sisters' gazes met, Vivi cut her eyes quickly to the kitchen
door, indicating Natalie should go. Natalie let out a small
puff of exasperation, but she did as Vivi requested.

"Yeah," said Anthony with a sarcastic frown. "I always
carry weaponry around in a paper bag."

Vivi eyed the bag curiously. "What do you have in
there?"

"You'll see in a minute. First I think we need to discuss
how unethical it is to steal a headwaiter from another
restaurant."

Vivi's jaw dropped. "You think I stole Aldo?"

"He's out there waiting tables, isn't he?"

"*He* came over here and asked *me* to hire him!"

"You could have said no."

"Why?" Vivi challenged, her body temperature beginning to inch up. "Good waiters are hard to come by, and
he's wonderful. If you can't hold on to your help, it's not
my fault." Her heart was beginning to race, unnerving her
as she realized sparring with him was arousing her.

Anthony flashed a triumphant smile. "Well, you can
kiss him good-bye at the end of the evening. He resumes
working at Dante's tomorrow."

"So you did threaten to shoot him."

"Can we stop with the shooting, please?" Anthony's
eyes lit on the two women working with Vivi. "Aren't you
going to introduce me to your staff?"

"That's Joanie"—Vivi pointed to a stout, busty woman
frying onions in a skillet—"and that's Charmaine." The
second woman, a dour-faced matchstick of a girl, was
busily whipping cream. "Ladies, this is Anthony Dante. He
owns the Italian restaurant across the street." They both
smiled in acknowledgment.

"Where did you find them?"

"My friend, Bernard. He knows many restaurateurs in the city, and asked around." Vivi tipped her head up proudly. "I lured them here with superior salaries. Plus, both were eager to work for a female chef rather than a male."

Anthony frowned. "Did you even bother to check their credentials? Or did you just take Bernie's word for it?"

"Do you think I'm a complete twat?" Vivi asked crossly.

"Twit," Anthony corrected quietly with a wince. "I'd be careful with that expression if I were you."

Vivi gave a curt nod of appreciation, warmth flooding her cheeks. He probably found her pathetic, still getting euphemisms wrong after all this time.

"I heard about the review," she ventured. She regretted it as soon as she saw his handsome face, a face she'd once cradled tenderly in her hands, fall.

"Yeah, well, enjoy it while you can," he replied with bravado. "A little tweak here and there and that reviewer will be eating his words."

"I think the reviewer was wrong. I think your restaurant is very good." She moved to one of the burners to give a good stir to some fish broth simmering there. "Of course, mine is better."

"Of course," Anthony responded sarcastically.

"Did you see how packed it is out there?" It was probably putting pepper in his wound, but she couldn't contain her excitement. "Your sister-in-law did a good job with the PR."

"She did," Anthony agreed. He joined her at the stove. "Much as it kills me to say this, you deserve this success, Vivi."

Vivi felt her eyes fill up. God, she hated the way she was at the mercy of her emotions. One kind word and she was on the verge of tears. Maybe it was because the compliment was coming from a fellow chef whom she respected. Or maybe it was because the compliment was coming from the man she still loved.

"Thank you," Vivi replied, managing to keep her tears at bay.

Anthony cleared his throat nervously, holding up the bag in his hand. "I brought you a small opening night present."

"You did?" Vivi couldn't hide her surprise. "You didn't have to."

"I wanted to," Anthony said softly.

He put his hand in the bag, pulling out a large, clear bottle filled with olive oil. "This is homemade and hand pressed. A branch of the Dantes still lives in Italy, and every year, they send us a big batch made from the olives in their grove. I think you'll find it exceptional to cook with."

"Oh, Anthony." Fingers trembling, Vivi reached out to take the bottle of oil. "This means a lot to me."

"Use it in good health." Anthony's expression was strained as he touched her shoulder lightly. "I'd better go back across the street."

"Have you tried any of the food?" Vivi asked, masking her disappointment at his departing so soon. It was slowly dawning on her that she wanted his approval. The realization troubled her.

"I have to go," Anthony repeated.

"Not without trying something!" Vivi insisted, suddenly convinced there was nothing in the world more important. She cut off a small piece of leek tart and, without thinking, brought it up to his mouth. Their eyes met, the intimacy of the act dawning on both of them at the same time. Vivi hesitated; then she gently pushed the morsel through his parted lips, her insides trembling. Dear God, she asked herself, why are you torturing him? Torturing yourself?

Anthony chewed carefully, thoughtfully, and deliberately slowly, Vivi thought. She put her hands on her hips. "Well?"

"Too salty," Anthony pronounced. "But passable."

Vivi frowned. "Do you really mean that? Or are you just saying that to get my hog?"

"Goat. And no, I'm not just saying it. You always use too much salt."

"You can go now."

She heard a chuckle as she turned back to the stove, and then he was gone. She remembered what Theresa had said to her that day she'd gone in to discuss PR, how the verbal jousting between her and Anthony was a form of foreplay. If the warmth still heating her body in the aftermath of his departure was any indication, Theresa was right. She didn't want to think about it right now. She had a restaurant to run, critics to dazzle. She went back to work.

People stood up and applauded when she emerged from the kitchen at the end of the opening. *Applauded.* She knew she deserved it, and yet to be so blatantly feted made her feel slightly uncomfortable. She said a quick prayer of gratitude while taking her bows, thanking God for allowing her to make her living doing something she loved. Glancing up, she quickly skimmed the well-fed crowd, a small, silly part of her hoping that perhaps Anthony had decided to stick around and share a meal with his brother and sister-in-law. After all, he'd taken the time to give her a gift; perhaps he'd give her the satisfaction of dining in her restaurant. But as soon as she saw he wasn't there, she chided herself for even wanting it. Vivi's was going to be a huge success. Nothing else really mattered.

Chapter 30

Until she became aware of the sweat dripping between her shoulder blades, Vivi hadn't noticed the seasons had turned. July had unleashed itself upon Brooklyn, with soaring temperatures shimmering up like a mirage from concrete and asphalt, and staggering humidity amplified by crowds.

Her tunnel vision of the year previous had paid off, however. Vivi's was an unqualified success. Reviews had been glowing, and there was a waiting list for reservations. Vivi had never worked as hard as she was working now. Each night, she fell into bed exhausted but hopeful. She was sure that within a year, she and Natalie would be turning a profit and they'd be able to repay Bernard much sooner than they'd planned.

The other good news was that Natalie had finally found her own flat. Living together hadn't been as hard as Vivi had feared. Still, when they heard the tenant in the apartment directly above, Roberta, had passed away, they jumped at the chance to get Natalie in there. Of course, the landlord raised the rent, but the price was still manageable with Natalie's salary and the tips she made. Natalie made a surprisingly good waitress, and even seemed to enjoy it.

Taking a break from moving Natalie's newly purchased futon into the apartment, the two sisters flopped down on it, chugging from their respective bottles of water. "Instead of buying a dining table I think I need to get an air conditioner," Natalie said as she panted lightly. "At least for the bedroom."

"I agree." Vivi said between gulps of water. She found herself smiling. Natalie had been doing well at managing her finances. She was still attending a group meeting once a week for "shopaholics," and had even made some friends. Vivi thought back to the person her sister had been over the winter, and was startled at the transformation. She had humility now, and was much less judgmental. Of course, she was still fully capable of snappishness now and then, especially when Quinn O'Brien strolled into the bistro. Vivi's had become one of his favorite local haunts. Vivi didn't dare mention how obvious it was that Natalie was Quinn's main reason for frequenting the bistro. She suspected Natalie already knew, which was why she was so biting to him.

"We need to talk, my dear."

The seriousness of Natalie's tone, coupled with the look of concern on her face, caught Vivi by surprise, and she immediately began to worry. Was Natalie going to quit? Go back to France? Had she incurred some more debt?

"What is it?" Vivi asked evenly.

"You don't seem as happy as you should be."

Natalie's words were like a sharp poke. Vivi was thrilled to be cooking, thrilled to be the proprietress of her own establishment, and yet, she still felt incomplete. That Natalie noticed was testament to how close they'd become.

Vivi pressed the bottle of cold water to her sweating

cheek. "It's silly, I know. I have everything a person could want."

"Except the one you love."

Vivi stared at her.

"I think you should get back together with Anthony Dante."

"What?"

"You heard me. You always look across the street wistfully at his restaurant. Each time his brother comes into Vivi's and you come out from the kitchen to say hello, I can tell you're dying to ask how Anthony is. I've even seen you watching Anthony when you catch sight of him on the street. I think you should go to him and see if he wants to get back together."

Was this really Natalie speaking? Natalie who'd once lectured her on avoiding widowers who also happened to be competitors? Natalie who told her to focus on the restaurant above all else?

Vivi slowly lowered the water bottle from her cheek. "I thought you hated him."

"I don't hate him. I just thought"—Natalie cast her eyes down in shame—"that he wasn't good enough for you." She looked back at Vivi, her gaze tender. "I was also afraid he'd hurt you."

"He did."

Vivi sank back against the futon, still stunned by the words of this new version of Natalie. "I don't know what to say."

"Admit I'm right, *cherie*. He's what's missing."

Vivi didn't want to miss Anthony, but she did. The way he made her laugh . . . the passion in his eyes when he looked at her . . . even his vehemence when he thought he was right and she was wrong—she missed all of it. They spoke the same language, both in and out of the kitchen. And she'd thrown it all away.

Vivi shook her head sadly. "I don't think he'd take me back."

"Of course he would," Natalie scoffed.

"I—I'm not sure I could manage it all. The cooking, the restaurant, a relationship . . . it's too complicated."

"Of course you can manage it," Natalie replied firmly. "Papa juggled a career and two families, didn't he?"

Vivi inhaled sharply, blowing out a long, slow breath. Granted, there were times when each of her father's families received short shrift, but overall, he had lived a very complicated life with grace and aplomb. What she faced was child's play in comparison.

"I don't know what to say, Natalie." Vivi closed her eyes, pressing the sweating bottle to the back of her neck.

"Do you want him?"

Vivi hesitated. "Yes."

"Then go after him. Don't worry about the small details right now, just think about the big picture: the two of you back together and happy, arguing about the sex of zucchini blossoms."

Vivi cracked open an eye, regarding her sister wryly. "You've become very philosophical in your newfound frugality."

"Maybe I've just figured out what really matters."

"What if he won't take me back?" Vivi asked again plaintively.

"He loves you. You know that."

She did know that, but that didn't save her from feeling fearful. Anthony was a passionate man, with a strong sense of pride and a temper to boot. What if he told her to go to hell, that he'd gotten on with his life and didn't want her anymore? It was possible.

Still, her father always said it was better to try and fail than never to try at all. She would speak her heart to

Anthony, but only after she consulted with another member of his family.

Following a map provided by the Fernwood Cemetery's office, Vivi made her way to the grave of Angie Dante.

The cemetery was nowhere near as grand and magnificent as Pere LeChaise where her father was buried, but there was a sense of peacefulness among the rolling green hills that made it an unexpected oasis of calm in the heart of industrial Brooklyn. She could see why some people came to cemeteries just to think, and why people long ago used to hold picnics in graveyards; the serenity was wonderful.

She was surprised by the simplicity of Angie's grave. The Dantes were so dramatic, she was expecting an elaborate headstone. Instead, it was a simple rectangular stone bearing Angie's full name, Angela Maria Dante, below which was inscribed, "Beloved Wife, Sister, Daughter." A bouquet of wilting rosebuds and baby's breath lay propped up against the stone, with a card that said "From Mama."

Vivi stood there for a long moment, feeling the warm breeze brush her face and hair, searching her heart for something to say. Thinking back to her talk with Natalie, it had occurred to Vivi that maybe it wasn't Anthony who couldn't let go of his dead wife. Maybe it was she who had to get over his past.

"I hope you don't mind my being here," she began, picturing in her mind's eye the dark-haired, curvaceous woman whose smiling face had looked out at her from photographs at Anthony's home. "There are some things I need to tell you. Anthony is a wonderful man. You know that, but I wanted you to hear me say it.

"I love him, and I hate the fact that I hurt him. If he takes me back, I will never, ever hurt him again, Angie." She swallowed. "I was afraid that deep down, you were still number one in his heart and that he couldn't commit to me the way I wanted."

She lightly touched the top of the stone. "I want you to know that you don't have to worry about him. I promise I'll take good care of him. I'll make him as happy as I can; as happy as he deserves to be." Vivi felt tears prick the corners of her eyes and she blinked them back. "Thank you for loving him first, and showing him how wonderful life can be when two people really love each other. Were it not for that, I don't think he ever would have been willing to try again." She took a step back, head bowed. "Rest in peace." She made the sign of the cross, and blew a gentle kiss. Immediately Vivi felt lighter. She turned her face to the spring sun, and set out to find Anthony.

Why couldn't God have designed human beings so they didn't need to exercise? Finishing his morning run, Anthony paused, catching his breath as he waited for the stitch tearing his side to abate. He'd pushed it. He always pushed it. He had to learn to slow down and let himself build up speed and endurance. Otherwise, he was going to blow out his knees or keel over from a massive coronary.

He squinted as he looked up the street, swearing he saw movement on his front stoop. Was someone sitting there? He squinted harder. "Shit," he muttered to himself. It had to be Insane Lorraine, returning to exact vengeance; selling hot dogs and beer to rowdy hockey fans had probably traumatized her. Or maybe she had traumatized them. It wasn't until he was two houses away that he realized it was Vivi, sitting there on the top step of the stoop, a foil-covered bowl resting in her lap.

She looked happy to see him, which helped ease his embarrassment over being so sweaty. "Hey," he said more casually than he was feeling, swiping a forearm across his forehead. It served a dual purpose—it allowed him to wipe away perspiration while at the same time catch a quick sniff of his armpit to see if he smelled rank. He didn't—at least he thought he didn't. "This is a surprise."

"It was intended to be."

He nodded at the bowl in her lap. "What you got there?"

"Hazelnut risotto pudding."

Hazelnut risotto pudding? The dessert he'd made in their cook-off—the cook-off he would have *won* were it not for his traitorous brother?

Anthony swiped his other forearm across his forehead. "And you made this because . . . ?"

"Because you should have won that day, and this is my way of admitting it." Her smile was tentative. "Think of it as a peace offering."

"I wasn't aware we were at war."

"I wanted to talk to you."

"I can see that." Anthony chuckled. "It's not very often I come home from a run and find a French woman on my stoop offering me dessert. You must really want to talk to me *bad*."

Her hands tightened around the bowl on her lap. "I do."

Anthony felt his pulse beginning to hammer, hard and primal, but his mind warned him not to get ahead of himself. "Well, let's go inside, then."

He tried not to think about the last time they'd been together at his house as he unlocked the door and ushered her inside. "Guess you're off today, too, huh?"

"Yes." There was a slight hesitation in her voice as she added, "Like you, I'm closed on Mondays."

"Yeah, I've noticed that."

He noticed everything that went on across the street: what time her deliveries came, the daily specials posted on the sidewalk chalkboard outside the restaurant, whether her business had gouged into his in any way. It hadn't, which was good. It would be hard to sit here and talk to her if her restaurant was seriously drawing away from his customer base. It was going to be hard to sit here and talk to her anyway—she looked gorgeous, her hair back in its usual functional braid, her long coltish legs poured into a pair of faded but form-fitting jeans. So simple. So beautiful. Did she even realize?

He followed in bemusement as she headed straight for his kitchen as if she'd been there a hundred times before. "Spoons?" she asked as she put the bowl down on the table.

"We're going to eat this now?"

"Yes. As we talk."

The same pushy Vivi. He was desperate to go upstairs and shower, but the resolute set of her jaw told him that wasn't going to fly. Sighing in resignation, he fetched two spoons. "You want bowls as well?" he asked her over his shoulder from the kitchen counter.

"No. We can just dig into this bowl."

"How informal."

She smiled shyly. "Are you teasing me?"

"Maybe." He walked back to the table and, peeling back the foil atop of the bowl, handed her a spoon.

"Sit."

They sat, Vivi eagerly sliding the bowl to him. "Taste. Please."

"You do know it's counterproductive for me to be eating this after working out, don't you?"

" 'Working out.' " Vivi clucked her tongue dismissively. "You Americans are so obsessed with fitness! If you just ate right and walked around more, you wouldn't have to 'work out.' "

"Yeah? Maybe if we all still smoked like the French that would be enough."

Her brows furrowed into a little scowl. "Just eat."

"As *mademoiselle* wishes." He dug into the custard, helping himself to a hearty spoonful, letting it slide around his mouth for a few seconds so he could appreciate the full taste before swallowing it down. Damn, it was good. As good as his. "This is fantastic."

Vivi's face lit up. "Thank you. It's the currants that make it, no?"

"Completely." *Ha! Put that in your pipe and smoke it, Mikey.* Wait until he told his brother that another chef agreed with him on the currant issue. "Where did you find a recipe for it?"

Vivi hesitated. "Your brother. I wanted to make it exactly like yours."

Now it was Anthony's turn to scowl. "My brother gave you a family recipe?"

"I promised him I wouldn't use it at Vivi's."

He'd gone from flattery to annoyance in a matter of seconds. Goddamn Michael. Anthony couldn't wait until he was back at Met Gar next month.

Vivi looked upset. "You're mad at me?"

"No, I'm not mad at you." Anthony sighed. How could he be mad at her? She'd gone out of her way to make something to please him, to restore some kind of link between them. The question was, why?

"What's this all about, Vivi?"

Vivi looked away nervously. "Us."

"Us," he murmured, his defenses immediately kicking in, despite the fact she obviously hadn't come to kick him in the teeth again, unless she was some kind of sadist. "What about us?"

Vivi looked at him. "I made a mistake in breaking things off. If you'll have me, I'd like another chance, please."

For a split second, Anthony felt as if his heart might burst free of his chest and throw a victory punch, but the pain she'd inflicted on him over the winter made him wary. He wanted to know why she'd changed her mind. He *deserved* to know why. And so, even though he longed to take what she said at face value and just gather her up in his arms, he asked for an explanation.

"Why the change of heart?" he asked suspiciously.

"I realized"—Vivi swallowed as she began toying with her spoon—"that *I* was the one who couldn't let go of Angie. Not you."

Dumbstruck, Anthony pushed his back up against his chair. "Why do you think that is?"

"I was scared, Anthony."

"What about your whole 'I can't handle a relationship and run a restaurant at the same time' schtick? You've suddenly changed your mind?"

"That was just an excuse," Vivi admitted softly, "though you do have to admit, many chefs' relationships don't last." She rubbed her temple. "I was afraid," she repeated, "especially after the bedroom thing." The mention of it made the air crackle. "I guess you could say I frogged out."

"Freaked out."

She began choking up. "Please say you forgive me and will give me another chance."

He could feel his defenses beginning to crumble, but continuing wariness stopped him from giving in. "You totally broke my heart, Vivi. You realize that, don't you?"

"Yes," Vivi said shakily. "To me, that's the worst part of all this. That I hurt you when you didn't deserve it."

"How do I know you won't do it again?"

"Because I swear to you," she said fiercely. "I love you, Anthony. This can work, if you'll just forgive and trust me."

He wanted to, but the memory of her abrupt change of heart still smarted. All those careful months of circling each other, only to open himself up to love again and have her push him off a cliff—there was no way he was going to go through a drama like that again. Getting kicked in the nuts once was tough to take. Getting kicked twice just proved you were a chump.

He stood up, pulling loose and shaking the damp, sweaty T-shirt that had pasted itself to his chest. "I need to think about this. Why don't you stay here and have some pudding while I run up and shower? Then we'll talk some more."

Vivi nodded, her eyes following him as he left the kitchen. He ran up the stairs, grabbing a towel from the linen closet before plunging into the shower. He turned his face up to the hot spray of water, letting it beat down on him. Him and Vivi, back together. It should have been a no-brainer, but he still couldn't make the leap of faith.

Chapter 31

Vivi sat in the silent kitchen, listening as Anthony padded upstairs to take his shower. Having asked for forgiveness and a second chance, she'd received wariness. But she knew Anthony—while his words were cautious, his smoldering eyes showed the love and desire he felt for her. Bodies never lied, and she was going to make his tell the truth.

Vivi felt a roiling within her. One minute, she was sitting at the kitchen table, docilely accepting Anthony's decision to ruminate while showering. The next she was climbing the stairs, stealthy as a cat, heartbeat accelerating at the very idea of seduction. She felt her nipples go hard; her breath was already beginning to come in short, staccato bursts.

She paused with her hand on the bathroom door to steady herself. She could hear the water of the shower pelting down on the bath tiles, strong and insistent. As quietly as she could, she opened the bathroom door and tiptoed inside, closing the door behind her. Through the frosted glass of the shower stall she could see the outline of Anthony's body, and her heart took another tumble as she thought, *How silly of him to work out.* His body was perfection to her, muscles where there should be, hard to the touch. Restless, she pulled her long-sleeved T-shirt over her head and shimmied out of her bra, jeans, and panties, still being careful to keep as silent as possible. She peered down at her own nakedness, assessing, appraising. She was nowhere near as thin as so many chiseled American women, but that didn't mean she wasn't sexy. Her hips were soft but firm, her breasts somewhat small yet girlishly voluptuous. She loosed her braid, shaking her blonde hair out. Her heart was now pounding so loudly she was shocked Anthony couldn't hear it over the rush of the water. Slow and steady, she approached the shower, gently pulling open the door and slipping inside.

Anthony looked shocked. "Vivi—"

Hungrily she pulled his face down to hers, steaming water rushing over both their bodies. Her kiss was ravenous and demanding; Anthony returned it, drawing her to him, the two of them pressed together, hard, beneath the glistening cascade.

Vivi splayed her palms against his hard chest, the water aiding her hands in sliding easily over the smooth surface of his skin. Anthony closed his eyes. He couldn't hide his arousal; it was there in full view, pulsing to life as she reached down to take him in her hand. Vivi was surprised when he moved to block her, his brown eyes dark with desire.

"Too soon," he said. "Let me enjoy *you* a little bit first."

He turned her gently so she faced away from him, anticipation spiraling through every cell of her body. How was it possible to feel so relaxed yet so aroused at the same time? The soft press of the soap against her back brought a mellow rush of pleasure. Anthony began soaping her in small, tender circles. She felt pampered, cared for. And then his teeth nipped the curve of her neck, and colors she'd never seen before began exploding in her head.

She heard the thump of the soap as it dropped from his hands and he drew her tightly to him, his strong hands pressing against her belly, his mouth planting butterfly kisses up and down her neck.

She let her head fall back on his shoulder, rocking and rubbing her buttocks against him, animal desire rising. Anthony's hands traveled up her body, cupping her breasts. His fingers began circling her nipples, while at her ear, his tongue flicked and played with her lobe, one minute tugging with his teeth, the next sucking.

"You like—?" Anthony whispered in her hand.

Vivi's body was beginning to quiver. "Oh, God . . . *oui*."

He bit down hard on her lobe and she cried out, pain mixing with pleasure. There was a current of wet both within and without her, as the eddying swirls of desire inside her began moving faster. Anthony's hands slipped low on her belly, then stopped. *God, please go lower. Please.* Vivi held her breath, burning shards of desire tumbling inside her as his hand reached down, parting her soft folds. Slowly, almost tauntingly, he began playing with her, his fingers caressing and teasing.

Vivi moaned, swelling with arousal. The water, his need pressing hard and hot now between the cheeks of her buttocks, the building tempo of his fingers—she could feel consciousness slipping off to some other place as she gave herself over to total sensation. *"Je t'aime,"* she moaned. *"Je t'aime."*

"Je t'aime," he whispered back in her ear, pulling the both of them against the far wall of the shower stall. His fingers were still circling her, but now, with his other hand, he adjusted the shower nozzle and opened her wide, pounding beads of water slapping against inner thighs.

Vivi gasped dizzily, tilting her hips upward for full sensation. Her legs were beginning to shake as Anthony's fingers continued weaving their magic, moving faster now as he panted in her ear, his breath ragged. Jagged bolts of fire seared her skin as the water pelted down on her, hot and endless. And then it happened—she felt herself plunging over her own waterfall, her body flying apart in the mist and roar of the water. She laughed joyfully as an avalanche of water poured down on her, sacred, baptismal. When the seismic shocks in her body finally abated, she turned to Anthony, cupping his face in her hands.

"Thank you," she said breathlessly.

"Which was better?" Anthony asked, grabbing one of her hands and kissing her fingers fervently. "That or my hazelnut risotto pudding?"

"That," Vivi said, snaking an index finger between his lips. He sucked hard, and Vivi felt another spasm inside her gaining momentum. She wanted more. Wanted to feel herself grasp him from inside. Wanted *him*.

"You now," she purred.

"I agree. But there's something I need to do first."

Vivi watched with cautious fascination as he turned off the shower, taking her by the hand and leading her out of the stall. He reached for the giant towel hanging nearby on the wall. Wrapping her in it, he picked her up in his arms, heading for the bathroom door.

"What are you doing?" Vivi squealed delightedly.

"Something I should have done months ago."

He carried her, himself naked and dripping wet, across the landing to his bedroom door. There was no hesitation at all as he kicked the door open and brought her inside, depositing her roughly on the bed. His gaze was almost feral as he tore open the damp towel covering her and climbed atop her, his mouth claiming hers with a masculine greediness that stunned her.

"Jesus Christ, Vivi, you drive me wild . . ." She could feel his body tensing with restraint. She didn't want restraint. She wanted abandon. Her voice was desperate as she strained upward against him, digging her nails into his damp back.

"Fuck me," she implored. "Please. Now."

A guttural groan escaped Anthony's lips as he raised himself up. Vivi waited breathlessly, knowing what was to come next, crying out as he drove himself deep inside her. She wrapped her legs around him, reveling in his fullness, in the passionate certainty with which he claimed her body.

"Harder," she commanded, beginning once again to feel the undertow of desire dragging her under. Pleasure punched its way through her blood as he began thrusting deeper, each slam of his hips against hers as much a proclamation as a demand.

Their eyes met and held as Anthony continued pumping, bringing her once again to the screaming precipice where there was no time to linger, only plunge. She tightened herself around him, urging him on, begging and whispering things that should never be said aloud in the full light of day. Anthony's eyes clouded over with lust before he closed them, giving himself over to pleasure in a way that made Vivi feel strangely triumphant. When his moment of release arrived, his body was taut as a bow, the planes of sunlight striking his face from the open window giving him the cast of a conquering warrior. He emptied himself into her with all the speed and urgency he had, the strangled cry of his orgasm echoing in her ears. It was a sound she knew she'd never tire of.

Deliciously decadent. Those were the first words that came to Vivi's mind as she slowly came awake after lying asleep in Anthony's arms. She could tell by the slant of the sun coming through the windows that it was close to noon, perhaps a little later. They'd slept long and deep, both of them sated, both of them finally at peace.

Vivi turned to look at him, surprised to see he was still asleep. She listened to the steady rise and fall of Anthony's breath, and prayed it would be the soundtrack of her life. She imagined them older, curled up together just like this, the walls of the room festooned with photos of their children, maybe even their grandchildren one day. She saw them out and about, holding hands in Paris, arguing about restaurants and ingredients. Their life would be a never-ending discussion, the conversation never, ever dull.

She kissed him softly, and his eyes opened as he smiled at her sleepily, pulling her closer. "Hey, beautiful."

"Hey."

"You been awake for long?"

"No."

Anthony lifted up his head, squinting at the alarm clock on the nightstand in surprise. "Jesus, it's almost noon."

"So what?" Vivi snuggled tighter against him. "It's our day off. What does it matter?"

"You're right." He kissed the top of her head. "You sleep?"

"I did." She gave a little yawn. "I am a bit hungry, though."

"Me, too. Just let me wake up a little bit more and I'll go down and make us some breakfast."

Vivi propped herself up on one elbow. "What will you make?"

"Coffee, maybe some biscuits."

"What kind of biscuits?"

"Biscuit biscuits—you know, with buttermilk, shortening?"

Vivi wrinkled her nose. "You should add some vanilla."

"What?" Anthony came up on his elbow. "You don't add vanilla to buttermilk biscuits."

"Well, they sound very dull otherwise." Vivi sat up, raking her hand through her hair. "I know, why don't you stay here and relax, and *I'll* go make us breakfast?"

"Yeah?" Anthony sounded dubious. "What do you have in mind?"

"Well, depending on what you have in your kitchen"—she gave him a pointed look—"I could make scrambled eggs."

"I'm perfectly capable of making scrambled eggs."

"Chere." Vivi put her hand on his arm. "Americans make terrible scrambled eggs. They're so dry. The French way is better; you make them over a gentle heat so they stay soft, like custard."

"Fine. Then I'll do the coffee."

"No, that's all right, I'll do the coffee, too," Vivi offered quickly.

Anthony narrowed his eyes. "You still think you do coffee better, huh?"

"Of course I do."

"Honey, you forget: I've had your coffee, and it's no great shakes."

Vivi snorted. "Whoever heard of shaking coffee? That's ridiculous!"

"No, no." Anthony looked charmed as he took her hand. "It's an expression we use when something is just run of the mill."

"The mill?" Vivi was more confused than ever.

"Okay, let me put it simply: your coffee is mediocre, Vivi. I love you, but it is."

"Savage." She flopped back down beside him, staring up at the ceiling. "You're wrong," she said after a few seconds.

Anthony covered his face with his hands and groaned. "This is it, isn't it?"

"What?"

"What the rest of our lives are going to look like."

Vivi thought a moment. "Probably," she agreed happily.

Anthony chuckled, rolling atop her. "How about this," he suggested, stroking her hair. "We go down to the deli to pick up lunch."

"That deli with the scalding coffee and soggy egg sandwiches?"

Anthony's shoulders sank. "Yes."

"I would love that!" Vivi bubbled.

"Great." He kissed the tip of her nose. "Then let's shower and get dressed—"

"And after lunch we can come back here and plan dinner!"

"If that's what you want."

"It is. I'll even let you help me," Vivi teased.

Anthony wrapped his arms around her again. "I'll be your sous chef anytime," he murmured.

Vivi kissed him softly. "And I yours."

Recipes inspired by

Vivi's Pineapple Flan

(Serves Eight)

1 vanilla bean
2 cups whole milk
1 fresh pineapple, about 2¾ pounds
3 large whole eggs
3 large egg yolks
⅔ cup vanilla sugar*
2 tablespoons unbleached all-purpose flour
2 tablespoons heavy cream

1) Preheat oven to 450°F. Butter a straight-sided 10½-inch round glass or porcelain baking dish.

2) Cut the vanilla bean in half lengthwise and, using a small spoon, scrape out the tiny black seeds. Combine the milk, vanilla seeds, and vanilla bean pod in a heavy saucepan. Scald over high heat. Remove from heat. Cover and let steep for fifteen minutes. Remove just the vanilla bean pod.

3) Meanwhile, prepare the pineapple: Using a large knife, slice off the top and the bottom of the pineapple. Slice off the prickly rind, being sure to discard all the "eyes," leaving a cylinder of pineapple. Cut the pineapple lengthwise into eighths. Remove and discard the pithy core. Cut the eighths into 1-inch wedges. (You should wind up with about 1½ pounds of pineapple wedges.)

4) Scatter the pineapple wedges in the prepared baking dish. Bake for 5 minutes. (You can actually bake the pineapple for a few minutes before adding the custard, so the juices are re-absorbed into the pineapple and don't seep into the custard.)

5) In a large mixing bowl, whisk together the eggs, egg yolks, vanilla sugar, flour, and heavy cream until well blended. Gradually whisk in the warm milk.

6) Pour the custard mixture over the pineapple wedges. Bake until golden, about 45 minutes. Cool on a rack. Serve at room temperature.

To make vanilla sugar, split 4 vanilla beans lengthwise and scrape the seeds out of the bean pods. Combine the bean pods, seeds, and 4 cups of sugar in a jar. Cover securely and allow to sit for several weeks until the sugar is scented and flavored by the vanilla. Use the vanilla sugar in place of regular sugar when baking desserts.

Anthony's Ricotta Fritters

(Serves Four)

½ pound fresh ricotta
2 eggs
⅓ cup flour
1½ tablespoons butter, softened to room temperature
Peel of one lemon, grated (without digging into the pith beneath)
Salt
Vegetable oil
Honey, of runny consistency

1) Put the ricotta in a bowl and crumble it, using two forks held in one hand.

2) Break eggs into the bowl, and mix them with the ricotta.

3) Add the flour a little at a time, working it into the ricotta and egg mixture with the two forks held in one hand, or a spatula.

4) Set the batter aside and let it rest for at least 2 hours, but no more than 3½ hours.

5) Pour enough oil into a frying pan to come ½ inch up its sides, and turn on the heat to medium high. When the oil is very hot (if a driblet of batter dropped in floats instantly to the surface, it is ready) put in the batter, a tablespoon full at a time. Push the batter off the spoon using the rounded corner of a spatula. Do not put in any

more at one time than will fit loosely without crowding the pan.

6) When the fritters have become golden brown on one side, turn them. If they are not puffing up slightly into little balls, the heat is too high; turn it down a little. When the fritters are brown on both sides, transfer them with a slotted spoon or spatula to a cooling rack to drain. If there is batter left over, repeat the procedure until it is all used.

7) Put the fritters on a serving platter, dribbling honey liberally over all of them, and serve. They taste best when served hot, but are still very good even when lukewarm or room temperature.

Be sure to visit the Blades' website at
www.nyblades.com

Hot romance featuring the **cool** hockey
players of the New York Blades

by Deirdre Martin

who "always delivers heat and romance."
(Romantic Times)

———————————————

Body Check

Fair Play

The Penalty Box

Chasing Stanley

———————————————

penguin.com

It's a...

Total Rush

Free spirit Gemma Dante wishes her love life were going as well as her New Age business. So she casts a spell to catch her Mr. Right. But when the cosmic wires get crossed, into her life walks a clean-cut fireman who's anything but her type.

Sean Kennealy doesn't know what to make of his pretty neighbor who burns incense. He only knows that being near her sparks a fire in him that even the guys at Ladder 29, Engine 34 can't put out.

From
USA Today Bestselling Author

Deirdre Martin

penguin.com

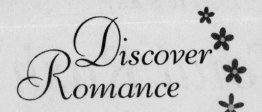